GREEN EYES
an erotic novel (sort of)

Michael Ampersant

Cover art: *Joe Phillips:* Latino Boy (digital painting, 2007)
Cover design: *Phil Haxo*

TABLE OF CONTENTS

FOR CHANG

The reign of error shall someday come to its end; we must enjoy it while it lasts.

Marquis de Sade

PROLOGUE   (INSTEAD OF CHAPTER 1)

R eaders, the first chapter of this story describes a casual encounter of three men in the dunes behind the gay beach of my town. It does so in overly graphic language—language that could discomfort or even harm some of you. I have therefore decided to replace it by a flat summary of the events related there, events that triggered the heartbreaking, murderous, but ultimately fortuitous story of the *Green Eyes*.

My name is *John Lee*. I live in *Georgia Beach*, GA, and teach French at *Southern Georgia College*, a small school 30 miles to the south-west near the Florida border.

I have issues. During my adolescence, I was diagnosed with bipolar disorder, a psychological condition characterized by difficult mood-swings. As I grew up, I became arrogant, shy, and homosexual, character traits that interact with my bipolarity. At my age—I'm 29 years old—I find myself in a downward spiral of disengagement, depression and neglect. I was outgoing and sexually active during my youth, but confine myself mostly now to my small apartment on the *Davis Canal*, where I—autoerotic efforts aside—play chess on the internet (losing), publish a blog (that nobody reads), and prepare classes (that students don't care for). A side effect of my bipolarity important here has to do with my language. Although I am averse to power-point expressions ("going forward"), I myself use various forms of new-speak (e.g., "un" as an antonym-shirking prefix), idiosyncratic expressions ("said" as adjective, "wise" as post-modifier), and am given to awkward metaphors and abundant bracketing (()). My mother is French, my father rarely spoke when I was young (he did other things), and English is not my first language.

We're in early July 2012 when the story begins. I wake up on a Sunday morning, feel the need for fresh air and decide to take a stroll along the beach. As I saunter past the gay section of said beach, I encounter a man of great physical attractiveness. He is roughly my age, but his most remarkable feature is a pair of green, mesmerizing eyes. We take note of each other. The man, let's call him *Green Eyes*, is somehow indicating his readiness for an immediate exchange of bodily fluids. I follow him into the dunes. We undress for, and engage in, a sexual act. A third man appears on the scene, undresses, and joins. All three of us reach a climax in due course. Green Eyes re-dresses and disappears. In a surprising turn of events—surprising at least for anybody familiar with the anonymous behavior of gay cruising—the third man invites me to a party at the house of a friend later in the evening. So far, *Chapter I.*

Hold on. Bowdlerization of Chapter I doesn't mean you can fool around. This is serious adult material. You'll see.

You haven't read Chapter I, but we had a thrilling encounter with a green-eyed man, who, following cruising conventions, has left the scene already, leaving me and an anonymous blond person behind, who has suggested that we meet up again later.

I'm sitting on the ground, he's hovering above me, his head tilted a bit, his feet planted apart in masturbatory position, his absent-minded hand still stroking his own, softening dick, both of us naked, the beach only a hundred yards away—and he's asking for a date.

"You are asking for a date?" I say.

He halts his pointless jerking. "Yes," he replies, "an acquaintance is having a do next to the *Blue Moon*, midnight. I'm certain you would be welcome. We could meet up and get laid. There's always a closet or a darkroom for the occasion."

I take visible note of my own naked body, then stare at his (this avoids a lot of explaining), and say: "We just had an anonymous sexual encounter, not really sex, but a sexual encounter. Spewing one's cum over a person amounts to a sexual encounter, and you ask for a date? How intimate can one get?"

"Come to think of it." He studies his own bare body, "Yes, that's what I have been doing. Sorry. Don't be offended. Stupid me." He has a British accent. His hand now plays with his short hair.

I get up, retrieve my clothes, re-dress. He looks around.

"You've no idea where my swimming trunks could be?" he asks with a helpless gesture.

I look around too. "You were wearing trunks, right? Where did you strip?" And, imbued with that particular sense of superiority of the dressed in front of the naked, I continue: "You were sneaking on us, weren't you, until the heat got the better of you?"

"Heat?"

"I mean your heat, your horniness."

He drops his head. "Horniness, that's an awkward word."

"We better find your trunks," I say, repeating myself: "Where did you strip?"

"Don't know, nearby, obviously."

We look around, walk around, we're in the dunes, or just behind the dunes, some trees planted on a sandy surface partially covered with dune grass and ground ivy, but there are no trunks in sight. The sense of dressed-ness still tickles: "You realize we're in the middle of a *calzonade?*" I say.

"Come to think of it," he says but then adds: "Swimming trunks are not strictly underwear."

We search some more. No swim suit nowhere to be seen.

"I'm screwed," he says (Brits, apparently, use four-letter words more selectively). I can't help it, I like him. Perhaps not in a sexual way, but I like him as a human being, enough at least to get concerned about his future as a naked alien on American soil.

"You're in trouble," I say. "You find yourself in the middle of public space, surrounded by more public space. You need a towel. There are enough towels on the beach, I'll go and get one for you."

"You would do that for me?"

"Yes, I will," I answer, already waving my hand in goodbye.

"Can you tell me your name?"

"John. And, yours?" I ask reflexively.

"Maurice."

Of course, I think. "I'll be back, Maurice," I say.

I'm back on the beach now. What am I to do? I will purloin a towel, dis-appropriate it and misplace it. And God will forgive me and remunerate the victim in a display of eternal justice. It could be in the victim's interest, in fact, my stealing his towel, if he needs eternal justice more than I do—which he possibly does, given that I'm not much of a believer.

This is the gay part of the beach, the rainbow flag plays proudly with the easterly breeze. Most visitors have ensconced themselves in some setup involving lovers, beach towels, beach umbrellas (for the sun), wind screens (for the breeze), and assorted paraphernalia such as colorful ice boxes for the booze, each party constituting a little island unto itself.

One particular island is empty, and between the umbrella and the windscreen there are three large beach towels in evidence. Who needs three large beach towels? I climb onto the island (the sandy patch between the umbrella and the wind screen), and it's my arrogance, as usual, that is my undoing. I'm getting choosy, hesitating over which towel to take back to the Brit. And so, before long, a shadow falls over my feet, a hand touches my shoulder, and a voice growls: "What are you doing here?" The voice belongs to a mature man, soft in the middle and elsewhere.

It's during the next second that I commit the next error of the day because I'm not only arrogant, I'm also slow-witted under duress. I should have risen above the occasion and ask the bear directly: 'Could you lend me a towel?' perhaps followed by some explanation, perhaps even the true explanation. He would possibly laugh a bearish laugh, his belly shaking. Everything would be fine, and I could walk away with a towel to save a British arse.

But I don't.

"I'm admiring your towels," I say. "Trying to find out about the brand, so I could order the same."

03 SEX ON THE BEACH

I don't believe you," the towel owner replies. "I think you are trying to steal something, possibly the booze."

"No," I say, "no, never." This round man isn't slow-witted, and he's developing dubious schemes behind his forehead.

"You were trying to get hold of the champagne, a *Bollinger* vintage, ten years old, that George and I brought to the beach to celebrate the first week of our friendship, worth a hundred bucks."

In retrospect, I could have said so many things, like 'What's your friendship worth?' or 'Bollinger is not my thing, I prefer *Moët*.' Or I could have confessed and plead for a towel for a hapless Brit. Instead I say: "Believe me."

That was the last thing this beach bear intended to do. "You're in trouble," he says with a clear sense of my apprehensiveness, "I'll get the Beach Guard, they'll take care of you." There's a brief, mutual pause as I consider my future as a convicted felon while the bear mulls over his dirty thoughts.

"OK, I'll show you the towels," he says. "Get down."

I sit. He does not sit with me, however, rearranges the windscreen and the umbrella instead. Our little island becomes an open-air cubicle with more privacy than I could care for. "The towels," he says, "are from *Nordstrom,* and they are very expensive, but also very useful, especially when you have to change out of your swimwear." He strips, picks up a towel, wraps it around his hips, posits himself above me, his legs apart, and says: "I'm ticklish."

"Do I need to know?" I ask.

"Tickle me," he says. It's clear what he means. 'Prison or sex,' I think a low-information thought. I raise my arm, get under his towel, and tickle what comes my way.

The beach bear grins, shakes his hips, and orders: "Wank me off."

We're long since past the point of return. I close my eyes, imagine a dark, dark room, and stroke his softish member. "You need to cooperate," I say.

Let's recall, I'm sitting on the ground, he's standing above me, legs apart. I'm reaching out to his parts under the towel, discerning his little sausage by my sense of touch, and now I'm fondling it, doing what I can to further a swelling, but nothing happens. 'This is not how erotic novels are meant to evolve,' I think to myself.

"Harder," he says, "we don't have much time."

"How so?" I ask.

"We don't have much time," he insists.

'We don't have much time,' I think, 'but we don't want to say why.' I sense the tables turning.

"Faster," he orders—he senses the tables turning, too.

My slow wit is coming to its senses. George, his partner of last week, is expected back soon, and this is not the moment to transform a one-week relationship into an open-air relationship while the champagne is still on ice. I abandon his willie, get up. Now or never. I grab his towel and run for the dunes. He's naked now, no way for him to run after me. Dog-eat-dog.

It's only hundred yards, I've escaped, I'm back in the dunes, waving the booty, but Maurice is gone. No Brit in sight. Shall I keep the towel? I hang it on a tree.

Y ou know I have issues. Bipolarity, arrogance, timidity, all this compounded by a minority role as aging homosexual. I was outgoing and sexually active in my youth, but these days I stay at home, except for the gym that I absolutely need for a look in the mirror, the occasional dash to the dunes, or a hurried embrace in the dark corner off the gym's locker room when both of you feel so hot after working out.

I was into tricks, brought them home most nights of the week, but the last one darkened my door I don't know when, four years ago. I'm caught in a downward spiral, arrogance and timidity feed on each other. I would have been better off in the past—before bipolarity went mainstream—when people instinctively shied away from maniacical-depressive conditions because they did bad things to their tongue. Plus, with my twenty-nine years, I'm also approaching the best sell date in the meat section. I don't wear the sticker on my sleeve, but people lie in your face and have sex with somebody else.

I need to do something about this, be more outgoing, see people. I must break the vicious circle of chronic depression. Yes, chronic, at least sometimes. Isn't it a fail-safe sign of depression that I feel slighted all the time? The way I felt slighted today by Maurice's disappearance? Although it's easy to conclude that he must have found his swimsuit, no need to wait for me after all. Why should he? Would I have waited?

Well, you have been more outgoing today, you saw enough people, did it help? First the morning excursion to the beach, and then the evening excursion to *Mamma Mia*. You were having a mediocre time at the counter for the loners opposite to the pizza stove and watched the crowd conversing and signifying until this guy appears whose face you somehow know, but can't place, with a woman. He's almost dragging her inside, holding her by her wrist, she's white trash, judging by her unkempt hair hanging flat down from her skull, she's too meaty for words, he wears shades, drags her to a booth and sits down opposite to her. Her body talk is just fidgeting, he keeps on exhorting her, I wonder whether they are married, it's not possible. He gets up, almost rolls across the table, plops down next to her, shifts his butt up to her ass, there's no oxygen left for her, his round flat face leans into her ear. She covers both ears with her hands, bends forward, hits the table-top with her forehead, repeatedly, then tries to get up, or out, but is stuck. Unexpectedly she dives under the table, scrambles on her knees to the aisle, lifts body and belly into the air, and flees, or waddles, and he stays behind and orders a beer while my undercooked pizza arrives. Not an encouraging pointer into the world of heterosexual relationships. Perhaps better to be a lonely gay on a Sunday evening.

Around ten PM I had already lost three games of chess on the *Internet Chess Club*. Several sex clips were better the first time I had seen them (although they weren't particularly good then either). I thought about a post for my neglected blog, but couldn't decide on a subject, I never really came out blog-wise, which creates all sorts of problems. Should I prepare myself for an early hand job? I came once today with the Green Eyes and Maurice. Yes. I can still come four times per day, so there is some elbow room in the hormonal department. Ten PM is the time when I go to the bedroom on a day like this, strip, and meet myself in the mirror for passable auto-sex. You know how this works. I try to avoid the mirror when I come, and it's icky to come over the floor or over the bed, all of which suggests an unstylish finale to the session, with me, dick throbbing, returning to the bathroom to ejaculate over the john. I know this in advance, it hurts my self-respect, the anticipation of the toilet bowl as the recipient of my erotic efforts, but the hormones are usually strong enough to keep me going, and when the job is done I wipe the last drop of cum and go back to work (during the term), or to bed (during the break). I'm working hard to prepare for my classes, you know, since I fear getting fired from this hippocampus of a college where I teach French to bulky students who hate my classes—they *know* something is wrong with me. But I will lose my job anyhow, nobody likes France anymore, and in my nightmares I have been fired already and eased into an after-life as a male prostitute by this proactive unemployment office ("You speak French, n'est pas, we can assure you, this escort service is completely above board"), until I find myself in soup kitchens at the age of thirty-nine.

So there we are, it's past ten on a Sunday evening, I had dinner already, nothing more to do, except that Maurice "invited" me to this "do" at the house of his friend next to the *Blue Moon*. I'm so out of touch, I didn't even know somebody moved in there to throw orgies and compete with the darkroom in the town's only gay haunt next door.

The party won't start before midnight (gay orgies never do). Maurice knew about the Blue Moon, despite his British accent, we must be world famous. Two more hours to go. How am I going to bridge the time? Next to the venue of course. On foot, the club is twenty five minutes away, and I should respect the drinking-driving regulations anyhow, in particular tonight, when we don't know where we will end up. Would we expect a textbook orgy with people naked and ready? This is Georgia Beach. It will be some compromising affair where people will try their best behind the flower pots or in the closets, Maurice mentioned the closets already. But what if there are not enough closets at hand, the opportunities for proper sex under polite circumstances having been eliminated, so we'll have to drink our time through the night instead. I'm briefly fantasizing about the real thing, the host receiving us in Adam's costume, his cock at the ready, a sexual slave fondling his rear with a life-size *fleur de lis*, everybody's giggling, you are encouraged to drop your guard and leave your clothes with a second slave and get laid on the kitchen table. You stay sober because there is no time for booze and discover that your wallet has disappeared from your abandoned pants when you leave.

The Blue Moon is fairly empty, as gay venues are when I arrive. I'm getting tired of this. Some people bring bad weather, I bring the absence of crowds. I arrive at a club, the crowd isn't singing and dancing to ABBA's "Give me a man after midnight." They are not laughing, cajoling, winking, alluding, anticipating. The champagne isn't flowing, the dicks are at rest. A few regulars with receding hair lines hold on to a can of *Heineken*, watching the non-crowd as they don't converse, or watching baseball on the overhead screen. They should return to the closet and get married.

There's nobody here tonight I know well, save *Ray*, who lives in the park when he does not live here. He is getting more and more smelly with the passing years, his hair graying, his pockets empty, but the management tolerates him because he is so innocent and helpless. I have to buy him a drink, we had sex so many times (I'll explain later). So I buy a drink for

Ray and myself, and we regurgitate small talk. I like him, but I don't like to talk to him. I feel a bit restless, despite my 10 PM session, so I want to finish the drink quickly and go to the darkroom. It's bad behavior to take your booze there, even though this joint hasn't placed the usual warning signs on the door about safe sex, alcohol, or prostitution

05   THE DARKROOM

L et's put this upfront: humor is always welcome, especially when it comes to bar room management. So the sign reads:

DARK ROOM
KEEP DOOR CLOSED
IF LEFT OPEN
ALL OF THE DARK
LEAKS OUT

We close the door. I should have known, Ray's presence near the bar has been a warning sign already, the room is empty, so to see. There's not much to see, of course, smells and sounds define the place, the infra-red bulb in the upper right corner produces just enough luminescence to discern shapes in fucking distance.

The place is quiet. I traipse through the infra-red air and hear my footsteps on the planks of the wooden floor—a redeeming feature of the Blue Moon, whose Victorian structure is made entirely from timber. Although, come to think of it, darkrooms often sport wooden floors, even when the venue is located in some alienating concrete building in downtown Manhattan, and even when other considerations would suggest linoleum, the sturdy kind found in hospitals. Perhaps this is by design, the gay club management lending a helpful, auditory hand to patrons in need of orientation.

To repeat, the place is quiet, and nothing would indicate the presence of particular people. The familiar stench of unused semen hovers in the air, easily out-stinking the lemon scent of its enemies, the chlorinated chemicals that hapless aboriginals pour over the floor every morning, unable to control their thoughts.

Many places are conducive to reflective thought, and empty darkrooms certainly fit the bill. Thoughts like, 'What am I doing here?' 'how could the world have come to this?' 'will I ever get laid again?' or 'don't stumble.' I'm traipsing in the direction of the bench that runs along the wall on the other side of the room, which I know is there, since I've used it before. It's stupid to stand in an empty room, much better to sit when the opportunity arises. The bench had been installed on the request of the more mature clientele who have come to prefer their sex in horizontal ways, I could be one of them. Plus, thinking is better done sitting. Well, perhaps not true. Anyhow, we are still traipsing, haven't reached the sex bench yet, dark rooms can be confusing. Think of your own bedroom at night.

I've just thought the 'What am I doing here'-thought when the answer strikes me like bad. 'You are killing time before you are going to gate-crash a party,' the answer is. Yes, that's right, gate crashing is what it amounts to. Invited by a random cruising acquaintance who isn't the host himself, and who has fled the sex scene as soon as he had found his swimming suit instead of waiting for me. Clearly, if he was at the party, he would disown me and laugh a camp, British laugh at the pointed question 'Do you know this guy'—if anybody could find Maurice, that is, 'Have you seen Maurice, we have this guy here?' answer: 'Maurice is busy,' yes, Maurice, more precisely "Maurice," anybody would know where "Maurice" is, Maurice, that's the *nom de guerre* he throws at hapless clingers who don't understand about casual sex.

Gate-crashing, me and my twenty-nine year old shyness, that would be that last thing I would do. What a *schnapsidee*, the thought alone that I would have to explain the whole thing to a gate-keeper who would listen with affected patience, let me finish my sentences that get longer and longer, and finally ask: 'We aren't gate-crashing, are we?'

I am blushing at the thought as I sit down on the bench for the elderly, wondering whether the infra-red light might somehow accentuate my skin-tone to the point where I was positively glowing in the dark so that people could see me and think I'm prudish and it's my first time to have modern sex with nobody.

19

An angel walked through the room—no, definitely not, there was no angel, not even a devil who's presence might have spruced things up a bit, it was only dark, and sad, and silent, like in the underworld of ancient religions, and it would always be like this, and I would die here, and nobody would take notice, and later during the night people would use my body as a prop for aberrant sexual positions until one pervert would realize my defunct state and do necromaniacal things to me, not to me, in fact, only my body, which would make it even worse. They would find me the next morning, raped to death, and there would be an inquiry by this ambitious young DA, *Hunnsbruck*, and the name of my family would be besmirched forever, and my mother would have to move away so that she would not have to care for my grave in the lost corner of the cemetery where darkroom victims are buried and tombstone inscriptions censored.

I sit on this bench, feeling confused. Wasn't it Maurice who asked for a date, wasn't it me who told him how absurd he was, wasn't it him who relented, but in a disarming way, as if he was eager to see me again? So I'm buried in thoughts as a passing light captures the floor in a circular movement. The door meows, the light retracts, and I'm no longer alone. Another guy has entered the darkroom.

T wo men in a darkroom. Alone. What does that mean? Nothing, relax, this must be Ray, who has finished his beer and expects me here, anticipating a brief session.

But it isn't Ray. It isn't him because I know Ray, who knows this room by heart, the only person with ray vision here, who discerns this room as clearly as I discern the beach in bright daylight. Ray was practically born here, or moved here as soon as his Malay parents would let him, and he would not hesitate (un-rhythmic squeaking of the wooden floor), or hesitate again (sounds cede) in his march to the sex bench where he would expect me. The squeaks are coming closer now, he's at most six feet away.

Two men in a darkroom, and nobody else. What does it mean? It means that standards will slip. In a normal darkroom encounter, when the meat market is efficient, you would be choosy and test the prospective meat until you're satisfied. You would feel his bottom (which needs to be tight), his abdomen (which needs to be tight), his nipples (which need to be tight), plus his hair, which needs to be there (rhymes). You would not be particularly interested in the shape of his nose, the color of his eyes, or his skin color (unless you are a racist, and even then).

Nipples, that's actually the most popular gauge. His hands get under your shirt and grope for your nipples. You have two, remember, arranged symmetrically on your chest. Your nipples are supposed to tell the entire story (I'm the lone skeptic here). Hard they must be, and mirror the erection that you are better having between your legs, otherwise the whole thing won't be fun.

Some people make more thorough attempts to gauge your defined-ness, but they are usually discouraged after a while and drop out of loop. Legs, yes, I forgot legs, people fondle your legs. It's to my advantage, I have strong, muscular legs because I did a lot of cycling in my youth, but I don't care about other people's legs, personally. Nipples. I've never had a successful darkroom encounter without the guy exploring my nipples (Ray excepted, of course). OK, so, with only two men in the room, the market is no longer efficient. You either have sex or you don't. And you do, of course.

The guy who's just entered is possibly not a regular, but he may have been here before, because I sense that he knows about this bench. I haven't made any noises but he's traipsing forward, as I did, and he's coming closer. He's in fucking distance now, one foot away (if you can fuck that far), and his outline appears in the dark. He may or may not be aware of my presence, lots of people have a sixth sense for physical proximity. He sits down, almost next to me. Some seventh sense must have told him about my location. He sits, no, he plunks down somehow. Something tells me he's exhausted, exhausted not only from his groping in the dark but something more fundamental.

Expect unexpected questions from me, that's my way to deal with my shyness. So I ask: "What are you doing here?"

"Huh," he says perplexed. But then: "What, *you* are here?" His voice sounds familiar.

"How do you mean?" I ask.

"It's you," he says with his British accent, "I'm so glad to see you." It's Maurice.

"Well, you don't actually see me," I say (this is typical me, this secondary cockiness for which I am getting too old).

"Never mind, I know it's you." There is some naiveté to him which doesn't fit his physical appearance at all—if memory serves, the crew-cut, the lank body, the voice, too. British accents are never naive.

"I found a towel for you," I say, "but you were gone. I figured you had found your swim suit after all."

"No," he says, "I didn't."

"So you went home stark naked? We are in America, boy, you can't do that sort of thing here."

"Believe me," he says.

"You're making this up because you think I'm cross."

"I understand you are cross, I would have waited for you, believe me."

I laugh. "Don't laugh," he says, "you don't want to know what happened to me."

"No, I don't," I say.

He's silent. I went too far, as usual. "I went too far," I say after a few seconds, "I didn't mean it." He grabs my arm.

"I got arrested on the spot, for indecency. You had barely left, and two cops appeared on the scene and took me in."

Y ou were talking about a calzonade, remember?" Maurice continues. "The real calzonade started after you left. Well, not quite, calzonades are supposed to be funny, this turned very ugly. I'm fearing for my life now."

"Why?" I interrupt.

"Let me tell. The police arrive in a jeep, step out, and start asking pertinent questions about my costume. I try to explain. How to explain your nakedness in an open, public space? I tell them I had to poop, and took off my trunks, and couldn't find them afterwards. 'Where's the evidence?' they ask, 'show us your feces.'

"It wasn't clear to me whether they were kidding or not. Anyhow, the question provided an opening, perhaps somebody else had taken the pains to defecate nearby. So we circle around a bit in search of poop. Just imagine the scene. I, still starkers, the two police men, overdressed, on my heels, not wanting to let me escape. Overdressed. They were in full armor, beepers, guns, intercoms, tactical equipment, everything held in place with tactical Velcro. There was a whiff of *Tom of Finland* right from the start.

"We can't find any poop, of course. I think about running away, but without shoes, on that ground, you couldn't run fast, and they looked reasonably fit.

"'So, we can't find your trunks, and we can't find your feces, either,' one of them says with his best attempt at irony. I realize the hopelessness of my situation. Better let the unexplainable unexplained. I fall silent. 'No other excuses?' the other cop asks perfunctorily, I will later learn his name, Dick. What's in a name, I tell you.

"I never learned the name of the second policeman. 'We'll have to take you in,' he says. They throw me into the rear of the jeep. Nameless throws a blanket over my private parts. We're off to the police station. Once there,

24

it's time for the—how do you say—mug shot. But the camera malfunctions (me, standing there, holding up the blanket, my rear exposed to the wall with the measurement scales, it was still kind of amusing in a slapstick kind of way). The camera malfunctions, everything stops. 'Somebody must have a mobile phone,' I say, 'why don't you take the picture with a mobile phone.' No-no, they can't do that, regulations. It's Sunday, you realize. They are understaffed, there are two other policemen there, the chief and some other chap. The chief stipulates that I'm arrested on some article of the Georgia code. I'm to be kept in custody until a mug shot has been taken, presumably tomorrow. I'm a legal alien, but that's where it ends.

"You see, animals, when they are cornered, when they know they are cornered, they just give in, birds, especially. When you pick them out of the water, some oil spill, they are covered in tar, they just relent. I once helped to clean up an oil spill near Torquay, I saved a few birds, I know how it is. I was covered in nakedness. I thought of these birds, I just folded. They read me the—what do you call it—*Miranda* rights. I take the fifth—I had to take a lesson in the UK how to protect my rights in America, I'll explain later.

"'I will need clothes,' I say to the chief, 'if you want to keep me all night.' The chief gets on the phone, can't reach anybody. He finally decides that he has the authority to send Dick to Walmart to buy some clothes, the money being added to my bail. Then he leaves. The fourth policeman also leaves. I'm alone with Dick and his nameless partner. Dick goes off to buy clothes at Walmart, and leaves as well.

"I'm alone with the nameless chap who tells me that he will lock me up. They have two jail cells right off the main office, along a small corridor. He takes me into the corridor, ceremonially unlocks the first cell, leads me into the cell. I expect him to leave, but he doesn't. Instead, he shuts the cell door from the inside, which is fairly pointless because the door isn't concealing anything, it's just an iron frame with vertical bars, old fashioned, homely almost. He shuts the door anyway. There is some symbolism to this. Perhaps he didn't do it consciously. So we're alone now, a twosome behind bars. It's getting awkward.

"'Show me how you do it,' he says.

25

'Do what,' I say.

'Your queer thing.'

"My God, we're still into queer here, I wondered whether he used the word on purpose. I understood what he meant, though. 'I took the fifth,' I tell him, 'no need to confess anything.'

'This is between you and me,' he replies. Hilarious, as if anything could happen just between him and me under these circumstances.

'OK,' I think, 'he could get violent, beat me up under some pretext.' So I answer:

'You want me to explain about casual gay sex, is that it?'

'Yes,' he replies, 'that queer thing.' It's like an off-Broadway piece from years gone by, some Tennessee Williams imitation.

'You need to learn about masturbation,' I say, somehow circumventing the issue, hoping to embarrass him. Most people are embarrassed about masturbation because they think they wank too much, although in reality they wank too little. But no.

'No,' he repeats, 'your queer thing.' When did we hear this kind of dialogue? Fifty years ago?"

"Are you a playwright?" I interrupt.

"I'm trying," Maurice replies. "You know," he says, "there's something about casual artistic activity, if that's the word, I'm not invoking Shakespeare here, but, you see, a West-End play, or off-Broadway, you see, or *Spielberg*, a lot of it is just context, changing context. A dialogue that worked 50 years ago doesn't work any longer because people have changed, they talk differently, they're clever-er."

"You know that the dialogue in the *Raider of the Lost Ark* was written by *Tom Stoppard*, even though he is not credited?" I ask.

"Yes, I know."

Souls meet for a split second, but Maurice isn't done with his story yet.

"I'm bringing this up, the dialogue, because I'm not convinced myself," Maurice continues. "Anyhow, the issue is masturbation, or not, since this chap wants to know about 'the queer thing.' 'I don't know about the queer thing,' I say. I use my words carefully, they read me Miranda, anything could be used against me, his word against mine, with my British accent, he's likely to prevail.

"'I'll show you,' he says. And, he drops his trousers. And, he has an erection, a delta-plus erection, if you will. Embarrassment, that's not the term I would use, I felt something much stronger, and I was scared. We have entered Tom of Finland territory now, a nasty, darker version of Tom. Who knows what he would have done next? Anyhow, we hear the door banging, and Dick is back. Prematurely. We're in the cell, the cell door is closed, I'm with my blanket, the nameless cop with his aroused member. Dick materializes in the corridor. Dick holds some togs. Something that resembles a defunct T-shirt, underpants, sweatpants, and some discordant leather brogues that one wouldn't be able to buy at Walmart, at least not the local one.

"The nameless cop clutches my blanket, covers his private parts, but fails to hide the trousers hanging on his knees. Dick scrutinizes this carefully. The nameless cop lowers the blanket a bit so as to cover the trousers as well, with little success. This was not Tom of Finland, of course, it was more *Tom and Jerry*. It would have helped, perhaps, if the anonymous cop would have said: 'we didn't expect you back so soon,' you see, he could have shifted the blame on the queer under arrest. I was starkers, remember? Perhaps it had been *me* who had started this. But he did not explain, he remained silent. Which put the onus on Dick, so perhaps it was a clever reaction of his not to react, after all.

"Dick has now to explain why he returned prematurely. Which he does. He saved the tax payer some money, he says, because his ex is living nearby, and he passed by her place, found some clothes, and is back now, peremptorily. Peremptorily wasn't the word he used, though, and the taxpayer was bollocks since the expense was supposed to be added to my bail, but anyhow. He's still holding the second-hand apparel, now he drops it. He's in our cubicle, right, with us. And, you know what he does? He closes the door. Ever so gingerly. The cell door. The door that had been closed before. We are a threesome behind bars. And, you know what he does next? I expect you can guess," Maurice says.

"Yes," I answer.

"He drops his trousers, brings out his dick, which is still soft, but hardens rapidly as I and his nameless partner stare at his crotch. Before I know it, he has thrown me on the ground, and is fucking me. Fucking me, okay. No gel, no condom. Just…nature. His name was Dick, right? His name should have been Cock, or *Artan*, or anything that denotes excessive manhood. This was the worst fuck of my life. He's pushing, and every stroke kills me. Kills me. I think they use rape a lot when they torture people. I tell you, they know what they are doing. You know, when your senses merge, when you can see pain, hear it, feel it, touch it, smell it, lick it? When you can't even groan? When all senses unite in despair? That was it. I was versatile, you know. I shan't be a bottom again, I think. Never."

"And then," I ask a bit heartlessly.

"I lie on the ground, being raped to death," he continues. "The nameless cop is standing next to my head. He's perhaps quite happy that Dick's outburst is helping him to escape from a tight situation. Anyhow, I see one nameless foot stepping back, and through my pain I feel the words 'Dick, your ex.' Dick doesn't pay attention at first, until we hear a scream, the scream of a woman.

"Dick unpops, gets up. I'm still on the ground, Dick's impressive member swings across the cell above me. I discern an under-class woman who's standing on the other side of the bars that hide nothing, and she screams. This happens between indigenous people in their local dialect, I hardly understand a word, but she came home apparently, and discovered the theft, and somehow deduced that Dick was the perpetrator, something about smells, 'I could smell you…' and some explanation that she came here because he's always on the Sunday shift, and she complains that he stole Martin's leather shoes. Martin, we might fathom, is the new man in her miserable life. 'Martin needs his shoes,' she explains, suddenly appearing very reasonable.

"I guess that did it. Her rationality upset him. The shoes, the shoes did it; he went off the cliff because of the shoes. He steps forward, his dick still throbbing. Some people can't really get rid of an erection unless they come, or he is on Viagra, he grabs her, starts manhandling her badly, and yells at her: 'You be quiet.' It's clear he's menacing her to shut up. He grabs her neck, starts to throttle her. She gags. He slaps her face, badly.

"It was obvious, he intended to shut her up, make clear that she must forget about the whole affair, go home, lick her wounds and never look back. I don't know what it was, her screaming, his heat, his irrepressible erection, I don't know, suddenly he grabs her skirt, tears it down, throws her on the ground, the same thing he did with me, gets on top, holds on to her shoulders, and bangs her viciously. He fucks, she howls. He fucks. It's rape. Unadulterated rape of the worst kind. Fortunately he's done quickly. After two minutes or so, he growls with a few discharging gestures of his hips as he comes. He's finished. He uncorks. He's still naked where it matters, he clutches her and her skirt, drags her along the corridor, sort of squat-shifting himself in his hanging trousers across the main office, and kicks her out. She must have crawled home.

"He comes back, his cock's still swinging, and a drop of semen plops onto the floor. I wonder whether they wiped the floor later, and if so, who did it. He raises his trousers, re-adjusts his tie. Yes, that's what he did, he re-adjusted his tie, they wear ties on Sunday, apparently. And he says, 'Now what?'

"He got back to normal very quickly. The nameless cop raises his trousers too, and adjusts his tie in sympathy. Both look at me. I think, 'They are going to kill me. They'll get rid of me, I'm the only witness.' But no. They look at each other, the nameless policeman collects Martin's clothes, hands them to me, I dress in this white-trash outfit with leather brogues for emphasis, and Dick says: 'You better go home now.' But then he grabs my neck, strangles me, for at least a minute, hard, I'll show you the marks—how long does it take before you die—and says: 'What happens in Vegas, stays in Vegas.' He releases his grip, shoves me across the office, and kicks me out."

Maurice has completely exhausted his breath, he gasps for air.

"Wow," I say.

"You can say that again," he says.

"How could they kick you out, you were under arrest?"
"I didn't dare to ask. They didn't think, I think."
"They will have some explaining to do."
"Or they come to their senses and come after me. I wasn't formally released, you know. Perhaps I'm listed as a fugitive now."

While Maurice was telling his story, the darkroom gradually filled up. Not really, but we were no longer alone, and Ray, the eternal Ray, sits at our feet, in his customary position, close enough to be seen.

"You want sex," Ray asks. I thought I would need at least a few minutes to recover from this, but Maurice says: "Let try."

"Cool," Ray says. Ray apparently assumes that I would join the fun and explain to Maurice what needs to be done.

"Give us a minute, Ray," I say.

So I explain to Maurice: "Ray is a sneaker, his best sex is when he sits on the ground and watches other guys. He just watches and jerks. So if you want to go ahead, do your thing. Ray will enjoy it. Ray has ray vision here, he can see you."

"Does he mind if I lie down," Maurice replies, "I feel a bit weak."

"He prefers when you stand, watching you from below, he's sort of a leg fetishist. He's interested in your legs more than in your dick. Your dick is just the icing on the cake."

"Okay," Maurice says and gets up. "Sorry," he adds, and sits down again.

"What's wrong?" I ask.

"Pain," he says, "pain in the tummy. Sorry."

"No sex?" Ray asks.

"Soon," Maurice says, "As soon as it gets better. Soon. A drink might help. Let's get a drink." He hauls himself up and we traipse across the room, holding hands. The bright lights of civilization greet us outside.

08 SHALL WE GO BACK TO THE DARKROOM?

I t's bright out here," Maurice says.
"Yes," I say. It's not clear to me where he's coming from.

"Anybody can recognize me here. Perhaps these police men are regulars, they would recognize me."

"I don't think so," I say, "they didn't play a comedy for your benefit. It went much too far for that. And if they do know they are gay, which I doubt, they are deep in the closet. They won't come out to the Blue Moon."

"Perhaps not, but they patrol the streets, the beach. I work in the tourist office, you see, on Georgia Avenue."

"Since when?" I ask, "You're not a local, obviously."

"I'm from *Torquay*, that's a seaside town in England, in *Devon*, on the south coast. I'm replacing an American here. Georgia Beach and Torquay are twinned, there are various exchange programs between the two towns, including the tourism offices, one Brit working during the summer here while an American replaces him in Torquay. I'm the lucky guy this year."

"How long have you been here?"

"Since a month, or so."

A young guy approaches us from behind, somewhat unsure on his feet. He slaps Maurice's shoulder.

"Hi, Maurice," he slurs.

"Bob," Maurice replies, "how do you do."

"I think I need a rest before Wagner's party kicks off," Bob replies and disappears in the direction of the darkroom. Another person, also young and attractive, steals a glance at me, he seems to know Maurice as well.

"Don't you spill your oats before the party," he says.

It's a conspiracy, Maurice knows everybody here, I know only Ray and the bartender. OK, there are two or three more people I recognize, although I've possibly forgotten their names, it's not funny.

"You seem to know everybody here," I say to Maurice.

"Yes, it's not safe here."

"Come on."

"I'm on display at the tourism office. If the police drive past, they can almost see me. Not to mention that I had to give them my address and my reason for staying in Georgia Beach. They can pursue me anytime, at their leisure."

He looks sickly, in more than one way.

"Relax," I say—the ultimate killer term in this situation, *relax*. I check my watch. It isn't even half past eleven. "Let's sit down somewhere, I'll get you the drink."

"I need more than a drink," he says.

I get drinks. I'm back, he has disappeared. Not again.

I have to strip-search the premises, find him finally outside in the garden hidden under a tree, crouched on a garden chair. "See, I knew you would find me, even in the dark. Anybody can find me here."

I hand him the beer can, sit down, and say: "I thought we covered that already. They have your address."

"Yes," he replies, takes a sip of his drink.

"I need your help," he says, "I can't stay at my place."

"Perhaps you should wear some disguise, shades plus a wide-rimmed fedora."

"Very amusing," he replies. "I will need some sort of protection, a cover. I have to disappear."

"Don't panic," I say, "think this through. You are a witness to a crime."

"Yes, a serious crime, committed under aggravating circumstances by a policeman on duty, at the police station, raping his ex-wife because she complained that he broke into her home. Not to mention my own case."

"There are three witnesses, I say, "you, the wife, and Dick's partner."

"Yes, so?"

32

"You are not the only witness. There are too many witnesses to get rid of."

"By no means. His ex-wife is scared to death. You should have seen her. I'm not really familiar with the social standing of American police, or their ex-wives, but she looked like under-class to me. These people have no faith in the judicial system. Where would she go? To the police?"

"And the nameless partner."

I started to realize how weak my case was. The nameless partner, he wouldn't raise hell because his own nameless behavior would get exposed, he would certainly prefer to let a serious crime go unpunished rather than being outed by his own testimony. Maurice was indeed the only witness that counted. Get rid of Maurice, and there would be no case.

Can I ask you a difficult question? How is one to balance the depressing truth of a prospective murder with the party excitement one is supposed to share with the prospective victim? Well, one is not. It is clear what Maurice wants, he wants to stay with me, at my place, until the threat is gone.

The choice is stark. I could promise to take him in. Or I could tell him to buzz off, which would mean that I could not go to the party. And it would mean throwing him under the bus for all practical purposes. Imagine, I have to hear on *TV Channel Two* about a body found in an advanced stage of decomposition at the local landfill whose identity somehow matches a missing Brit from the local tourism office. I couldn't. I would have to reach higher ground here, take Maurice in, even though he would work terribly on my nerves after a few hours, and my place is too small, and what not. I will suffer. Maurice will suffer—although, don't forget, there is an immediate payoff in terms of the upcoming party.

"Shall we go back to the darkroom?" Maurice asks, "I'd feel safer there." Me, having now opted for being a good person, I feel like Santa Claus, and a substantial erection is building in my pants (Napoleon was also known for this kind of tumescence). So I say, "I'll take you in. You stay at my place until this blows over."

33

09 RICHARD WAGNER AND LUDWIG THE SECOND

M aurice exhales. "Would you really do that for me?" he says.
"It's not a big place, we need some ground rules," I say to
Maurice. "I have a spare room."

I suddenly realize that my father is expected this week, my parents are
divorced, my father visits once a year, in the summer of course, for a few
days, until we have a terrible fight and he is forced to leave.
"I don't have a spare room, actually, at least not next week. My father
is coming." I say.
"Did you come out to your parents?"
"Yes."

I came out, of course, you're not a full citizen rainbow-wise if you don't,
but I kept it very official, and my parents never met any of my friends, or
partners, or whatever you call people you have sex with.

"Your bed is large enough, I presume, or do you want me to sleep with
your father?
"The bed in the spare room is very small," I say.
"Your father is gay?"
"Give it a try," I say lightly. I have no idea how to handle this situation,
my father won't be amused, who knows, perhaps we have our fight on the
first evening and Dad would have to leave, which would solve our
problems.

"Look," he says, "we're here so we can go to a gay party where we are
supposed to have sex, isn't it? Wasn't that the idea? Your bed should be
large enough for the two of us."
"You know how it is with casual sex," I say, "even with repeats, you
don't know whether you want to see that person again. Normally, you
don't."

"We don't have to have sex, if I can beat the bishop in private."

"Wank?"

"Wank."

"It's more than that, you just don't want to be in touch anymore."

"But you already promised." he says. "Didn't you?"

He's uncool in his British ways. Is he always like this? He's not your usual trick. Tom Stoppard, Tennessee Williams, off-Broadway, if he would match the usual one-night stand I would know by now.

"I can stay chaste," he adds. "I lie next to you, and you lie next to me, and I have an erection, and you have an erection, but nothing happens since we did it before, twice even, or three times, depending how often we'll do it tonight, and depending on whether our first encounter qualifies as proper sex, but nothing happens because we *did it* already, and gays can't go steady, they must change partners like dependent undergarment, so we don't have sex, and stay chaste while lying next to each other with our stiffies, until each of us sneaks out to the bathroom to get off, unsuccessfully trying to hide his biggy from the other in the process."

"In the process," I echo. He laughs.

"Going forward," he answers.

"Touching base." We both laugh.

"Do you take people home a lot?" he asks.

"I used to, but not any longer."

"Look, it might be only for a few days, I'll have to make something up, go back to Torquay. I can't stay here."

"Okay," I say.

Ray interrupts, he's taking his usual break from the darkroom, looking for somebody to buy him another drink. Apparently he couldn't find anybody else, that's why he ends up outside, under our tree. His hair's salt and pepper, he's covered with the stench of back alleys, and worse, nobody to buy him a drink. It's tragic, literally, if you think this through, a human being on the road to perdition, right in front of your eyes. I've just saved Maurice's life, I can buy Ray another beer.

I'm back with the drinks. I wonder whether Ray knows about this party, I guess not. No, he has no idea. There's a generation gap now in Georgia Beach, or something to do with trends, or in-crowds, to which neither Ray nor I belong. I'll ask Maurice about the party. Who's the host? "Godehart Wagner," he says, "a minted bloke from Germany. He inherited this house a few months ago. This is his house warming party."

"Wagner," I say, "like the composer."

"Yes, they are related, really, but he belongs to a secondary branch of the family, in the fifth generation."

"How do you know him?" I ask.

"Sheer coincidence, as usual, we were changing planes in Atlanta. We met in the waiting room for the commute down here. His gait. My raised eyebrows. His hesitation. 'Is this seat taken,' he asks with an accent that holds the middle between German and camp. 'It's not, of course,' I reply, drawing out the 'not' and the 'course.' There's no time to think. 'Will you excuse me,' I say, I have to go to the loo.' 'So do I,' he plays back. Off we go, I lead, he follows, eyes are following us, especially female eyes.

"Atlanta provides good privacy in its toilet stalls, most airports do these days, everybody wants to be the best airport in the world, a fair bit of airline personnel are around, all of them gay, supposedly, they need these facilities dearly, it's better to provide privacy to those in need than to leave innocent travelers exposed to the things that happen when less innocent people meet in poorly isolated stalls."

"So the stall isolate?" Ray asks.

"Yes, we were quite satisfied. His penis is long and thin, like the dong of a chimpanzee. What can I say? Intercourse is intercourse. You want to know more?"

"Yes," Ray answers. Visual or verbal, he always wants to know more (that's Ray's other thing, if he isn't watching, he's kibitzing).

"Well, trousers drop, the usual top-bottom question, he hands me the condom which I put on as he watches, which constitutes *Act I*. Wait, let me retract briefly. They do a fair bit of background music at the Atlanta airport, also in the toilets, and you know what they played for us? Wagner, Valkyrie. So he raises the toilet seat, climbs on the edge of the bare bowl, turns around, squats, I put my hands under his arm pits for stability, *Act II*. Penetration, excitement to the score of Valkyrie, *Act III*. Some suppressed heavy breathing, I come, release, *Act IV*. He jerks, turns

36

around, comes in my mouth, *Finale*. Very thoughtful of him not to come over my face or body, I wouldn't have had much time to clean up. We arrive back at the gate just in time, eyes following us. People have a sixth sense for sex, especially women.

"There's no seat assignment on this commute, so we sit together. He tells me his life story. He's from this minor branch of the Wagner family, but somehow he still holds some rights to the Wagner name. Not for the music, of course, that belongs to the public domain, but in some way Wagner's name is still protected under German law, some special provisions enacted by the Nazis, and he makes his money with Wagner mugs, and Wagner busts, and this themed stuff that you find in tourists shops. And he sells leather shorts, Bavarian leather shorts, emblazoned with the Wagner motif. You know—these garments that they wear with Tyrolean hats when appearing on the telly where they dance to the tune of Bavarian square dances, jodlers, if you will, and slap their thighs to the rhythm of the music. You are aware of that folly if you ever watched German television. It's of no importance when you switch to a German channel, there shall always be men in Bavarian shorts and Tyrolean hats, slapping their thighs."

"Impossible."

"Mind you, they don't dance to Wagner music, just a jodler."

"But the Wagner theme, how do you combine this with leather shorts?"

"Good question, no idea."

"Do you know whether Wagner was gay, too?"

"Actually I asked Godehart. Wagner wasn't officially gay, but he had an affair with the young king of Bavaria, Ludwig the Second, Godehart told me. Ludwig furthered Wagner's career, in fact, he underwrote his productions and built opera houses for him. Wagner would not have succeeded without Ludwig. So perhaps Wagner wasn't gay, perhaps it was just the casting-couch behavior of an ambitious composer. But we can't be so sure. Wagner and Ludwig exchanged quite a few letters, quite explicit, passionate ones, the jury is out on that one."

"How do you know?"

"Well, Godehart told me, I asked pointed questions."

"Nobody asks pointed questions anymore."

"I do," he says.

Both of us laugh. Ray doesn't laugh (although he is capable of asking pointed questions if people let him), but he's happy too and swills his beer.

"You kept in touch," I observe.

"We didn't exchange phone numbers, but I told him that I would work at the tourist office. He dropped by the other day and invited me. In the meantime, I had seen him a few times here at the club. We're friendly." He looks at his watch. "Let's go," he said. He hauls himself upright. He's still unwell.

"You go to party, everybody invited, not me?" Ray asks.

"I wasn't invited either," I tell Ray, "I just happened upon this British gentlemen in the morning who extended an invite on behalf of the host."

Ray is low information, but sensitive. "I figure," he says.

"You want to come?" Maurice asks Ray.

"Sure," Ray answers.

I'm almost at the point of saying to Maurice, 'Can I have a word with you,' but Maurice has already understood. "It will go swimmingly, I'll explain to Godehart."

We're off to the party next door. We're not the only ones. The Blue Moon empties.

10   BAVARIAN LEATHER SHORTS

There's a reception line. My first reception line in two years (I skipped last New Year's function at the college). One and a half years, to be precise. People. Lots. Maurice is ahead of me, Ray is behind. Six people in front of us. Ray is smelly, I'm embarrassed, Maurice is confident.

Godehart (don't ask about the pronunciation), the genial host, is also the bouncer. The place must have been spruced up since Godehart moved in. Normal places in Georgia Beach don't look like this. I like it, though, light timber, hardwood floors, more timber, colors, designer classics, not much ornamentation, and not a single Wagner bust in evidence. Instead, we behold tasty gay art with explicit flavors. The person standing next to Godehart is not exactly the sex slave of your dreams, but he's obviously some professional, a person who spends too much time in the gym for a daytime job. He's not a boy, he may have my age, but my re-awaking instincts tell me he is an escort, a rented boy, or man, and I'm mulling thoughts as to whether he is from the same agency that the employment office was thinking about when they were trying to ease me into this escort job, although they didn't so far, it was just a bad dream.

The boy-man is naked—another indication of professionalism—save for the Wagner-themed Bavarian leather shorts, which are held in place by leather suspenders. Godehart is still dressed, and nobody fondles his rear with ostrich plumes. The Wagner theme on the leather shorts (let's get this straight immediately), is espoused in ways that suggest a conspiracy. Richard Wagner's image is stitched onto the very front center of these black shorts, exactly where the crotch is located. They are very tight (tighter and softer than the standard issue, I'm informed later), so penis lines are in evidence. Imagine what an erection could do to the composer's stern portraiture, how his Germanic nose could be bent in unspeakable ways. Well, erections have gone mainstream, it's possibly the way to make money these days, selling crotch-enhancing, nose-bending Wagner shorts, this stuff is possibly hot merchandise at Bloomingdale's, I don't know.

OK, there's a redeeming feature to this. Wagner's image is also on the suspenders, little one-inch Wagner icons in matching colors that run from the belt, along the escort's washboard tummy, across an inviting pectoris (almost as inviting as *Green Eyes*), continue past the biceps and up to the shoulder where they bend into the invisible part of the spectrum behind the escort's back. The escort's penis is at rest, so Wagner's face on the crotch and Wagner's icon on the suspenders match reasonably well.

Godehart ("call me Gohard") is vigorously greeting Maurice, who explains about me and Ray. John, I'm almost his roommate, and Ray is in dire need of a shower since he had a difficult day. Gohard—I think one really needs to be fifth generation for this level of nicknaming—Gohard is very pleased. A second escort is dispatched to help Ray out of his clothes and into the shower. We know he's an escort because he matches the first one in appearance. Ray is taken off our hands, and we plunge into a pool of anticipated lust. More Bavarian rent boys are serving champagne on large silver trays, along with canapés, donuts, and pieces of pineapple, which, on special order (we presume), have been cut into obscene shapes. An orgy is in preparation.

"It's a conspiracy," these Bavarian shorts, I say to Maurice. I'm not saying this out of conviction, just using Maurice as a sound-board. What is a person like him going to think, a person who has seen more of the world more recently? Is this the new normal, crotch-enhancing composer shorts?

"Perhaps he had them ordered especially for this event," Maurice suggests.

"It would be impolite to ask Godehart, I guess."

"No, it wouldn't," Maurice replies, "event-consciousness, event-management at the level of merchandise bespokeness..." he hesitates. He hasn't lost his train of thought, he's just searching for words. "It's all about events these day," he resets. "It will certainly raise your standing if people know that you have specially ordered Bavarian crotch shorts for your special event, it shows latitude, it makes you a special person. A latitudinal person, so to speak."

Conveniently, Gohard swings by. We ask.

"Oh, no," Gohard answers, "I would have ordered them as special editions, but therefore was no necessity. The shorts are a part of my standard sortiment. They sell themselves, how do you say in English, they sell themselves like hot rolls."

"To gays?" I ask.

"Gay, straight, metrosexual, what you can think of. People find it fun to enhance their crotches in special ways. Everybody does it, or?"

He falls silent briefly. "Come to think of it," he resumes. "About that I did not think at all. I am glad to have made your acquaintance. You are very inspiring. Fantastic idea, or? Naturally. We transcendent the Richard. We enlarge the sortiment. Which other famous people would you like on your shorts? Let's have ideas." He's the passionate businessman all of a sudden, I begin to understand his success.

"Tiger Woods," I say meekly, knowing already that's not a good idea.

"Well," Gohard replies.

"Lady Gaga, Beyoncé, Michelle Obama," Maurice adds.

"Now I get more clear why we haven't done that one beforehand," he says. "We have juridicial problems. We need the copyrights for these people, and that is dear."

"Michelle Obama might be in the public domain," a passing rent boy adds jokingly, he must have overheard our conversation. With a remark like this, he's not your standard prostitute, he's probably an unemployed French teacher from a defunct Southern college who has been eased into his new job by a proactive employment office. I will have to spend more time in the gym, methinks. My mood swings again.

"We must keep in contact," Gohard says. "We should meet for a brainstorm. I need you, boys. Yet excuse me now, I must tend to my social network." He's off with a blown kiss.

Another rent boy passes, this one even more attractive than the others, the definition of defined-ness, if you will. "I have to go to the bathroom," Maurice says. I think he plays his usual trick for the benefit of the escort in hearing distance, but no, there's nothing seductive in his movements, he trudges away in unsuggestive ways, and the escort, either out of sheer professionalism, or out of laziness, stays put.

11 PUKE

I 'm alone now, alone at a party. Ray's still showering, Maurice's on the john, and Gohard is off to the relevant nodes of his network. How did this guy make so many friends, didn't he arrive together with Maurice just one month ago, when both met at the gate for the Georgia Beach commute in Atlanta? And I know practically nobody.

This was a day of mood swings, as usual, well, the day's over now, we're past midnight, and I'm on the downswing again. I know nobody, I'm out of touch, I'm a lonesome squirrel on a lonely tree in the garden while the bright lights in the house speak of cheerful togetherness of folks who wouldn't even throw me an acorn. I'm a member of the out-crowd, which isn't a crowd, just a meager set of me, Ray, and a few balding regulars at the Blue Moon. I realize why I have come to avoid parties (except that I'm rarely invited), you have to be in the right mood, the sing-and-dance mood, the *ABBA* mood, to successfully get your man after midnight and split the infinitive in the process, going forward.

I can't stand here alone, in the middle of a cheerful crowd of four-and-six-somes. Wasn't it Shakespeare who observed that this not a good situation to be in? Yes, in his famous soliloquy from *A Streetcar Named Desire*, doesn't he open with the words, 'To be or not to be in a situation?' It's a sure sign of my low that I contemplate my hippocampus and the confusion I could still create among post-adolescent obesity by spreading literary falsehood before I'm fired.

I can't stand here alone as a degenerate network of *one* while everybody else is making new friends. I cannot. I must not. I clench my fist, literally. Then I intercept a leather-clad rent boy, withdraw two flutes from his silver tray, gulp them down ruthlessly—not letting the bubbles play any tricks with my taste buds—and await the champagne's wanton, disinhibiting arrival in my stomach. Swoosh.

The network next to me consists of two elderly men, and two youngish rent boys. Love is in the air. The men are much older than me. I recognize one of them from the distant past, when I was still a young regular at the Blue Moon. He was running a place off the Coastal Highway, on Route 24, a large *Thai* place with an upper, more secluded, floor above the main restaurant, awful food, and willful oriental boys, who were waiting on tables in the meantime. Patrons came from all over the place, even from Atlanta, to taste one or more of his waiters. Yes, now I remember his name, *Neill Palmer*. He kept a website back in those days that was quite revolutionary. Poorly aligned text in colorful, meandering hues and pictures of his staff, ranked according to their state of sexual arousal, the apex being the climax, boys caught with their cum coming *in flagrante*. I remember that he had never managed to eternalize the moment of the squirt (white ropes flying from the penis). His cum-shots were always a bit off, the cum caught already dispersed into milky drops in the empty, or not so empty, space in front of his oriental masturbators.

Last time I came across Neill's site, the boy pictures were gone, the oriental nakedness had vanished, nothing but text remaining, loose talk about the "gay condition" and some such. Then his site had disappeared altogether. To my knowledge, the guy had been a pure rice queen, he would not touch a Caucasian dick. What's this guy doing in fucking distance of two white prostitutes?

While I am thinking this, Neill has time to raise his eyebrows in an apparent attempt to signal the discordant asymmetry that my joining them has created in the numbers of his network. But I am still on a high with my bubbly stomach, and say "Remember me, Neill?" and, without waiting for an answer, add, "What happened to your home page, it has disappeared from the net."

Now, let me interrupt myself here. The last time I used *Southeast Airlines* on a commute to Atlanta, we had a rough time in the air, and I sat next to this middle-aged man who was explaining to a person in the row behind us how he had been invited to this party, and the girls, semi-hookers apparently, were getting hotter and hotter as they were talked up by him and his able friends. Then one of the men, some stupid guy named Herbert, started a monologue about his encounter with the tax man. Nothing could stop him, and the girls would remain polite, and listen, ("uhuh, uhuh"), and Herbert would go on-and-on, and the girls would go on-and-on (listening), until all sexual overtones and undertones had left the room and the orgy died prematurely in gawks and annoyance.

Flashback reset: I am Herbert, the internet has replaced the tax man, and the rent boys have replaced the semi-hookers. Except that analogies always break down somewhere, with the Bavarian escorts showing more that polite interest in my questions, and welcoming me to their charmed circle with all their body language. Which I interpret as their attempt to replace the prospect of an unattractive closet partner with the prospect of a less unattractive closet partner in the orgy's near future (this assuming you had to use a closet, I guess you could also take them for a ride upstairs). So they tell me their names, Jason and something. Jason, on closer inspection, has dense, black straight hair, olive-shaped dark eyes, darker skin, and the Wagnerian penis line indicates very little. He was an Asian mutt, after all.

As you can imagine, my presence is not appreciated by Neill, in particular because statistics would suggest that Jason is the only Asian escort at the party, the only fuckable ass from Neill's point of view. But what could he do? This is a party thrown by a fifth-generation member of the Wagner family, a dynasty of *Siegfrieds, Wielands, Friedelinds, Gottfrieds, Winnifrieds*, (I looked this up on the internet) and now *Godehart*. We are in heavily polite society, so Neill has to stay polite and play along. I ask more questions and get more answers—he had come into some money, a whole family fortune, no longer needed the restaurant, had gotten tired of blogging, and of playing the madam (he knows I know), and retired to some country estate nearby. The hookers, contracted to accommodate any reasonable sexual wish by any conceivable invitee, they are trying to unwiggle. This is so funny, my spirits rise, and I am almost about to make a move, which could have ended with me and Jason retiring together immediately, when Maurice reappears, his face ashen, his movements slowed down, as if he has spent much too much time in the bathroom. Which he has.

But not with anybody we knew, or didn't know. No, he had been alone in the bathroom, on the john. He had felt abdominal pain during the entire evening, after the immediate hurt of the rape-fuck had subsided somewhat. But when he arrived on the john he couldn't even shit. Instead, he had to throw up, got sick beyond belief, vomiting his entire body content until nothing was nothing left. Puke, nothing but puke.

A s Maurice is saying this he's grabbing my shoulder. His knees fold, his body folds. He's falling to the ground, now he's just lying there, eyes shut. I touch his shoulder,

"Maurice, Maurice," I say. No reaction. I slap his cheeks. No reaction. He's unconscious.

"He's unconscious," Neill observes, "a bad fuck probably." This will be the last time that anybody uses those words at the party.

"Gohard," I shout, "we need an ambulance."

"We need an ambulance," Godehart answers.

"Somebody must call an ambulance," he continues.

"What's the number?" the rent waiter asks. Godehart doesn't know, of course.

"Nine-one-one," somebody suggests helpfully.

"No, no," I plead, "that's the police, we need an ambulance. Call them directly, that's faster."

The police would take Maurice directly to the landfill, better still, they would take his unconscious body to the hospital, with RapeDick in the back blocking Maurice's neck artery expertly with his thumb, leaving no marks. We've seen this in the movies. Maurice will arrive *dead on arrival* at the hospital, having died of *badfuck,* a contagious disease, and the night shift directs the body to the morgue where it can chill forever.

I am thinking this very quickly. "Please call an ambulance," I plead in Neill's direction while squatting next to Maurice; I'm trying to feel his pulse. Neill must have been through this before as a restaurant owner, not to mention bad fucks in the upstairs department, he must know how to avoid the police.

And he does. Neill's possibly thinking that Maurice's collapse would lead to my timely departure. If the ambulance takes Maurice and me off his hands, Neill himself could resume his flirt with oriental Jason. He brings out his cell phone. The emergency room wants to know the address.

"Next to the Blue Moon," Neill replies, "on the left." That seems to suffice. "It's urgent," Neill bellows into the phone. "Eight minutes," Neill informs us. I'm still on the ground, still not feeling Maurice's pulse.

"I can't feel his pulse," I blurt.

The news spreads quickly across the proto-orgy. This is not a bad crowd. This is a well-brought up crowd that knows how to share sorrow and concern, *chapeau*, Gohard, you know how to invite people. The four- and sixsomes dissolve and each person, more or less by himself, joins the evolving circle around Maurice and myself. We are silent at first. Another person kneels down to explore Maurice's vital signs, without result. Everybody is half-bent forward, the whispering starts (they could do the choir of a contemporary opera production). "Blood," "anus," "internal." The unmentionable words "bad fuck" are suspended in the air. No more fucking. Everybody is really concerned about Maurice and about everybody else, it could happen to all of us. They have no idea how badly Maurice was raped this afternoon.

The host shows initiative. "Can somebody bring a cold towel," he bellows. A willing escort hastens to the kitchen, and returns with a wet towel that is applied pointlessly to Maurice's forehead. "We need a thermometer," the host bellows again. A thermometer is duly found and handed to me. I insert it into Maurice's mouth. It's an old-fashioned one with an analog, quicksilver readout. The red bar rises quickly, stops finally at 103°. "One-oh-three," I say. "One-oh-three, what does that mean," Gohard wants to know. We're panicking, nobody is able to think German Celsius. High, I say, very high. "He's still warm," a heartless wit remarks in the background, he will never be invited again.

Eight minutes is a long time. Sirens approach, then stop. The concerned circle of party guests regroups to get a view of the door in expectation of the paramedics. Gohard opens the door. We hear the noise of the ambulance's rear door, the rolling sound of an emergency stretcher, steps. The first paramedic appears in the door, followed by the stretcher, followed by the second paramedic. The second paramedic sports shiny black hair cut short on the side, a well-defined body under a tight, white

47

T-shirt, and a well-proportioned butt in white, narrow sweatpants. He surveys the scene. His green eyes recognize me immediately.

He furrows his brows. I explain.

"Did he have any bowel movement during the last couple of hours?"

"No, he couldn't, but he got sick on the john and threw up in a bad way."

"Bowel could be torn, bowel content spilled into the peritoneal space, sepsis, septic shock," Green Eyes replies.

The first medic feels Maurice's pulse, nods. "Fast, weak," he says.

"Oxygen, the works," Green Eyes replies. They ease Maurice's body onto the stretcher and fasten the straps.

"You come with us," Green Eyes says to me. I follow. We're in the ambulance, sirens wail, we're off. While we are speeding across Georgia Beach, an oxygen mask is applied to Maurice's face, an IV pouch is fixed to the ceiling and connected to his inner elbow. "Volume," Green Eyes says, then continues: "A truly bad fuck is like an appendicitis, only more so."

"What's your name," I ask him for the second time (the first time was this morning, in very different circumstances).

"Alexander, Alex."

"Ruptured bowel?" I ask. "That could be serious." Alex fails to reply, adjusts the oxygen mask instead and checks the IV tube. He takes the pulse again.

"Normalizing a bit," he says. Somebody's talking on the intercom. "And you name?" he asks. Why am I surprised he wants to know my name?

"John," I say.

We've already arrived at the emergency room of the *Baptist Memorial Hospital,* the local institution. A woman, obviously the doctor in command, is expecting us. Her hair's cut short, her hips are too wide, her glasses are manly. She's a dyke. Maurice is hauled onto a rolling bed.

"I know this guy," Dr. Dyke exclaims, "I've seen him before. Atlanta airport. I saw him in the waiting room for the commute, with Godehart Wagner. I'm unsurprised."

"Anal penetration, ruptured bowel, peritonitis," Alex comments.

"Tell me something new," she says, muttering over the unconscious Maurice.

She raises her head, points her glasses at me. "Your work?" Informality reigns at this hour.

"No," I reply.

"You were around?"

"No."

"You know nothing," she says.

"It has to stay secret."

"We can keep a secret."

"He was raped today, in a bad way."

"By whom?"

"That's the secret," I say.

"It won't stay a secret for long, this is a serious crime...It wasn't Godehart Wagner?" Like the first time, she pronounces his name as if she's a textbook, 'Gooh-duuh-heart' rolls effortlessly from her tongue.

"How do you know about Godehart Wagner?"

"That not important," she replies. "Not Godehart?"

"Not Godehart, no," I confirm, imitating her pronunciation.

"Just a mischievous hunch," she says.

I'm getting upset. "Listen," I say, "listen..."

"We have to deal with a ruptured bowel," she interrupts. "We don't have much time. When was he raped?"

"Around noon, I would guess."

"That's more than 12 hours."

Yes."

"Not good."

"Is it bad?" I ask.

"He's still alive," she says, raising her shoulders.

Maurice, body and soul, is rushed away by a nurse. Dr. Dyke follows.

"What should I do?" I ask Alex.

"You'll have to wait here," Alex replies, "you're not allowed in the trauma room."

He points to a row of bluish waiting room seats and disappears. The seats are shaped like in airports, tasked to preclude horizontal relaxation. I plop down vertically.

First I think nothing. Then I think that I don't know Maurice that well. Then I wonder how Dr. Dyke would know about Godehart Wagner, since, after all, despite the official rainbow ideology, gays and lesbians rarely connect. Then I think about the party. What's going to happen? Would they be able to reset, resume their gay ways? Flirting, anticipating, singin' and dancin,' touchin' and feelin,' until the proto-orgy morphs into the real thing, when they embrace on the ground, and suck cock, and fuck, and lick cum, and relax, until they are ready for a second round of the same? No, I think, it won't happen, it's impossible. Everybody has to fear for Maurice's death now. There will be no orgy revival. Some elder statesman will suggest that this should stop, that we should go home, although I don't know how he would word it since I'm not an elder statesman. Godehart will concur, and the rent boys will start clearing the tables, moving trays, and making other noises that we know from venues about to unload their patrons.

People will start to leave, everybody apologizing to everybody else, sad, sad expressions will predominate, except among the escorts, whose faces are not sad enough because they are all too happy to go home early and have no fun with Neill. Good night, people will say and promise to be in touch as Godehart's network withers away into the night. Neill will cast a longing, hopeless glance at oriental Jason. Jason will escape to the kitchen and change clothes. Yes, that's the final signal. The escorts will change back into their normal clothes, and reappear among the crowd in their customary blue jeans and white, tattoo-free T-shirts, the way *Giorgio Armani* dresses, they're working for an A-list outfit, after all—that's the final signal. Everybody will leave immediately. Some non-wit will shake Godehart's hand and say, "We'll have to do this again," then realize the *contre-sens*, blush, unable to retract, because he's not only stupid, he's stupid enough not to admit a mistake. Good night.

While it may have taken you two minutes to read the last two paragraphs, it took me two hours to think them up. It's early morning now, not particularly late by gay standards, but I'm no longer gay, I'm sad. And very tired. And I have to wait until Maurice dies.

I cast a glance at the emergency receptionist. She's seen me before in all the people who spent a desperate night in her presence. I don't know how many sobs she's witnessed, cries, hurls, how many desperate men and women ended up in her arms. I don't dare to ask whether I should wait. She dares to tell me that I can go home, I should leave my number, and they will call in the morning. I can't, of course.

We're back to square one when Alex appears out of the blue (I've possibly dozed off in the meantime, fuck the seats). "You should go home," he says, "leave your number, they'll keep you posted." My resistance is for show now, I keep it short.

"I give you a ride," he says.

A meaningful good-bye from the receptionist follows us into the early morning outside.

13 DO YOU WANT TO SEE MY LATEST PROLOG PROGRAM?

H e asks about my place, I give him my address. "It's not far," I apologize.

"No sweat," he replies. We're cruising along the Coastal Highway at moderate speed. "Surprise, surprise," he says.

"You're cruising a lot on the beach?" I ask.
"Fairly moderate to moderate."
"In the morning?"
"I'm always on the night shift."
"Since when?"
"Since forever," he says. And then: "I'm lonely, I'm terribly lonely."
"Strange we never met," I say.
"You're on the day shift, I'm on the night shift."
"I couldn't do it," I say.
"At the college, I met rich kids, I mean children of medical doctors, who were studying computer science because their parents had told them too much about night shifts, and special shifts, and being on the beeper for 36 hours, *et cetera.*"
"Well, computer science is also a good choice, money-wise."
"I dropped out after a while, found it boring."
"Then you decided to become a paramedic?"
"Yes."
"Why didn't you go the whole nine yards, become an MD."
"I can still do it, they have special entry exams for paramedics at some schools."

I did a spell of computer science as well, I tell him, before I dropped out. "Found it too difficult."
"Computational complexity theory," he interrupts, "pathetic. And they cheat, they cut corners."

"How do you mean?"

"Theory-wise, they cut corners. It's bad mathematics."

"Never knew."

"Now you do."

"I shouldn't ask for an explanation, you mean."

"You're welcome," he replies and rolls his head.

We've arrived at *Row Boat Lane*, where the lonely squirrel lives. It's off the Coastal Highway, on the *Davis Canal*, quite nice, just the condo (I don't own the apartment, of course, rented it from an elderly lady who lives somewhere in northern Vermont where she migrated unwisely; perhaps I can explain later). You exit the highway, make a turn, dive down a ramp, and arrive at an oversized parking lot at the back of the building. That's what Alex does. He halts. No, he stops. It's somewhere in between.

If you've ever seen a movie, you've seen this one. The engine is running. I should open the door and say 'Thanks for the ride, I did appreciate.' He should say: 'You're welcome,' or perhaps say again 'No sweat,' because that's his style, then turn around, and leave. But he doesn't.

You never have much time in movies, not even in art-house flicks, so he can't stay silent in meaningful ways for more than a second (unless it's really one of those films that win *Golden Palms* in *Cannes*). Neither can I. So we observe regulations and stay silent for a second. Now the *washed-up scriptwriter* has a wealth of choices, the most important ones being (a) the driver turns off the engine; (b) the driver (or his passenger) bends over in pursuit of a passionate embrace, followed by a kiss of which we won't see the ending before the next cut; (c) the driver says: 'It's late, I'm tired, I'll see you,' followed either by the passenger's departure, or more complications; (d) the passenger opens the door and says 'Well, good-bye then,' followed by his departure and no complications, at least no immediate ones; (e) everything else.

He must have opted for (a), since the engine has stopped. "You don't have a stamp collection, do you," he says.

"No."

"Other collectibles?"

He's somewhat old-fashioned, I think. "No."

"What did you do in computer science?" he asks.

"Not much, introduction, operating systems, some languages."

"Which languages?"

"C, Perl, Prolog."

"*Prolog*, that's funny. Must have been ten years ago, or more. Completely outdated. But interesting, the most interesting language I've learned."

Yes, I think, how do we go on from here, moving forward. "How do we go on from here, moving forward?" I say.

"Moving forward...," the words melt on his tongue. "Why don't you show me your latest Prolog program?"

I laugh. He laughs. We hear a distant echo of the classroom laughter back when this joke was told for the umpteenth time. He parks the car for the night.

T he elevator is broken. We climb the stairs, and I'm hit by a pang of guilt. I was supposed to take Maurice home, not Alex. How is it that in the space of one day two casual sex-acquaintances turn into potential soul-mates? I didn't have a single soul-mate in years, and now I have two, and one is dying already?

Hold on, with Alex we haven't even arrived in our bed, the dune fuck doesn't count, the moving-forward-thing, it could be a misunder-standing, *comp-sci* is all very well but you couldn't handle it, and his loneliness, his loneliness doesn't make him a soul mate either, most people are lonely, if that made them soul mates, they wouldn't be lonely (John's paradox). With Maurice it went further, we had reasonably extended conversations by present-day standards, he's practically locked in soul-wise, and the sex part is not important, it'll work out, with his physique and all, except that he's dead now.

Another pang of guilt. Maurice is dying in the hospital, I'm running away with the nurse. It's not as bad as this senator, this running mate, from North Carolina who's telling his mistress that everything is all-right because his wife will soon die of cancer. It's not *that* bad. Good luck and good night.

But then, I think, did you ever make any promises to Maurice? A marriage vow? Not at all, you warned him of your gayish inability to bind to a partner, told him of emotional fire-walls that were to run right through the middle of your bed like a Chinese monument. Not your fault, not his fault, and his death isn't your fault either, you were trying to help him out with a towel, it was just bad luck that RapeDick appeared at the wrong moment. Plus, Maurice isn't dead yet.

Yes, correct, but how am I to convince the other side of the brain? We are confused, and it's not just Maurice, it's several people in *boyXboy* dimensions, sexual orientation, overhead morals, sheer happenstance, what not. Can you betray your lover with a casual sex acquaintance? *Yes.* Can you betray a sex acquaintance with your lover? *No.* Can you betray a casual sex acquaintance with another casual sex acquaintance? Let bring in the logicians. Nothing happens in four years, and then, in the space of one day, my life changes from Alex to Maurice and back, and I'm stuck. What do you get when you combine a trick and soul-mate, do you get a lover? Well, you don't, Maurice is dying. Hold on, didn't you meet Alex *before* you met Maurice, during the same encounter, isn't there some temporal order to this? It's a silly little thought, but it's alive and well and scales the stairs like a troll. I follow.

It's a good thing that the space-time continuum has a time element. As time progresses and you climb the stairs, you will eventually arrive at a door, hopefully yours. Then you have to find the key, open the door for your fuck-trick-mate, concentrate on his well-being, or your own, and think newer, better thoughts.

My apartment isn't large of course. A kitchen den, one bedroom, and the spare room where I work, with a desk that I move elsewhere when I have visitors, which I didn't have for years, except for my father.

So we enter my apartment. It's for higher reasons that entrances and exits are so important in life. Life, death, penetration, doors opening or slammed shut, actors barely do anything else, playwrights barely write anything else. We enter my apartment. "This is my place," I say redundantly.

We could shut the door and enter a passionate, somewhat artificial embrace (artificial because it's passionate), hasten to the bedroom, strip, and make love. If you need to know more, get hold of champagne commercials on *YouTube*. The clothes are shed on the way to the tiger skin rug enhanced (tiger-skin-rug-enhanced) super bed, the red pumps of the lady being shed first, his black bow-tie is next, the champagne is in holding mode (waiting). Gays can do it, straights can do it, bees and flowers can do it.

However, in doing so, you've set the relays for the future. If Alex embraces me passionately, it would mean that he's here for a good fuck.

If he does *not* embrace me, he's here for either *more*, or *less*. He may not know, at this point, what it will be.

He does not embrace me, instead hovers about the place, holding on to a Baptist-themed sweatshirt in his hand, with "PARAMEDIC" printed on the back. He looks around, looks out of the window where he beholds the contours of a large water tower on the other side of the canal that most people find pretty (I hate it of course, the tower resembles the sky-scraper-sized frog from Disney World). I offer him a chair at the kitchen table. He sits down, without emphasis. He stretches his arms, gapes, like cats do, well, the analogy breaks down soon, you know what I mean. He looks at me as if we've known each other for years. We could be brothers, except that his eyes, even when completely relaxed, still radiate bright intelligence, whereas Jim, my hopeless twin, never looks intelligent, even during casual sex (I presume). Jim and John, what a choice of names, my lazy parents.

"A drink," I say. "Sure," he says. Two beers are left in the fridge.

Under normal circumstances, I would put the can on the table, more or less in front of Alex, and leave him to his own devices. Instead, I search for a tumbler, and, since symmetry is a good thing, I search for a second tumbler. Awaiting decomposition in the dishwasher, the tumblers are not in evidence. I open the dishwasher, fetch the only two beer-sized glasses (always awkward fetching something specific from a dishwasher), and clean them thoroughly.

I could go too far now, like a conscientious hostess would, anxiously open the can, anxiously pouring the beer in pursuit of the optimal foam, then gingerly positioning can and tumbler near Alex on the table. Instead, I open the can, anxiously pour the beer, gingerly put the tumbler in Alex's reach, but forget about the can, which remains on the kitchen counter. I'm not doing this consciously.

Can I ask you a question? Let's not talk about love. Let's talk about a crush. You've developed a crush on this hot guy. He looks great. He's willing to follow you home. He's smart, penis lines promising (in this particular case we know much more already). Now what? You know that you want to see him again, right? And to be inside him, and outside him, and around him, now or never. And go on vacation together, and for long walks on the beach. Right, that's crush level. So you have a crush because he's beautiful and cool and so on. No, that's not how it works. You know it's a crush because he hovered effortlessly next to your kitchen table, because he stretched like a cat, because he held on to his sweatshirt. That's a crush.

Now, symmetry is a good thing, and the most crush-enhancing thing would be a crush of your crush on you. He's having a crush on you? Impossible. This paramedic demigod, this accomplished critic of computational complexity theory, he's so much above you with his green eyes—you, who dropped out of computer science for band-width reasons, you were forced to take up French, the language spoken at the kitchen table by your mother whom you still have to consult on matters French, the language you teach at this hippocampus of the worst repute, there's no way this guy could feel more for you than opportunistic desire, you're just the nearest person in fucking distance tonight.

15 HARMONIOUSLY MARRIED

Although … we don't fuck. If he wanted less than sex, why did he bring up stamps and Prolog programs? Perhaps he wants friendship, friendship *sans* Facebook account. You wanted chastity with Maurice, now you get it with Alex. Fuck yourself on the safe side of your Chinese fire-wall.

Alex drinks his beer slowly, I drink my beer slowly. He's rolling his head, which he does a lot (crushes are about mannerisms, not performance). So, he's rolling his head, first to the left, then to the right, and says: "Tell me about this guy."
"His name is Maurice."
"Maurice."
"Yes, it's not his fault, he's a Brit."
"Indeed," Alex replies, as if he were British himself. "You wouldn't say, with this crew cut."
"I don't know either, I was wondering too, I didn't get a chance to ask him, he died prematurely."

This is now typical John, a silly remark, neither witty nor correct, just banal and brutal, upsetting everybody, in particular the demigods. This is why nobody likes me.

The demigod doesn't seem to care, though. "He isn't dead yet," Alex replies. I think we caught him just in time."
"You think he'll survive?"
"No promises, but Dr. Dyke is very good."

I interrupt: "Dr. Dyke, Dr. Dyke, that's her real name?"
"Not officially, no. Her real name is Sandeman. Alice Sandeman, but you wouldn't know, she never wears her name tag. When she arrived two years ago, and the night receptionist, the one you met, got nosy, which she is, and asked too many questions, Alice replied: 'Call me Dr. Dyke'."

I explain to him that 'Dr. Dyke' was the moniker I invented myself. "Sure," he says, "It happened to her before. She preempted it at the Memorial by bringing it up herself. Alice is great, she's very good. I think they've beeped up one of the surgeons, haven't seen her since, she's possibly assisting the surgeon. They cut Maurice open, clean the abdominal cavity, and fix the bowel where it's torn. Maurice's likely to survive. Eighty, ninety percent, I'd say."

"When do you think we'll have him back?"

"Have him back, we, WE?" He's upset all of a sudden. "This was a trap, in the dunes, right? He waiting in bushes until you've got yourself laid by a passing cruiser, then relieving himself cum-wise in a detached threesome, because that's his thing, while you watch from your perch at the bottom, because that's your thing, and otherwise we're harmoniously married?"

I realize through the haze of his anger that he has just constructed one of my hopeless sentences.

"I didn't even know it was a cruising area," I lie.

"Well, it's semi, it's too open." He retracts quickly: "Well, sure, it's absurd, unlikely, at least. It was a coincidence." His eyes are back on cruise control.

"Happenstance is destiny," he adds.

(Did he say it was destiny we met?)

He wants to know more about Maurice, the rape. I tell the entire story.

"Bad," he says, "bad. I know this Dick, of course. You meet these cops all the time, accidents, trouble, when you have a dead body, you have us and the cops. Dick what, Dick Benson is his name. I tell you something terrible. I'm not surprised. I've seen this guy losing it before. He's quite a character. He's a psychopath. He's an accident waiting to happen. Now he was an accident waiting to happen."

"Huh?"

"Because it happened, the accident."

"If you call it an accident."

"Why—not of course. An accident waiting to happen isn't an accident. Psychopaths come in gradations, like everybody else. From serial killers to Ponzi schemers to small-time mad hatters. Benson is somewhere in between. But he has the traits, the glibness, callousness, lack of empathy, impulsiveness. And he's violent. I've seen him losing it before. In front of the police chief. Beating up somebody. A crime victim, by the way. One wrong word, he hits the guy in the face. In front of the chief. It's never his fault, of course. The guy almost choked on his vomit. You would flap your ears. The chief actually flapped his ears. This guy is capable of anything."

"OK."

"Until this thing is official, and recorded," he continues, "Maurice may have to fear for his life. Officer Benson has a motive. Aggravated rape is a capital offence in Georgia. He's looking at the electric chair, I mean the needle. And he's not stupid. Lots of psychopaths score high on IQ scales. Maurice is the only witness, the ex-wife is muted. The mate, it was possibly Blake, that's his partner, Blake will keep his mouth wide shut, for obvious reasons. Maurice needs to make a deposition, as quickly as possible. Somebody must start asking pertinent questions. At the very least."

"He can't go to the police."

"He can't go anywhere for some time, at least a week."

"What should he do?"

"File this, as soon as possible, with the local DA. With Hunnsbruck, or one of his minions. Have us call the DA, have them come to the Memorial. Alice knows about the rape, right?"

"Yes."

We had been talking for an hour now, during the dawn, and the virgin sun had started kissing the ugly water tower across the canal (to no effect, sadly).

"Can I clear the air of Benson," Alex asks, "open the window?" Sure he can. Warm, moist air invades the kitchen. It feels good, this cloud of humidity, it's like you're entering a sauna on a cold day. I realize how chilly I felt from fatigue. Birds are singing outside. Alex raises his head and a finger. "That's a martin, possibly a purple martin," he says.

"I didn't know the name," I say, "I don't know about birds, but it lives here. It sings every morning."

"During the summer. They migrate to the Amazon delta during the winter."

"How do you know?"

"Learned it from my mother."

"I learned French from my mother."

"You learn everything from your mother, don't you?"

"You think?" I ask politely.

"My mother died when I was ten. That's when the trouble started." He wavers. "I'll explain later," he adds.

Later, he said, "later." The washed-up scriptwriter's heavy-handed handle on the future.

More birds sing, Alex stays mum. Something is passing through the room, he tracks it with his eyes, it's not an angel. This isn't the moment to suggest any transition into my bed, if that's the word. The sun persists in its embrace of the water tower as if it wants to force the issue. It's seven AM.

It must have been this silly word "later," he somehow caught himself in flagrante. "Let's go for a walk," he breaks the silence.

So much for more than sex. He must know what he is doing. I shake my head. More body language. "Let's go to the beach," he persists.

"For sex?" I laugh a desperate laugh. His eye brows are puzzled.

"No, for a walk. You know about beach walks, don't you?"

"Yes, but I go later, around nine." Nine minus seven is two hours that we could spend in bed together. I am about to share my arithmetic results, but he has already risen and grabbed the sweat shirt, he's a mathematician himself.

I am so desperate now. "I'm really tired now," I say, "I don't have to explain, I think." He could end our relationship with the words 'You don't have to come.'

"Look," he finally says, "I understand."

"Look," I reply, "you don't have to explain about your mother" (a one-liner, off-Broadway design, one line from a famous play, context rules, the audience gasps, you could hear a pin drop).

Another pause. "This morning thing, I really mean it, it isn't an excuse. You can't miss out on this morning, it's too good. You've never been to the beach at seven 'clock in the morning, in early July?" He sings the opening cadences from this song from Uriah Heep, "July Morning," which isn't that great, I remember another song, A new life, a new

62

morning, from a forgotten act from the 60's, much better than Uriah Heep, (can't find it on the internet).

"Come on." He sits down. He gets up again. He's doing a pirouette on his left sneaker.

I cry. I cry, suddenly and uncontrollably. Tears roll down my nose. I bend forward over the table (where the tears would form little puddles if this would go on for long). Alex sits down, next to me. He puts his arm on my shoulder.

16   VASOCONGESTION

T his is not exactly what happened, though. I didn't get it at first,
this turn of events, ("reversal," to *intimi*). I left the room in
complete desperation, stumbled into the bedroom, sat down on the bed,
and cried. It was when I felt his touch on my shoulder, Alex's touch, that
I realized my survival at the hands of the washed-up scriptwriter.

We sit on my bed, next to each other. I really need to pee. I didn't go
to the bathroom since when? Perhaps I hit the urinal at the Blue Moon, I
don't remember. In the hospital, I didn't dare to ask for the men's room,
I felt that the emergency receptionist felt that I had to be instantaneously
available for the bad news, like you can't miss the moment that they
fish *John-John* out of the water, remember, when the hottest scion of the
Kennedy dynasty, who had just saluted the coffin of his presidential father
at the tender age of three, had gone missing with his wife and his airplane.
We were watching *CNN*, and were shown nothing but a beach (plus the
sea), for hours, and the anchor tried to keep us entertained (ratings), but
not too much (propriety), for hours, and it was *Search & Rescue* (John-
John, by now, had disappeared for 18 hours or so, supposedly here, in the
sea off this beach, because pieces of his luggage had already been retrieved,
here). So we are watching S&R ("search and rescue"), the beach, the sea,
bright sunshine, the anchor bubbling haltingly. And then, without prior
warning (they could have warned us that the coast guard is now changing
from S&R to a more somber recovery mode), suddenly the anchor's face
pales, and he announces that the rescue mode has switched from S&R to
this more somber mode—you were glued to the screen, you couldn't miss
that moment, your bladder be damned. "I need to pee," I say.

"I need to pee, too," Alex says. We trot to the bathroom. We're buddies
now, serious sex pals, we will fuck together, we will pee together. I lower
my pants. It's not that I really have an erection, but my ding-dong is not
at rest. Alex lowers his pants as well, and my ding-dong does ding. Alex
stands next to me, my penis stands at an angle of 50° above the floor, ca.
20 degrees in erection country. I cannot pee. His semi-erection is milder

at a more modest 35 degrees (there was no ding), but he can't pee either. Why can't you pee with an erection?

Nothing happens. Alex laughs. "We're in a s*exual response cycle*," he says, "and we've already entered the *excitement phase,* with our genitals experiencing *vasocongestion*. The penis is a pendulous organ that swells when blood fills its principal tissues, spongy structures that expand under blood pressure. They exert pressure on the *urethra*, which sends messages to the internal sphincter of the bladder to that effect, informing it of its encumbrance. The sphincter closes. You can't will the internal sphincter, it's autonomous. That's why you stand there. And me, or I."

"What can we do about it," I ask like a little brother, "I have to pee."

"The internal sphincter is controlled by an autonomous part of the brain. But this part reacts to contexts, as any reasonably-designed, autonomous agent does. So you have to change the context. Don't think sexual arousal. Think something absolutely detumescent."

"Like, like..."

"What's your worst nightmare?"

"A faculty meeting. A meeting of the faculty of my department."

"You mean you're a professor?"

"Well," I say, "I teach at SSC, Southern Georgia College, I teach French."

"I know that place, in *Brantley*, I once had a fling with a student, against all odds. I had to drop him off, unseen, behind the Buckthorn bushes, hush hush, touch and go."

"Yes, the place is still in the closet, but that's the least of its problems."

"Elaborate," he says, "it'll help."

"For starters, it's a hippocampus, you may have realized."

"Hippocampus? That's another part of the brain, involved with memory."

"I mean, the campus crawls with hippos; obesity rules the college sea."

"Obesity rules the college sea," he repeats. The words melt on his tongue, or not.

"You get the gist."

"And you are a professor."

There I stand, unable to relieve myself, and am lectured on mixed metaphors.

"You better release your dick, let it swing freely," Alex says, "the swelling is sensitive to tactile stimulation, that's how masturbation works."

I release the dinger. He releases his dinger in sympathy. Both dingers are swinging freely in bathroom space. There would be the suggestion of some coupling, were it not for the fact that his penis is more pendulous than mine. "You'll have to continue a bit," Alex says, "tell us more about the campus."

"It doesn't work," I say.

"Well," he answers, "the thought of rotund post-adolescents may stimulate your kinky side."

"Your detumescence isn't happening either," I say, but it's not true. His pendulous organ is fairly pendulous now.

"Wait," he says, resumes manual control of his pecker and starts to pee. A thin urine jet steadies quickly into a healthy gush.

He's proud of it, as if this were *Brokeback Mountain*. I'm not into pee sex at all, I don't even like watching this, in public toilets, when I really have to pee, I always seek the urinal away from the crowd. So this helps, detumescence strikes, and I can pee again. Not as convincingly as Alex, but we are done in the bathroom.

17 MY PENIS HAS NEVER BEEN THIS LARGE

W e're back in the bedroom. We finally embrace, kiss. This is it, this is the moment. Should Alex expect me to sink to my knees now, unbutton his fly, like in the porn flicks? Or unzip his zipper, most porn flicks are so cheap, they don't have money for the more expensive, button-holed *Levis*—unzip his cheaper jeans and start caressing his briefs with my lips, drawing the attention to his budding tumescence under the cotton?

Well, I might, at least in the sense that my bedroom looks almost as bad as the motel rooms where those flicks are shot. A chest, two wooden bedside tables, two wooden chairs. A timber-framed bed done in cherry imitation, a mattress and dirty sheets, a discordant collection of things that speak of my financial (and mental) condition.

Yet Alex isn't waiting for the cotton kiss (besides, he doesn't wear any fly-enhanced leg-wear but is still clad in his hospital sweatpants). Instead, he undresses unceremoniously. T-shirt, pants, briefs, shoes, socks are all arranged into a neat pile on the second chair.

He climbs onto the bed, folds himself into some relaxed, unassuming position, like a model in a drawing class, but without the attitude. The simplicity of his movements I will never forget, they changed my life.

I follow his example and make an unusual effort at apparel-folding. Although we had fairly rough sex the previous morning, there is not the least suggestion of anything untoward between us in the past, for all practical purposes we could be virgins. I lie next to him.

"You're beautiful," he says, caressing my face. I'm caressing back. This would be the moment to say 'I love you,' although you never know what you get back, like 'moi non plus,' statistically the most honest answer (*moi non plus*, French, used by *Serge Gainsbourg*, the one and only basis for his fame, this noun phrase, meaning "me neither"), or 'I love you too,' but uttered unconvincingly, or 'I love you too,' uttered more convincingly, although you know it's bullshit.

(I hold back.)

(I cannot hold back.)

"I love you," I say.

"No sweat," Alex comes back—bypassing world literature from *Homer* to *Spielberg*. Have you ever heard anybody saying 'no sweat' in this situation? There's a teasing movement of his eyelashes, although his green eyes stay neutral as if it's head or tail. "In human sexual behavior," he says, "foreplay is a set of emotionally and physically intimate acts between two or more people meant to create desire for sexual activity and sexual arousal." Ooh, he's so sweet!

He does what he can. He caresses my pecs, my tummy, my nipples, retracts to my shoulders with his versatile hands, pays attention to my biceps. "You are still quite OK, gym-wise."

"Thank you," I reply, not reciprocating further—there are no words for his Adonis *corpus*. His eyes appear to know this while they are kissing other parts of my body. We're in for the longer haul. He bends over, caresses my thighs, my legs, teasingly avoiding my package or other private parts, all of which have reached a state of extreme arousal. My penis has never been this large.

Should I tell him? It wouldn't go with the romantic flow of his movements, or would it? I know, I know, but this is me, John, always ready for a silly remark. "My penis has never been this large," I say.

"There's no significant correlation between penis size and sexual satisfaction, save in extreme cases," he comes back. "King Farouk of Egypt had a two-inch penis, yet hookers loved it." He laughs. I could say something back, about kings and hookers, perhaps he's a bit naive here, but I don't. More caressing. "You're OK, though," he adds, "it's not *too* large, like mine." The teasing, tactile neglect of my sexual organs, Oh My God. Touch and go, silence.

"The average sexual intercourse lasts sixteen point two minutes," he says, breaking the spell.

"That's long."

"I can't believe it either, but that's what the medical literature says."

He could say something to the effect that we should help the statistics along by compensating for apparent over-reporting by making love forever, but he doesn't. Instead, he moves—yes, he moves to embrace the cliché—he moves to a higher level. He takes hold of my cock, strokes it gently. We're in familiar territory now, well, we've been in familiar territory the whole time, except for his 'no sweat,' remark, or for the size of his (uncut) dick (however irrelevant), or the record size of mine at this moment, or his beauty, or the touch of his fingertips, or his smooth, supple skin that I'm now caressing.

He bends over, and my cock disappears in his mouth. He has full, sensual lips, naturally, and his sensual tongue plays with my sensual soul. There's a flush in my abdomen, emanating, radiating, spreading through the known universe. We haven't changed positions so far as if we will always be side by side, fluent movements rule. He's at it. He's at it.

"Hold on," I say, "I'm about to pop already, not so fast." He can't speak now, due to anatomical constraints. He must have heard me, though, but isn't relenting, he continues, effortlessly—this is really something, how effortlessly he sucks cock. There are no special effects, he's taking his time, there's no rush, only…(rhymes)…my crush.

I explode in his mouth. I'm cumming, I'm cumming, finally, too early, squirting, shooting, exploding, no superlative is spared. He's still sucking, quaffing my load, holding on to my dick. He relents. His position has changed, he's next to me, his dick throbbing above my face. He's so sweet. He's stroking it now, his member, we're in for a facial. His ministrations continue fluently. He doesn't groan, he doesn't make any noise whatsoever, except for the squishy remarks of his foreskin (supplemented by uppity comments from my mattress, which are not his fault).

"Ready," he says. A first contraction, his body spurts back. A second contraction, a first spurt of cum spouts from his knob and ends up on my face. More contractions, more cum everywhere, we've been there before, you get the picture. Still holding his dick, he touches my face with his left hand, wiping his cum over my features, then licking it off with his alpha-tongue.

He sits. "Time for a cigarette," he says.
"I don't smoke," I say.
"It's a poem by *Tennessee Williams*."

We're silent for some time, and now, finally, our angel walks through the room, Alex stretches, another embrace. He's on top of me now, where he unfolds, as if we are forever suspended in a better space and a better time. Infinity.

ne two three, infinity (I'll explain later). My ass.

Alex has already left his perch as a *grand horizontal* when I wake up. Better even, or worse, the sheer fact that I could fall asleep testified to his untimely departure, since nobody, not even straight people, would be able to do so with the *Green Eyes* on top of them. And I did sleep, because I have my usual morning glory, and I am alone, as outlined already, no external stimuli present, only my sleep, and sweet dreams perhaps that I don't remember. I'm too old for spontaneous erections, it's either sexual or it's sleep (not quite true, I remember now, I had one just yesterday, but still).

Sometimes I have trouble falling asleep, and sometimes I don't know whether I did actually fall asleep before waking up in the middle of the night, but then I feel my boner, and know I slept, realizing that my sleeping is better than feared, and thus comforted fall asleep again (only to wake up at a later time with another boner (I think I should stop now)).

Alex is gone, at least he is not the cause of my erection, and my bed is otherwise empty. Where is Alex? Perhaps he's brewing coffee in the kitchen. I get up, and my pendulous organ—I had learned the term "pendulous organ" from Alex only hours earlier—my organ was still *not* very pendulous on the way to the kitchen, the place where Alex was *not* brewing coffee.

My world falls apart, and it's only the second or third time in 24 hours. Through the haze of my upcoming tears I look around. There's a sheet of paper on the kitchen table, a location where experienced tricks in my days—in the days I still brought tricks home—used to leave their goodbye messages when they had been brought up well-enough to signal goodbye before leaving—after getting up as quietly as possible, hoping to undisturb my sleep, getting dressed quietly, not using the bathroom in order to avoid noises, finding some reusable sheet of paper, and a pen, and then writing in very readable hands, usually, like, like drawing a Valentine heart, signed "M," or perhaps even signed "Michael," or, in extreme cases, writing a grammatically well-formed sentence along the lines of "Sorry that I have to leave early, Michael." Sometimes even the word love was used, carelessly, perhaps, but carefully written, since most tricks live near the literacy threshold, rarely write anything, whence their writing hand is unblemished by later excesses.

Where was I? Yes, In the place where experienced, well-brought-up tricks would leave their messages (Mother: "Michael, there is another thing that you should never forget, your exit should always be graceful, and should it happen that genetic destiny strikes and you end up as a loose homosexual, so loose that his nights are spent as one night stands in the company of other loose men, even then your exit should always be proper and good-byed"), in said place I find a re-used sheet of paper with the not-so-readable words *"Dear John, I had to go, I love you, Alex,"* and a little Valentine heart drawn under the text (he could have encircled the text with the Valentine heart, it would have been prettier, but he didn't).

No home number, address, email, homepage link, twitter, tweet, something. Alex is gone.

Now, the situation isn't completely hopeless, at least in the technical sense that I know where he works, so I could try to retrieve him by calling the hospital and ask for Alex, the alpha-god paramedic, ("Alexander, you know, I don't know his last name, the paramedic with the green eyes") and it's anyone's guess what the result would be. Perhaps he is a medical secret, ("We cannot divulge the names or other coordinates of our staff, by law"), or not a medical secret ("You're not the first person asking for Alex in this way, you know"). Or I could, in anticipation of such answers avoid any contact by telephone and position myself around dawn near the staff entrance of the hospital, waiting for Alex like fans wait at the *bühnenausgang* of Wagner's opera burgh in Bayreuth for a famous singer, and ask for an autograph when the alpha-god finally appears.

There are other possibilities as well, think hospital email etc. Let's do some hand-waving here (an expression I had yet to learn from Alex), you get the gist. Email, stop. Internet, Google. You know, I can't think in panic, so I type "Alex" in Google's main search window of my computer, today enhanced for unclear reasons by a *Sherlock Holmes* motif. Only more than one billion answers. Without thinking I click on the first link, which connects me to ALEX, the *Alabama Learning Exchange*. Good, I think, that's in the South. But not in Georgia, I realize, then my thinking stops again since the terrible truth strikes again, that I have lost the *Green Eyes* to a hopeless, lonesome future in *confirmed bachelor county*, GA, USA.

I would normally make coffee once detumescence (what a useful word) has commenced, but don't feel like it. Instead, I get my thoughts together and start a systematic search for "Alex," the "paramedic" of the "Memorial Baptist Hospital" in "Georgia Beach," in "Glynn county," "GA," "US," which yields nothing. A hospital is not a university, they won't list all their staff in unreadable, smallish fonts, even people who died 20 years ago of disappearance, like Alex had died of disappearance, this morning, between eight and ten o'clock.

I read the message again. "Dear John, I had to go, I love you, Alex." Nothing, nothing in this message would speak of the future. There are no undertones, no overtones, the message is as neutral as his green eyes were (used to be) when his own studied ambivalence was undecided about a course of action. In the meager space of a few hours I had seen this neutrality more than a few times already, if his eyes talked, something was at hand, and there was nothing of the surreptitious eye language that tends to accompany the meaning-challenged behavior of people who have nothing to say, eyes too open, eyes too small, eyes winking, squinting, and so on.

A message as neutral as his eyes. Why didn't he say anything about a date tomorrow, or on Saturday, or the Blue Moon, or the beach. Why did he "have" to go. He was sleeping next to me, or on top of me, or whatever, his next shift starting, what, possibly at 10 PM or later. Why did he have to "go?" Why did he "love you," why did he "I love you," if he loved me, he would not be gone but embrace me tenderly while sticking his penis into my ass, a routine that we had practice already once, although, during our earlier cruisin' encounter, he had refrained from the poignant anatomical commentary that accompanied his later work.

73

"I love your work," he could have written, if I'd only shown him my blog. I mean the blog I talked about earlier, about everything and nothing, even the gay condition, perhaps he would have liked it (although I have no followers), and decided that he cannot ditch a person that's not only 'OK, gym-wise,' as he had said during foreplay, but also OK blog-wise, and he would now put his penis into my ass, or at least leave his number, and everything would be all-right.

There is a movement now in trendy USA, of which even I am aware, to replace the words "blogger," "blogging," etc. by better, nicer words, and if such words are ever found, I would not only be a good blogger, I would also be a *nicer word*, and Alex would be sure to stay, but he's already gone.

I stare at the Sherlock-Homes-themed Google search window and realize that there is no *deerstalker*. It's not about Holmes at all. It honors *Agatha Christie*, perhaps her thousandth birthday, and her biography comes to mind, how she had married this racing pilot, much handsomer than plain Agatha herself, and how the relationship had soured, and how she, famous already, had suddenly disappeared, gone, *futsch*, with search and rescue teams (S&R) in hot pursuit, until she had suddenly and without prior warning reappeared in some country inn, and never returned to her handsomer husband, and later marry a handsomer archaeologist, 14 years her junior, and they would write books together in the sense that when she would write a book he would take time away from his other obligations and also write a book, in the room next to hers.

This is the future that Alex and I deserve. He an accomplished sexologist with a lucrative clinic next door, I an accomplished *nicer word* behind my laptop, and we would happily live ever after, and he pays the bills.

19 NAKED GIRLS

I brew coffee without further justification. I drink a cup and don't know what to do. The sun is still at it, embracing the ugly water tower, it is almost on top of it now, what's the name of this position? I should take pictures for my blog, and mention in the post that the tower is an ugly frog, how do we say, 'in attendance,' 'in expectation,' 'in dire need of,' what? 'Relief,' 'transcendence,' perhaps. I could use an older trick and insinuate lightly that the tower is, in reality, a spaceship, which is awaiting trans-whatever into an ugly frog. We're not getting anywhere. My blog, that's the blog that could have saved me if I would only have shown it to Alex, so that he could have liked it, and liked me more, and leave his number behind, I'm repeating myself.

The blog lives in the spare room, on the ambulant desk, in my computer (I'm still stuck with a PC). I leave kitchen and coffee behind and turn the switch. Starting up takes forever, my PC is four years old (why did everything happen four years ago?).

Let me see, I don't quite remember when I posted the last post, like what, three days ago? About what? I forgot as well. This blog, confusingly named *Freedom Fries*, is about everything and nothing. It includes loose talk about the gay condition and risqué pictures of the semi-graphical kind. But the soft porn never angles more than 35°, we're barely in erection country, not because I'm prudish, but because I want to avoid a *content warning*, which, I fear, would discourage the last of my regulars of whose sexuality I know little. Beyond the pendulous porn there are posts with shots of the acidic type, and political posts against slavery and the Confederacy. Sometimes somebody emails a new joke, I find a fitting picture, you name it. There are millions of these blogs, perhaps more than potential visitors (some guy from the computer science department told me that 20 thousand new porn sites go on line each day, I can't believe it, but then I never believe other faculty).

I have *80* to *100* unique visitors per day. Outsiders expect me to have thousands of viewers, and sometimes somebody tries to get me to post a nasty post on some *Assistant Secretary* of the *Environment* in the expectation that this will finally change *Washington's* ways and keep the Confederacy intact. However, eighty percent of the visits are for one single post, a hilarious bunch of naked girls holding trophies in their hands. You keep these girls because they save your ass click-wise in an unbalanced world when you have to speak about unique visits to un-unique visitors (this sentence meanders too well in its muddy delta; it's quite typical for the blog).

My thoughts are uninterrupted by Window's duh-daah-duh-daah, and the blog is finally awakening (terrible sentence). My last post was posted ten days ago. Not good. Not for the first time. If you don't post, the search engines lose interest, your visits drop off the cliff a few days later, like *Wile E. Coyote*. It's hard to resurrect the score, you have to post like hell to re-awaken the crawlers. The terrible blog syndrome is raising its ugly head, you're tired, tired of blogging, and not only that.

When you start playing with the settings—which is what I'm doing at the moment—it could be a good sign, but usually it's a bad sign. We shouldn't only change our ways party-wise, and meet new friends, and marry Alex, we should also change something about the blog. Its content perhaps? Doing the opposite of what we are doing? Or at least improve the presentation, the whole set-up, it hasn't changed in four years, the world has moved on. Let's change the settings. We can "customize," or do "HTML." We click on "customize."

Another list appears, choices, choices. "Dynamic View" is the first option. *Dynamic View*, we don't remember that one in particular. Let's see. We click. A pop-up displays your blog in new ways, but the window is shaded, you don't see enough. "Apply to blog?" an inviting button asks in orange. You'd like to know, right, so you click *Apply to Blog*. Two wheels of patience appear, little cogwheels turning in opposite directions, embracing each other (to the extent that cogwheels can do that). Nothing happens for a while, the wheels still making love.

Then, all of a sudden, the wheels die the *liebestod*. The screen yields a flicker, and a casual text in the upper left corner reads in unassuming *Times*

New Roman, without further embellishments, or icons, or anything else, there's just one large white page (white as #FFFFFF), where your blog used to be. It reads, "Service unavailable, Error 503." We've seen this before, so we click on the *renew page* icon on the navigation bar. "Not found, Error 404," Blogger replies. You try again. You try different browsers. Nothing works.

You type the link, "http://freedomfris.blogspot.com." Blogger comes back in a better mood now, colors, flags, offers for help, plus the orange-colored button-offer to register freedomfris immediately ("Start the blogs, start the blogs!"). A typo of course. I retype, more carefully. Times New Roman and #FFFFFF are back. Error 404. We try all sorts of things. Resets, restarts, and so on. Error 404. Error 404. Freedom Fries, my blog, is unavailable, inaccessible, frozen. Like Alex. *Futsch*, gone, dead.

The phone rings.

20 MY FATHER AND YOUR FATHER WERE FATHERS

T he phone rings.

It's not that simple, of course, the phone doesn't ring. Instead, it sings a pop song to me, or, more precisely, speaks like your future ex would speak to you in a failed marriage.

"It's coming back to me now," the cell sings again.

It's the hospital. Maurice. We killed Maurice and now he's dead. A neutral voice informs me about my identity. "We have you down here as next of kin," the voice continues. My parents are still alive, my stupid brother is, tricks never die. This is the first death notice of my life. *Next of kin.* This is the moment. "I would like to provide you with an update on the condition of our patient. Mr. Dymond has undergone surgery."

"Wait," I interrupt, "is that Maurice? Maurice Dymond?" A pause. Yes, it is.

"Mr. Maurice Dymond received blood transfusions and is now in stable condition, but still under intensive care. He has regained consciousness after surgery, and is sleeping now."

"Wait," I say, "wait."

I put the phone down, pour myself another cup of coffee. Then I put the cup next to the cell phone, go to the bathroom, and wash my hands. I'm back in the kitchen, where cup and cell-phone await my return. Did I kill Maurice or not? The voice is still there, no sign of impatience. He's possibly used to this, even trained for it in case the news would be different. I apologize for the intermission.

"Mr. Lee," the voice continues, "there is something more. I have a message for you, from Dr. Sandeman, the MD of the ER. She's asking you to see her, urgently, at the beginning of her next shift, tonight around ten o'clock. She must discuss important matters with you, concerning Mr. Dymond. She absolutely hopes you can make it, despite the late hour. She apologizes for the inconvenience. You might then briefly visit with Mr. Dymond, the IC unit is always open to next of kin in emergency cases. Would you please confirm?"

"How do you mean, confirm?"

"That you will come."

"Yes, sure. Maurice okay?"

"Considering the circumstances."

"He's going to live?"

"His condition is stable. He's under IC. Any problem, any situation, we know within seconds."

I'm going to ask more questions, it's like you've won the lottery big time, and they call you, and you want to know how they are going to pay, and when, by check, or wire, and whether you should get a haircut. The voice cuts me off.

"Please confirm," it asks.

"Can I ask you one more question."

"One more."

"Who are you?"

"I'm Quinton Hayes, the head nurse of the IC ward. You did invite me once to your premises, four years ago." He was possibly my last trick. I confirm.

I sip the degrading brew; a new bird is singing outside, perhaps another martin. The sound is faint, the windows are closed now (air conditioning). You suffer when you look at the heat outside, the water tower is suffering too. I'm a selfish person, and could stay in character by thinking that Maurice isn't a bad substitute for Alex. He has no nick name, right, it's just Maurice. What is it about "Maurice?" Yeah, right, a gay story with a happy ending. The Brits sometimes play with their surnames, Dymond, perhaps he's *Dy*, or *Lady Dy*. I'm not thinking at all.

The doorbell rings. Alex is back! It must be him. Nobody else knows where I live. He's back from the convenience store and brings cigarettes and love and fresh condoms for an extreme fuck. No need to answer the

79

intercom, I have an erection already. I'll buzz the buzzer. I hear the push-click of the entrance door below, then heavy steps. As if somebody carries a heavy load. Slow, onomatopoetic steps. Something is wrong. The steps turn at the penultimate landing, I can see them now. It's my father.

The blog is frozen, I'm frozen. Usually I swing from one uncool state to the next, but my father does wonders, he makes me freeze so fast, I would make a good guinea pig for cryopreservation efforts.

I await my father on my landing as he climbs the last flight of steps. I stay motionless, focus on him as if he doesn't exist, looking through him. His bag is heavy, heavier than last time, he's a year older. I step backward into my apartment. He puts his bag down, gasps, heavy breathing of the unerotic kind. He's waiting for me to say something, I reciprocate. He isn't saying 'hello,' or 'howdy,' he doesn't know how to overcome my threshold. He explains why he has come earlier, he couldn't reach my voice mail, something to do with his boss. No embrace. I'm thinking whether I should submit him to an awkward handshake, shoulders and body stiff, the arm bent at an acute angle, you've seen this in Nazi-flicks. I did the Nazi shake to him on some occasions but won't do so today. I retreat further into the kitchen, he follows with his bag.

"You want coffee," I state, my first words. Yes, he wants coffee. I hand him the poisonous brew. Let his visit commence.

"Joe sends you his greetings," he says.
"How's Joe doing."
"Fine," my father answers, "he's finally got on with his divorce."

It isn't complete clear what he wants to say, as usual, it's rarely clear to me what he wants to say. I've learned a lot from him though, how stupid people are—not that he ever explained, although he's complaining a lot how stupid people are. I'm more stupid than him, for sure, so I've completely given up on syllogisms, or other debating tools. When we fight, it's not a debate. I really try hard not to argue, and when I succeed, it's because I get him so mad, he runs after me, I jump off the cliff (Wile E. Coyote), and he follows. It's easy to make him mad, that's my weapon of choice, NRA, take note. I make him mad about everything, then I'm off to bed, he's off the cliff, no beer left in the fridge. We do this for three days, then we have a real fight, body talk from the street. I'm five times stronger than him, we had a real fight once, he keeps me going at the gym. When we had that fight, he rolled down the stairs, some ribs were broken, he had to drag himself to the emergency room, I did not follow up, nobody wanted to know. Mother and him are divorced, he left town, found a job in Atlanta.

Why does he always come back?

Perhaps his skin is so thick, he feels nothing. He spends a holiday week on the beach (cut short to three days), and I feed him one hamburger each night, plus not enough booze. Perhaps he comes here for weight loss. Perhaps it's just a pretext, his beach towel time under the melting sun. Perhaps it's plain guilt, self-flagellation, or it's just for show. Perhaps he wants his boss or Joe to believe in his family life, he's a father, my father, my father and your father were fathers, he has sons, my son, John junior. Who knows. Or he likes to talk about his vacation, he vacations in Paris, TX, and Georgia Beach, France.

He drinks the poisonous coffee (it's so bitter now *Miss Marple* should urgently plan on a visit). He shakes his head, puts the dirty cup back on the table, and survives. "You know what," he says without prior warning, "I'm with the *Tea Party* now."

Does he really mean it? Should I say anything back? Sarcasm is the lowest form of wit, right? "Cool," I say.

I should have left it at that. "You're a Tea Party activist, or passivist," I go on.
"Both," he replies.

I lost. I should beat him up now.

I get the spare room ready without further comment. The desk is on wheels. It goes into my own bedroom, there's just enough space. I re-drape the sheets of the spare bed, don't change them. Let a dirty old man sleep in dirty old sheets. I didn't change them since last year. He used them before, perhaps he's still sexually active, don't let's go there.

81

How to abuse a father in the meantime? Step *one*, no welcome. Done. Step *two*, offer poison. Done. Step *two-a*, let him die. Fail. Step *three*, let him ask for the booze. Step *four*, there's no booze left (Alex helped). Step *five*, be unpredictable. On some occasions, I go and fetch a few cans of beer from the nearest convenience store. On others, I don't, I'm off, busy, see you later, there is no spare key. He's off to the beach, he returns, he can't get in, there are no flower pots, my cell-phone is on voice mail. The first day is almost over, two more days to go.

You want to know whether he ever abused me? Well, he didn't rape me. My mother once caught him on the wrong side of my body, when the thing stopped. I'm politically incorrect in a terrible way, I know. I didn't really care. He sucked my dick, it didn't hurt. I've never been asked to suck his. I wasn't hurt, or devastated, at least subjectively I wasn't. But I think my bipolarity has something to do with it, I learned to compartmentalize, or my brain did, my father in one compartment, other things in others compartments, and myself somewhere else. These compartments are still there. I always have to think outside some boxes, go back and forth from box to box. These boxes will possibly stay with me for the rest of my life. This back and forth all the time, it must have something to do with my mood swings, I don't know.

I never talked about it. He never talked about it. My mother never talked about it. But when I came out, mother divorced. I never asked her why. But I'm sure she thought it was his fault, that he "initiated" me somehow, like some people get initiated to poor argumentation techniques by a third-rate teacher who raises two fingers to signal a quote when he can't find the right word (that's obviously not what she thought, bear with me). Yet sometimes, when I cannot sleep, when all barriers are down, I agree with my mother and think that my life would be so much easier in the arms of a naked girl who's just won a trophy for fucking me to death.

We're still at step five of the relationship therapy. Be unpredictable. Head or head. It's head, we'll go fetch some booze, I need fresh air.

21   THE GERMAN CEMETERY

I'm on my way to the convenience store, except that I'm not, because the truck won't start. Father is in his box, I can forget about him, but my truck is in a different box, in particular when it acts up. I never knew it was a truck until Joe, a neighbor, told me so—*I* thought I had bought an *SUV* from a stupid lemon dealer, an antique *Mercedes 320 ML* from another millennium. But after a few miles it transpired that the fine line between arrogance and hubris had been crossed once again by my autonomous brain in that the lemon dealer turned out to be right, and I turned out to be wrong. It helps a bit, though, that Joe—a wealthy oil man from Louisiana who owns the penthouse on the roof and the latest version of my model at a six-digit price point—that Joe calls his ML a truck, it makes a difference in the delusion compartment whether it's your *truck* that breaks down, or your *premium-brand SUV* with leather seats and other deluxe options.

Some options still work, but the ignition is not among them. I'm not a technician, I try what I can, but give up after a few minutes. This would be serious, I wouldn't even get this piece of junk to the repair shop, I would have to pay the towing service on top of a hefty Mercedes bill, and it does not help either that the proactive employment office from my dreams comes back to mind, with their suggestion I should join an escort agency for pecuniary reasons—perhaps I should take it as a compliment gym-wise.

It speaks of my gym that I'm still able to think while swimming to the convenience store through 90 percent humidity. The place is in a bad location for a convenience store, right next to the largest mall on the Coastal Highway, but it's only seven minutes from my place on foot. The store had gone out of business several times before, but *Luke*, the new owner, had extended the convenience range smartly with vampire equipment, sex toys (free speech), and very good condoms, gays come for miles for the *Iliad Premium Latex*.

Sales have certainly improved, I'm not the only customer despite the hour, and last night's host Godehart has apparently run out of latex stock because he has already arrived (perhaps the orgy has seen resuscitation after our emergency departure). *Luke*, behind the counter, greets me with his vampire smile (I'll explain later). Godehart is ensconced in the toy department where he is practically exposing himself with a large double dildo in his hand. I'm describing this thing in case you don't know. Thick, rippled, skin-colored phalli extending in both directions, angled at roughly 150 degrees, attached to a sturdy handle to hold on to, and suggestively shaped in the form of a scrotum, the handle. Godehart is entirely in his element, despite the hour, holding on to the plastic balls, studying the thing as if he has never seen one, turning it this way and that way, knowing that people would watch. He is happy to see me, overjoyed almost, extending the dildo arm invitingly as if he would expect a *baise-coc*.

He wants to know about Maurice. He has called the hospital, but they weren't willing to divulge anything, except that Maurice is still alive. The orgy had been canceled, or at least postponed, and we all dearly hope that Maurice will be able to attend next time. I fill him in on the survival part but avoid any mention of rape, a bad fuck is bad enough.

"I stand here as a flamboyant homosexual with a double phallus in my hand," he says, pointing his Wagnerian nose at the toy, "but do not misunderstand me, I am truly concerned about the events of yesterday, and this is the first time that such a thing has passed at any of my feasts. It is for that reason that I came here at this early hour, since I wonder myself if next time we should not propose a certain test to our guests, before..." his voice drops off.

"GooDuuharrt," I say, imitating Dr. Dyke's pronunciation of his name, "That's not a good idea."

He is somewhat taken aback. "How do you know how to pronounce well my un-shortened fore-name?" he asks, receding a bit into the superficially secluded sex department.
"I learned it from Dr. Sandeman, she was in charge when we arrived at the emergency room."

"Alice, ach," he says. "Alice will think that everything is my fault. She has no concept of my member. He is long, but he is thin, and he never causes problems inside an anus."

"How does she know about you?"

"Alice was the girl-friend of my wife, of Eleanor. Eleanor died, I mean she is dead, she performed a suicide. Eleanor lived here, in Georgia Beach. She was an artist, a fine art painter, and she was well-to-do by herself, she did not need to live near an urban center. Alice moved down here to live with her."

"You were married?"

"Well, yes, Eleanor and I were married."

"You're bisexual?"

"No, entirely not, that is a misunderstanding."

"But you were married."

"It was a marriage of convenience. The coming-out process was inhibited in my case. Have you come out to your family?"

"Yes."

"To whom?"

"My parents."

"Could you tell me their names?"

"Mary and John."

Godehart nods. "I understand, that explains everything. It is impossible, however, to come out to somebody with the name Winnifried. Believe me. For bearers of the name Winnifried, or Friedelind, even Wieland, it is impossible to be comed-out to. So I had to find a wedding partner. I met Eleanor in Bayreuth. Eleanor was a great admirer of the Richard, and she was also rather vain, so that it appealed to her to become a Wagner herself through marriage. I think she would even have consented to sexual intercourse, if that would have been the requirement."

"But that wasn't the requirement."

"No, it was not. She never had an opportunity to see my penis. And I never raised the subject with her—the subject of the actual length, or shape, or other properties of him—that was not necessary. We always slept in separate rooms and used different bath rooms. Eleanor cannot have formed true ideas about the size of my member. Consequently, Alice cannot have formed true ideas of his size, since Eleanor could not have passed true informations to her. From the one follows the other. But our

85

marriage was rather successful. We started the company together, with her money. We co-owned the company."

"Why did she move here?"

"She was not German, she was American, out of the South, she was a *southern belle* in her own lesbian ways, and she was homesick. When her aunt died, she left her her house, which is located next to the Blue Moon bar, as you know. So she decided to move down here. She and Alice had already begun their relationship. Alice followed her down here when she obtained a position at the hospital. It is very terrible that we lost Eleanor to a self-murder, and that Alice was not in the position to protect her."

"Eleanor was depressive?"

"In truth, it was not the first time. She had made a suicide attempt earlier. That was when we still lived in Bayreuth. I blamed it on Bayreuth, and on Godelind, my bisexual sister. They had an affair, of course, but Godelind ended the relationship in that she said that she couldn't undergo Eleanor's American accent any longer, and she critiqued Eleanor's fine painting work. Eleanor had a sensible soul, she was a real artist, at least in that respect. When Eleanor was resuscitated, I suggested that she should move away. She moved to New York, where she met Alice."

"You know Alice well?"

"I knew her quite well. But we do not speak with each other anymore."

"Since the suicide?"

"You understand, perhaps."

There never has been any suicide in my family, perhaps that's why it is so dysfunctional. "I can imagine," I say.

"I should not make any false accusations, so much is clear."

During the entire conversation, Godehart had slowly lowered the sex toy until it was dangling from his hand like a hockey stick. He caught himself when it touched the ground at the tip of the other phallus, and his now-pensive face reverted to normal, with a wistful, slightly debauched expression on his lips. "If I understand you right, you think that this double dildo would be unpractical," he says, bringing the conversation back into familiar territory.

"I think this thing could do more harm than a live penis."

"I think I understand your argumentation, I should have bethought this before. We need to find another solution. But we should not discard this toy entirely, we should bring it home, perhaps for ourselves."

"What?" I splutter.

"You are very welcome to accompany me, we could spend an interesting afternoon together, including you, and myself, and the dildo."

Now, folks, are you still there? You want to know what happened next? I got an erection. And the fact that Gohard was picking up on my dynamic penis lines with his frolicking eyes did not help, the tumescence stabilized under his gaze into a solid bulge. "How interesting," he said to my crotch, drawing my attention to his own dynamic pendle inside his elegant slacks.

One is never too old to learn, I think to myself, and didn't you promise yourself to change your life? Besides, Godehart, perhaps 15 years my senior, had abruptly trans-*whatever'd* into the seductive appearance of a younger elder statesman, and the neon overhead lights kissed his face in the most convincing ways, bringing out all the charm of his laughter lines.

We proceed to the cash-out counter. Luke sees us coming. Luke, like all undead, has a sixth sense for everything, which he doesn't need in this case. As we approach the counter, he catches himself, raises his eyes a bit too late, but is all politeness. "Shall I wrap it up, or do you want to use it immediately," he asks with his vampire sense of humor.

"There is no requirement to wrap," Godehart replies, "but I must refresh my reserves of *Iliad Premium Latex*, please."

"Iliad, always an excellent choice," Luke retorts as if he were Godehart's butler. "You might be pleased to learn that Iliad has issued a new size category for its range, Magnum XL, it may even fit onto the dildo."

Godehart is very pleased, indeed. Rubber reserves are replenished, extended. I buy two cans of beer.

We leave the shop together. Outside, the heat greets us like another vampire, this one without any sense of humor. Godehart points to a high-shine Mercedes SUV parked near the entrance, same type as mine, ML, but the newest model, painted in metallic not-quite-turquoise. The thing looks as if it won the lottery. We mount the ascent to the fine leather seats. There is no need to start the ignition, the thing is telepathic, it just rolls off the parking lot.

At this moment I have to think very quickly. Fortunately, the appearance of my father has reset my panic button, I'm as calm as a cloud. And I think *German Cemetery,* Rome, Italy. I once met a man in unquestionable circumstances, a world-famous composer, from Europe, a composer of contemporary music, world famous, his operas would premier by default at the *Met* or in *Covent Garden,* and he had already written more symphonies than Beethoven, let's call him *Hans Werner* (not Wagner). Hans lived in Rome, where this cemetery is conveniently located (wait), a burial ground for German nationals since ages. The cemetery is world-famous in Germany since it holds the remains of *Goethe*'s son, the one-and-only son of the German *dichterfürst* (the spell checker suggests "Lichtenstein"). Every German school child knows about this. What they don't know, it's also a cruisin' ground. So Hans pays an urgent visit to Goethe's grave (the son), meets new friends, and has a "quick embrace" (his words), with an American, apparently, who flips his wallet and hands the world-famous composer a hundred dollar bill. Hans accepts the money and leaves the grounds elated, with one more anecdote in his pockets. I'm not making this up.

I'm still thinking, bear with me. Hans is world famous, you are world-*un*famous. But that's not your fault, your blog is frozen, not your fault. And you need the money more urgently than Hans. Perhaps you could ask him to lend you the hundred dollars, but you've never seen him again, he won't remember you. Hundred dollars won't be enough, by the way, for the Mercedes repair job.

As I said, I finished this thought very quickly, and before Godehart has a chance to take the wrong turn. "Wait," I say to Godehart, "I must show you something." Godehart is slightly disoriented, weren't we heading toward his home? "I'm in trouble," I add (like an impostor would when he makes his move, although the impostor would speak more like Godehart than me ("I have encountered temporary pecuniary problems that are inconveniencing me absolutely at this midday hour")).

"Turn right," I say to Godehart, who follows his dick. It's seven minutes on foot, one minute on the cruiser. We arrive on my parking lot, where my truck is waiting like a poor relative of the Mercedes family. "It won't start, can you help me?" I say.

You get it? 'Can you help me?' It's ambiguous, right? But the immediate context is one of innocence, suggesting nothing but a consultation among Mercedes *confrères*, my asking him for advice as to how to resuscitate a poor relative of the Mercedes family. It's absolutely above board, no suggestion of prostitution.

I don't know whether Godehart got it immediately, but I think he did. I hand him the ignition key, he ascends to the driver seat of the junk truck, inserts the key in his casual-ceremonial ways, turns it, and listens to very contemporary music, short bursts of engine sound followed by silence. He goes through the motions, repeats his ignition efforts just enough times to keep up appearances, when he shakes his head and says: "We must contact Mercedes." He gets on the cell-phone and calls the Mercedes emergency HQ on the moon where they speak German. Godehart speaks German himself, not for long, he's interrupting himself already, tells me that they will need the car key. I don't quite understand. They will send a towing truck, per space shuttle, since he, Godehart, is a member of the galactic black-card Daimler club, and it's all free of charge. Now I understand. My useless father, I explain in turn, will have the key ready when they come, the name on the doorbell is *Lee*, I give him the address. A few more words in German.

"They'll send someone now, liftoff," he says, locks the SUV. I'm running upstairs with the key to hand it to dad, who is waiting for his beer.

We're off to Godehart's homestead, driving on the Coastal Highway again (that's all you do in Georgia Beach), when a large towing truck transcends from the sky, with a large, revolving, dark-blue neon Mercedes star mounted to the roof of the cabin, while a choir of flying Valkyries intones the famous Wagner song *"Dein guter Stern auf allen Strassen."*

I'm making this up.

So, we're on our way to Godehart's homestead next to the Blue Moon. I am quiet, Godehart is quiet. That's typical at this point in a budding relationship with a trick. You're in the car now, and you either talk a lot, or you don't talk at all. Except, I'm not a trick, I'm a prostitute. And he's the john. John and john, John is not a practical name for a sex worker. Well, too late. He's delivered on his part of the deal, it's my turn. Relax, there is no law that says johns have to be old and ugly, that's just a self-serving prejudice. I once met this guy, an Italian, not even *that* handsome, fairly average, who was really into anal penetration, the first thing he told everybody was that he was a *top*, and this guy would travel to Thailand on a regular basis, to places like *Pattaya* and *Phuket*, and the boys—that's what he told me at least—the boys would ask about his hotel room and tell him: 'You don't have to pay.' He never had to pay, that's what he said at least. He was on his way to Thailand again, I gave him a ride to the airport.

Let's think more profound thoughts. This is my first time, never done it for money before. Possibly not the last time. Hold on, did he actually pay me? Like Werner was paid, the American flips his wallet, and 100 dollars enter your pocket? Well, Godehart's help is worth much more, potentially, you don't know what the problem is with the ignition, it could be thousands of dollars. So this is actually a good start of my escort career, I'm with my own agency now, we can assure you, John, your agency is completely above board, please change your name. It would be worse if it isn't prostitution at all, in hindsight, if they find out that my truck is a non-starter and has nothing to do with Godehart and his galactic membership, pun not intended. And they will. We have your vehicle here, Mr. Lee, it has undergone surgery and is now in stable condition. Please bring the checkbook.

"Godehart" I say, "my truck has nothing to do with you, they'll find out and send me the bill."

"We will cross that bridge when we reached it," he replies. Is he offering me a pension as kept boy, paid every time my piece of junk breaks down? What am I bringing to the table? My junk. He will know how to think outside the box and use tables in creative ways.

"Why did you decide to get settled here in the hinterland?" I ask.

"It will not be for the full-time, I will naturally behold my bureau in Bayreuth."

"Still."

"Well, to my surprise, I inherited Eleanor's house."

"To your surprise? You were her husband."

"I had expected that she would leave it to Alice."

"Alice might have expected that, too."

"I will not make false accusations."

"Did she leave anything to Alice?"

"Yes, she left her her art work, all the paintings. They are still in the basement. Everything."

"But not the house."

"No."

"The house would have been more practical."

"That you can say."

"Is it good, her artwork?"

"How shall I express myself, my tastes are more traditional."

"You are not convinced by Eleanor's work?"

"Ach, her most recent interest lay in spots. Mostly she painted two or three spots. One white spot, and one black spot, for example, on a white background."

"How can you see a white spot on a white background."

"That is a good question. That is perhaps why she killed herself."

I look at him for any signs of an oops-moment, but to no avail. Anyway, we have arrived at his place as the SUV, in a final inspired effort, turns onto the driveway a bit too fast. Squeak. Something is wrong.

"You weren't driving," I say, "you didn't have your hands on the wheel." Godehart raises his index finger in an *amerto* gesture and purses his lips.

"Have you heard from the autonomous Google vehicle design?"

"Yes."

"This is it. This is the first model that is licensed in Georgia under a secret say-so of the government. The director of Daimler is a spirited fan of my fore-father. And the governor of Georgia is also a spirited fan of my fore-father. From the one the other follows. Do not tell anybody, though, it has to stay a secret for a while, lest misunderstandings take hold with the *hoi polloi*."

"The color is a bit out of the ordinary for a secret."

"*Meryl Streep* invented this color in her entertainment film, 'The Devil Wears Prada.' It's the only color that does not appear in the rainbow. She called it *cerulean blue*. She is also a great fan of my fore-father. It is always best to hide secrets in the public view."

"She looks like she's won the lottery, your Google truck."

"Truck," he says, "you call her a truck? She is a *Mercedes 500 ML Brabus Google beta edition*."

"That's a mouthful."

He grins his grin. "She listens to the name *Isolde* when nobody is present. She is, how do you say, she is a scout's secret."

With this, he grabs Luke's plastic bag and leads me up to porch of his charming Victorian lady, prettier today even in bright daylight than yesterday night.

We know Godehart's interior already, more *Bauhaus* than Wagner, save for the art on the wall, which isn't exactly Wagner either, you recall the two boys on a jetty in a meaningful embrace. "Your interior isn't really Wagnerian." I say.

"That appears to be a question of perspective. Most of these designs, what the educated burgher calls modern design, that was already invented almost a hundred years ago. But I didn't appoint the interior. Eleanor did. I changed the paintings on the wall and made the beds more multi-purpose. Lesbian sex is less demanding. I left her interior ideas untouched. I know I have bad taste."

He draws my attention to another painting, hanging above the couch opposite to the pond boys. "This is a *Ross Watson*," he says, as if he's expecting a reaction. I feel like a young pupil at the hands of the a wise pederast, well, not quite. I am eager, though. "This is a play on *Caravaggio*," I answer.

"Yes," he replies, "even though no penises are there to see, or?"

Come on, does he expect me to say that there aren't any penises on the Caravaggio either? The A-plus escort will go the extra mile: "The real things have more vibes," I say.

"That you have said well," Gohard replies.

My career is progressing, I am ready for anything now, upstairs, downstairs, in between. Gohard points at the leather couch and says: "This is the right place, or? I will be so back soon."

What's the experienced escort to do momentarily? Porn-wise, I shouldn't undress until he's back, the stripping is part of the game, but prostitution and porn are not the same thing. Anyhow, I stay clothed since the air conditioning is overdoing it. He is back with an industrial bottle of lubricant, and he's already naked. I should perhaps strip now, but he has already unpacked the double dildo, handed it to me, and is sitting on the couch. Sitting is not the word. He's recumbent with his back against the backrest of the couch, his bum on the edge of the seat, legs stretched into the air. He's a picture himself now, and the picture says: "anus."

That's what we are here for, us escorts, always glad to help. He pours the lube, greases the anatomy between his legs.

"The dildo," he says, and hands me the bottle.

"Shall I grease both," I ask foolishly, but his mind is already set, so I lubricate just one of the phalli—just imagine, perish the thought.

"This is the largest dildo ever, wish me luck."

He splays his legs, I've never seen an asshole as expectant as this one. An angel is looking over my shoulder as I lower the dildo into place.

Ay, there's the rub. How are we going to tell the dildos apart? We're dealing with a Siamese contraption, two plastic phalli pointing away from each other at 150 degrees. It doesn't make sense to speak of a left- and a right dildo, or a west- and an east dildo, or an up- and a down dildo? Okay let's go for the last option, *up-and-down* it is.

So, holding on to the up-dildo, I apply the tip of the gooey down-dildo to his sphincter. I aim, I push.

"Uugh, uugh," Gohard reacts prematurely, I haven't achieved anything. A second try, a second fail, the wide tip of the plastic phallus has taken up residence in his perineum and doesn't want to go any further. More pressure, more resistance.

"Let me fetch the poppers," Gohard says. He gets up and returns with a bottle of Rush, the best poppers there are. He unscrews the top and takes a deep, long sniff. The stuff works very quickly, you have three minutes max, so he hauls himself back onto the couch.

Amyl nitrate (the poppers) is strongly relaxing, we're always glad to help, the A-level escort goes the extra mile, and in one swoosh the thing goes in. He screams, but he's happy—hurt turns into lust, that's the idea. The Rush-effect wanes quickly, though, and Gohard's countenance shifts from silly happiness to silly pain. "Get it out, get it out," he yells.

I grab the dildo by its other horn (the up-dildo) and pull. The down-dildo loves Gohard and has no plans to move. I pull harder, but the thing is really into Wagner (pun intended). Gohard screams, yells, gurgles. "Get it out," he is trying to say again but his voice fails him.

It's real bad. It's unbearable. Long, feeble, Wagner-groans fill the living room of tasty art and unassuming light-wood paneling.

The doorbell rings.

T here isn't much left of Gohard's casual-ceremonial ways, the dildo has him in its grip, or counter grip, whatever. And while the situation is serious enough, I can't suppress another collateral thought, this one involving the washed-up scriptwriter and an art house flick in which Gohard would try to answer the doorbell now, dildo and all, somehow haunching to the door, shifting from leg to leg, perhaps groaning. He reaches the door, opens it, and gulps "*Hilfe*." (Come to think of it, didn't *Godard* (*Jean-Luc*, not Gohard) make a movie exactly like this, with *Woody Allen* as a peripatetic porn star and a peripatetic flower pot that's always blotting the view of the adult parts of the unfolding drama? Did Allen survive?)

The doorbell rings again. So it's the postman. No, it's Sunday. No, it's Monday. It's not for nothing that us escorts are paid well—if we are paid at all—there's so much learning by doing involved. Shall we open the door? My budging A-level instincts tell me to stay put. Godehart moans softly, it's unclear whether he's praying or trying to say something. He rolls his head, that's what Buddhist monks do a lot.

We expect the echo of a failed doorbell initiative, silence followed by departing footfalls. Instead we get the clanky noise of metal on metal. There's something tentative to this, perhaps it's a burglar who's been pushing the bell to see whether the residents are at home and is wielding a picklock now. Godehart can't really roll his head any more. *In flagrante* master class.

I wonder whether the burglar could sue us for emotional damage done to him as he unsuspectingly tumbles upon harmful obscenity. While I thus wonder, the door swings open and clear, female eyes, enhanced by manly glasses, come into focus. Dr. Dyke.

Godehart can't speak at the moment, but Dyke can, presumably, although she doesn't. She ceases all activity whilst her medical mind assesses the situation. There she stands. It would be an understatement to say that we stared at each other (the more so because Godehart cannot really participate, his eyes left to dangle at the pond boys on the wall).

What's the washed-up scriptwriter doing in all this? He has a writer's block, I have to carry on alone. When you're in a hole, stop digging. That's perhaps a good idea, the more so since you're in panic and can't recall Dyke's real name, it could be a bad idea to use her moniker at this delicate hour. When we met for the first time, Dyke and I, her first words were "Your work?" That was twelve hours ago. What will she say now? Will she ever speak again?

"Your work?" she asks.
"Welcome to Godehart Wagner's home," I reply, one of my better lines today.
"I'm unsurprised," she says.
"*Que sera, sera*," I say—what can I say, there's no way to take this seriously. Even the dildo victim sports a smirk on his lips, a painful smirk at that, but a smirk nonetheless. And even the washed-up scriptwriter chimes in, *Doris Day* is singing in the background.

"He needs help," Dyke says and disappears hurriedly. My first concern is frivolous, as so often. I approach Godehart, who cannot speak, and ask him heartlessly: "What's Dyke's real name, I forgot."
"Sandeman, Dr. Sandeman," he moans. I sit down next to him and hold his hand, I feel so guilty.

The doctor returns with a medical bag, plops down on Godehart's other side, opens the bag, and produces a large syringe. It's obvious, the syringe will hurt Godehart more than the dildo even. Further research in Dyke's bag leads to the discovery of a medical vial of unclear denomination whose content is transferred into the syringe.

"This is very strong stuff," the doctor says so that people will listen. "It's used at executions in some states. An overdose kills easily." She orders me to hold Godehart's left arm, cleans the inside bend of his elbow with a cotton swab, and pushes the entire content of the syringe into his brachial artery. The effect is almost instantaneous. Godehart folds, losing control of his muscles, apparently. "It acts as a relaxant until it kills," Dr.

Sandeman says. Godehart's facial features fold as well, he appears reconciled with any final solution.

"You'll lift his feet into the air," she orders, and, while I do as told, grabs the up-dildo, (now the down-dildo). A whooshing crescendo accompanies her success, it's as if Richard himself had a hand in this.

She closely inspects the dildo for debris. "He may survive," she says. I lower Godehart's legs and align his body on the couch. "Now for the antitoxin," she says. She fumbles in her bag. Precious seconds elapse, minutes, perhaps. She says nothing, but the expression of her manly glasses moves from stern to sterner.

"How much time do we have," I ask. She does not answer.

I nstead, she gets on the cell-phone. "I need dada-hexa-dada-oid," she says to the phone. "We have 6 minutes."

Last night we had eight minutes to wait for the same ambulance. That took a long time. Six minutes takes longer. Godehart has left for dream country, an elated expression has taken hold of his Wagnerian features. His small eyes are closed.

"He looks like a younger, elder statesman who has made peace with the world," I say to Alice (in reality I said something more banal).
"Elder statesmen live forever," she replies, "possibly our only hope."

Silence. "You believe in God?"
"Us escorts believe in anything," I utter reflexively.
"He pays you?"
"No, no, I misspoke."
"Let's hope he paid you in advance."
"He did, actually."
"How much?"
I explain about the galactic Benz service.
"On the moon?" she asks.
"Yes."
"Closer to God, then."
"Yes."
"Good. We need somebody with direct access."
"Last time it took them eight minutes," I say. "That was yesterday with Alex on board."

"Alex won't be on board," she says. "The six minutes, I was making a motivational effort here, I need them to break every speed limit in town. If Godehart goes, my license goes. Stupid, I forgot. Stupid."

The manly glasses stare into infinity, or at the tasty pond art. "As an emergency room MD I'm not supposed to carry a doctor's bag around, let alone administer secret drugs, let alone forget about anti-toxins." she continues, "Keep Godehart awake, just slap his cheeks on a regular basis."

"He might think of it as a new kind of sex."

"Let's hope. It might revive his spirits," she comes back, "why don't you give it a try, you know how to do this. Anything to keep his vital functions active."

So I slap and slap Godehart's cheeks. Let's hope he's not getting used to this.

"You know Alex well?" I ask. Not the question she expected, but perhaps better than to ask whether she knows the way to the nearest unemployment office.

"Yes, I do," she says.

"I thought MD's and normal folks rarely mingle."

"Alex isn't normal folks. He would be an MD if it weren't...we have a rainbow table in the canteen."

"I thought you were working night shifts."

"That's how it works. The canteen's closed, the vending machines are open, the perverts mingle."

"You're on first-name basis?"

"When nobody's around."

Two minutes left of Godehart's life. The moment of truth is approaching. "You know I took Alex home, last night," I say.

"Good," she says.

"But the next morning he was gone."

"I know."

"He told you?"

"Of course not, but I know. It's part of his problem. He knows it himself."

"Lots of us are like that though, perhaps fifty percent, or more."

"His case is different."

"How so?"

She rolls her eyes, first at me, then at the dying Godehart, then at the doctor's bag. "Had I come home earlier," she says, "Eleanor might still be alive." Her eyes are moist.

Sirens wail, I answer the door, the toxin, or anti-, is delivered. Godehart, exactly the kind to panic at the sight of an approaching syringe, has departed to seventh heaven and couldn't care less when Alice pushes the life-saving stuff into his artery. "Oxygen," she orders the paramedic who's *not* Alex of course. The guy returns quickly with a pressure bottle and a breathing cap that is now applied to Godehart's happy face. Godehart's mimic shifts, he's becoming increasingly aware of the termination of his dreams.

"A cup of coffee would be a good thing for all of us," Alice suggests as she moves back into character. The ambulance has left, I'm off to the kitchen which is spic and span. Yesterday's Armani boys knew what they were doing. Coffee is being prepared and served by *Lee's A-level Escort Service*, the senior management getting into the act himself.

Godehart is coming to his senses. "I almost killed you," Alice breaks the spell.
"Shall I say thank you for that?" Godehart replies, "I was in seventh heaven." He affects a casual gesture at the world, "and now that."
"I got you there in the first place, you wouldn't have lasted. You would be dead by now."
"That would be then eight heaven, or?"

Alice removes her glasses. Her eyes are drying.
"That you don't know?" Godehart persists.
"No idea."
"In Hinduism, there is an eighth heaven, which means escape from the eternal wheel of re-incarnation."
"Interesting."
"And you know what its content is? What happens in eighth heaven?"
"No."
"Dreamless sleep. The afterlife that every atheist gets for free. The Hindu must work for it during all his life, and the atheist gets it for free."
"So I should apologize."

"Never apologize unless you know you'll be forgiven," Godehart says. Alice laughs dryly, some kind of inside joke, apparently.

"Perhaps you should get dressed," she says to him and looks at me. I hasten upstairs and find a bathrobe. Godehart's parts are being covered, and I will recall later that Alice had a chance finally to appreciate the Germanic peen-hammer penis. She must have been curious (or perhaps not).

"Perhaps we should talk," Alice says.

"Perhaps should we talk," Godehart says.

"Listen," Alice says, "I did not kill Eleanor. I loved her. I had absolutely no incentive to kill her."

"Did she still love you?" Godehart asks.

"It wasn't clear to me. She still loved *you* though, in her own way."

"I never knew."

"The situation got more and more out of hand," Alice said. "It was a downward spiral, Eleanor's artistic pretensions, the booze, *Special K*, *Ritalin*, *Georgia Home Boy*, all the medication she took behind my back. You can't control somebody who has lost control of herself. There was nothing I could do, short of sending her to a rehab. Which I tried."

"She became more and more addicted, or?"

"Yes."

"We should not have had that stupid strife," Godehart says. "I had time to think about it, you know. You know of her suicide attempt in Bayreuth, not true? That was an omen. But she should have left you her house."

"She changed her will four days before her death. 'I've changed my mind, I leave you all my art,' she said to me. She knew what she was doing, she was sort of getting even. What could I have said? That I prefer her house to her art?"

"There was no suicide letter, or?"

"Changing her will *was* her suicide letter. I didn't get it at the time."

"You should have forewarned me."

"It didn't make sense. We are the only two people who think it was suicide. Officially, it was a deadly interaction of drugs. Like in *Michael Jackson*'s case."

"Yes, I know."

"I wasn't her doctor. That was the first thing I thought when I met her. I want to be your lover, but not your doctor."

"I must apologize to you," Godehart says, his eyes wet, and knowing that he will be forgiven.

"I should do so, too," Alice replies, "I failed your wife. And you. I failed both of you."

They are trying to embrace, not an obvious thing to do when you are sitting on a soft couch next to each other. The escort is no longer needed.

"I should go now," I say, eyes also wet.

"No, no, you stay," Dyke says. Then, to Godehart: "I have to exchange a few words with this young man here. But before I do, let me tell you why I came. Some gallery in Manhattan called, they are interested in Eleanor's work. Dead artist stirs spirits. The pictures are still the basement, I hope. That's why I still have your key. Please find three pictures for me, decent ones, representative of her work. Stick to The Dots variety, it's more typical of her recent work."

"You want them now?"

"That's why I came. I rang the bell, remember, I thought you were not at home."

"You want me to select the pictures myself?"

"Yes sure, it doesn't really matter," she says, "if you can walk. I have to have a word with him here."

"John," I add helpfully.

Godehart gets up, marches a few steps. You can see he still hurts a lot. "You can walk," she diagnoses, "Not too large, the pictures, they have to fit into my car." Godehart is dismissed.

"Alex needs help," she says to me. "He needs help. And he's not the only one. All your friends need help, as far as I can see, Maurice in particular. Go see Maurice tonight and talk to him about the rape. This should not pass. We need to report this crime."

"He doesn't want to?"

"I talked to him briefly after he woke up. He's scared. And he is still very weak."

"I understand."

"It's important, don't miss it. I'll join you briefly. Use the emergency entrance."

"I will, I promise." She's done. We await Godehart's return.

How to say this. "Can I call you Alice?"

"Go ahead."

"Alice, I don't know how to say this."

"All fences are down, just go ahead."

I get up and turn my back to the tasty pond-art on Godehart's wall, then realize that this is the wrong move and sit down again. She abstracts her gaze from the pond-boys and looks at me. "Alex," I say, "Alex is really important."

"I know," she says.

"It's not only his beauty."

"I know," she says, "although, sometimes I think his beauty is his undoing. He looks in the mirror and sees his mother."

"Yes, he lost his mother at ten."

"He told you?"

"Yes."

"Mmh."

"He told me he's terribly lonely."

"He has me but that's not enough", she says. "I see what I can do. You can lead a horse to the water. That's where the buck stops."

Godehart has somehow managed to retrieve three oils on canvas from the basement.

"Help me with the paintings," Alice says to me, "store them in the car."

"Could you give me a ride," I ask, "it's not far, but it's so hot, my car broke."

"Sure," she says.

We store The Dots in her car, each painting taking its own seat, I would have to sit on The Dots. "I'll ask Godehart to give you a ride," she says and summons Wagner.

"No problem," he says, "my new SUV will take him home." He points at Isolde, disappears, and returns with something that holds the middle between a credit card and an iPhone. He pushes a red button. "Say something nice to her, voice recognition bootstrap."

"I love you, Isolde," I say.

"Good," Godehart says, "she'll like that. Now tell her your address."

I do as told. He hands the gadget to me. "She'll know how to get back on her own. Scouts secret, promise," he says, and waves his hand at the departing Alice. I'm off as well.

25 THE HITCHHIKER'S GUIDE TO GAY SEX

T here's this black guy standing on the sidewalk....wait, not yet, give it a paragraph or two.

Godehart evoked this spy rule that secrets are best hidden in public view; perhaps he's a spy himself and the Wagner thing is just a hoax, how could he otherwise have Isolde painted in, what, "cerulean blue," I've never seen this on any vehicle, let alone on an SUV, which, through its premium size, multiplies the hue's effect to obscene proportions.

We've backed out of Godehart's driveway, and Isolde has already shown her autonomous mettle by coasting down Atlanta Street's rows of antebellum miniatures and Victorian ladies. This is so beautiful, folks, the care-free proportions, the windows talking to you like the eyes of a trustful dog. Fluted columns, ornamental pediments, occasional gingerbread, muted colors, daring colors that speak to the neighbors, manicured lawns (green), comely hedges planted at the base of creaky porches decked with patient rocking chairs, the dwellings lined up along the street like invitees at a banquet. This is America at its best.

So we've coasted down Atlanta Street, and then turned left on Second without a hitch, and then turned right on Georgia Avenue where we meet the rush-hour back-up around the downtown traffic circle. Isolde takes note and eases neatly into the file of slowly-crawling afternoon vehicles. This could take some time, the jam may continue all the way up to the junction of Church and Route One. We're passing *Lupo di Mare*, the smarter Italian restaurant, and there's this black guy standing on the sidewalk, facing the traffic, raising his right arm with an extended hand, the thumb pointing forward. What's this guy doing? Hailing a taxi? No, you would do that differently, you wouldn't use your thumb. We haven't seen this since I was born, he is hitch-hiking. He *must* be hitchhiking, he's holding a chain saw. No, he's not holding a chainsaw, he's unencumbered, but he wants a ride.

Isolde is crawling, so we have time to study him. He's slender, but in the solid way of someone with perfect proportions. Long legs, long arms, he is long, but not too long, just ectomorphic. And his butt, folks. I learned this expression from my racist French mother, *cul de nègre*. It's as round as the moon, his butt under the snug jeans that he wears despite the tropical heat. Fortunately, his light shirt is wide open, and we get a glimpse of the perfect torso, including the washboard tummy and other definitions. The short sleeves can't hide his biceps—it's not the gym, nothing in the way of prison meat, but something else. His features are very symmetric; the nose is from Michelangelo, the eyes, too. And the lips! You need serious painters to do those lips justice. They are *jababa*, of course, with a touch of *Angelina Jolie* thrown in, and they would leave perfect hickeys on your neck, but they hide nothing of his perfect teeth. He's smiling shyly, he's not at ease, it's a criminal offense not to own a car, many people are in prison.

Isolde is still crawling, some progress has been made moving forward, ten yards are left between us and the African looker. Is Google gay? Isolde exits the file of backed-up cars and finds a space right in front of our man. The passenger window lowers itself, I have to bend across a few miles of SUV space to make eye contact.

"Where're you headed?" I ask.
"Ocean View," he says.
That's to the south of Georgia Beach. You have to turn left on Route One, cross the canal bridge next to my condo, and continue for a few miles through the Georgia Seashore State Park. It's in my direction, but only for a mile or so, he would have to catch another ride pretty soon.

You know, I have my moments. So I explain to him where I live, where my place is located with respect to the canal bridge, where I would have to drop him off, and so on. He's not from the neighborhood, he says. It's freakin' hot, tiny, shiny beads of sweat are conspiring on his perfect forehead, he mounts Isolde and is seated on the passenger throne next to me. He must be thinking I'm rich.

106

Let's talk probabilities. You know, we are discussing this all the time. How many gays, what's the percentage, isn't it unfair. Ten percent, or less? Let's be optimistic. Ten percent. Provided he is gay, what would be the probability that he is interested in my latest Prolog program? Or my frozen blog, or my father, who fell asleep on the couch. Your father, I think.

Does he want to have a look at my father? "Father," is that another euphemism? My God, I have an erection already. The pendulous organ, it must be the most euphemized object on the planet, and only in part because it has to do with sex. The thing is so funny all by itself, its erratic behavior, its willfulness, it's like an unruly pet always ready to get its owner into trouble. It's getting me into trouble now.

"My name is John," I tell him, "What's yours."
"John," he replies. Good move, perfect. We have a subject of conversation now, name-sharing, a touch of intimacy. In China, you can't have sex with a person who shares your last name, at least you can't marry. It would be an interesting research question, perhaps I could get a grant from the sociology department and investigate whether sex-having is biased name-wise, in the sense that your probability of having sex with a person of the same name is higher than...(will somebody please interrupt me).

Let's sort this out. Assume he's gay and has an hour to spare. What's the probability that he'll follow me upstairs for a ride? High, very high. What else can he do, he has an empty hour to fill, he's young, hormones flow, glands fire. It's eighty percent at least, ninety percent perhaps that we'll end up in a quick embrace, let's leave the remaining percentage to idiosyncrasies, perhaps he doesn't like gray eyes. Duh, duh, duh. *Ooh point one* times *ooh point eight*, it's eight percent we'll end up in my bed *pronto*, provided we can overcome the father-hurdle. My father is in the way. Or he is at the beach, where he usually stays until six o'clock. We have one hour, almost two, even. Perhaps John is in a hurry and has no time for sex. Yet if you *are* in a hurry, you don't hitchhike. OK, we've narrowed this down, we own eight percent of his probability space already. How about the remaining 92 percent? Does it matter? He wasn't promised to you the way Alex was, no offense taken, you drop him off at the bridge, or he accepts a glass of fresh orange juice at your place because that's a good idea, and he's thirsty, and then he's off, and if he's world-wise he has you down already, but he's a modern metrosexual man, he drinks your juice like *David Beckham* poses for gay magazines. He might even give you his number, or his email address, because you discovered a common interest in orange juice, and chess, and people.

Traffic is still backed up, all the way to the junction on the Coastal Highway, that gives us time to think. We can offer him Prolog, but that's not drinkable, so we have to hit Luke's store for the second time today, for the perfect orange juice. So we have to explain the excursion to the convenience store. And if he's not interested in juice? In fact, I don't have to ask him about the juice, I'll just tell him whether he minds the detour via the convenience store. No hitchhiker in the world would mind.

We will detour, I will shop, and then return with this juicy, fresh orange juice, and a bottle of wine. Like in most states, convenience stores cannot sell real booze in Georgia, which is a pity, because it's more effective. You never know, perhaps he's alcoholic, he really needs a drink, so when I return from the shop, he's waiting in the Google-SUV, I turn the bottle this way and that way when I mount Isolde, he's game, even if he's not gay, he'll follow his addiction up into my place where I feed him the whiskey that I can't buy until he loses all inhibitions. His sexual preference joins the other sexual preference, they melt, they unite, like natural forces at very high energy states, they discovered the god-particle yesterday, remember, which will also get in on the act. He's drunk, but not too smashed, three quarter of a bottle say. He no longer cares, and I suck cock, or he's still up to it, completely loose now, and I show him some porn, and perhaps pictures of prison cells and muscles, and he wants to fuck now, fuck, and there's no pussy, save mine. John doesn't look alcoholic, though. Perhaps that's even better, even wine may do the trick. Trick a non-trick into a trick—duh, duh, duh.

Relax, we'll cross the bridge when we get there. You explain the detour to him. Sure.

Shall we have him wait in the SUV? Maybe I should drag him along, he's never seen a convenience store before, not one with a toy sex department annex vampire section. So I will mention our common interest in vampires that we'll discover as we speak, and take him into the store, because it's another opportunity for interaction, five more minutes to change his sexual orientation. He's shy, and sweet, and intelligent, if I spring the sex department on him he wouldn't say no. Would he be embarrassed? No, he's too young, he's seen too much internet porn, regardless, even if he's the religious type. Context rules, the more we talk about sex the more we want to have it, porn provides an instantaneous stimulus for everybody, the dildos will give him more ideas, he's suddenly feeling horny, and he's thirsty, and he's a metrosexual, as usual, and I ask him whether he's metrosexual, and he says yes, and then I put the gun to his head and ask whether he means it. Everybody does it, including *David Beckham*, I explain, and I will have a terrible erection at that moment, even worse than now…

We've reached the junction now, one minute to Luke's store, no traffic jam on Route One. I spring the sex toys on him when we arrive at the parking lot. He laughs obligingly. Cool, man.

We enter the store. Should I go first, or, in a display of Southern etiquette, open the door for him—it would also be a *reverence* from a white guy for a black guy. I'm always polite when it doesn't matter, so I usher him through the swinging glass doors into Luke's ice room. Luke is behind the counter and sees us coming. I think he's a bit jealous now. Anyhow, there is only one thing I can do. I put a bright smile on my face. And there's only one thing that Luke can do, put a bright smile on his. He's seen it all, and he's happy to see me again.

Another twist comes to mind, I will introduce them to each other. So, I say: "This is Luke, he's the vampire." Luke is always happy when somebody brings up his immortality, and he would be welcome to hand his moonlight vampire agency card to John (birthdays, church functions, funerals). However, I won't tell Luke that this is John. We have some sort of vacuum now that nature abhors. Luke chooses the easy way out and asks him: "You're from here?" No, John is not. He doesn't explain, however, which is perhaps a good thing because Luke, in the absence of further information, must conclude that John is a trick, the first one he's seen me with, which will induce some suggestive familiarity in his behavior which may help things along. John is politely interested in vampires, tells about a party at his sister's, vampire-themed, it was hilarious. Luke hands his card, finally, "What's your name?" *John*. So, we know each other really well now, a reunion of the Iliad clan, will somebody please tell John our family name. "Got any new toys?" I ask Luke suggestively, who is hands-on when it comes to sex shop terminology, *Ben Wa balls*, *butt plugs*, *docking sleeves*, and so on, words which might loosen our John further, if he understands what they mean. I try to move the conversation into comprehensive territory. "How about the Siamese dildo's," I ask, "anything new." Luke flashes his vampire smile and takes us to the sex department. Explanations of the graphical kind flow, John is politely impressed and asks a funny question about "frictional coefficients." Luke asks whether he should wrap it up, for us, the last frictional dildo on the shelf. I decline gently. We don't need it today, (*we, today*), another time perhaps (*another time*), I say it lightly, John has a sense of humor, today we need orange juice, because we (*we*) are thirsty. And a bottle of chardonnay, because we are frictional. Make that three bottles.

What's the chance John is alcoholic, one percent? Zero, I guess. You like chardonnay, I ask him as we leave the store. He may never have heard of the grape of white Burgundy wine, an excellent opportunity to explain, to taste, to imbibe, in particular if he doesn't drink, three, four glasses, and he is the mood. And if he does (drink), I will point out that Luke's chardonnay is real good, which is almost true, I'm drinking too much of the stuff myself.

So, now, we're back in the Google cruiser. You must be thirsty, I tell him, how about a glass of orange juice? I'm not talking about drinks. These are shifting sands, folks, until we sink into the ground and make love. "Orange juice," I say again, "a drink, you know my place isn't far," (*a drink, my place*). The wording, the ambivalence. We reach the next decision node now. It would be for me to push the brakes and drop him off, just before we arrive at the ramp to my apartment down next to the canal. What if I don't stop, what can he do? And it's not me, it's the autonomous cruiser that knows what to do, because Isolde is gay, although he doesn't know because it's a secret, I pretend I'm driving myself. He can't be aware of the spot, the decision point, he doesn't know the place, he'll find out when he drinks my orange juice, so Isolde dives down the ramp to the parking lot. We're parked already, I grab the bag with the wine and the juice. Come on, you must be thirsty. What he doesn't see, fortunately, Isolde has already turned around and is on her autonomous way back to the Wagners.

It's hot as we climb the stairs. Now what? It's unlikely, but not impossible that my father is around, that he fell asleep, too lazy to drive to the beach, or he came back early and has somehow managed to get inside without key. Only the sturdiest trick, some real hard-core rainbow supremacist would be able to handle my father. We march through the kitchen den into the bedroom and close the door (slam it). The mattress squeaks alarmingly, more noises ("uurghh," "ooohh,"), less noise, the door swings open, I march my man back to the exit, a last sturdy kiss, then he's off, father is upset, that's modern life at the end of the rainbow. Let's face it, even if John is a straight gay with nothing to hide, my father's presence would mean the end of our lust. He would drink a glass of juice and flee the scene at his earliest convenience. I should have killed my father long ago. I should kill him now. Do we hear anything snoring, sounds crossing the door? Perhaps a squeaking mattress, somebody getting off? No, the place is as quiet as father is when he sits at the kitchen table lost in admiration of the water tower. I unlock the door, and the place is…

(That's a cliffhanger, right?)

...empty.

The place is empty. No father anywhere to be seen. I check everywhere.

There are a few loose ends here, like the wealth gap between the truck's cerulean color and the duff brownish gray of my 1.5 bedroom kitchen den. I should explain this gap away, or excuse it by telling the truth. But we have reached the point where a little mystery comes in handy, so let the explainable unexplained. And just as I'm thinking this, another thought swings by: I could have used an attractive car to attract an attractive man in the same way that an attractive man could have used an attractive man—himself—to attract an attractive car. Symmetry rules again.

You, John, you could be a serial sex addict who's entire inheritance went into a man-eating Mercedes fly-catcher. And this black looker, what did he do? His whole effort went into an equally absurd approach, hitchhiking. Nobody hitchhikes, he isn't hitchhiking at all. He's standing there in your kitchen because he's a serial sex addict like you. Perhaps he's a prostitute? No, that would be a first at 4 PM on Georgia Avenue, there are better venues for paid sex. But sex of the unpaid kind—there's always implicit cruising, thousands of eyes have met there before and changed their mind. Prostitution is a calculating business, but wild sex is *not*, you're overrun by insurgent urges, that's the whole idea. John must have been overcome by those urges, and his only solution was to put his fabulous body on display, raise his thumb, and hope for the best. That's why he was hitchhiking and followed you home. Eight percent we'll get laid? No, John, it's much more. We should know within 20 seconds.

Countdown. Twenty, nineteen, eighteen. Will he shuck his pants? No. He will make a step forward—he can be certain of my intentions now (fourteen seconds)—take control of my nipples and squeeze them through the cotton of my T-shirt, or raise his hand to my neck, tasting me with his fingers, perhaps for the optimal location of his love bites (seven seconds). I reciprocate somehow (zero seconds, ignition). Embrace, dropping pants, rising dicks. Perhaps we'll lean into each other, or, without embrace, free-style, our dicks touch, and he joins them with his well-proportioned left hand. It's gorgeous, do it yourself, gently stroking up and down both brothers, one is yours, one is his, the sensual effect of touching both kin in one go, sensing yours in two ways, sensing his in a different way, this hilarious sense-confusion. We even learned this in school (using only fingers, of course, although I never trusted this teacher who died of disappearance later). Life is about ambiguity.

Something must have gone wrong. The countdown is over, and he's standing next to Alex's chair, contemplating the water tower, or the room, or me, perhaps anticipating more Southern etiquette. He's well-brought up, so much is clear already, he's waiting for me to offer him a seat. No sweat. He wasn't promised to me, right, so I offer him the seat where Alex used to live in my life for an hour, and pour him a glass of orange juice, not even thinking of the wine, all second thoughts are suspended for a few seconds.

He's slightly disoriented, my behavior is out of kilter. Did he upset me in some way? Not at all, not at all, my boy, I'm relieved, in fact. You are sitting in Alex's chair, I see his posture in your posture, his beauty in your beauty, and there's a big difference, I have no crush on you at all. It's purely physical, just heat, unadulterated, irresponsible gay heat—that's why us gays are gay, it happens all the time, perhaps 100 million times per day worldwide, one thousand times *per second*, a gay *rush*, exuberant lust, lust with many adjectives—but it's not a crush, let alone love. I want cum spouted over my face, his dick in my ass and mouth, I want four letter words in action. And I want Alex.

I still want fuck, fuck, but I'm used to these letdowns like every gay person. So I recover quickly, and John, the innocent, senses my recovery. I sit down and pour myself a glass of juice. All this has taken less than a minute.

Reset. I look around. Something is still out of kilter. Yes, the kitchen table is *not* empty, it's cramped by more than the usual debris. It's loaded with a stack of papers of some sort, flyers. There are lots of pictures, I cast sideways glances while thinking what to say next. Another sideway glance,

113

John tracks my eyes. It's too late for a cover-up. The flyers, it's all pictures of placards, with hippos holding them, or people dressed up for Gettysburg. They read something like "NO PUBIC OPTION," or "REMEMBER DESCENT, THE HIGHEST FORM of PATRIOTIC," or "MORE FUN, LESS TAXIS," or "GET A BRAIN, MORANS," and so on. The head line says "TEA PARTY," which is not misspelled.

That's why his bag was so heavy. My father brought this stuff to save the Confederacy in Georgia Beach, canvassing or something. Fail, I think, fail, there's no way to explain this away, and whatever John would have been willing to do for you, he's not going to have sex with the Tea Party.

John, however, in a reversal that must have been thought up by the washed-up scriptwriter, John just laughs.

"Your work?" he asks. "Cool, perhaps a bit too subtle, not everybody will get it, people need to know some orthography."

I tell him a guy from Atlanta printed this and wants me to canvas the stuff but I have no time. "Can I take some home?" he asks. "It's hilarious, we know how to spell in Monroeville."

Great, I think, but not yet, we have more important things to do.

"Where you from," I ask. He just told me, but he's patient, he's from Monaville (Monaville?), that's down in the rural south-west, on the other side of the Okefenokee swamp. What are you doing up here? Something to do with college basketball. Why are you hitchhiking? His car broke down, there's a Greyhound terminal in *South View* where he could catch a bus home. We have something in common, I tell him, my car broke down too, somebody lent me the SUV, I know, the color is ridiculous.

Should I relent? Impossible. The hormones flow, the tide is rising, and when the tide goes out we must be naked. But an effective schemer will need more information to make his next move. What's your background? He's still living with his parents, his father is a minister with his own church. Yes, exactly, come to think of it. I'm not having a crush, but his effortless formality, his bearing, accentuated and tender, somehow letting others know how important they are, where have we seen this before? Yes, in this black sergeant, for example, or whatever they are called in the Navy, dressed up like a modern magi, who lifts a baby from the arms of its mother, entrusts baby Jesus to a waiting sailor on the tender, then takes Maria's hand as if they are at the altar, and helps her with this *one* step from the quay onto the bobbing boat, only children of black ministers can save the world like this.

Oh, John, you are so low (I mean myself). You're only thinking about one thing. Does he drink? Of course not. Stop, they drink wine at holy communion. But the stuff is red. How about his mother? How about her cooking, does she cook with white wine (won't fly). How about his siblings? Are they all married? How old is he? Does he have a girlfriend?

You're twenty, you've grown up in an isolated rural community, you may not know about your own sexuality unless you are really a victim of your hormones, like *Truman Capote*, say. Does he have a girlfriend? No, he doesn't, he says with a timid grin. Shall I ask why? Hold it, John. The wine, the chardonnay, it's my only chance. Another glass of orange juice? You're still thirsty, right? You know what—not the most subtle transition, but what can we do?—you know what, white wine is even better against thirst than orange juice. You mean it. Especially the stuff I bought. It's called chardonnay, it's the grape of white Burgundy wines. He knows about

Burgundy, he has a Mormon friend who has been there as a missionary. You know what, I tell him (all hippocampus professor now), you know when the Romans conquered Burgundy and started to grow vines, they cultivated grapes that would quench thirst because they did not trust the water of the *Saone*. The Saone? Yes, that's the local river. You mean it. Yes, it really works, the chardonnay. You'll see. We are into *thirst quenching* now, and you don't quench thirst by sipping. You *quaff* the stuff. I find two large tumblers in the dishwasher, clean them, and pour the wine.

We raise the glasses. You have to drink the stuff like water, I tell him. He does. Sputters a bit, chokes a bit but swallows it obligingly. Perhaps he's surprised it goes down much easier than liquor. His glass is already empty. Mine is empty, too, but I can handle the stuff. Two glasses and he'll be tipsy. Three glasses and I have to make my move. Focus, John, focus. Let's cross the bridge when we get there.

"They say," I invent, "that the third glass is always the best"—save the fourth one, if we need it—because it brings out the honey flavors of the barrel, you don't want to miss that, wine that quenches thirst like water and tastes like honey. Can you taste the honey? Yes, his mother is a great cook. He's a bit *lala* already. Don't take chances. He's tipsy enough to accept another glass. I don't even have to drink. Talk a bit about France, John, give the stuff some time to work. My mother is French, I tell him. He's interested, though his concentration is slipping slightly. Listen, I tell him, I want to show you something. I have a blog, which sleeps in my bedroom. You're interested in blogs? He's interested in everything, although his voice has lost the perfect diction of a black minister's son. Naked girls, LOL.

He gets up, I lead the way to my bed. "Sit here," I point to my mattress. I start the computer. He sits there. The computer start-up takes forever, as usual, he sips and quaffs the wine. He has some trouble with his bed-side equilibrium, it can be difficult to sit on an exhausted mattress. My computer cooperates, and you know what, Google cooperates too, the blog unfreezes, comes alive again—cryopreservation works, folks—the naked girls are back and smile their calculating smile at my new lover.

This isn't the time to discuss sexual preferences in any meaningful way. You're horny, right? How many people in the world must have jerked on your naked girls, they've got more than 60 thousand page views in four years, how many orgasm did you help along, you've done a good job, John (me, the bad one), missionaries quench hunger, you quench libido. You're horny, right. Yeah, he slurs.

He's recumbent on the bed now, needs help. I undo his belt, unzip his fly, pull his jeans from under his *cul de nègre*. The briefs come off at the same time (very pretty ones, printed with colorful graffiti cartoons, his mother must have bought them for him), his loose shirt is not in the way. I suck cock. Is he aware of it? Autonomous stimulation takes its toll, his erection is coming along nicely. He has a very decent dick. Shall we embrace the cliché and move to a higher level? Can he still stand? I shuck my shorts, take his hands, help him to rise, fold myself into doggy position.

"You know what to do, right?" Does he hear me? He can't have HIV, impossible. I wiggle my butt, he must know how to do this, and he does, he's in already. I'm so excited, my anus is an open book, he reads it like the Bible. He's in. Whether he's a virgin or not, he's in, and he's no longer a virgin. His thrusting movements are very much to the point. A facial? Don't overdo it. Let him come. Let him come. He comes (heaven), unpops. I turn around, a few jerks, semen spurts, the tide is outgoing, we're both naked. He sinks back onto the bed, laughs a Kenyan laugh, rises again, gives me a kiss. Fulfillment, holy communion.

What happened to Alex? Why did he give me a kiss?

We unfold. Time for cigarette, I think. I'm becoming old-fashioned, too.

The doorbell rings.

27   I CHARGE 100 DOLLARS BUT AM WILLING TO NEGOTIATE

I t's father, it must be him. He's back from the beach.

John (the other one), hasn't become fully aware of the problem, he has raised his head briefly—he's lying on the bed, still recovering—but hasn't made the connection yet. The doorbell rings again.

Father. We don't even know. The tide is out, I'm naked, but it doesn't matter since he's still waiting for the buzzer downstairs. We're not at home, are we? In the best of all worlds, *Candide* is now in love with his *Pangloss*, who will tell him that this is the best of all worlds because they made love, and they made love because this is the best of all worlds. Which is a tautology, so it's always true, which is even better. Has John seen the light, in colors? For the first time? Like *Andrew Sullivan* did when he kissed a boy, for the first time? We kissed, right? The doorbell rings again.

It's an advantage of shredded relationships that you no longer have to care about conventions. Happy families are all alike and will answer the bell either immediately or not at all (if they are *too* happy right this moment). Every unhappy family is unhappy in its own way, and answers the bell as they see fit. I've gotten up now, I've planted a bond-preserving peck on John's forehead, closed the bedroom door, am standing in the kitchen den, and the doorbell has died. Father always rings three times.

Option one, I buzz now. It would be a first, provoking an *in flagrante* father-wise, we covered this already. We sacrifice the good John on the altar of a shredded relationship, use him as a prop in a bitter *calzonade*, just to embarrass my father, who wouldn't know what to do if a lightly dressed *black-man* (my father uses other terms) emerged from my chamber without explanation. I would have to kiss John goodbye, who would flee. Not good. There are limits to my hatred, at least in the sense that I'm still aware of other priorities. The problem is, I'm no longer so sure, crush-wise. It's not that we don't want to see my father see John, we don't want to see John see my father. *Option two*, we don't buzz at all. John—perhaps he has a nickname, I should ask—John needs to recover. He's feeling the near past in his bones and other organs. Let him rest, let him feel guilty. Yeah, that's basically it. Let him sleep.

I feel a hand on my shoulder, and not for the first time during the last 24 hours. It's John, who's still naked, like me. I—even though I have more pressing things on my mind—can't help but check with my own eyes about his pendibility. John follows my eyes, it's one of his things. I won't tell you the results, though, since there are some thriller elements to this story. Anyhow, John appears to recover very quickly, I've seen this before, I have a colleague who gets completely drunk on a single glass of wine inside less than ten minutes. He slurs obscenities at the edge of the precipice, then makes a big step forward and ten minutes later makes a big step backwards—and is sober again. Everybody loves him except bar tenders and his wife. John must be like this, or will soon be if he falls under my spell.

John needs to go home, he says, his parents are expecting him. Call them, I say—you get the idea, he tells his parents he's delayed, and I cook eggs, you need proteins in our situation. "Can I call you Jojo," I ask.

"What?" he says. He's livid all of a sudden, "Yoyo? Why do you want to insult me?"

"We're both called John, that's confusing."

"You call me Yoyo, you call me a weak, stupid person. In ebony talk."

"I didn't know. Forgive me. I didn't know. I'm not black."

"I can see that." He stares at me.

"I'm really sorry, John. Trust me."

"Trust you," he laughs. "Call me Ben, that's my pet name. I'm, the Benjamin of Dr. and Mrs. Martin Luther Fletcher. The youngest child, if you get the idea. I'm sorry."

He's sorry about what? I'm sorry too that I can't take him home, or at least to the bus terminal in Ocean View. Then I think about myself again. John, the bad one, I will be sorry that I didn't take him to the bus terminal. I send him downstairs like this, Ben may not even find the ramp to Route

One. There is another road off the parking lot, along the canal, he might get confused. And he's not going to get another ride until he puts up a sign that he's charging hundred dollars but is willing to negotiate. Even if he leaves his cell number, what am I going to ask him when I call? Why he got lost? Why his mother cried? Why he never got home and is with this escort agency now?

I will need a car, and the only one in reach belongs to my father. I think *Gilbert & Sullivan, Rossini* comes to mind, the whole nine yards. But I can't think up anything remotely resembling a comedy of errors that would meet the required constraints: (1) I get hold of the car keys; (2) Ben (John) is kept unaware of my father; (3) the make-believe survives Ben's scrutiny long enough.

Ben's just too smart. He's already having second thoughts about the flyers on the table, I can see it, he's perusing them with that African grin. He may wonder whether I can spell "public," or "moron."

You, reader, you might be able to think something up here. A better, funnier story, where I tell Ben that there's this stalker who is also a schizophrenic, but in a pleasant way, and who thinks he's my father but he's not, at least not all the time. He's a nice guy, basically, except that he's Tea Party when he's not my father, that's why he left the flyers. And he owns a Chevy, and he's stalking as we speak. He is a so-called *loud stalker*, a stalking subspecies, quire rare. He even rings doorbells, and he's downstairs, but he owns a car, and he would possibly lend us his car—it doesn't fly. So let's cut corners. "It's possibly my father," I say, "and he...wait, Ben, wait...he has a car, I borrow his car and drive you to the Greyhound terminal."
"How about the SUV," Ben asks.
"It's already gone," I say.

He waits, he thinks. He doesn't quite understand. Why is the truth always brutal? It must be the booze.

"OK, he says. Shall I get dressed?"
"It's an option," I say.
"Cool. These flyers, that's your father, right?"
"How do you know?"

"I can smell him."

"Take a few with you anyhow, they are pathetic."

He grins. He's less shy now.

We're dressed, ready to roll. Ben's got hold of an inch of the flyers, how do we get hold of my father? He has a cell-phone, right? Let's hope he's not behind on the payments. Technology works, so I tell him the truck is broken, I need to borrow his car, right now, to drive a friend to the Greyhound terminal in Ocean View. I'll be at the parking lot in two minutes. As we exit the main entrance his back is turned to us. We walk around him in a semi-circle, perimeter of 20 feet, Ben flashing his stack of flyers, grinning. Let a little mystery prevail, Ben was born in Kenya, right? I extend my hand, say nothing until it holds the car keys, hand father the apartment key. We get into his crappy Chevy. We've not said hello, we've not said goodbye. We're good.

"You've any idea of the bus schedule," I ask. Yes, he has. There's a bus at six seventeen PM—in fifteen minutes. The last one. That'll be tight.

We're speeding down Route One past the big lonely sycamore tree someone must have planted there with ulterior motives. I slow down. I always slow down here, I'm scared of this tree. I cannot explain this to Ben who casts a glance at the speedometer. I speed up again. How to speed in a jalopy? I've no clear idea where the bus terminal is located. Another two minutes are lost. It's six fourteen as the terminal appears on the horizon. There's only one way to get this straight, leave it to Ben-John to make up his mind. He's heard of *coordinates*, right, phone numbers, emails. It would be silly to impose myself. And I'm shy, don't forget. Even if my autonomous brain had calculated that it would be a smart move to ask about his future and his cell-phone, other parts of my body might not cooperate once I got the number, they might postpone the call until tomorrow, until tomorrow again, and until John has all forgotten about me and my parts. Six fifteen, we're driving up the Greyhound lot, through the WRONG WAY sign, a bus driver clanks the grey-horn at us. I stop. That's it, I think. "That's it," I say. Precious seconds crawl. "Nice meeting you," he says. This is quite a day.

More seconds crawl. Another hound-blow. "John," he says, "you're a nice guy, I did really appreciate." The space-time continuum crawls all around us now. "Why don't we exchange emails?" he finally adds. "I'll be up in Georgia Beach when my car is ready." That's not the most committal of postures, but *Wile E. Coyote* climbs gladly back onto the cliff. "Sure," I breathe.

How do you find a pen in an adjective-challenged Chevy? You don't. There is none in the glove compartment, nothing glued to the dashboard, Ben is pen-less, I'm pen-less, and I can't think in panic. If he tells me, 'J, O, H, N, 6, 5, 3, 9, 6 at, gmail, dot, com,' my mind gets fucked up on the numbers, and I won't be able to recall them five minutes from now.

"I tell you," he says, and he starts "J, O, H, N," and so on, when I become aware of a ball-point rolling on the foot well carpet under my feet. It barely works. Ben is throwing good time after bad time. The ball-point starts up. I write down his address, double-check on the digits. Ben's gotten out of the car. One Greyhound sweeps off the lot with energetic gestures. He runs after the bus for a few yards, then returns. "That was mine," he says. He's standing there now, the passenger door's still open, we're intruding on Greyhound space. Another bus crosses the lot, the driver is trying to kill us.

"I'll drive you home," I say. There's some token resistance on his part, but we're a happy family, conventions work. We're off to, what was the name?

28 THE HAROLD HALMA PHOTOGRAPH SCANDAL

M onaville," I say to Ben, "would you know how to find it?"
"No," he says.
"You don't know where you live?"
"Yes I do."
"But you can't find it."
"No, I do."
"You're sure you cannot find it?"
"It's Monroeville," he says, "not Monaville."

"You'd better ask for directions," he adds after a few seconds.
"Yes," I say.
"Now, are you going to ask for directions or not?"

He's so sweet, we've met only two hours ago and we're in screwball country already. How will the washed-up scriptwriter handle this? He will let me stay quiet for a second, five seconds, ten seconds, ignition. He will wait, in fact, until the producer suffers a fit. There's some off-Broadway expression on my face, but only in the mildest of ways. Not a grin. A Mona Lisa smile. That would be perfect. He would be overdosing it a bit, though, if he would then let Ben say: 'You smile like Mona Lisa,'—which Ben conceivably could say, they must know about her in Monaville—but the scriptwriter writes true to form.
"You smile like Mona Lisa," Ben says. This can't last.

It doesn't. Ben is eager to get home and explains that we have to continue south, on One, until we cross the bridge, then turn right on Route 82. I thought so already. It's my commute to the hippocampus, the only practical way to get to the south-west. We're silent for a while. Ben shows none of the signs of guilt that country boys are supposed to exhibit after having been tricked into gay sex by assistant professors from small schools who haven't completed their Ph.D.

Okay, let's press the issue. "These directions," I say, "they're for Monaville, or for Monroeville?"

"Yes," he says.

"Capote was born in Monroeville," I say.

"*Truman Capote?*"

"Yes. Your Monaville?"

"No," he says, "I would know."

"Monaville or Monroeville?"

"Yes," he says.

I'm trying to flirt, that's obvious, but is he flirting back? All these yes's and no's, what do they mean? Reader, do you realize—perhaps not a big insight, but anyhow—do you realize that in our situation a flirt means *more* than a fuck? Much more?

I can't ask him whether he's flirting, of course. "You're like the Bible, it's yes, yes, or no, no," I flirt.

"Yes."

It's coming back to me now. And I don't mean the *Bonny Tyler* song "A Total Eclipse of the Heart," I mean the *Harold Halma* photograph scandal.

Yes, that's the way to go, much better than to ask him to carefully evaluate our homosexual encounter retrospectively and split the infinitive in the process. "You know about Truman Capote?" I ask.

"Yes."

"You've heard about the *Harold Halma* photograph scandal?"

"No."

"Capote was already a budding young author, after World War Two, when Harold Halma, a photographer in New York City, was commissioned to take an author picture of the prodigy, Capote recumbent on a winged settee, eyes staring into the camera, the hand resting on his abdomen. Halma's picture caused a scandal at the time, people got very upset, even though Capote was fully dressed, mind you, since, since there was this suggestion that he *quote*, was dreamily contemplating some outrage against conventional morality, *unquote*. Because, evidently, he had one hand in talking distance of his crotch. Quote, contemplating some

124

outrage against conventional morality, unquote. Pathetic. Imagine this happening today."

Let's see what Ben's going to say. I guess he masturbates a lot. Two times per day. Three times on Sundays.

"It's not yes," he says, "it's yea....'But let your communication be, Yea, yea; Nay, nay: for whatsoever is more than these cometh of evil.' Matthew, five-thirty seven."

"It took you a while," I say, deeply disappointed.
"The Bible at your fingertips," he answers.
"Well, it took you several minutes."
"Think first, then ask the Lawd."

No more flirting. "You're headed for the ministry, like your father?"
"Nah," he says, "I have no talent."
"Never knew you needed talent."
"More than ever. The suspension of disbelief, not an easy matter. It's called spirituality, the talent."
"You're an atheist?"
"Nah, I wouldn't dare. I'm mom's baby."
"So you *are* an atheist."
"It's not only spirituality, it's real difficult. You must be a good preacher, speaker, organizer, business man, analyst—I mean as in *psycho*—you must be patient, forgiving, people-loving, corpse-resistant, a good husband, I'm not up to it."
"What are you up to?"
"Engineering. My father isn't up to it either. He's a good husband, but he's not up to it. He's losing members, they drift to the mega-churches. And some even to *Fox News*, even though they are black."
"Why?"
"Ask him, you'll have ample time to ask him tonight."
"You mean I'm invited for supper?"
"Invited is not the word."
"I'll have to be back, I have an appointment at ten, at the hospital. It's important."
"Forget it."
"I really have to be back."

"It's you pitted against Mom, forget it."

We'll cross the bridge when we get there, I think. By the way, the *Sidney Lanier Bridge* is looming large ahead as we are approaching its ramp from the north. The bridge gets us across Simons River that bulges for a mile here before turning north and reaching the sea five miles south of Georgia Beach.

"Could you build this," I ask.

"I will. It's a cable-stayed harp design. The standard design for new bridges. I will build bridges like this one. You build bridges, you leave something behind."

I teach French, I leave something behind, I think.

"You want me to explain?" he asks.

"Next time."

"Compared to the traditional suspension bridge, like the *Golden Gate* Bridge, the downside is that the deck needs to be stronger, because the cables pull at it at various angles. But the whole thing is self-balancing, the horizontal forces balance if you arrange the cables symmetrically. That's the main advantage. It's more stable, so the support structure can be lighter."

"Symmetry is a good thing," I say.

"Symmetry is a good thing," he confirms.

"It's official, people with symmetrical features have more sex."

"I know," he says.

His features are very symmetrical, remember, so I ask: "What do they don't know in Monaville?"

"I don't know."

"Monroeville, then."

"Lots of things, in particular the unknown unknowns."

I could ask whether he does a *minor* in epistemology, or whether he's an admirer of *Donald Rumsfeld*. He can't be, he must have been eleven years old then. I'm not good at transitions, you know, so I say: "What do they know about sex in Monroeville?"

"They are learning," he replies.

We've descended the Lanier ramp and turned right, where Georgia really begins. Route 82 is a straight stretch of tarmac into the wilderness, space shuttles could use it for landing. Shrubs, construction sites, trees, farms, muddy river basins, *What-A-burger*-burgers, car dealers, homesteads, crossings, gas stations, driveways, motels, fields, churches, mini malls, junkyards, each one giving way to the next strictly at random. Towns mixed up with junk yards, junk yards with malls, malls with people milling around as if they enjoy their entropy. I didn't sleep last night, feel suddenly dead tired, and ask Ben to take over. We stop at an abandoned construction site. Both of us have to pee, each one is chastely using his own tree. I don't peek at Ben, he doesn't peek back. No peeking. Ben takes the wheel. Time for thought.

I'm reaching the plus-pole of my polarity, which is always a bad start. Three men in twenty-four hours, one of them not even gay. Well, Alex left you (unless he comes back, Alice only said she'll take the horse to the water), and Maurice will go back to England. But Ben's too young, even if you manage to turn him around, the age gap wouldn't work. You'll see him a few times, invite him out to Lupo di Mare, except you don't have the money. The unknowns become known, he'll graduate and is off to the *Castro district*, where the Golden Gate Bridge needs urgent repair work, replacement even, by a harp bridge. And Ben has become so good at playing his instruments, they'll eventually build him a monument, right next to the Fletcher Bridge, in classical Greek style, the torso *al fresco*. And because the pendulum finally swung, and the Confederacy lost, and slavery's finally abandoned, he's proudly wearing a nice marble penis, much larger than the willie that Michelangelo felt obliged to equip David with under the scrutinous eye of Pope Leo, perhaps even at 35°, the willie.

"Welcome, John," a sonorous voice sings into my ear. "Welcome to Monroeville." A mature carbon copy of Ben looms large over my crouched, sleepy body. Dr. Fletcher practically carries me into the house, announcing our arrival to his happy family by superfluously calling out "Gracelyn, Gracelyn, honey," across the front yard of his post-colonial cottage, porch and all—a small place though—"meet John," as if I'm the redeemer in person.

Gracelyn, almost as beautiful as her son, materializes on the porch, takes hold of my hands, and touches my arm at the elbow as if I were *Bill Clinton*,

I mean as if *she* were Bill Clinton, and sings: "We are so grateful that you've been brought our son home."

Then she takes tactile possession of Ben, who has already positioned himself next to his mother in anticipation of this, and explains: "We been so proud of Ben, he *bin* our Benjamin, you know." Then, rolling her head and addressing her son directly: "You *bin* lost, my son, ain't you, and John, here, been saved you."

Although there are no undertones, I have the feeling she can read thoughts. Clutching my arm again, she goes: "You better be hungry. We gonna have cornbread, ham hocks, black-eyed peas, and pie, sweet potato pie. You been known soul food, ain't you?"

This is the moment to cross the bridge. "I'm afraid, Ma'am," I say, "that I cannot stay. I'm really sorry, it is not my fault. I need to be back in Georgia Beach at 10 PM."

"That's not possible, young man," she replies.

"I have an urgent appointment at the hospital," I say.

She's too intelligent to tell me that nobody has appointments at hospitals at 10 PM. Instead, she asks: "Have you been sleeping last night?" My sense is, if I were to lie, she would come back 'You are not telling the truth.' So I slept two hours, I say.

"And tell me, what you been doing during the day?" The first sideways glance of this evening is being directed at Ben. Can black people blush?

I painted myself into a corner already. "These roads are dangerous, you know," she says, "especially during the night. We can't let you go, the Lawd won't forgive us." She's getting physical again, so I am trying to make a mental note to self that I must call the hospital and explain.

This is apparently the wrong moment for mental notes. It will be ten o'clock when a message drops into the voice box of a neglected cell phone sleeping between the Tea Party flyers on my kitchen table.

The dinner is delicious, including the ice-tea. Dr. Fletcher explains about his church, and the mega-churches, and the Gospel, and the difference between the Gospel and Fox News. They had to sell their house, move into this place, which is nice, but much smaller. I'm very interested, and very tired. Maurice had explained to me that intelligent animals fold at the right moment. The cat nap in the car didn't help at all, made my fatigue only worse, and there's no booze to prop me up. Gracelyn reads thoughts, and understands, and explains to her husband that John is tired and needs to go to bed. Ben begins to suppresses a grin.

"We're sorry we have no spare bedroom," she says. "I hope you won't mind sleeping with Ben," pointing at her son next to her, who's in full grin-suppression mode now.

"I can sleep on the couch," I say, "or find a motel room, I shouldn't inconvenience you at this late hour."

"You ain't, you ain't, my boy" Mrs. Fletcher says, "Ben's used to this." I feel much less tired all of a sudden.

Ben's bed turns out to be very narrow. I have a cold shower, except that the water is lukewarm, they're possibly filtering it from a local pond. Just to be on the safe side, I put on my boxers again. Ben isn't naked either, he wears a fresh pair of underwear with another colorful graffiti cartoon. You can judge the love of a mother by the underwear of her sons, right? His bed is barely three feet wide; we're lying side by side on our back. "Sleep tight, don't let the mosquitoes bite," he says.

I can't sleep. Ben can't sleep.

What would you do in my situation? You know this has never happened to me before? I had a few bisexual partners, sure, but I never, ever, I swear, made a pass at an innocent kid of unclear sexual preferences nine years younger. A cuckoo clock and the air conditioning are in animated conversation. Should I say 'I love you?' I love Alex. Should I say 'Let's have sex'? I love sex. It's his turn. His body would speak. Or should. Or doesn't. I try to fall asleep.

I must have slept, since I have a boner now. I had a boner before, but the new one has all the clarity of a night glory. I'm lying on my side, another indication I slept. And I feel Ben not only next to me, but also between my thighs. Let's verify. The sense of touch gets involved. Yes, it's his dong, between my thighs. He knows that I know—provided he is awake, perhaps it's just his own night glory while he dreams sweet dreams of beautiful cheer leaders that can't take their eyes away from him as he's happenin' on the basketball court. Let's whisper inaudibly, we'll see.

"You know that's what they did during the Middle Ages?"

"No," he whispers back.

"They didn't have enough beds then. People would routinely share beds and put their dong between their legs."

"That's where they already are."

"*Vice versa*, I mean." He whispers a chuckle.

"You're serious about the middle ages?" he asks.

"The Church disapproved strongly, it was a big issue at the time, two people in one bed," I say. I feel his hand on my boxers, which come off under his ministrations.

"Does your mother know?" I whisper.

"Mothers know everything, especially mine."

"You think she likes me?"

"Yes."

"Do *you* like me?"

"Yes."

"I like you, too."

"I thought so," he whispers back.

Nothing happens for a while. How to move forward. "Have you heard about the Knights of Malta?" I ask.

"Vaguely."

"They had a special technique, such that they would penetrate their partner, and then do nothing, just do nothing, for hours, just stay in place, frozen in time, as it were."

"And the erections, did they freeze too?"

"Good question. More historical research will be needed," I whisper.

"There's perhaps another way to find out," he whispers back.

He adjusts his position slightly, moves his body up a bit, something is playing with my sphincter. Penetration is in the air, except that he can't get in. He gets up, boner throbbing in the fuzzy moonlight of the net-curtained window. "I'll get some butter from the kitchen," he whispers.

"The butter will leave stains on the sheets," I say.

"Saliva, then." He's on a mission now. "Spit. Help me." He sits up, cross-legged, his dick pointing at the moon. "Just spit," he says.

We spit, his knob is getting real shiny. There you sit, cross-legged, trolling decisively into gay territory, your dick reflecting the pale lunar light, and all inhibitions are gone. Spit, spit. Mysterious noises are possibly being heard on the other side of the thin bedroom wall where Dr. and Mrs. Martin Luther Fletcher try to sleep.

People run out of spit after a while. That's the sign. I find myself in our original position, on my side, and feel him clearly (as you might guess). He's drilling, if that's the word, or screwing, anyhow, he's making himself at home. He moans a bit, embraces me from behind, I feel the tension in his triceps mount, then relax. And there you have it, the Knight of Harp Bridges settles in for the long haul.

"Don't you think it's a bit too early in our relationship to start experimenting," I whisper after a while, "shouldn't we follow more conventional paths, fuck inside the box, as it were?"

"You call this fucking?"

An all-pervasive touch embalms me and goes on vacation with me and for long walks on the beach as I am trying to stay awake.

I realized too late what I had done, or not done. In the confusion of my father's arrival, I left the cell phone behind, and then, despite all the mental notes to self, had completely forgotten about Alice, because it had been exactly ten PM when Gracelyn suggested that I sleep in the same bed with Ben. The *mental notes to self*, that must have been it. The deities of the English language are taking offence and punish me dearly (or it's other deities with more pressing concerns).

I'm no longer at Ben's place, I'm in the Chevy heading home. I had left Ben and his parents behind, waking up in the morning not stricken with the usual morning glory but the thought of Alice (or, more precisely, her thoughts). I got so upset with myself, it was not a happy good bye, I turned down the breakfast invitation and left. Others think I hate them when I hate myself—perhaps Ben thought that I had risen with a sexual hangover and under the illusion that it had been *him* who had somehow seduced *me*—it was so stupid and arrogant not to explain about the missed appointment, the Fletchers would have understood. Gracelyn made her best efforts and got the situation under control somehow, but it was not a pretty picture, regardless, and Ben is never going to see me again. Bipolar downswing is not the word, my inner thesaurus fails me.

So I'm returning home, having crossed the Sidney Lanier Bridge already, entering the Georgia Seashore Park. The sycamore tree is on my mind, it's coming up shortly, and there it is, on the left side of the road, with its arrogant canopy printed onto the blue sky. Somebody must have planted it there—this isn't its natural habitat here—a park bureaucrat with murderous instincts possibly, I wouldn't be the first victim.

One fine day, I drive past on my commute, and a motor vehicle had taken aim, crashed into the tree, and wrapped its Detroit steel conclusively around the stem. It's a mystery how they got the suicider out of the wreck and why they left it in its deadly tree-hug for a week, all this during the college term when I had to pass the scene twice per day. I always slow down here, but I've never been this slow. This tree, with the ghost of this wreck, it always makes me think of *Nine-Eleven*. Each time I drive past I'm trying to get into the heads of these people, the lone passenger in the sycamore vehicle, or the "martyrs" on Flight 11 or *Flight 93*; in the movie, they pray.

I'll never make it home at this speed—as if I *wanted* to go home, my father expecting me, he's too lazy to walk to the beach, he needs the Chevy. He's possibly assuming I'm dead and feels too guilty to call the police.

So, there we are. My father in his underwear—no clichés being spared as usual—sitting at the kitchen table—*idem*—he's sitting there and is possibly trying to express concerns for his Chevy or whatever. I don't listen, although his magic still works, his presence cools me down. I feel a bit better, but not for long, the cell-phone is waiting and there is no way not to listen to the voice mail this time. And we are not yet done, father says something. A man had rang the bell at an ungodly hour—where did he pick up the term *ungodly*, is he getting married again—and asked for me, and he had told the guy, he forgot the name, of course, and he had told the guy that I had taken a black-man (he used a different word, as usual, we'll get to that) taken a black guy to the Greyhound terminal, and I was supposed to be back soon, but never returned. Alex, right, that was his name. Alex.

I think I don't have to explain. I'm asking absurd questions, like if Alex left a phone number, or maybe an email address across the intercom. My state is purely physical now, I feel the need to breathe. And I haven't even remotely dealt with the messages that must be waiting in my voice box like road-side bombs wait for the G.I.s in *Hurt Locker*.

Have you been through this? Sure you have. Knowing that somebody has left a message about this cancer test, say, I know, it can be worse, I'm out of my mind, but that's what we bipolars do. *Pelican Brief* comes to mind, the *Grisham* thriller, when the cover's blow off the conspiracy and one of bad guys heads to his office with only one thought in mind. Kill yourself, focus, kill yourself *now*. Compassion with self, that's what it is, John. Anyhow, I fish the cell from among the Tea Party flyers still on the kitchen table, take a good look at my father in the hope that his cryo-magic still works, and head for the bedroom.

I push the voicemail button, and there are two messages. The first is just Alice, she's wondering where I am, and would I please call back, she's very official, but friendly, she's still expecting the world from me, and whether I would please call back immediately. The second message, we can place the voice now, it's my last trick (except for Ben, if you will, and except for Alex, if this goes wrong)—my last trick. Quinton Hayes, the head nurse of IC, evenhandedly informing me that Dr. Sandeman has expressed her concerns as to my non-appearance at the hospital despite repeated assurances on my part of my ability to be present on time. He's not asking for a return call. Basically he's saying that they'll never going to throw an acorn again at this scum-squirrel that we met at Godehart's party. Go fuck yourself.

So I call back. I have to do this immediately. My window is only a few second wide, it's like this Pelican character, you do it now or never. Quinton Hayes' number is from an unknown source, though, I can't return the call. Alice's number—the first call—is known, but I abort the effort after the first ring. I just don't dare, and she must be sleeping now.

I go on the internet, even find the hospital's intensive care ward listed separately, call, but Quinton Hayes got lost in the hallway, though the female voice that answers my call is still there and sounds unhinged by my insisting on talking to Hayes since she's the deputy head nurse and will insist on helping me. So I tell her I need to pay a visit to Maurice Dymond, the British patient in intensive care whose next-of-kin I am, despite my American accent.

"Please hold the line," she says, "I have to check." I am trying to interrupt her, but she's already on the computer, and she cannot listen to the computer and chew gum at the same time until the computer says no (it's very unfair what I'm saying here, we'll see soon). NO.

That must be an error, I tell her, and refer to Quinton's phone call 24 hours ago. "So 24 hours ago you got a phone call about Mr. Dymond as his next-of-kin, but haven't been able to visit him in the meantime despite the severity of his condition and your purported kinship?" She's right, my

God, she's right, finally somebody who is right. If the whole world were like this, black presidents would get reelected.

My numbness is gone, you know I have my moments. "You are right", I say, "you are absolutely right"—she was expecting something else, we might guess—"if the whole world would be like you, black presidents would get reelected."

She mulls the thought briefly. "Come to think of it," she says.

You know, when I'm really desperate, I do really bizarre things.

So I say: "Would you marry me."

She must have gotten proposed to before. "I'm in a same-sex relationship at the moment," she replies, "but there's light in the tunnel." It doesn't make complete sense to me, but she isn't done yet. "You surprise me, John, you know, Quinton told me about you."

This can't last, of course, these few seconds of bliss, and it doesn't. She's pushing the reset button and says: "you are not listed." It's even crueler this time.

When you are in a hole, stop digging. How do you know you're in a hole? Your sentences get longer and longer, so the worst thing is that somebody does *not* interrupt you. Nurses are better paid than college teachers, their sentences are curt and to the point. But I can rest assured, Quinton will call back.

On a normal day I would know what this means, but today I cling to every straw. I sit down on my bed and wait for the call. I slept reasonably well last night, Ben's efforts—or the pointed absence thereof—must have replenished my hormones. Did I come? I don't remember, I woke up in panic, no time to check. I can still come 4 times per day. Should I lock the bedroom door? Nah, he doesn't dare to intrude, and it would be more awkward for him than for me. Besides, there is some departing noise, he's possibly off to the beach.

So I drop my pants and engage in the first auto-erotic effort since ages, two days at least. My dick is stroke-resistant at first, all autonomous spirits have left my body. It really takes five, six minutes before the swelling of the spongy, cavernous tissue is felt by an already tired hand. I'm usually a quick masturbator, but not today. I set my mind to the task and imagine the silly little picture on the *Iliad* condom package, the one for anal practice, with a nice little dick already wrapped up in the jonny, and an inviting little ass putting itself in the right position for immediate use, it always turns me on. But not today.

I try to imagine Alex, first his dick, then his soul, then his dick again. Maurice. Nada. Ben. Ben's dick had filled this space quite a lot only yesterday, give or take a few inches. Nada. I finally give up and get dressed again.

The doorbell rings.

They are please to inform me they have been able to deliver my vehicle by Galactic Merc Service, and whether I could take time away from my other pressing obligations and sign the delivery form. I hasten downstairs, somewhat to the Benz-man's astonishment, who would have been ready and willing to take the elevator (which is still broken) and pay a visit to my premises. That's one of the things I regret in this soap opera, that I didn't let this guy pay a visit to my premises.

An attractive hunk, clad in the gray-bluish Mercedes color, awaits me downstairs, Merc definitions, Benz profile, Merc penis lines on the Benz crotch, he's barely able to hold on to his virility, everything's ready, the key, a pad for the form, the ball-point, and the self, although any hint of tumescence is stylishly kept to the *Armani minimum*.

"Free of charge," he intones. As you know, I'm slow-witted under duress, so I don't get the signals, or didn't get them in time, not before my man—a touch of I-could-stay-around-a-bit-longer in his poise—has taken off again in his galactic truck. It was his body talk, in fact, that made me realize what not had happened. So sorry. Next installment, promise, more Benz men.

I dance around the wonder truck as if it is the golden calf. They haven't only repaired it, they've bathed it in magic Benz lotion and manicured its edges. I'm on the upswing again (technically almost forced, given where I was in before), mobile again. I could go visit Maurice. I'm next-of-kin, who's going to stop me now? I'm with my SUV, the Mercedes with inbuilt priority. The hospital is eight minutes away. The SUV suvs like an SUV.

The *Memorial Baptist Hospital* is located on the corner of the Coastal Highway and Route 24. It's a mid-sized institution, serving Georgia Beach and environs. The parking lot is half empty. I find a space that's visible from most parts of the building. I could point at the high-shine Mercedes if anybody is going to question my credentials.

The summer heat has somehow subverted the air conditioning, the building appears deserted, like people have gone fishing. I enter through the sliding doors of the main gate, a sole receptionist tends to an urgent phone call. A board next to the stairs decodes the hospital's layout in exemplary *Geneva font*, the Intensive Care *Unit* (ICU) is located on the second floor. My sneakers squeak interestingly enough on the sturdy linoleum. The IC ward is separated from common mortality by a sci-fi lock, a glass wall with sliding doors, access is controlled via magnetic badges. There's a bell. Let's exploit common ambiguity here, Hayes's never revoked yesterday's request to come and see Maurice, he only expressed dismay at the lack of follow-up on my part. I push the visitor button. Everything is see-through, I can peek into a glass-paneled control room where nurses spend their time behind computers like everybody else.

I push the button again. *Nada,* the internet rules. An idea. I finger the call-again sequence on my cell and am connected to the voice of my future wife, I can see her talking to me, she gets up, she can see me too, she's waving her hand. Maurice Dymond has been transferred to the Trauma Ward, he's better now, he doesn't need intensive care any longer.

"John, is that you?" she asks.

"Yes, it's me," I say.

"I thought so," she says, "you match Quinton's description. It's a shame all attractive men are either married or gay," then terminates the conversation cruelly and disappears behind her screen.

Another movie flash strikes me on the steps to the trauma ward, featuring *Casanova* (yes, him), who implausibly appears in the French movie *La nuit de Varennes* and says to a queen riding with him on the stagecoach to said Varennes (the town north of Paris where the fugitive King *Louis XVI*, on his way to exile during the French revolution, had just been intercepted by the toiling masses), so Casanova says to the queen, who has just made him an offer he could resist, but doesn't, he says: "Sure, why not, one should try everything."

This is a modern hospital, there are few access restrictions regarding normal patients. Maurice has been assigned to room 3-16, I'm told by the trauma control room, and he's really happy to see me. He's quite upbeat.

I forgot the flowers. "I forgot the flowers," I say, "I brought the towel but forgot the flowers."

"That almost rhymes," he says, "it rhymes internally,' I brought the *towel* but forgot the *flower*."

"I forgot the *flower* but brought the *tower*."

"No word is safe in English," he replies.

"Don't do the Lady *Dy* on me," I say.

"My moniker, did you discover this yourself?"

"Not so difficult, once I knew your last name."

"Can I tell you," he says, "when they began calling me 'Lady Dy' in school, I didn't quite understand."

"So you've been pushed into homosexuality by heartless bullies."

"And now I'm kept there by heartless hotties like you, darling."

I explain about the truck, I couldn't come yesterday because of the truck, and I tell him the story of Godehart's Merc-service and the Armani Minimum. He tells me he's feeling much better. I ask how long he's planning to stay in the hospital. He laughs—"planning,"—it'll be a few more days, they told him. You still want to move in with me, I ask, I feel guilty and Alex-less and what not. He looks great with his cropped blond hair, a bit pale though, like all aspiring playwrights from the tourist office. I don't let him answer.

"Why do you wear a crew-cut," I ask.

"To look more American."

"You want to look more American, you should eat more."

"Don't say that," he says, "look at you and Alex."

"How do you know his name, 'Alex'?" I ask.

Dr. Sandeman came to see him, Alex in tow. Surprise, surprise. They tell him he must make a deposition, but he's not so sure. I tell him about Alice's concerns. Yes, he knows, still, he isn't sure. What's a deposition worth? He's heard stories how court cases in America collapsed because somebody died, a car accident, something unforeseen, the key witness is gone—what's the expression—*blotted out*, taken care of. The jury's bored, case dismissed. "Even if my deposition holds full legal status after my death, somebody will have to read it out in court, what with attention spans and everything, the jury will fall asleep."

"Not if Benson manages to come up with a thrilling homicide," I say stupidly. Maurice is not amused.

I can't fault him. But I tell him he should think about his contract, the exchange arrangement between Torquay and Georgia Beach, he may not be able to quit his appointment here on his own volition just like that, and he can stay at my place. "My bed is large enough."

"That's not how it sounded last time."

"I'm changing my ways."

"How can one change one's ways?" he asks.

"Masturbate more, have more sex in general, be more outgoing, and love the world."

"New Year's over since six month, isn't it?"

(I'm getting cheesy, that's new:) "When I met you, I decided to change my ways."

"So, tell me, how often did you beat the bishop since my death?"

"Well, I tried."

"And otherwise?"

"You don't want to know"—I'm exploiting common ambiguity here, but that doesn't work with aspiring playwrights from the tourist office.

"I *do* want to know."

"I don't really know."

"If people remember anything, it's sex."

I give in and explain about Alex on top of me and Ben between my legs. "Simultaneously?"

I have to explain further (about Godehart, for example), no secrets are being spared.

"And all this while I was dead, practically speaking," he says.

I suddenly realize (a) I love him, but (b) I'm not in love with him. "I love you, but I'm not in love with you," I say.

"Do you have pen and paper?"

"Huh?"

"I must write this down."

"It's not so deep, somebody must have thought this up before," I say (we'll discover later that it's on the Urban Dictionary, not to mention various psycho sites).

"I might use it for my new script, if I could buy the copyright from you."

140

"I sell French, and my body, and one-liners, but I thought you were writing plays," I say.

"Plays, or scripts, what's the difference. This is a script because it's an action comedy, there are too many locations for a single stage."

"What is it about, your script?"

"It's political," he says, "*Dr. Strangelove* meets the *Naked Gun*, but I might be able to use your idea nonetheless, one should always have a boy-meets-girl thing in the background."

He's actually insisting I get pen and paper for him.

"You don't need to write it down, you can remember it," I say.

"Yes, but you might have more witticisms *in petto*."

I glow a bit inside. The first compliment in years (almost).

So I'm off to the control room. "We're fully digitized," the head geek says (who looks like a younger *Bill Gates*), "But we can lend an iPad to Mr. Dymond." Really? Yes, "iPads are known to further the healing process. I-padded patients recover more quickly. By 35 percent." He hands me an i-thing (35% of what?).

"Do I have to sign for this?" I ask. No, the iPad knows when it is stolen, it's linked to the hospital coordinates and shuts itself down when carried off the premises. "Somebody steals it, it's gone, even if it doesn't work," I say.

"But the moral universe remains intact," he replies, "and we add it to the patient's bill, they don't notice 400 bucks in the larger scheme of digits."

I'm back with the borrowed iPad and tell Maurice about the blog and how it froze. He's already i-connected and has it on the screen.

"I could publish my script on your blog," he says. "Could I do that?"

"Tell me more about your script."

He doesn't answer. Instead, he throws a hysterical fit: "Faboo," "Blimey," "Stupendous," he cries, and wraps up: "PLEASE, let me use this, FREEDOM FRIES, John, Freedom Fries, please let me use this."

"Us escorts is always glad to help," I say.

"This is it, this is what I need."

"Sex?"

"This is better than sex. This is about eternity. About *George W. Bush.*"

Turns out, he's planning a script about the aftermath of the Bush presidency, number 43, that is, the bushier Bush. Bush gets killed—almost—by *Dr. Strangelove* or *Mel Gibson.*

"Only almost?" I ask.

"This is how it starts, Bush is having second thoughts about the Freedom Fries. He'll say to Laura, they are watching a show on Lynx, you get it, don't you, on LYNX, about his presidency, a hagiography about his presidency, and he'll say," (Maurice's typing already) "and he says: 'Well, make no mistake, the Freedom Fries were stupid,' and then Laura answers: 'The house canteen isn't edible anyhow, whether French or liberated,' and then he comes back, he comes back: 'I wonder whether they are still called Freedom Fries,' and she comes back 'No, they are not,' because she knows those things, and then it's turtles all the way down until there's some sort of happy ending, this thing *must* happy-end, it's so improbable, and Freedom Fries *must* be the title, that's a happy ending in itself, please, John, pretty please."

"I don't know whether you realize the door is open," I answer, "people can hear you."

"Then close it," he says—we're actually alone in this room, the other bed is empty. So I close the door and say: "Okay."

"Can I publish it on your blog? I must publish it on your blog. Please, pretty please."

If I give him permission, he can post the posts that I don't post. "For the permission I have to log in under my name," I tell him. He hands me the i-ding, I arrive on a page about the weather in *Copacabana* in under two seconds. I hand it back, spell my login name for him. A few seconds more, and he has obtained the permission to post on my blog.

"Why don't you start your own blog? It takes thirty seconds," I ask.

"Your blog is already established, it has readers."

I laugh, he'll find out soon enough: "I haven't come out blog-wise, not fully."

"What is this," he interrupts me, points at the screen with the blog. A

142

banner (the blog has a few commercial banners from *AdSense*), a red banner is blinking: "MAURICE CUMMING."

"This targeting really goes too, far," Maurice says, "how could they possibly know? And, sadly, it isn't even true."

Both of us study the screen now, the banner is a book ad for a spy novel, *Maurice Cumming* is the name of the author.

"Let's impart a romantic edge," he says. "We sit on your bed, you're masturbating all by yourself, you're cumming momentarily, even though you are *not* Maurice, and Maurice is not cumming, even though he *is* Maurice, because he's doing your blogging, although he may steal glances at the cumming non-Maurice once in a while."

"Blogging *is* masturbation."
"Perfect," he says, "symmetry restored."

Fragment of an email alert from the *New York Times* (international edition), arriving in our mailbox *at the very moment* (8AM EST on Aug. 8, 2012) (*I swear*) that we were writing in the first draft (where Maurice's character was still called "Charles"): "'I came, I came,' he [Charles] exclaims, 'I came just by myself, it's like a wet dream.'"

It's completely unclear to me whether he's serious or not. "They told me explicitly not to masturbate," he says. "The cut from the surgery must heal first, but I could give you a blow-job."

I'm still young, I drop my pants. These hospital beds are higher than normal beds, the bed line is just at the right level blow-wise, especially if the active partner is lying on the bed, on his side, horizontally, whereas the passive partner is standing, vertically, not on the bed, but on the semen-resistant floor next to the bed, facing the active partner with his no-longer-private parts.

Maurice is already at it, gently befuddling my dick with his left hand. Do I have to go into details? Okay, you get the idea. The usual adjectives apply. Maurice's making sure I'll stay inside so nothing gets wasted, his Adam's apple tells the story. "I came, I came," he exclaims as soon as anatomical conditions allow, "I came just by myself, it's like a wet dream. Maurice cumming, John cumming. There is no author with the name *John Cumming*, right?" Why don't you look it up, I say. Yes, yes, the iPad knows, there was a 19th century Scottish clergyman of that name, who published 180 books during his lifetime and got obsessed with the concept of *Rapture* (the metaphysical variety), but who, judging by the overall vibes of his Wikipedia entry, never had sex in a hospital: John Cumming.

We're done in the happy sense that both of us came. But we're not done in the sense that my pants are still hanging on my knees when the door opens and a nurse enters. He's bringing something for Maurice, yes, three tiny pills on a little saucer, one tablet oblong, the others roundish, they look like a happy family. "Do you want to change you pajamas?" the nurse says to Maurice while studiously ignoring the unorthodox positioning of my pants.

"How do you know?" Maurice asks.

"Nurses know everything," the nurse answers, "especially if there are clues." I raise my pants, buckle my belt.

"I think I had a wet dream," Maurice says. The nurse smiles, exits, and, while closing the door, says: "Don't overdo it."

"I don't understand why you're not in love with me," Maurice says.

"You're not in love with me, either."

"How do you know?"

"This was just too passionate. It was great, but sort of staged."

"I tried," he says.

"Don't try too hard."

"You know how it is. I *have* been in love."

"Often?"

"Too often."

"For how long?"

"That's the problem. And you?"

I bring up Alex (again). And Alice. And the missed appointment. So, you got yourself into a fine mess," he says.

"You can say that."

"How can I help you?"

"You can help me by making a deposition."

"Alice left a phone number, I can call her anytime."

Alice's calling card, I realize, is waiting on the bed-side table. Maurice dials, is connected, explains.

"Tell her I'm with you at the moment," I interject—physical proximity is always suggestive—but there's no apparent reaction Dyke-wise, she doesn't send her regards.

"She'll pop in later, today," Maurice says.

Where does this leave us? We're done now, right? I shouldn't bring this up: "You were scared at the Blue Moon, scared of RapeDick. You're not scared here?"

Stupid. He wasn't scared but now he is. "How did *you* get here," he asks. What can I say?

"You'll stay at my place," I tell him, and kiss him good-bye. "Tomorrow," I say.

I've almost reached my high-shine truck when I realize that I had passed a police uniform on the way down the staircase—I had been too impatient to wait for the elevator, as usual—some guy in full armor, wearing shades. A guy perhaps six feet tall, not obese by Southern standards, quite strong. Brandishing his uniform like they all do, perhaps a bit more. I had seen this guy, I had seen this guy before. Why, obviously, I had, this is a small town, you know the cops, at least by sight. No, I had seen him recently. I have a bad memory for faces.

I unlock the truck per beep, then lock it again. Forty yards perhaps to the main entrance, sixty yards inside the building. I dart across the parking lot. Five, six seconds into the sprint. The sliding doors stay shut, apparently programmed to slow down speeding crazies. Another two or three seconds tick until the doors change their mind. The receptionist is still on the phone, but she takes interest as I accelerate across the deserted reception hall, throwing a "Sir, Sir," after me, let's hope she alerts security. Two flights of steps. How much time has elapsed since I've passed the cop? Thirty seconds, one minute? My shoes squeak on the sturdy linoleum, I slip. How would the guy know where to find Maurice? Perhaps he just asked. The door to Maurice's room is closed.

A uniform hovers over Maurice's bed, I see erratic jerks and a pillow. I yell. The uniform turns around. I know this guy, sure, it's the guy from the diner, the same shades, absent nose, narrow lips. He's stepping forward. He will kill me. I think of my father. I yell again, or try at least. He does not reach for the gun. He ducks, one foot in front, the left arm stretched forward, he knows how to fight. I don't think, mimic his movements. He dives forward, is on the other foot, rams his knee into my gut. Like a piston. The pain kills my voice. His boot hits my knees. I fold. I'm on the ground, lying on the side, holding my abdomen like an embryo. I can still think. Only noise can save me. I yell, I yell, sure I yell. He kicks. I yell. He stops kicking, is on top of me now. His face is on my face, spit drips from his mouth. My arm still works. I hit his ear with my thumb, his inner ear. I do it again. I clutch his hair. I can still yell. It's getting dark, I feel much better.

**

I must have slept. I'm waking up. I'm lying on the ground. Feet are planted around my head, white coats hover above. A uniform is on top of me, restricting me. I did something wrong. "Why did you try to kill him?" I understand. I cannot speak. "Why did you try to kill him," the white coat says again. "He's injured," another voice says.

31 I EXPECT YOU TO DIE, MR. BOND

W e've been here before, I've seen these eyes before and I know this room, a hospital room. There is a bed to the left, and lying on the bed is a person, wait, it's Maurice. My field of views widens until I realize that I'm a patient myself. Alex is standing next to my bed, and there's a hint of concern in his green eyes.

My head is between the ears of a pillow. The head rest is inclined somewhat. "This head rest, it's inclined at 35 degrees, right," I say.
"You're getting dangerous," Alex says.
"What am I doing here?"
"You *were* getting dangerous."

A spy flick comes to mind, a German accent hovering above an encumbered spy who's strapped to some torture bench but asks in an odd gesture of helplessness: 'What do you expect me to do?' and the German accent replies: 'I expect you to die, Mr. Bond.'

I tell Alex. He laughs his dry laugh. The more I make him laugh, the more he'll give me his email address. I raise my arm, try to clutch his hand. He understands. We never held hands before. "Why don't you give me your email address," I ask.
"I have nothing to write."
"I'll remember it."
"It's Alex-six-five-five-three-seven at gmail dot com. What's yours?"
"That's almost a phone number."
"Two digits are missing."
"You want my email," I ask, "really?"
"If I give you mine…"

Mine is a difficult, outdated address, I'm not sure he's trying to remember. 'Alex-Five-five-six-three-seven,' I'm telling myself. "Five-five-six-three-seven," I'm saying.

"It's six-five-five-three-seven," Alex corrects me, "the largest *Fermat prime* known."

"That'll help."

"You can look it up on Wikipedia."

"The number?"

"Yes."

"Until a larger one is found."

"Not bad," he says, "but no new one has been found in 350 years." He smiles. He's the man of my life.

"Not 35 years, mind you," he adds.

I'll have to get my act together. I do this wrong, everything will be lost.

"Alex, I'm in the hospital, right?" I say.

"Yes."

"The guy from the diner tried to kill Maurice, right?"

"The guy from the diner?"

"Yes, the guy from the diner."

"You sound confused."

"I am confused."

"Maurice says it was RapeDick. Dick Benson."

Did I dream it? This is the man I saw the other day in Mamma Mia. On Sunday evening. Sun glasses, absent nose, small eyes, mean, narrow lips. A familiar face. Not the first time I had seen the guy. A cop, sure, you know the cops from sight, this is not a big town.

"I saw this guy having a beef with a woman in Mamma Mia, on Sunday evening," I say.

"On Sunday evening?"

"Yes."

"After the rape, then."

"I guess so."

"Perhaps his ex," Alex says, "Benson tightening the screws on her to stay mum."

Yes, right, the woman did fit Maurice's description.

"It was him," I repeat, "he was wearing the same shades."

"Three witnesses," Alex interrupts me, "Maurice, the ex, and Blake, his partner, three witnesses. Maurice almost gone."

"It's not possible," I say. "How could he expect to get away with this?"

"If you hadn't shown up Maurice would be dead by now. And Benson could have gotten away with it. Figure this: Nurse enters room with dinner tray. Patient is asleep. Patient refuses to wake up. Patient appears dead. Patient *is* dead. Patient had emergency surgery, was one day out of intensive care. Patient suffered post-surgery *exitus*. Not quite *in tabula*, but almost. Stuff happens. Not even sure they would perform a *post mortem*."

"Benson wouldn't know."

"He knew enough to find Maurice. Few murders are calculated on a strictly rational basis. Benson has lost it. He's groping in psychotic space."

"Groping in psychotic space," I echo.

"Well, excuse me."

"Sounds like a one-liner I could sell to Maurice."

"Well, try."

"I think he's sleeping."

"He had a sedative."

"And you, Alex, what are you doing here?"

"I am guarding you, both of you."

"Why don't you let security do it, you have security personnel in this hospital, right?"

"Yes, we do," he says.

"So?"

"They are not convinced."

"That Benson tried to kill Maurice?"

"Yes."

"Did you try?"

"Have you ever tried to convince security of anything?"

"Why can't we just go to..."—I'm interrupting myself.

"We've contacted the DA office. They are sending somebody, tomorrow. Somebody must take care of Benson."

I need a clear head. Alex is easily derailed by a wrong word. I need a cup of coffee. He will get it for me from the vending machine. I'm briefly alone with Maurice. Should I wake him up? Will I be able to get up? What's wrong with me? No bandages, so to see. Alex is back.

"I'm not hurt in a serious way, right?"

"No, you are not."

"No concussion?"

"Headache?"

"No."

"Fuzzy or blurred vision?"

"No."

"He must have hit you fairly badly, though. You lost consciousness."

I realize some bad hurt in my groin.

"My groin," I say. He laughs.

"Yeah, it can wipe you out." He has this paramedic look on his face. "You should be fairly groin-resistant, though, with your amount of practicing. You've been all over the map, haven't you?"

"What was I doing, sleeping?"

"You got a sedative as well, a milder one."

"Why?"

"You were talking gobbledygook, security thought it was you who tried to kill Maurice."

"And?"

"Maurice recovered just in time to save your ass and explain."

"Can you take me home?" I ask.

"I have to take care of Maurice until he's back in IC. He's relatively safe there."

"Will I see you again?"

"You're seeing a lot of people."

I fall silent. What can I do? I hide behind a used one-liner: "Fifty ways to leave your lover."

"Alice talked to me," he says, "about you."

"I have been trolling."

"Apparently."

"Will you forgive me?"

"I don't have to forgive you anything."

We're interrupted. In walks a nurse who knows how to make an entrance. He has aged bit in the last four years.

150

"Quinton," Alex says, all alpha dog now, his green eyes fixed on my former trick, "there you are."

"It took quite some doing," Quinton says, "It's 3500 bucks per night, I had to find somebody to sign off on this."

"And who was it?"

"Myself. The head intensivist is off playing golf in Palm Springs, and his replacement is C2."

"C2," I ask.

"You don't want to know, John," Quinton replies, unblocks the wheels of Maurice's bed, and disappears with the English patient.

"What's going on?" I ask.

"He's going back to Intensive Care, he's safer there, you can go home."

"I don't want to go home."

"This is the trauma ward, we have no jurisdiction here, we've called in too many favors already. Tomorrow at 10 AM...the DA, we need you. You're an indirect witness, you were the first one to be told about the rape by Maurice. Be there, or be square."

He's gone. An MD appears, examines me briefly, and declares me discharged.

I 'm on the Coastal Highway again, driving home. Some new billboards have gone up, or changed their tune. Next week is *Georgia Beach Week*, the so-so attempt of the local business community to replicate *Woodstock*, or *Burning Man*, or whatever, and put our town on the map by means of a local festival. It's always themed, and this year it's vampires. I forgot. Men and women with extreme fangs have replaced dental paste and *Pampers* on some billboards, the undead appearing with their fangs next to the ever-reborn face of the new mayor. And I haven't even seen the latest installment of *Twilight*. I have to ask Luke about this when I fetch food for the night.

So I tell Luke about the truck and the galactic Merc man. Then I ask: "The *Week* is coming up, with vampires. Your work?"

"I'm a tiny cogwheel in the larger machinery of meaning," he replies, "I'm not even a member of the country club, but yes, sure, the mayor asks for ideas, I answer his call. Alerted them to a fortuitous coincidence. You've heard of the *End-of-the-World?*"

"Who hasn't."

"No, I mean next week."

"Really?"

"Last time was in May last year, remember?"

"But that didn't go through."

"A regrettable error in the calculations."

"They should have hired Alex," I say absent-mindedly, Luke doesn't even know him.

"Well, they hired *Barbette Bienpensant.*"

"Never heard of."

"She's some professor at the *Metaphysical University*, and she's predicting the End for next week."

"Cool."

"Cool, isn't it. Vampires and Rapture, dovetails neatly."

"You're more on the vampire end, I guess."

"No-no, I'm broad-minded, have a look." He points across the main aisle at a row of life-sized sex toys, inflatable puppets, blown-up already, the vulvas invitingly open for business.

"So?" I say.

"I'll have them fitted with a timer and dressed in neighborhood wear, you know, the clothes people wear when getting raptured while mowing the lawn or watching TV. And then, *poom*, I don't know when exactly, Professor Bienpensant hasn't finished her calculations yet, *poom*, the timer goes off, they deflate, the puppets, *pooff*. They will look almost real, you know, empty clothes, neatly aligned on the lawn, or the couch, the empty puppet inside practically invisible. Neat, isn't it?"

"Cool," I repeat. "You think they sell?"

"I know what you think," he says, "but people are not stupid. They are useful, these toys, they are re-inflatable. Rapture fun is a nice pretext to purchase one. The wife cannot complain."

I buy a few cans of beer and two microwavable hamburgers, plus a bag of microwavable fries, plus ketchup.

"Don't you need some hands during the Week? For your stall at the Festival venue?" I ask.

"You need money?"

"I need money, yes. I'm not paid during the break."

"You'll be running off with the Count," he says.

"The Count?"

"Well, yes, Dracula."

"No, no," I say, "not Dracula, especially not Dracula, I need the money."

"I'll think about it," he deflects. "This black guy," his words follow me as I'm leaving, "yesterday's black guy, John, he would be a nice twist, can't you ask him. Ask him if he's interested, he looked like a college kid in need of a summer job." I sidestep, he understands. Of course.

I arrive at home. Father's mis-parked, as usual, I park my own vehicle as far away as possible from his clunker. I don't feel great and have trouble climbing the stairs. Let's hope it's not a concussion after all. The groin still hurts. Father has the spare key now. Will he be sitting at the kitchen table?

Will he be doing nothing with his life? Will people always sit in their underwear at kitchen tables doing nothing with their lives?

Father is indeed sitting at the kitchen table, but he is doing something, he reads his flyers. I lost yesterday's Tea Party exchange in the second round on points, but there is something beyond the content of this shit that's aggravating. The stuff take up too much space on the table.

"You haven't had a chance to do something about your canvassing material, right," I ask.
"I was at the beach," he answers.

We should have a fight now, but it's vital that we don't get into an argument. Any attempt to prevail through argumentation must and will fail. How to start a fight then? How to send him off the cliff? I pop hamburgers and fries into the microwave, get hold of two plates, the ketchup, salt, and put his plate ever so gently on the table in front of him. I'm teasing him, it's sort of obvious, but what can a poor body do. He asks for knife and fork. Is he getting married again? "Can't you eat with your hands?" I say.

He's crouched over the table, both elbows propped up, his mouth hovering above the food. And now he's killing a fry with his fork, and a second one, and a third one, and now he's munching himself to death while a score of slaughtered fries are sticking out of his maw like trapped fish or other bad metaphors. "Why can't you eat with your nose," I say. He groans something back. I'm about to share a flashback to *Monty Python's* 'A Fish Called Wanda,' (nose, fries, ketchup, oral orifice taped shut, death by asphyxiation, almost) but the doorbell rings.

The doorbell, what else would you expect from us. It's Ben. Ben! The soap must go on! Perhaps I should tell Ben that my father is around, but father can overhear me on the intercom. "Sure," I say to the intercom, "come on up." He won't be able to stay long, whether that's OK. Sure, it is. With a father like this, everything is fine, even non-sex. "My father is here," I let him know.

Ben makes his entrance in a holy sort of way, only children of black ministers can do this. He's very polite, obviously, he's even trying to greet father formally, but Dad remains immersed in his flyers. "Can I offer you a beer?" I ask Ben. He has to drive home, no alcohol, a cup of coffee would be fine.

He has recouped his car, crossed the overpass, made a U-turn, and swings by. He left my phone number at home, couldn't call in advance. Did I give him my phone number? We exchanged email addresses. I guess Ben changed his mind on the spot when crossing the overpass. *Dr. Freud*, can you hear us?

"I thought I would never see you again," I say. This is something I would not have said only three days ago, in particular not in the presence of my father. I tell Ben about the missed appointment at the hospital, about the missed mental notes, my stupid behavior the next morning, about my feeling terribly sorry, whether he would please, please convey my sincere apologies to his parents. My father raises his reading glasses— tomorrow I will tell him that Ben has a big dick. Ben is getting up, he's already done, apparently, it's as if he's just been waiting for me to say something in the future tense.

"How long is you father staying..." he asks—this is like soccer, folks, the right wing man passing the ball, and—"until tomorrow," I say (goal).
"Great," Ben replies. "I have another meeting in Georgia Beach next week, I'll send you an email."

He's almost off already, I ask him whether he needs money. Always, of course. Luke wants to hire him, the convenience store vampire. He's all ear.
"I'll go see Luke right now, if he's there," he says, "and we'll talk next week."

He blows a departing kiss, somehow managing to include my father. This must be the first time my father has received a blown kiss from a *nigger*—bear with me (I know), just a few paragraphs. Where's John going to stay if he comes to work in Georgia Beach?

You wonder how I'm going to start a fight now. So do I. I could disappoint everybody and go to bed. Or I could collect the flyers, stack them in some histrionic gesture and create a neat pile that contrasts neatly with my next move, dumping everything into the trash can. So we have a fallback option now. The flyers, we do that tomorrow when we kick him out. I dump the flyers, collect his things, open the door, and haul his belongings outside. The bag will tumble down the steps. I'll be in a foul mood, I kick ass. No words, just kicks. Second time to get physical. Last time to see him. Change my life. Tea Party. Asshole.

Where was I? The flyers. The threat is stronger than the execution, they say in chess. So I say: "If this shit isn't gone by tomorrow, I'll dump it in the garbage."

I don't get the expected reaction, though. On his standard form we could expect the re-enactment of some *Candid Camera* scene that I may or may not win on points. But no, he just sits there, glancing longingly at his flyers. Something has changed in that man. The tide went out, including Boston harbor, and the muddy ground of the nation is packed with naked clowns, wrapped in the flag. And if they are not angry, angry, about this guy from Kenya who spends their hard-earned $$$, they sit at my kitchen table and do things with their life. Or my life. I can't win this.

So I retire to the bedroom. I activate the computer and read my email, and have a message from Nick, chain mail. It's a bunch of Anti-Obama cartoons, plus some language about *real* Americans, real *Americans*, and accompanied by the complaint that the nation is under siege because all these cartoons couldn't be published in the US. I look closer. This one (Obama dressed up as *Al-Qaida* in front of the White House dressed up as *Kremlin*) appeared in the *Washington Times*. The next one (Obama dressed up as a shaman) it's a bit difficult to see, was published in the *Times-Picayune*. The third one appeared in the *New York Post*. And so on. It's trivial, and it's not, because this is how they operate, claiming the high grounds of patriotism and victimhood, supported by nothing but lies and ignorance, assuming that the rest of the world is even more stupid than they are. Where have we seen this before? Ever taken a class in European history? The rise of the Nazis, for example? It's exactly, EXACTLY the way the NAZIS operated on their march to power.

I need to pee, and I need a drink. So I'm back in the kitchen. Father still immersed in his flyers. I grab a can of beer from the fridge, and say: "Perhaps you need a spell-checker."

Zero points. "I gave some of your flyers to Ben," I continue, "the black guy you've just met, he liked them." Mild blood pressure symptoms father-wise. "He thought they were anti-Tea-Party," I add. Pressure rising? "Ben is from Monaville," I continue, "a former slave refuge, and he's telling me, *we* can *spell* in Monaville…" (I'm on to something, father reddens).

"It's Obama's fault," he says, "he's the govment. The govment is the problem."

(What else.)

"You're a patriot, right," I say.

Don't go there John, you are getting argumentative, that's not the idea. But he's a patriot, sure, you bet, his outfit, it's even named *Tea Party Patriots*, but hey, *Holt*, his pal, who was tasked to print the stuff, forgot the 'patriots' in a last-minute effort. "You're supporting the troops, right?" I ask. He nods solemnly ("You bet.")

From premises to conclusion, how do we do this? Don't John, don't. "You know, your troops are also part of the government," I say.

He possibly didn't hear me but performs a few speech acts just to maintain mammal bonding ('What do you know,' 'Listen to me,' 'You moron'). "Would you spell moron with an 'a' or with an 'o'?" I ask. No reaction. "Your *Medicaid*," I add, "that's also the government"—ain't, ain't, what do you know, keep the govment out of my Medicaid.

You painted yourself into a corner, John, as usual. How to get out of this, how to move forward? We're lucky for a change, we don't have to do anything, father gets up as if he has been preparing for this (we're both standing now), and goes:

"Call this a govment! why, just look at it and see what it's like. Just as that man has got a few cents in his pockets, and they start raisin taxes. They call that govment! A man can't get his rights in a govment like this. Sometimes I've a mighty notion to just leave the country for good and all. Yes, and I told 'em so; I told that muslim in his face, by email. Says I, for two cents I'd leave the blamed country and never come a-near

it agin. Oh, yes, this is a wonderful govment, wonderful. Why, looky here. There was a nigger there from Ohio -- a mulatter, most as white as a white man...”

(What's going on?)

“...He had the whitest shirt on you ever see, too, and the shiniest hat; and there ain't a man in that neighborhood that's got as fine clothes as what he had; and he had a gold watch. And what do you think?”
(This cannot be.)

“...He's a p'fessor in a college, and talks all kinds of languages, and know everything. And that ain't the wust. And he votes? For who? Thinks I, what is the country a-coming to? It's 'lection day, and I'm just about to go and this guy crosses my path. I'll never vote agin...”

(This can't be him.)

“...The country may rot for all me -- I'll never vote agin as long as I live. And to see the cool way of these niggers -- why, they wouldn't give me the road if don't shove them out o' the way. I says to the people, why ain't these niggers put up at auction and sold? -- that's what I want to know. And what do you reckon people say?”

(Something is wrong.)

“Why, they say slavery has been abandoned. There, now -- that's a specimen. Here's a govment that calls itself a govment, and lets on to be a govment, and thinks it is a govment, and they give money to the thieving, white-shirted niggers, and ...”

He sits down. He must have lost his train of thought.

Let me think. The humble worm *C. Elegans* is the third-best researched organism on the planet, so we know it possesses exactly 302 neurons which make up its brain. *E. Coli*, a bacteria, is even better researched, so we know it resides in mammal bowels and has no brain at all. I always thought that my father, who is considerably less-researched, would be located somewhere between the two, yet how is it possible that such an organism learns, retains, and recalls an entire page from the book of *Huckleberry Finn*, including some editorial modifications? A tirade of Huck's father, to wit, that template of alcohol-addled, redneck lucidity?

Shall I make my contribution to the wealth of human knowledge and ask this organism how he does it? It's a bit complicated, but he knows a lot about worms and bowels. So I sit down at the table, and say: "The humble *WORM* C. Elegans is the third-best researched organism on the planet, so we know it possesses exactly 302 neurons, which make up its brain. E. Coli, a bacteria, is even better researched, so we know it resides in mammal *BOWELS* and has no brain at all. I always thought that *YOU*, who is considerably less well-researched, would be somewhere located between the two, yet how is it possible that *YOUR* organism learns, retains, and recalls an entire page from the book of Huckleberry Finn, including some editorial modifications? A tirade of Huck's father, to wit, that template of alcohol-addled, redneck *STUPIDITY*?"

Thomas Mann was famous for taking entire pages from some humble govment document, the report on a cholera epidemic, say, change a word here, a word there, and turn it into Nobel-winning prose. Am I anything near that? I've accented the words "worm," and "bowel," I've switched to the second person, and changed the last word, lucidity became stupidity, just to be on the safe side. Can one win prizes for insults? "Can one win prizes for insults?" I ask.

(John, you *did* it, you did *it*! Bingo! Change of plan. We must have him back next year.)

And now I go too far, as usual, and ruin the entire evening. So I say to him: "Do they have entry exams at the Tea Party? Or Sunday Schools? Did you have to learn this by heart to get in? Perhaps it's required reading in other places as well, perhaps you cannot get a job at the *American Enterprise Institute*, or the *Heritage Foundation* without proof that you know this by heart."

He smiles, he smiles. He knows nothing. He won.

33 SOME PEOPLE EXPEND ENORMOUS ENERGY MERELY TO BE NORMAL

The doorbell rings twice.

You may have learned in high school about certain experiments involving dogs, behavior, and a scientist called *Pavlov,* who trained dogs to respond to a signal, a doorbell, say, and rewarded them with a cookie if they would react in a particular way, push a button with their paw, say, until one fine day there would be no cookie, the bell would ring, the dogs would push the button, but there would be no cookie, and the pooches would howl and cry and die in despair.

I'm exaggerating here, not only regarding all the canines that survived, but also regarding Alex, who rang the bell only yesterday when I was still cheating on him in Ben's arms. Anyhow, it's six AM, the sun is embracing the water tower, I'm not negotiating on the intercom. I don't want to know, I just push the buzzer, leave the main door ajar and go find some clean underwear in the bedroom. It takes a little while, my search, and when I've finally returned to the kitchen in the last pair of passable boxers, it's him who's hovering next to the table, holding on to his Baptist-themed sweatshirt, not seeking eye contact *per se,* but not looking at my crotch either.

This, folks, this is why gay novels are different, and why you should read us. What happens next simply couldn't happen between straight people.

"Your name is Alex," I say, "right?"

Just imagine this were Alexis, my date since three days. She wouldn't ring the bell at six AM, and if she did, we would assume she has issues, serious ones, so I would react very differently to her morning visit, and if, for the sake of argument, we assume that she didn't have issues, I would definitely not open the conversation with the line 'your name is Alexis, right?'

Let's start this all over again. "Your name is Alex," I say, "right?"

"Yes," he says.

"You're done with you shift?"

"Yes."

There's something between his brows that keeps me from asking more questions, so I say: "I'll make us a cup of coffee."

He sits down at the kitchen table and stretches like a cat.

"Your non-concussion," he asks, "headaches, drowsiness?"

"No."

"Did you sleep well?"

"Yes."

"Good. Did you drink last night?"

"No. One beer, with my father."

"Good."

"My father will depart today," I say.

"He's sleeping?"

"I guess so." I'm listening, yes, a familiar snore emanates from the spare room. Why is it that all rednecks always sleep through all doorbells while snoring like rednecks? We both listen in.

"Why is it that all rednecks always sleep through all doorbells while snoring like rednecks?" I say.

"You and the universal quantifier, you're quite a pair," he replies. "Why did you say *depart*, why didn't you say *leave*?"

"Because he's not going to leave. But he's going to depart, because I'll kick him out."

"Oh, that's it," he says, "why do you have him, then?"

"I'll explain later," I say.

We're sipping my questionable coffee. Something walks through the room, it's not quite an angel. I'm trying to mimic the trademark neutrality of his eyes with my own peepers, not sure I succeed. It doesn't come naturally, his expression, he's making an effort, and if he would let go, his regard wouldn't turn into insouciance, or nonchalance, but into something darker, considerably darker.

161

We're sitting next to each other at the table, brothers again. I'm not a sensitive person, or a good observer, but when I'm idling, waiting somewhere, say, I tend to observe people at a distance, trying to gauge their relationship, whether they are friends, or married, whether the marriage is happy or not, and when I get feedback—one of them departing, the other staying behind, clarifying goodbyes being exchanged—yeah, right, you know this already, Mamma Mia, clarifying goodbyes being exchanged, LOL. Anyhow, if somebody would look at the two of us, he would take us for brothers, one or both adopted, possibly—but brothers.

"You're the only child?" he asks.
"I have a twin brother, Joe."
"Joe is more like you or like him?"
"More like him"—there are exceptions to the brother rule, I realize.
"I'm an only child," he says, "I think."
Then he thinks. We're both facing the water tower. The sun is already at it.
"You like that thing?" he asks with a nod at the tripedal reservoir.
"I'm the only person in the world who doesn't like the Sidney opera house," I say. He laughs.
"Never thought about it."

Another cup of coffee, I always need two cups at least. "Let's go for a walk," I say.
"Sure," he says.

I get dressed, shorts and sneakers. We close the door gently, let father sleep, he's going to have a rough day. Alex's car is parked right next to my truck. I realize for the first time it's a Toyota Prius.

"This is yours, the SUV?" he asks.
"How do you know?"
"I'm a bit telepathic."
"You can read thoughts?"
"Nothing in the way of complete sentences, but when I'm close to a person, sometimes I know, I just know. Trivial things, flashes, like 'truck,' or 'hamburger.' It isn't always helpful."
"Shall we take my truck," I say.

We take my truck. His car stays behind, parked on my parking lot, which is an excellent location for his Prius, there's space enough.

"The beach?" I ask. "Yes."

Talking about SUV's. I tell Alex about Godehart and the galactic Merc service. He seems to know quite a lot about Godehart, except for the Google truck. Alice must have told him about Wagner but not about Isolde. He's very interested, wants to know everything about the vehicle, how autonomous it is, and whether you can steer it via remote control. I tell him I drove it myself, in the sense that it drove me.

"You said you're lonely," I say, "perhaps you should meet Godehart, he's fun."

"Yes."

"You want to meet Godehart?"

"You've read Grisham, Pelican Brief?" he asks.

"Yes."

"This character, one of the bad guys, he decides to kill himself when their cover is blown, he tells himself, 'Kill yourself now, now, don't wait. You have ten seconds'."

"I know. Especially on a bad day."

"I have lots of bad days."

"How do you mean."

"I have a few minutes per day to meet a person, of a few seconds, or nothing."

"But at work," I ask, "how do you do it, how do you work."

"I don't meet people, they are there."

"And Alice?"

"She was there, too, or, more precisely, she arrived, and then she was there."

"Hospitals are hierarchies," I say, "It's strange you are close."

"That's right," he says, "I don't understand it either, but Alice appears to understand."

"Alice knows you are an accomplished critic of computational complexity theory?" I ask. He laughs.

"How about mixed metaphors?"

He laughs again.

I tell him about my latest finding, yesterday, the 'fries trapped like fish or other bad metaphors.' He laughs: "You un-wiggled nicely there," (alpha dog compliments beta dog).

We've arrived at the head of Georgia Avenue, which ends right on the beach. There are no parking spaces left, despite the early hour. We circle around the giant statue of *Peggy Noonan*, the famous columnist, a gift of the *Republican Club* to its hometown, and find a space in front of the Tourist Office hundred yards up the road. I explain about Maurice, the exchange with Torquay, his ambitions as a playwright.

"How long is it," he says, "that we met. Three days?" I have to count. We walk back to the beach, past the Noonan statue, which, in its better days, had an endless voice loop about *George DoubleYou*, him of the Freedom Fries, educating tourists and natives about the 43rd president ("Mr. Bush is the triumph of the seemingly average American man"), but a mechanical failure had silenced the sculpture some time ago, and the repair work had been delayed for unclear reasons.

We've rounded the corner of Nick's restaurant and are heading south on the beach. A long stretch of crystalline sand extends past *Dewey Beach* and runs for more than five miles to the northern mouth of Simons River. It's surely one of the finest beaches on the East Coast. The sea breeze is picking up already—the land of Georgia heating up, the warming air rising, cooler air hastening in from the sea to replace it. We're walking past the gay beach which is still empty. This is where we met, in the no-man's land between the beach and the dunes of the cruising area. I want to say something about the dunes, then think better of it. He, too, casts a furtive glance at the location of our first encounter.

We're alone on the beach, but we are not. It starts with a charming, spotted, long-beaked bird picking in the sand.
"Spotted Sand Piper," Alex says. The next bird is sort of salt-and-pepper, and a bit fatter on its legs. "Great Yellowlegs," he says. A white bird touches down, flamingo-like, but smaller. "Georgia Flamingo," he says.
"Tell me anything."
"The Georgia Flamingo, I made that up," he says, "I felt your thought."

A long pause, half an hour, or more (the longer the better). We could be holding hands.
"We could be holding hands," I say.
"Yes," he answers.

164

I'm telling him about me and observing people. "Anybody would look at us from a distance, I swear, they would think we are brothers."

"Not if we were holding hands."

I grab his right hand. "Better?" I ask.
"That wasn't my point," he says.

I withdraw my hand. He raises one of his long, wide eye-brows. "We're done now?" he asks.

I grab his hand again. "We can't be done," I say. He withdraws his hand, looks at me.
"*You* could *use* a brother. An older brother."
"You're up to the job?"
"How old are you?"
"Twenty-nine."
He laughs. "We're the same age."
"Don't duck the question," I say.
"Naah," he laughs, "I wouldn't be up to the job. You're quite something. Possibly better holding hands." He grabs my hand again.
"Are we flirting?" I ask.

He scans me from top to bottom, then says: "Children would also do the job. You would have to make an effort, possibly, but then you could become a loving father. You would change. For the better."
"A guy I know," I tell him, "a photographer, Jack, he had a career as a Hollywood facilitator, helping other people to market their scripts. He would spend his time in the company of martinis next to the pool of the Beverley Hills Hotel, and then he got married and became a loving father," (I'm not making this up; Jack lives nearby, we'll meet him again).
"See," Alex says.

More birds. "Why are we here, walking in the direction of the South Pole?" he says, putting his right arm around my shoulder.
"You say," I say.
"Maurice," he almost interrupts himself, "Maurice brought us together, his collapse at Godehart's party, sheer happenstance, destiny."
"Aren't they each other's opposite, destiny and happenstance?"
"They constitute an identity under competing ontologies."

165

"Aha."

"One deterministic, the other indeterministic," (beta dogs asks question, alpha dog answers).

More birds, sand, surf. I untie my sneakers, arrange them next to a piece of driftwood. He does the same. "They'll be there when we come back," he says, "nobody is going to steal those." We're walking on the edge of the surf now, the water plays with our feet. The tide is rising.

"The tide is rising," I say, "it could steal the sneakers."

"Tide is almost at the top now."

"How do you know?"

"I know those things."

"When the tide goes out, we must be naked," I say. He laughs.

"Seriously," he resets, "we were *thrown* together, you *had* to accompany Maurice to the hospital. And I *had* to give you a ride, if only to tease Roxanne."

"Roxanne?"

"The nosy receptionist."

"You are clinically depressed, that's right?"

"Yes."

"Since when."

"Since forever, since my mother left me, dying."

"You were ten years old, then, you said."

"Yes."

"Nineteen years since."

"Yes, nineteen years," he says, "it's too much."

Another pause. "You may know this," he says. "Some French sage, who said: 'some people expend enormous energy merely to be normal…' "

"Yes, I say, *Camus*, Albert Camus, one of his famous lines."

"Right, I'm one of those people."

Across the wide mouth of Simon's river, *Jekyll Island* glints on the horizon like the promise of a better world. I don't know how we did it, we've walked five miles already. My bare feet start to hurt. This distance, it's almost two hours normally, I forgot my watch. "It's eight o'clock," he says, "we have to go back, don't forget the appointment. The DA, Maurice."

166

We turn around. His pace accelerates, he had probably forgotten about the appointment as well. "You're never late?" I ask.

"Sure," he says, "we're late all the time. Meat wagon arrives, patient's dead."

"Why didn't you go for an MD?"

"My condition. I couldn't handle it."

"Any perspective that it'll get better one day?"

"Nobody knows. I'm not strictly unipolar, I have better days, sometimes, like today."

"You take medication?"

"Sure."

"Alice trying to help you?"

"Sure."

More birds. Our piece of driftwood appears on the horizon, his sneakers parked to the left, my sneakers parked to the right, mine turned toward each other at the tip, his turned outward, all laces in post-adolescent confusion. "It's a metaphor, these sneakers, a metaphor of us," he says. I don't quite get it but happily agree (*us*). "Say something first, find out later what it means," he adds.

"You surprise me," I say.

"Not for the first time, I take it."

"I mean, you're normally very strict with language."

"Extensional semantics have their limits," he answers (alpha dog speaks, beta dog is mystified).

We put the sneakers back on, we're faster now. "Let's put in a sprint," he says. We sprint.

It wasn't clear to me in retrospect whether he had planned this, but we're back at the gay beach around half past nine, somewhat out of breath. "You're pumped out, right," he says. "I think you need a rest." He gives a nod to the dunes. I was already thinking.

He's so sweet. I'm an extreme materialist, you know, and tend to think of humans in terms of molecules and chemical reactions (unless I think of them as idiots), but life can be beautiful. A few queens have already arrived on the beach for the early sun, and their eyes follow us as we head toward the cruising area. I wave at them. They wave back. That's why we are gay, folks, that's the upside.

We continue a bit deeper into the woods, well past the point of our first encounter. What will it be? We don't have much time, we shed the clothes. "Fuck me," he says, and is lying on the ground already. I penetrate with soul and body. I'm so excited, I come almost immediately, which isn't good from the point of porn writing, but it saves time. I pop and unload. I'm staying with him while he's doing his own thing. What a load. Cum everywhere. A furtive glance at his watch. Get ready, he says. We re-dress, we're back on the beach, eyes expecting us, one queen saying: "That was quick, but profound. More profound than a quickie."

"How do you know?" Alex asks.

"I have a sixth sense for sex," the queen replies. General hilarity. I blow kisses, I'm getting less shy by the day. Alex doesn't blow kisses since alpha dogs don't blow kisses, but he grabs my hand.

The gay beach, I've always thought of it as next to the head of Georgia Avenue, but it's not when you are in a hurry. Another five minutes or so. We're running now, we shouldn't be late. It's exactly ten on the large clock above the entrance of the tourism office when we reach my truck. Eight minutes to the hospital on a normal day, but not today, since some event with flags and a parade is blocking the main road, people wearing lots of make-up, capes, and fangs. Vampires, right, a dress rehearsal for the Festival Week, perhaps.

Georgia Avenue is closed. We have to take a circuitous detour involving Atlanta Street (driving past the Blue Moon and Godehart's homestead), Second Street, Gerard Street, and so on. It's fifteen past ten when we arrive at the hospital, sprint-climbing the stairs as if Maurice is about to be burked again. Alex's ID gets us through the lock of the Intensive Care Unit. We burst into Maurice's room, where a congregation of Maurice, Alice, and an anonymous suit are awaiting us as if we were the missing bridegrooms of the wedding. Maurice is reclined on the bed, still chained to his IC equipment. Chairs have been arranged, possibly by Alice herself, two empty chairs speak for themselves. We plop down, breezy, happy, sand in our tousled hair, on the legs, the clothes, the adolescent sneakers. There are wet-dark stains on my T-shirt, possibly Alex's cum

168

soaking through from the inside. We're so sexy, Maurice's monitors can't quite handle it. I sit next to Alice, who is not amused.

Something is smelly. I realize that it is sticking to my shorts. It smells like shit and looks like shit. The door flings open, a nurse enters in haste. I've seen her before, vaguely, through the distortion of two glass panes, it's the deputy head nurse, my future wife, at least in some possible worlds she would be, and I don't even know her name.

"Anything wrong with Mr. Dymond," she says, "we're getting alerts." A brief look at Maurice, who shakes his head, a longer look at Alex and myself. She can read thoughts, or smells, especially when she wriggles her nose, which she does now. "We haven't had an accident, Mr. Dymond?" Maurice shakes his head. She opens the window—this is a very modern institution, you can even open the windows. On her way back to the door she sidles up to me, rests her hand on my shoulder, and says: "John?"

"Sure," I say, as if I had my doubts.

"We talked on the phone, twice," she says, "I'm *Amy-Lou*, I did appreciate your frankness." Then she turns around, smiles at Alice, almost puts in the hint of a mock-curtsey, and says "Dr. Sandeman." It's not exactly clear to me what's going on here, the IC ward is apparently a world unto itself. This is so innocent, folks, I can't understand why Alice is upset. Anyhow, Amy-Lou exits. I don't exchange glances with Alex.

But we're not yet done. The door opens again, Amy Lou reappears, tiptoes up to me, and whispers: "If you need a fresh T-shirt, let me know." I have to look at Alex this time and there's a mischievous grin on his face.

S o, there we are, from left to right, Maurice, Alice, John, Alex, and the legal suit. Alice is angry, you can practically see her fist clenched in her white-coat pocket, but we're all adults, so she is doing the honors and introduces us to *Trevor Howard*, the Assistant DA, who has been so kind to come all the way from Waycross to listen to our case.

Attempts are being made to shake hands across laps, it would be awkward to get up again. Alex has a last name, Iglesias, which I learn on this occasion (come to think of it, the black hair, the eyebrows, the warmer-colored skin, it must have been his mother then, the eyes, Irish?). Maurice's IC gear is going quiet, I wonder whether they've installed a tumescence meter as well.

"Apologies for us being late," Alex says. He owns the room, I don't know how he does it with this depression on his shoulders—he doesn't know it either, I guess, that's his secret. Alice explains the reason for our presence, we're indirect witnesses, she points out.

"Let me introduce myself and our office briefly," the suit commences, "I am the assistant district attorney of the South-Eastern Judicial District charged with cases of sexual and related offenses, working closely with Doyle-Ray Hunnsbruck, the esteemed district attorney, who is committed to achieving justice for our district's most vulnerable residents, working tirelessly to hold offenders accountable, upholding the laws and statutes of Georgia, and working closely with our police and communities to develop inventive strategies for making the district ever safer. May I inform you that the DA has been apprised of your request. He sends word of regrets, since he has to visit to the Georgia Assembly this morning where he will brief lawmakers on his latest innovative efforts."

Maurice is impressed. You see him asking for pen and paper to write this down. Where is his iPad? Come to think of it, the suit isn't wielding a (yellow) pad either; he must have an excellent memory. I'm also impressed, in particular by the gap between the suit's boiler plate and his outfit. At this level of civic buzz you would expect a button down shirt in magnolia white, worsted wool as the fabric of a summer costume, a Windsor-half-knotted tie and so on, but instead you get a silky suit with sheen in the wrong places, a shirt also worn yesterday, a string (*string*) tie, and terrible shoes. Trevor Howard isn't the budding young Assistant DA who will go far, he's someone pushing fifty with shadows under the eyes and an unspeakable touch of yellow on his right forefingers. There's also a slight tremor to his hand. This guy isn't going home to a loving family tonight.

"If I understand you correctly," the suit continues, "you are making reference to serious felonies of a sexual nature."

"Yes," Maurice, answers, "I have been raped."

"Raped, you say."

"Indeed."

"Raped by a male person?"

"Yes, of course."

"Well, then it would appear that you haven't been raped."

"Huh?"

"Title sixteen of the Georgia statute stipulates rape as an act of a person gaining carnal knowledge of a female person, Mister Dymond."

"Carnal knowledge," Maurice echoes.

"The penetration of the female sex organ by the male sex organ."

"I was penetrated viciously," Maurice says, "It almost killed me, that's why I'm here."

"So it has been determined," the Assistant DA replies with an indefinable expression on his narrow but not unsensual lips, "that rape in itself has not occurred."

Maurice casts a pleading glance in my direction. "Perhaps it's defined differently," I interject, "what happened to Maurice."

"In point of fact," the suit answers.

"How do you define anal penetration by the male organ in legal terms?" Alex asks, while wiping some sandy grains off his upper bare legs.

"We define it as sodomy. Sixteen-six-two of the Georgia Code, 'a person commits the offense of sodomy when he or she performs or submits to any sexual act involving the sex organs of one person and the mouth or anus of another'."

171

"Sodomy then," Alex says.

"Unfortunately, young man, the consensus of opinion would be," Howard continues, "that sodomy obtains vice versa. Mr. Dymond submitted to a sexual act involving his anus and the sex organs of another person, so he committed sodomy as well. Sodomy isn't necessarily a felony, but the onus is on the probandi."

"I was raped," Maurice protests, "I was raped by any measure, it almost killed me."

"Cui bono, I ask you, Mr. Dymond, cui bono?"

Alice and I share a regard—the enemies of your enemies are your friends after all. Alice is not going to sit idly by, I trust, no, she is about to get into the act, but her cell phone rings. An emergency. "I am not on duty, I am in an important meeting with the DA office," she answers, but the situation at the other end of the line is a matter of life and death and they know she is around. She departs with a critical look at the entire room, and in particular at Alex, who reciprocates.

"I'm not a lawyer," Alex says, "but I recall the term aggravated sodomy. That might be the term to apply in this case."

"Contingently, yes," the suit answers.

"Would you mind educating us," Alex says, all the while brushing more sand off his legs. His T-shirt is stained too, I realize, some cum must have missed its target and ended up on his own body.

The suit bends forward, apparently taking some interest in the stains (later, when we've become allies of sorts, we will learn that Howard got intrigued by the cum-scent), and says: "A person commits the offense of aggravated sodomy when he or she commits sodomy with force and against the will of the other person."

"There you have it," Alex says, "that's what we want to report."

"You employ the first plural pronoun, Mr. Iglesias," the suit replies, "may I use the occasion and I inquire about your involvement in this case."

"I am an indirect witness," Alex says, "as Dr. Sandeman already informed you."

"Meaning that Mr. Dymond confided to you under circumstances that leave no reasonable doubt as to the veracity of his statements."

"Nicely put," Alex replies.

172

The suit isn't pleased. "Mr. Iglesias," he says, "you should not make gratuitous remarks. Allegations of aggravated sodomy carry sentences of twenty-five years or more. Conversely, false accusations of said felony are also sanctioned severely."

Alex gets up: "I think I made a mistake. I didn't prepare this properly," he says to Howard. "Excuse me, I'll be back soon." He is on his way to the door when he adds: "Carry on," as if Maurice and I couldn't do much harm without him.

A threesome behind IC doors. Poor Maurice, who didn't care for a deposition in the first place, he is now more or less left to his own devices. His monitors aren't happy either, the pings speak of cardiovascular aggravation. I feel guilty, really.

"Mr. Howard," I say, "the rape of Maurice is only part of the story..."— the suit is trying to interrupt, but I talk through it, I feel so guilty—"...the rape of Maurice is not the only crime to report. Of equal importance, at least, is the rape of Officer Benson's ex-wife."

Howard doesn't understand. "Hasn't he been told?" I ask Maurice. Maurice has no idea.

"Perhaps," I say, "it might be a good idea if Maurice tells the story from the beginning." Next thing, I bite my lips. Maurice is not stupid, so he skips the beginning and starts with him being taken into custody and held on account of the malfunctioning mug-shot camera, but then has to backtrack because he has to explain why Benson left for Walmart and returned prematurely, but Howard, who, on previous form, should have taken the opportunity to move the conversation into non-territory again, listens attentively, while Maurice explains how Benson came back with the clothes picked up at his ex's place, raped Maurice, then Dick's ex crashes the party, ex is raped as well, then kicked out.

Maurice has barely finished when Alex returns, an iPad in his hand. I'm perhaps not the only person to realize that Alex has changed into a new, stainless T-shirt. If he can do it, I think, and excuse myself. But Amy-Lou, the promiser of fresh T-shirts, has vanished, and only Quinton and some other guy are manning the control room. Should I ask Quinton for a fresh T-shirt? Nah, Quinton gives me this look ('I am not amused by your future with Amy-Lou, let alone by your past with Alex') so I retire to the bathroom and wipe the brown smelly substance off my shorts, with decidedly mixed results.

I'm back in Maurice's room but have missed nothing. Alex and Howard have entered a sparring match about the Georgia law code, Alex pointing to the iPad with pages of the code on display, the suit pointing with his yellowish index finger at his (own) temple. In Georgia, we learn, any sex outside the marriage is "technically" illegal, be it fornication ('an unmarried person commits the offense of fornication when he voluntarily has sexual intercourse with another person'), or adultery ('a married person commits the offense of adultery when he voluntarily has sexual intercourse with a person other than his spouse'). "They should modernize the clause, make it gender-neutral," I throw in, but am ignored, as usual.

In the meantime, the suit has begun his cross-examination. How did Maurice end up at the police department? Why had he been arrested? So, he was naked. Would Maurice mind explaining? Is he aware of paragraph sixteen of the criminal code, prescribing the punishment of (i) public indecency in cases of public sexual intercourse, (ii) lewd exposure of sexual organs, (iii) lewd appearance in a state of partial or complete nudity, or (iv) lewd caresses and indecent fondling?

Howard's digging unearths fairly minute details recently committed in the South-Eastern Judicial District, involving a lewd encounter of three people in a public space, all of whom are present as we speak, isn't that remarkable.
"We're not the elephant in the room," I say, idiotically.
"Could you arrest us," Maurice asks, and the suit affirms in the positive ("technically, yes"), citing another article of the Georgia Code.

Does anybody mind bringing up the minute detail of Benson showing up at the hospital and attempting first-degree homicide of Maurice by means of a pillow? Yes, Alex does, and is refuted on the spot, with Howard reiterating how serious false allegations would be, in particular allegations invoking the reputation of a police officer in good standing. Any witnesses to the attempted murder? Yes, Maurice (the victim), and John. There we go again. Haven't we met these people before? The Georgia Code has

174

much to say about conspiracies, we can take his word for it. And if we can't, we can go to the police.

This silky suit is quite a dog, you think of alpha-animals in terms of huskies or Alex, but prematurely aging, unfashionably-dressed assistant DAs know how to bite back. Alice is finally returning from her emergency. There's no need to explain the situation, she understands immediately, with Alex and Howard standing in the middle of the room, both slightly red-faced, Maurice sulking on his bed, dead-pale, his monitors beeping. I'm testing in the meantime with two fingers whether the cum stains on my T-shirt have finally dried (yes).

Would it have been different if Alice had not been called away? Hard to tell. Happenstance, destiny, you name it. So, Alice is back, everybody calms down, including the monitors. Alice sits down, Alex and the suit sit down.

"The discussion got a bit heated," Howard says, "I had to explain quite a few things to these fine young men, but we've finally reached consensus, I take it."

I could kill him. Suddenly it strikes me, the guy is gay himself, deep in the closet, but active, juices flowing, the *pizzicato* of his movements, the taint of camp in his voice under duress (Alex's counterpunches) the suit is gay, gay, and he will go home tonight and get off on his memory of Alex (we will later learn that his actual jerking involved a fantasy of all four of us).

"The District Attorney is proud of the fact that his office maintains a conviction rate of 88 percent," Howard says after a moment of contemplation. "We owe it to the people of Georgia to maintain the highest judicial standards. We cannot befoul our success rate with frivolous cases. Any case that we take on will answer to the plausible standards of probable cause. In lieu of the improbable cause constituted by the case sub judice."

"Sub judice?" Maurice asks.

"Yours."

So, there we are. Benson won't be taken off the street (if that's what Howard meant). Benson's first attempt failed. How about a second attempt to silence Maurice? How long will we be able to keep Maurice protected behind IC locks. Who's going to pay for the 3500 bucks per night?

Perhaps we should spread the news how the DA walked away from us, so RapeDick would know he has nothing to fear (why should a well-respected police officer in good standing go about the task of murdering an innocent non-witness?). "Would you do us a favor," I ask the suit, "and inform the local police office of the results of our discussion?"

No, he wouldn't, the content of an indictment, or anything leading up to an indictment, is confidential until filed in court, article whatever.

We're back to square one. Alex rolls his eyes and then his head, gets up. I get up, but the suit remains seated.

"The DA and I are closely working together on this." Howard says, "Doyle-Ray has earned a statewide reputation as a law enforcement leader of the highest caliber. He is a trail-blazing jurist and knows how important it is to serve. He has been awarded the *Trumpet Award* and many other important awards. The *Atlanta Business Chronicle* has recognized him in its annual *Who's Who in Law and Accounting*." And then he adds, somewhat out of character: "The DA knows what he's doing. Trust me."

With this he rises, shakes hands, and departs.

35 TWO VISIBLE SPOTS

With an inquisitive look at Maurice, Alice gets up as well. She's about to explode, explode at us, who have blown it, "completely." We're little boys who can't hold their cum when the situation requires grown-up behavior. We've besmirched the hospital, and the medical profession, and ourselves, literally. And since she's a medical doctor, she is going into details, and wants to know how many spermatozoa we've killed needlessly with our—she'll have to look this up in a thesaurus, it's not that she's shy, she's just too upset to find the right word—with our irresponsible behavior. "You thought you were sexy, right," she says, "you were just feckless, harebrained, immature, undependable, untrustworthy, inexcusably, both of you," and she means Alex in particular since she has given up on the cum-squirrel anyhow.

People sometimes say sensible things just before they die, and Maurice, along those lines, he's just trying to help Alice with her thesaurus. He says "wasteful," as if this is his last word, and starts to cry, tears rolling down his face, more and more tears coming until he succumbs to what appears to be a full-blown nervous breakdown; needless to say, his IC-equipment acts up as well. Quinton reappears, summoned by the monitors presumably, and seems to have an inkling of what has happened, since he says: "This is enough. The patient needs rest." Alice, a bit overtaken by her own reaction possibly, grabs Alex's arm and pulls him out of the room, leaving the cum-squirrel to its own devices, which follows the pair meekly into the hallway, where all three of us are presently standing, not knowing what to do.

The only thing that can save us now is the washed-up scriptwriter. So the phone rings, Alice's cell phone. Not that she is going to share anything with us, she'll possibly never speak to us again, but she's so upset, things have to be repeated. So we learn that this gallery in Manhattan needs more of Eleanor's work. Two of the three pieces that arrived this morning are already sold, on account of the fact that Eleanor is a real Wagner, and what with the new *Tristan* in the *Met* performing to rave reviews, everybody wants a piece of the cake, or of Eleanor Wagner-Beasley, or of her paintings. And, the fact that she's dead now is truly regrettable, but "helps, in view of the price-points." Alice doesn't know whether she should pale or redden. We learn that Eleanor had explicitly forbidden the use of her status as a Wagner-in-law in the marketing of her paintings, it's in her will and in any letter she ever wrote to any gallery that turned down her work. She had to be an artist in her own right, despite her own admiration for Wagner's work, *Richard* Wagner's work (to avoid any confusion with the Bavarian leather shorts), any mention of the W-word was strictly forbidden in the vicinity of her paintings. Oh, so sorry, they didn't know that on the other end of the line, and you can see a twenty-two year old, just-so-art-history-graduate from Columbia wielding her voice and explaining that's all a regrettable misunderstanding, and that the word is out now, and could they have the paintings by yesterday, *Federal Express?* Like last time, that's faster. They would like at least three large paintings, oil on canvas, larger than the last ones, and they would prefer paintings with two dots, or three, but not more than three, because the stage decoration at the Met is also dot-oriented. A perfect fit, but not too many dots, that's confusing, and we're looking at a price point of forty kay per piece, including their commission, which is stellar.

Alice is now really in trouble, and both of us (Alex, John) grapple with the implications in our favor, at least in the sense that Alice has something else to worry about than the punishment she'll mete out at the besmirched beach boys. This is at least how I took it, Alex took it differently.

Reset. Alice in a dilemma—what can the thesaurus tell us—bind, fix, jam (to keep it short), or conundrum (to think in style). Alex is clever enough to think this through very quickly, and even I am up to the task. It's not going to help anybody if she's going to refuse. Eleanor is dead. It's not her fault she was a Wagner, although it is, but still. So Alice will be saying *yes*; we know this before the fact, not to mention the money.

Let me remind you of two minor events already accounted for: (1) the moment that Ben sat down at my kitchen table and I saw Alex's beauty in Ben's beauty, and (2) the moment that Ben and I arrived at his home in Monaville and he took up position next to his mother in anticipation of her next move. Combine these two events and by analogy—very much by analogy given Alice's anger and Alex's clinical depression—by analogy we see Alex taking up position next to Alice, awaiting events. And these events will be (1) Alice is going to contact *FedEx*, only to find out that they won't be able to pick up three large paintings today since one of their delivery vans is too small and the other one is broken, and (2) Alice's own car is too small for three large paintings, so the conclusion will be that she needs our help. Or Godehart's help. Since she hates us forthwith, she's not going to ask us, she is contacting Godehart instead, who's on voicemail. So she hates us even more (in fact, whom she really hates is herself—she had lost the patient who triggered the emergency call, a fact we didn't know at that point).

"Spots no. 65," *Eleanor-Wagner Beasley*

It's a matter of timing now. Offering help within the next two seconds will meet a wall of refusal and contempt, but the passage of a few more seconds could change things significantly. So we wait a little bit until Alex nods imperceptibly, and I say "We will help you." Well done, John, not saying "we could help you," or some such, which would force a choice upon her in the sense that she has no choice but to say "no." Yes, we will help you and that's it. She still has the key to Godehart's house. We'll go with two vehicles, her car and my truck, she selects the paintings, we load the paintings into my truck, I'll go to the FedEx office in *Lewes* (that's to the north of Georgia Beach, a few miles). She will follow in her Toyota Prius, and Alex will accompany her, since the rear view of the Prius sucks.

Let's hope nobody is going to have an accident, in particular not me, since this could entail the destruction of irreplaceable art by a great masteress.

Godehart is not at home. We descend to the basement where Alice grabs three oils on canvas without much ado. "Grabs" is not the right word since there are too many paintings to choose from. Not only dotted ones, several racks are filled with plain gray canvas-squares, other racks contain French flags, or German ones, give and take a color. The paintings are large and require the input of two reasonably agile men. They barely fit into the truck, we have to lower the rear seats, but—as you may have observed on other occasions—there is a galactic metaphysics at work in that it's almost impossible not to fit anything into an aging Mercedes ML.

When we arrive at the FedEx outfit in Lewes, the situation has changed significantly. Alice is in trouble maintaining her anger—let's throw in a really tasteless analogy here, think of maintaining an erection during a faculty meeting at my school. There are credibility problems with Alice's indignation, and you only have to look at Alex to understand why. Save for his eyes, Alex has disappeared. While Alice negotiates the FedEx bureaucracy, Alex is standing next to her, hands folded behind the back, and you can feel how he's forcing himself to stay in place. Alice has trouble getting her act together with Alex in this state.

We keep it short and skip a few jokes at the expense of the FedEx bureaucracy. Alice keeps it short, too. Instead of saying goodbye, she says "I'm sorry, Alex." Alex reciprocates, but purely *pro forma*. "I see you tonight," Alice says (one wonders when these people actually sleep).

"I'll have to recoup my car," Alex says to nobody and mounts my truck. We drive back to my place, but not in expectation of more sex, or love, or anything, although Alex says "I love you," when he gets out of my SUV and into his Prius and is gone.

S o there we are again, standing on our parking lot, the apartment building on one side with the canal behind it, the overpass almost above us, the road off the lot along the Davis Canal on the other side—a pretty, verdant, almost enchanted spot. We are Alex-less once more, this is now what? The fourth time in three days he left us. It's two o'clock in the afternoon, early July, early millennium, at the top of the Georgia summer. While I'm climbing the stairs, I realize that I haven't dealt with my father yet. It's the third day of his visit, I have to defenestrate him today, but it's the middle of the day, so he must have fled to the beach to squeeze a few more tropical hours into his miserable life. But no, I open the door, and he's sitting there, at the kitchen table and all that, the flyers are gone, he's dressed and all that (I'm re-reading the *Catcher in the Rye*). He's sitting there like one of Pavlov's dogs. He's actually trying to tell me something, it's almost heart-breaking, that he's getting married again, or having been diagnosed with interminable cancer, or that he still loves Mom, or regrets what happened between us (and all that), but I need to think about Alex and not to think about Alex and won't listen.

He's babbling along while I think about Pavlov. Father's expecting the out-throw? The bell rings? You are a-waiting your turn? Bark bark, old man, you won't get the cookie, I'm having a nap. So I ignore him, not even ostentatiously, I just ignore him, hit the john, and then the bedroom.

The idea is to have a nap, as I said, and forget about Alex and everything. You realize what's going to happen next. I'm lying there, on my bed, and masturbate, all the while eating a rotten tomato that I brought from the kitchen because I need to motivate the next line ("you call it pornography, I call it *new realism*").

The self-sex takes only five minutes, so the question remains what I am going to do next. I lie there some more. At *Holden Caulfield's* age, the hero of the Catcher in the Rye, I could come three times in a row, just like that (and all that). I'm still young, so I try a second time (to masturbate), but fail miserably. Why is it that we never learn about self-sex at *Pencey*, old Holden's prep school, everybody's sixteen, they must have been floating in cum there, literally, what's wrong with old *J.D. Salinger*? He is a realistic author, flow of consciousness, first person, minute-by-minute account of non-events, and nobody's masturbating! You can buy twenty e-books about the Catcher on Amazon (but not the book itself, that's only available as a dead tree @ *$0.01* plus shipping charges). Any of these meta-books raise the question why there's no wanking at Pencey? What are these literary critics doing all day? You were almost Salinger's neighbor in *Cornish* for a year, you had a scholarship at *Dartmouth*, you were a member of the *Militant Grammarians of Massachusetts* nearby. How is it possible you end up as a despised teacher of French at this hippocampus? Whining all the time, like Holden, but masturbating unlike Holden? If Alice ever chides me again cum-wise, I'm going to ask her whether she's read Salinger, that'll shut her up (I'm mixed up here, I know).

Yes, we need more tasteful thoughts. My God, I feel like shit, drowsy, it's as if the a/c has stopped working, although that would be too much, that's not going to happen. But we still feel like shit, drowsy, sleepy, unable to sleep, hot, de-cumed (ugly, very ugly). It's three o'clock in the afternoon. There were some departing noises from father. What's going on?

There's a goodbye message on the kitchen table, right where Alex had left his message. It's from father, I presume, I don't remember his handwriting. It reads almost like a suicide letter: "Dear John, I have to go now. I feel sorry. Let's stay in touch." Why do we have to stay in touch? There's no need to stay in touch, you know? Go to hell! You're Tea Party now, right, why can't you just undress and have yourself raptured like any good Tea Party Patriot? You sneak out on me as if nothing has happened, unbeaten, un-whatever. I fall in love, I lose, I have a father, I lose. What would Salinger say? ("Awful.")

Did you ever try to drink my coffee on a weekday afternoon during the summer in Georgia? Did you ever try to activate a computer at the same time? And go on the internet? And discover that Maurice has already posted the first installment of his Freedom-Fries script on your blog. Presumably before he entered a state of nervous breakdown, or, more likely, *after* he entered a state of nervous breakdown, the way it reads.

(Excerpt: "GEORGE W. BUSH (first clip): We do not torture. GEORGE W. BUSH (second clip): We do not torture. GEORGE W. BUSH (third clip): We do not torture..."). Did you ever go to the first home page of CNN, which speaks of nothing but *Fifty Shades of Grey*, the bestseller of the decade, a play of fan fiction on the *Twilight Saga* (and all that)? How about fan fiction Salinger-wise? Where would we start? With Holden's failed essay on the Egyptians perhaps ("The Egyptians were an ancient race of Caucasians residing in one of the northern sections of Africa. The latter as we all know is the largest continent in the Eastern Hemisphere...")? How would we do that? We're getting really dangerous now, and long-winded, and grab another cup of coffee. So we write: "*George Clooney* was born in 1692, when Columbus sailed the ocean blue. His mother and father were both on the Mayflower heading east. His father was native to Spain, while his mother was native to Spain..." Isn't this much funnier? And we could go on and on, we copied this from the internet, there's much more to copy (Clooney has an affair with Paul Revere). The Catcher still sells two hundred fifty thousand copies per year, world-wide. How many would we sell? Good question. How many did we sell today? Let's have a look. Forty three page loads on the stats counter so far, fifty one on Blogger's own statistics. Focus, John, focus, you'll never get anywhere unless you focus.

F ocus. FF as a literature blog? Nobody's interested in literature. Porn? We type "How many porn sites are there on the internet?" into Google's search window. "Four-point-two million" is the answer. We add our site, it's still *4.2* million. Business is bad, it's murderous, regardless of our attempt to out-porn everybody this morning, we failed miserably because Alice didn't care for it, and the DA didn't care for it, and nobody cared for it. The locals just can't handle it. Right. Local. How about a local blog? All politics is local, everything. More about local restaurants, the latest anecdote from the gay beach, an interview with Gooduuhaard who has recently moved into town and has a German accent and a pencil penis. What's the competition local-wise? So we type "local blogs Georgia Beach," into the search window. The answer is zero of course, since Georgia Beach is our invention. Let's try *Rehoboth Beach* (DE) then, the place on which our town is modeled. There's only one local blog, strictly speaking, run by the charming *Hadley McGregor*, whose picture disambiguates her gender beyond belief.

More search results point to more interesting non-blogs. We learn, for example, that the temperature in Delaware is 30° below ours here in Georgia, or that the average housing prices have dropped alarmingly by 10,000 bucks in the last four weeks. So there would be room for us, the poorer people get, the more blogs they read. We study this more carefully. *Channel Two* Action News has its own site (Georgia Beach has its own TV station since it's larger than Rehoboth), which informs us that a body was found in the parking lot of *Mamma Mia*, the pizzeria. Not quite a body but a female person almost dead, who was then urgently transported to the Baptist Memorial Hospital where she was not declared dead on arrival on account of heroic resuscitation efforts which tragically failed after an hour. A case of hit and run, apparently, but we can be assured of a happy ending since the capable arm of the law is on the case, represented by officer *Richard Benson* of the local police force and other Georgia Beach Finest. There's even a clip of Benson with his slap-my-face face, the thin lips, the smallish eyes, the stubby, I-can't-hold-these-shades nose, the discordant gestures, Officer Benson, who was the first on the scene and has secured all the evidence and handed it to the homicide investigation unit, and you know what, it's really tragic, the victim was his ex-wife, he recognized her immediately when he saw her lying there, obviously hit by a vehicle on the run, and the evidence points nowhere, except that it's possibly a random event, somebody under the influence of substance abuse, but evidence has been secured, meticulously, carefully, responsibly, which will surely lead to the apprehension of the perpetrator soon, and Benson, the loving ex-husband, will never forgive that son-of-a-bitch. How do you feel about that?

So that's what we could blog about, like really tragic local events, like heartbreaking, and we could even mix our own juice into the dish by alluding to the occasionally neglected fact that the understanding between exes is not always what one might hope for.

I'm still doing the Wile E. Coyote thing when the cell phone rings. Alice. She has seen the local news. Benson obviously killed his wife by means of some hit-and-run and subsequently destroyed the evidence in his role as the first cop on the scene. And she had been the failed doctor of the resuscitation efforts, not knowing with whom she was dealing, a female, approximately 40-year-old, victim of a car accident.

Yes. Has she tried to contact Alex? Alex is on voice-mail. Coincidences don't happen, right, or whatever *Hercule Poirot* is thinking when bodies pile up. No, she hasn't contacted the DA office again. She has contacted the hospital administration, however, which is off to the *National Convention of Creative Health Care Management* in *Palm Springs*. They will call her back as soon as they're done with the nineteenth hole. Maurice, how about Maurice. Can he stay in IC? Who knows? Clinically, he's no longer in need of IC, and the billing department isn't happy with Maurice in IC, it's $3500 per night and some phone call to Torquay wasn't returned.

Why did Quinton sign off in the first place? Well, he didn't, it's always an MD, except if somebody of authority signed a blank form, that happens. So why did Quinton use a blank form for Maurice's name? She's getting brutal now, "Cherchez la femme" she replies, apparently assuming that I not only speak French but am also able to grasp the triple meaning of her statement—let's hope there's is triple meaning because it would otherwise mean that Alex had offered sex to Quinton in exchange for the deal, something fairly stupid to do if Quinton was actually in love with Alex, and not something I would expect Alex to go for, but you never know, the hormones flow, etc., and Quinton had been a good fuck four years ago, perhaps his reputation had spread in the meantime.

Who's going to be the next person to "convince" Quinton? Who's going to be that person? That wouldn't be me, right, ex-tricks are no longer susceptible to your tricks. Maurice himself couldn't do it, of course, with his abdomen still in bandages, right?

Only an idiot is going to ask her a question like this: 'Why don't you (*you*) lend us (*us*) the money, you've just hit an Eleanor windfall?' (I'm wording this a bit more carefully). Well, the forty kay per canvas would include a stellar commission, but she would be willing to do it anyhow, the situation is desperate enough. But it's not only about money. You can't actually pay your way into the *Intensive Care Unit*, you need a medical reason for it—it transpires that there is some residual professionalism still lingering at the Baptist Memorial Hospital in the sense that money can't buy everything. So we can fuck our way into IC, but not pay our way into IC, I say (I actually say it). She retracts, I misunderstood her remark. Which one? Well, I know, she's not going to repeat it. Will Alex show up for work, I ask. She's not sure, sometimes he doesn't.

"Will Alex show up at the bottom of a depressive cycle?" I ask.
"It's my fault," she answers.
"Is Alex suicidal?" I ask.
"Yes," she says, "sometimes he is."

"I don't even have his phone number," I say, "I thought his email would be more useful."
"He's on voice mail now," she replies.
"You know where he lives," I ask. Yes, she does. Would it make sense to go see him?
"Anything makes sense in this situation, anything and nothing." Should we go together, I ask.
"No," she says, "you should go."
"Whose life are we going to save now, Alex's or Maurice'?"
"Both," she answers, and gives me his address.

186

Listen, folks, I have my moments. And even though every second could count, I go to the fridge and recoup the third bottle of chardonnay, left mysteriously untouched by the Tea Party, still half-empty, pour the wine into one large glass, and swallow it as if we're at one of Godehart's orgies. And while I'm awaiting the swoosh effect, I go on the internet and find the number of the DA office in Waycross. I dial the number and ask for Trevor Howard, the Assistant DA for sexual orientation. I'm asked my name and sexual orientation. No, not the sexual orientation, only my name, but am put on a holding loop with *Jonny Rebel* playing in the background (an instrumental version, no lyrics), occasionally interrupted by informative messages about the mission of the office spoken by a soft-voiced lady with just the right amount of drawl. It takes forever, this looping, this is DA-ing in style, what else would you expect from us.

"John," Howard's voice says breezily.

To repeat, I have my moments. So I say: "Trevor."
"How are you doing," he replies.
"I'm good," I say.
"Good," he says.

"Trevor," I say, "do you have three minutes?" Yes, he has. I tell him about Benson and the hit-and-run on his ex, and about Hercule Poirot, the detective. He's heard of Hercule Poirot. But he wants to hear more. It just so happens, he's planning to come to Georgia Beach anyhow to spend an hour on the beach, and we could meet up at the Lupo di Mare, he has an expense account, at, say, seven o'clock. Done deal.

I have to share this thought with you before we move on. 'What are you doing, John,' I think, '*cherchez la femme*,' (French, meaning, 'look for the girl' ('woman,' actually)), 'what are you doing?'

Alice has given me Alex's address, which is two minutes from the hospital. It takes nine minutes to get there. Four minutes elapse till the next John-thought, namely that I will have to cancel the appointment with Howard if Alex is dead. Five more minutes until I arrive at Alex's place. Alice explained he'd rented the second floor of a small Dutch revival, no street number outside, there's a bell, no name tag. I push the bell. No answer. I push the bell again.

187

This is a fairly rickety timber construction, I crash the door and run up the stairs where a drowsy Alex awaits me alive. He's just been woken up by the doorbell.

"How long did you sleep?"

"A couple of hours."

"When do you people actually sleep?" I say, relieved.

"Before somebody disturbs them," he says.

"Do you take sleeping pills?"

"Sometimes."

"Did you take any other medication?"

"Yes."

"How are you feeling," I say (I once had a black lover, and when he sang 'how are you feelin',' I loved him more).

"How are you feeling," I say again and grab his arm. We should kiss now but we don't.

"Okayish," he says.

"You're still mad at Alice," I ask disingenuously.

"I wasn't mad at Alice, Alice was mad at me."

"Alice is concerned about you."

"Did you talk to her?"

"Yes." I don't tell him about the hit-and-run, let him think that Alice and I talked only about him.

"It's OK," he says, "I'll get over it."

He disappears into a small corner, where I hear the gurgling noises of what turns out to be an espresso machine. He reappears with two filled espresso cups. He disappears again and returns with an iPad in his hand, possibly the one that was supposed to beat Trevor Howard this morning. He sits down and puts the iPad on the table, then picks it up again, fidgeting with it reflexively. It's as if he's interrupting himself when he says to me: "Listen, John, listen carefully. Whatever happens, I really love you." For the first time this afternoon he looks into my eyes. He's really making an effort. He peepers are no quite as forlorn as earlier today, but still. You may recall those medieval paintings, *Hieronymus Bosch*, perhaps, where tiny demons sit on the shoulders of cursed people. That's how he is sitting there, not as a tiny demon, but as a cursed person, fidgeting with his iPad.

Then, in a where-was-I gesture, he changes tack, hands the iPad to me and says: "You are the only person in the world who doesn't like the

Sydney Opera House, right? You're also the only person in the world who doesn't know how to use an iPad. Get used to it."

"How do you know?" I ask.

"I know those things," he answers.

Then he gets up and says: "Let me go back to bed. I need more sleep."

I get up, too. "I love you," he says (again), and disappears into the other room. I follow him after a few seconds, he's lying on a bed already, a single bed (when have we seen this last time?), and he's busy swallowing pills. He crouches under a sheet, assumes a fetal position, and closes his eyes. I wait for a few minutes, just standing there next to him. He's falling asleep. I kiss his forehead as if he's dead already, and whisper "Good bye." I make it down the stairs, realizing that I am carrying the iPad.

38 WHAT'S PAUL KRUGMAN'S PENIS SIZE?

*L*upo *di mare* means sea-wolf, possibly an allusion to the cat fish being served in an upscale hotel-restaurant at the heart of Georgia Beach on Georgia Avenue. It's where we tend to pick up black lookers of uncertain sexual preferences. Lupo di Mare, like most outfits, falls short of its web site, the pictures on the site are sheer food porn, whereas the actual food—not another mixed metaphor John, please—is dressed up too much (narrow escape). I'm already seated at the enormous bar that testifies to serious problems with alcohol and waiting times. I rarely come here for pecuniary reasons, but the bar tender knows me well.

I share another John-thought with you, namely that I will take my tab with me if-and-when Trevor Howard shows up with his expense account. Perhaps I should drink less, just in case he doesn't. This, reader, is your first serious foray into my ~~alcoholism~~ substance abuse, so let's keep it short. I arrived much too early (we have an appointment at seven, I arrived at six), and had already ordered a double gin tonic, a whiskey sour, and one glass of the better chardonnay, this on top of the half-bottle I had gulped an hour ago. If Howard stands me up, I'll have to wash dishes in the kitchen—if that's still the way to deal with the problem—or be arrested, possibly by Dick Benson. Since I will be fairly smashed by then, the dish-washing is out anyhow, and it will be Benson's turn. Will he rape me or kill me or both?

Once in a while you really need the booze, especially when you have to think this through, whether you want to die, how you want to die, and where you want to take your A-level escort service in the meantime. The first rent assignment, with Godehart, had its problems, let's hope Howard is not into dildos. Now, why should Howard want to rent me? He's fifteen years older, there's an asymmetry that nature abhors, perhaps he dislikes asymmetry too. How often did you come today? Twice? So there is room for at least one more ejaculation, possibly two. Would that be enough?

Should I warn him ("Trevor, let me share this upfront, I can come twice tonight, is that all-right with you?"). Not really A-level stuff, but what can we do, we're understaffed.

We begin a conversation with the beefy guy next to us, or ask the washed-up scriptwriter what to do next. He's in a good mood and has Howard show up early. That's a good sign. It's always a good sign, the person first showing up for a date is always the loser. I'm just (*just*) sober enough to recall belatedly that it had been me who showed up first, but never mind.

How am I doing this, I'm already 29 years old, near the minus-pole of my bipolarity, but Howard is really pleased to see me. He is dressed differently now in a colorful post-beach outfit which clings to his gaunt body. He looks ridiculous like all failed bureaucrats, but he's also looking vulnerable, like I must be looking vulnerable at the moment. As an assistant DA he should be a connoisseur of human nature, let's see how this is going to pan out.

I have been courageous enough to ask for a table for two to be ready at seven, we'll have to wait some more. Howard will have a drink at the bar. Let's get this on track immediately, let's talk about the gym. I didn't have a chance to go to the gym during the last couple of days, too busy. You can't imagine how busy life is for a hippocampus teacher during the college break, but tomorrow I'll be going (duh, duh, duh). So I'm teaching French. How interesting. Interesting, indeed. How to turn the conversation to murder? I seemingly can't make the transition, bubbling instead about the influence of French on the evolution of English, or hiding the many weaknesses of my résumé.

I see two tables cleared next to the central window on the street side, very good tables indeed, when I notice two people to my left, who have replaced the beefy guy. I've seen the face of the man before, on my blog, actually. We're famous in Georgia Beach, seriously, folks. Will I tell Trevor? You think Trevor would be interested in politics, or the New York Times, or economics, or Nobel prizes? Possibly not—you have other problems when you're a confirmed bachelor without a future. Trevor, who must be looking right into the eyes of *Paul Krugman* behind me, shows no signs of recognition what-so-ever. It's crystal-clear, he's not attracted to the fifty-nine year old Nobel laureate.

In the distant past, when penises had average size, there was talk in some quarters that IQs would be sexy, but we have proof now (sample-of-one!) that Krugman either does not look the part or that IQs are out. What's Krugman's penis size? Krugman, I realize, is drinking sparkling water, which is actually penis-enhancing, at least in the sense that alcohol induces impotence. That's what I should do, drink sparkling water, do they award Nobel prices for French? Should I raise my voice so that Krugman can hear me and admire what I have to say about the Normans and their conquest of the Anglo-Saxon tongue? Where am I now, 0.13 BAC? Did you know that French has more words for booze than English? Or *vice versa*?

Our tables are ready, Trevor and me at one of them, Krugman and his wife (happy marriage, I guess) at the other one. Krugman and I are seated back to back. Krugman has his tweed jacket draped over his *Thonet* seat, whereas I don't since it's not my seat and I don't own a tweed jacket. It's clear, I'm going to blow this unless I change tack, so I am making a major effort, think of *Scott Fitzgerald, Ernest Hemingway, Jack Kerouac, Truman Capote* (perhaps the saddest case), and so on, until I get to *Eminem, Amy Winehouse, Lance Armstrong*—and finally find the strength to order sparkling water. As planned, I've taken the bar tab with me, but Trevor doesn't know what's on it, it'll blow his expense account, he'll get fired, and Maurice will get killed.

"Did you have a chance to think about Hercule Poirot?" I ask.
"Yes," he says.
"What do you think?"
"I think nothing," he answers as he is being handed the menu, which requests his full attention (too large, too wordy, printed in RSVP font). We're both having lupo di mare, the waiter casts a benevolent-campy look. We recognize each other. The guy had been at Godehart's party. "May I remind you of Sherlock Holmes' dictum," Trevor continues post-menu, "and avoid theory-forming prior to fact gathering?" I start to like Trevor more (although Krugman, at the other table, could inform him that theory-less fact-gathering will drown you in trivia, but never mind).
"Why did you block us this morning?" I ask.

"Did I?" he answers.

"It was fairly clear."

"I think I was fairly clear, too."

"I don't understand."

"You are intelligent enough to understand my position," he answers. "How many hints did I drop? Did you hear my introduction, did you hear my extroduction, did you listen to my language? We're supposed to speak user-friendly now. I almost could get fired for this."

'Extroduction,' I think, great, he's one of us (I later realize that the Urban Dictionary had the scoop in 2009), but am eager not to interrupt the flow of conversation, say instead: "I took them at face value."

"We take the side of the victims, so you should never take us at face value."

"Bodies are piling up," I say, lowering my voice, although I should possibly raise it if I want to force the DA's hand.

"Maurice is still alive," he says.

"Listen," I say, "where have we seen this before, a hospital patient is practically murdered with his own pillow by a police officer on a rampage and nothing happens."

"But the patient had sex in a public space before."

"That has nothing to do with it."

"What do you think Peach State voters care more about, Maurice's death, or his lewd behavior?"

And I thought I'd seen it all. "You want to know what I think," he says, "I think a lot of murders go undetected. My personal theory, five percent of the bodies in the morgue, they are there for extraneous reasons, pillows, weed killers in a broth fed to an Alzheimer patient, electrocutions, what not. Don't think your case is special. One percent of the American population is already in prison. You want to add another five percent?"

"So you aren't pursuing Officer Benson because you want to save America?"

"Look at it any which way you want."

"Could you make an exception for us?" I ask (the way Maurice would have asked this himself).

"In the way of looking at it?"

"No, in the way of handling it."

"And bring the American civilization to its knees?"
"Yes."

He leans back. "Depends," he answers—DEPENDS, that's what we
wanted to hear, folks, us escorts is always ready, and I really don't want to
split the bill—but then he continues: "depends, but not on yours truly
only. Indictment decisions at homicide level are made by the DA, and the
DA answers to the voters, not to me."
"He hasn't decided yet?"
"You think he wants to know?"
"He doesn't know?"
"Why should he."
"You said he knows."
"Did I?"
"He sent us his regards, you said."
"He always sends his regards."
"He's in charge."
"Exactly, so why should he know. Credible deniability, or whatever it's
called. You think I'm going to risk my non-career by telling him about
this? I would force him to say 'I don't want to know,' or 'let's move on,'
and he hates to say 'I don't want to know,' he really hates it, although he
actually likes to say 'let's move on.' Don't you see he's the recipient of the
Trumpet Award? The youngest DA in the history of the world? The
youngest governor in the future of mankind? You want to get into the way
of a rising sun? Be my guest."

I shouldn't be speechless, I know. Anyhow, the catfish is being served,
we have a break. It's Howard who's drinking now. The first bottle of
Chablis is already empty, a second has been ordered, and it doesn't help
at all that I've become abstinent under the influence of my hero at the next
table who drinks *Perrier* and knows nothing of me. Should I make a pass
at Krugman? Ask his wife whether there is some space in their marriage—
'there are three of us in this marriage,' she could unexpectedly say from
table to table and point to the empty chair between her and her husband
as if this were a play by *Pinocchio*, no, not Pinocchio, what was the name,
Ionesco, right. Must tell Lady Dy.

The food looks great and the catfish (how did this beast jump from
"wolf" to "cat" when it crossed the Channel?) is soft and juicy and goes

194

extremely well with sparkling water. I'm already considering a new career as fish-eating temperist, although I would have better done helping Trevor with his second bottle (and third), we'll soon see why.

"What can we do then..." I ask, (*we*).

"I can't promise anything." He'll place a phone call to Dick Benson tomorrow, and will try to get a message across, although he doesn't know yet what the message will be. So that's it, a phone call for a horse, a sex call for a country (don't tell Alex).

I'm getting more sober, Trevor is getting more drunk. A third bottle has arrived. Robin, Krugman's wife, takes note and whispers to her husband. Krugman, who always thinks that nobody recognizes him anyway, turns around discreetly and wipes his loosely hanging jacket off his seat. The tweed thing falls on the ground, one sleeve draped over my sneakers. I pick it up, hand it to the grateful NYT columnist, and say "I know you, I know you, you are, wait, you are writing for the New York Times..."— Krugman patiently waiting—"you are the guy who wrote 'The world is flat,' you are Thomas Friedman."

Krugman, to whom this has happened on numerous occasions, if we can believe his blog, Krugman is not amused at all. He grabs his jacket, turns around, and ignores me forthwith. Fail, John, fail.

39   DRIVING WHILE INTOXICATED

How about dessert?" Trevor says with Chablis in his voice—this is real Chablis, folks, from the French village of *Chablis*, technically a Burgundy white wine, but dryer than other wines from the region. Very light, a touch greenish in color, perfect with fish, and only the best bottles are real good. I, foolish enough to proffer advice on the basis of my French background, had suggested the *Premier Cru Les Fourchaumes*, which will mean the untimely termination of Trevor's expense account by the Georgia tax payer, or by transitivity, if you understand what I mean.

"How about dessert?" Trevor says again. I like him more and more. I like people on the other side of the trenches anyhow, one of the reasons nobody likes me, and I'm realizing that he's talking about the dessert because of me, because I might actually want one. There's something unselfish about this guy that possibly explains his bottomless cynicism. I really could do without dessert, we're deep into the third or fourth day of this soap, I'm as exhausted as a bad metaphor but feel the need to keep my side of the bargain, which implies more energy-draining, you know how it is, I'd better be done with this as soon as possible, so I say: "Let me be your dessert." No cliché is being spared, folks, as usual, what else would you expect from us.

Let's get serious for just one paragraph. Alex, knowing Benson, took Maurice's fears very serious from the start. Alice did. Then Benson comes to visit Maurice to smother him for good with a hospital pillow, only to be interrupted by yours truly (a typical Krugman expression). Then, Benson's ex expires in a hit and run and Benson himself is the first cop on the scene. And to top it, the DA won't touch the case.

What do you make of this? Maurice is still in hospital, one more day under IC protection, let's hope, then they'll move him back to some other ward where anybody can "visit" him, and Maurice isn't ambulant at all. He'll have to stay in hospital at least three more days. We must stop

Benson now, Trevor is our only hope, Alice would never forgive me if I don't fuck Trevor to death in exchange for a phone call. "Let me be your *peach and cream*," I raise the ante.

Alcohol induces stubbornness. It takes some doing to convince Trevor of my qualities as an immediate substitute for the *dolce* that we don't need, and since Trevor is getting loud, the Krugmans are getting embarrassed. Our waiter grasps the implications, shows up, and wipes Trevor's expense account clean.

Trevor has some trouble getting up. I should have taken this as a warning sign, changed tack, and suggested we'd just use my truck, but I didn't. So I explain to him that I would take him with my SUV to his car, which is parked near the beach, so he can follow me home, since it's too complicated to explain my address.

We're off. I'm taking the route via Church Street, the sneaky direct shortcut through the black neighborhood would be too circuitous for serious Driving While Intoxicated. This is my next mistake, the only mistake, in a sense. We're on Route One, southbound, 500 yards to go, Trevor's still behind me in his Buick, swerving a bit, but following, when another car appears in the rear view mirror, white, marked with red-blue stripes and rooftop alert gear. Next thing, the cops are falling behind, and the Buick is falling behind as well. Trevor is being pulled over. Would it make sense to stop now, help or assist Trevor in some way, perhaps explain to the cops that they've got the wrong guy, a real-life assistant DA without a future, they should better arrest me? No, it wouldn't make sense. My involvement would make matters worse, perhaps they know him anyhow, he knew Benson, didn't he? So I continue apace, trying not to change my speed or show any other symptoms of driving under the influence of being aware of the cops. What will Alice say? Shall I turn around, go to the hospital, talk to Alice, or Alex? Not a good idea either, I'm still DWI. They'll arrest me as well, or confiscate my truck, or whatever the Georgia code allows them to do. So I go home and get on the phone, but Alice is already in the trauma room, and Alex didn't show up for work. Alex didn't show up for work. And I still don't have his phone number.

How fast does an aging Mercedes ML 320 go when you want it to? Faster than the average police vehicle? I'm up the ramp, cross the median strip of Route One as if we're in a B-movie, merge into the north-bound traffic, and accelerate up to 100 miles per hour or more. People must be thinking I'm crazy, which is the idea, cops don't do crazies. I arrive at Alex's place in under four minutes. The tranquility of the neighborhood provides the perfect backdrop for my efforts, they can hear me coming, dogs bark. I brake the truck and slide onto the driveway as if this were an exercise in squealing tires. I don't bother about the bell, the lock is broken anyhow. I race upstairs and stumble into Alex's dark apartment.

It's very dark. I can be as upset as I want, it's very dark. It takes more time to cross the den than it took to cross Georgia Beach. Alex's bedroom is dark too, no idea where the light switch could be. Another movement and I've hurt myself somehow, and stumble, and I've hurt Alex, who was sleeping, and who is now squeezed by a disoriented scum-squirrel sitting on his lap.

We make noises, partially sympathetic ones. Alex finds the switch on his bed-side lamp. He'll forgive me. Yes, he took sleeping pills. He's upset that he slept through the alarm and didn't show up for work. They don't care for this at all at the hospital, it could get him fired. In fact, it's amazing how easygoing they are. He would have fired himself a long time ago. It's difficult to gauge his eyes, or more precisely his eyebrows in this light, but the situation is so-so at best. I give him a kiss, anyhow. He's making an effort, kisses back. "I was concerned about you," I say.
"Don't you worry," he mumbles.

I tell him the Trevor story, starting with Alice's remark 'cherchez la femme.' "I don't know whether I should laugh or cry," he says. "Do me a favor, call the hospital and tell them I'll be there in 30 minutes. I have to ask you a few questions." I call the hospital, he disappears into the kitchen corner and reappears with two filled espresso cups. Then I realize Alex doesn't even know about the hit-and-run on Benson's ex. I tell him. He's impressed, and he's not. "Maurice is the last hurdle," he says. "Somebody has to take care of Benson."

"Yes," I reply, "I tried."
"Indirectly."
"I can't go and take him out."

198

"Would it stop Benson if we get this out into the open? Blow the whistle? What would his reaction be?" he asks. "Would he stop trying? Would he try harder?"

He sips his espresso. "Your blog," he continues.

"Yes," I say.

"You don't have many visitors, right?"

"How do you know?"

"I had a look at it." He finishes his cup.

"I know, I say, "it has no focus."

"You could start a new one, more focused."

"I thought about a new one, with local focus, actually, that's how I learned about the hit and run on Benson's former wife. But the new blog would have even less readers, at least in the beginning."

"Fewer readers," he says.

"Yes."

"It's not a mass term."

"Thank you."

"Fewer readers," he repeats and rolls his head.

"Fewer readers."

"Why?"

"The search engines wouldn't know it. Most new visitors come through search results."

"How long would it take for the crawlers to discover a new blog?"

"Hard to tell, days, months."

"Can't you tell them?"

"Yes, you can, but they don't always listen."

"But they know the old one?"

"Yes."

"Why don't you turn the old one into a new one? Change the name, and so on. You can do that, right?"

"The name change wouldn't do much."

"You can suppress old posts, right?"

"Sure."

"Hide your identity?"

"Yes."

"You post this tell-all about Benson, the rape, the pillow, the hit-and-run, how long does this take to show up on Google's search results?"

"Ten to thirty minutes."

"Somebody searches for say, 'Benson plus murder'."

"Ten to thirty minutes."

"They don't crawl that often, or do they?"

"No, but Google gets the direct RSS feed."

"Why doesn't it show up immediately?"

"Don't know."

"Where would it show up, the result?"

"Possibly on the first page, unless there are other Bensons involved in murder cases recently, or if there's a Benson so famous his name is associated with everything. Like if his name would be *Bieber*, say. Otherwise, it would possibly be the first page."

"You can remain anonymous, right, he can't trace you."

"The FBI could."

"But not a local cop without investigative authority."

"Don't think so."

"Well," he said, "I go to work, and you go home and turn your blog into some local vigilante site with a few explicit posts on Benson's activities. And then we move from there. Give it some steamy name. *Georgia Beach Secrets*, or something. Mobilize the invisible hand of an open society."

I kiss him passionately without much of a result, go home, to bed, and fall asleep.

I'm asleep, but not for long. I'm not good at sleep anyhow, and this whole situation works on my nerves. I wake up around three AM, brew some coffee. Alex's idea could work.

Plus, I have little choice. This is the first time of my life I am truly in love. And, it just so happens, I am truly in love with an alpha-god. Perhaps one fine day I know better, but for the time being I am the *Scarlett* to his *Ashley*, *Apollo 13* to his *Houston*, the tiny brother to the big, big brother who knows everything and has a big dick.

Plus, it's actually the rational thing to do, outing Benson via the internet. Mobilize the invisible hands of an open society, or whatever Alex says.

So we forget about the coffee, get on the internet and into Google's Blogger, change our name into an a.k.a., and relegate all older posts to draft status with four clicks (it takes a few more because there is a bug, but anyhow). The old header, a distorted picture of *French fries*, goes as well. I'm vain enough to want some sort of non-standard header, think of deerstalkers, then of Agatha Christie, it's all terrible, we're in a hurry, so we hazard a *potpourri* of pictures with a screen shot of Benson on Channel Two, a gun, the picture of an ambulance, and the words GEORGIA BEACH SECRETS emblazoned in white *Baskerville Old Face* all over it, "Baskerville" is in the right ballpark.

And then I have a really bad idea. I want to attract traffic, and the term "secret," won't do much search-wise. What are popular search terms these days? Except for *Walmart* and *Facebook* and *Drudge Report*? How about vampires? I don't even check, I just know. So I change the name again, this time to GEORGIA BEACH VAMPIRE. Isn't that what Benson has become? It's four AM.

We need four posts, one for the context and the rape, one for Benson in the hospital, one for the hit-and-run, and one for dire predictions about

Benson's future. I'm not gifted enough for *murder-she-wrote* flourishes, so I write this down in the hopeless vernacular that you know from these pages.

Click, publish. It's there, it's up, it's typo-ridden (*Lichtenstein, masterclass*). We'll double-check in twenty minutes and drink a cup of coffee in the meantime, it's too late to go back to bed now.

Morning has arrived, the sun has a-risen and does its thing to the water tower. The cell rings.

It's Ray. Of all people, it's Ray, who's never called me before. Did I ever give him my number? Yes, he answers, I'm actually the only person who ever gave him a number, that's why he remembers it so well, and this is the only phone call he's allowed to make. They booked him in last night. He had been trying to have a nap on his usual bench in *Lake Gerard Park*, an early slumber in preparation for the darkroom. The cops had warned him they would book him in next time for serious sleeping, or loitering, a promise they finally kept. He's at the police office, but that's not the main thing. He can't speak now, they won't let him, would I please come and help, I'm the only person he has. This isn't a trap right? Is this a trap? I hit the return call button and ask for Dick Benson. Benson is not around, they regret, they are busy. It's not a trap. I go.

Something is wrong. Cars parked at odd angles—some marked, others unmarked, bubble lights still flashing—share the lot with a fat white cubicle on wheels. There would be the suggestion of a crime scene if this weren't the entrance to the police department. Inside, an excited official wants to know my business. More uniforms are milling about. Confusion reigns, someone of *Tommy Lee Jones'* stature is clearly missing. I'm led into a small interrogation room, window-less except for the mirror on the wall. Ray sits at a lonely desk as if this were *Total Recall*, or whatever that *Sharon Stone* movie is called where she bares her pussy to a shocked world audience.

Ray had been booked in for the night, he tells me. "I allow to make one phone call, and call the number from you, but no answer. I say I can't reach friend. They very unhappy about this, but they not care, tomorrow try again. One cop give me cold hamburger and blanket, and say they keep

202

me for night and take mug-shot tomorrow, and I can expect things. I scared, you know, I never booked before. I not even know if I illegal, I born in Malaysia, no passport, driver license, you know. So I sit in my cell. Sometimes, something is going on in the main office. Cops sign in, cops sign out, that sort. After an hour, or what, somebody else is booked. The guy drunk, hammered, they not nice to him, and throw him in next cell and say we do you tomorrow cuz you smashed. The guy know a lot, he talk some law-talk about codes and paragraphs, but they not listen. He talk to me through the bars. I listen, but he give up soon, cuz I not know what to say. I think the guy is gay, but he not in the mood. He lie on bed, and snore. I no idea how long he snore, an hour or so. Like the darkroom late, people sleep. I still not sleep, I never sleep at night, you know."

"You need to change your life style," I say.
"You hear the story?"
"Yes."

"So I not sleep. That the story. Cuz, next thing, I sleep or what, I wake up with the cops all over me. And in the other cell, the drunk from last night, he sit on the bed, a cop with a gun point at the guy. And on the floor, there is the cop from the office, the cop from the counter lie there, and blood, lots of blood all over him, the guy is freeze, or what. And the drunk is sober, he say something that he not do it. He say like 'I prefess innocence, I prefess innocence,' and he really upset. They ask me I see anything, or hear anything, but I say no, but I have terrible headache. I say I have terrible headache, but they not care. They point to piece on the ground in the other cell next to the bed where the guy sit, if I know anything about the piece. I dunno, I say. Then somebody in space suit come, and pick up the gun and spray the gun with somethin' from a spray can, like in movie, like he look for fingerprint. And he say to the guy on the bed, 'we know soon.' They drag me to this room. And I call you. I have terrible headache." Ray points to a big bruise on his cranium, he must have hit himself very badly.

"And the dead guy was a police officer?" I ask. Yes, the guy who manned the counter during the night.

I get hold of the bouncer at the entrance and ask whether I can take Ray home. Well, they have to interrogate him first, he's the witness to a serious crime, involving the homicide of a police officer on duty. Who's the victim, I ask. The bounce doesn't know himself, but he'll ask (this shows how confused they must be, entertaining murder tourists). He actually does ask, and the answer is some Blake, Blake whatever. Why did I want to know? What was the name of Benson's partner? What was the name of Alex's phone number? I call Alice, who is done with her shift. Blake, she has no idea, but gives me Alex's cell number. Alex is not on voicemail. Blake, yes, Blake Jackson, Benson's partner. Benson's partner. "He is dead?"

"He is dead."

"Killed?"

"Shot."

I tell Alex about Ray.

"He's on a rampage," Alex says. "Nobody is safe. Somebody has to take care of Benson."

I tell him that Howard is being framed for Blake Jackson's death. "It's ironic," Alex says. "Perhaps there is something like justice out there, once in a while. Perhaps a bit too much of it, justice."

Where is Maurice now, is Maurice still in IC? "You should know," I say. He doesn't. I have no idea. He'll talk to Quinton.

Maurice is the missing link, the only hurdle. Maurice must stay under IC protection, absolutely, Benson's capable of anything, regardless of the odds. Benson lost it, framing Howard won't stand, his game will be up soon. But we can't wait for eternal justice, in the long run we're all dead. He'll get back to me.

How about Ray? I'm trying to talk to the bouncer again, but Tommy Lee Jones has arrived. Mouths are shut, curt replies prevail, Ray will be held for interrogation and I am kindly shown the door. Rays casts a desperate look in my direction, he's crying. "I'll be back," I say.

Outside, yellow crime tape has been wrapped around the entire scene and Channel Two has taken up position with its uplink dish. They (that is, *Charleze*, their local reporter) want to talk to anybody, especially to people who are just leaving the building. I just don't have the guts to tell her about

Benson and wave my hands. If I only would have talked, things might have turned out differently.

Back at home I do a Google search and discover that my blog is *number one* on Google's search on Benson's name plus "murder," or "hit-and-run."

I lie down on the bed and fall asleep.

T he doorbell rings.

It's neither Ben nor Alex, though. The voice on the intercom belongs to somebody we don't know. He would have called, had he been in possession of my phone number. "You would have rung the bell, had you been in possession of my address," I suggest. Well, lawyers have their ways of finding out. "You're not Dick Benson," I say foolishly, as if Benson would tell me via the intercom in unaccented East Coast delivery. I trust phonology and push the buzzer.

He mounts the stairs ~~in protest~~ and wears a gray suit and complains about the elevator. I apologize and offer him a cup of coffee that he ~~gracelessly~~ gracefully accepts.

He's representing Mr. Howard. He's a friend of Mr. Howard, but he's also representing him, because Mr. Howard has few lawyers, or *vice versa*. He had a chance to speak to Mr. Howard earlier this morning in extenuating circumstances, and he has a message. For me. Four messages, to be precise. He paws his suit, produces a leathery kit of lawyerly writing things—he must have studied this in law school a long time ago, this display of analogue tools—opens an appointment book, and, with a thespian touch you'd never achieve with a mere iPhone, tears a page from the last part of said book, from where the *Mayan* calendar has ended, and hands it to me, and bids his farewell.

So he's gone. I'm doing what I often do in situations like this, I do something else, and visit an internet site with lawyer jokes. I can't remember jokes actually, I can study a joke ten times and still forget, but it doesn't matter, all lawyer jokes are the same.

So I'm looking at this torn page of vat paper, four lines scribbled by a nervous, substance-dependent hand (there are a few British actors always getting the parts of aging homosexuals, they all must scribble like this). Anyhow, the lines run:

(1) "http://a-happy-family-blogspot.com,"
(2) March 22, 2010,
(3) "Manhunt.net mec_____ (six lying dashes)," and
(4) "Cherchez la femme."

This is a message about blogs, right? Yes, blogs. Now, if *Tolstoy* were still with us, he would tell us that there are basically two types of blogs, happy family blogs, and unhappy family blogs.

Happy family blogs are all the same. They are called "The Jones family," and "The Smith Family," and have lots of posts about family outings and babies, and lots of pictures of happy families standing next to camping chairs on a meadow holding babies up in the air against the backdrop of Appalachian mountain ridges (there's also something about the language of these blogs too complicated to get into because I don't understand it myself), but—happy family blogs are *never* called "A Happy Family Blog." So we know already something is wrong. And we discover soon—we're on the interwebs now—that the name behind the happy-family-blog is "Hunnsbruck."

Blogs are organized as push-down stacks, with the latest post on top, and older posts below in descending chronological order, so the second message, about March 2010, points to a post down the stack. There is more happy family on display with more babies (or fewer, if they had another one in the meantime). Sometimes I really need a break from this world, and these family blogs always do it for me—you need sex, you watch porn, the analogy holds.

How about the third message? Well, *Manhunt*, that *is* porn, the ads certainly are, it's a large dating site for gays, lots of explicit pictures, I don't think I have to explain this, but imagine you are 28 years old and in urgent need of a date that lives nearby, how would you present yourself to the world? Don't be shy.

Now, how would you present yourself if you were married? And I don't mean married in the way that Godehart was married to Eleanor. I mean in the way that the youngest DA of the South-Eastern Judicial District is married to *Caroline*, his lovely wife. Well, you would stay incognito, aka anonymous. There would be pictures of your body, but none of your face. You would look young and hale, but happy only in ways that your poise can suggest without your facial input. And that's what the post of "mec_____" does, who is 28 years old, top/versatile (position), 6 feet (height) , defined (built), white (ethnicity), brown (hair), blue (eyes), ask me (cock), sometimes (availability), ask me (place), and negative (HIV status). And the pictures, there are several pictures of his torso, in sweatpants in front of a mirror, in sweatpants in front of a mountain, in swimming suit in front of the sea, *mec*_____ is looking great each time, even without face or baby. The guy is fairly hot, Trevor possibly had a crush on him in the beginning. How do you know it's Hunnsbruck? Because there's this identical picture from the family outing of March 22, 2010, identical from the collarbone on down, the bared torso nicely stretched upwards, accentuating the definitions of his washboard, you'd say the guy is procreating and making babies and holding them aloft just to look great.

So Hunnsbruck is gay, and he's deep in the closet. Well, who isn't (gay)? There was a prior probability of ten percent that he's gay anyhow, what the heck.

That's where the fourth line of Trevor's message comes in. "Cherchez la femme."

This cannot be. I wasn't stupid enough to mention this to Trevor. Or was I? I mean, my upfront talk about the gym, this Marilyn Monroe line 'let me be your dessert,' (Monroe would never have said that), you really had to lay in on and tell him that Alice told you to cherchez la femme? Alice never told you that, right? You were just drunk, you don't remember what you said.

How do we move from here? I don't even have a Manhunt account (people these days possibly split their lives in two, the part *before* they got a Manhunt account (or Grindr, or Craigslist), and the part *after* they got a Manhunt (or Grindr, or Craigslist) account. So I get a Manhunt account.

And then what? I don't even have cool pictures. OK, let's assume I have cool pictures (hot would be better). I contact the guy, I don't know what Manhunt calls it, but there will be ways to poke somebody's listing and say 'Hey, I'm the lay of the land, and I'm living down the road, have a look at my pictures.' (chat). And then what? Have him come over ('sometimes'), get laid ('bottom/versatile'), and while we do the pillow talk I discreetly suggest he'd take care of Benson? And what if he says 'No,' and informs me that a fuck is a fuck and the law is the law? He's a DA with principles, right? And then he fucks me again (new condom), and I come again, and he wipes the cum over my lips and cheeks and says "great" because sex with Manhunt is always great, and looks at his watch (DAs wear their watch during sex), and says "later," and is gone.

So, pillow talk won't suffice. We need to *blackmail* him. We turn my scrappy abode into a boudoir, with one-sided mirrors on the wall and candid cameras, and later send him a screenshot from a clip that we could post on *RedTube* in all innocence, like *Oscar Wilde*'s last lover would send the torn corner of the writer's last *billet d'amour* as a reminder of an ailing uncle who needs ten more guineas. 'TAKE CARE OF BENSON,' we would write, 'A FRIEND.' That's how it, like, looks like. Candid cameras, Manhunt memberships, capital letters, plus, what if the guy isn't attracted to your defined body because he's a rice queen? We go back to *mec_____*'s ad. Nothing that would indicate any racial preferences. I'm still OK, gym-wise, *n'est-ce pas*?

How about the candid cameras? I have no idea. *Jack Horn* would know, the Beverly Hotel poolside facilitator, who's happily married now and lives nearby, but Jack is a night owl and still sleeping. You can send him an email and move from there. What else? Register for Manhunt.

This, right in the middle of this mess, this is the perfect moment for Manhunt, looking in the mirror while not looking in the mirror. Nobody knows what will come after Alex, except that it will be Manhunt (or Grindr, or Craigslist). "Manhunt," the name alone, I once came across a picture of the two founders, they really looked the part. Manhunt will structure my sex life forthwith, so it's best to be utterly distracted by other things when you have to admit to yourself that you are pushing thirty, eternity starts now.

Manhunt, unfortunately, appears a bit disappointed re my inability to post some hot pictures at this juncture for the 49,415 members currently online, and some algorithm discovers that the avatar I'm trying to upload instead (a really hot Brazilian model three quarters my age) is, in fact, not me, and refused per-ti-nent-ly. *Mañana*, then.

Anyhow, I send an email message to Jack, and, while we are at it, I also send a message from my new, anonymous account to TV Channel Two, referring to the blog and the Google page where we're proudly the *Number One* on the search term "Dick Benson + Murder."

Briefly, I feel better.

The sun is up and pulsing and doing its thing to the water tower. I realize I shouldn't have looked outside—it all comes back to me now. *Making love in the dark*. What's blackmailable here? Is it enough, the DA in an embrace with a man? Do we need frontal nudity? Cum-shots? Let's hope he doesn't shoot his load at the cat cam. Or perhaps he should, in a dramatic finale, so the scene ends poignantly like in this movie, *Sliver*, with a black screen, and we send Jack Horn back to Hollywood to sell the script. Maurice will write it.

The credits roll, the sound's still on ('What's going on here?' 'Where is my underwear,' 'You little piece of shit, you think you can sell this?' 'You cannot do this', 'Blackmail me like that, it's a felony,' 'Hold on, where's my check book'). This is…I will have to keep this very much under wraps and swear Jack into secrecy. It's illegal, John, it's plainly criminal what you're doing here, Hollywood will love it, and Hunnsbruck will love it, too.

Maurice. Haven't we promised to pay him a visit?

42   500 MILLION SPERMATOZOA CAN'T BE WRONG

They know me now at the *Memorial*, it's amazing how quickly you become a regular in a hospital, even when you're just a visitor. After a few days people greet you with this *Cerberus grin*—'eternity starts now' it seems to say today, or perhaps 'the road to heaven starts in hell.' I push the bell to the IC ward, and Amy-Lou, peeking through the glass panes, waves her hand before even pushing the buzzer. She must have forgiven the cum-squirrel his soiled T-shirt, well, she was never mad at me anyhow, five hundred million spermatozoa can't be wrong (that includes Alex's count).

"I was expecting you," she says cheerfully.
"I should have brought flowers," I reply.
"For me or for Maurice?"
"For both of you."
"Only for the two of us?"
"For the three of us," I reply reflexively.
"I like orchids," she says and points at her desk in the control cubicle where a collection of potted long-steeled plants with butterfly blooms queue up like a reception line.
"They don't need much light, and they live forever if you water them properly."
"White or pink ones?" I ask (both colors are in evidence).
"Any color of the rainbow will do," she replies, "especially from you."
"Rhymes," I say.
"That's what Maurice would say too, although it's not quite true."
"*That* rhymes," I say.
"You can't always win," she laughs.

So we *are* a threesome now. She's right. It's hard not to fall for Maurice. It's hard not to fall for hunks anyhow, but injured hunks, pale enough to make aspiring writers, there's no glass ceiling, the sky's the limit.

Amy-Lou has good news, Maurice is much better, although it's also bad news, for she will see less of us when he goes back to the trauma ward. "Can't you keep him for a few more days," I ask, "he'll write you into his new script."

"He has already," she replies.

"How."

"I'm on *Team Cheney*, as a nurse."

"He's potentially blackmailing you."

"Ooh, if Maurice would only blackmail me more, but it's still 3500 bucks per night."

"Perhaps we can find a medical reason."

"There are always reasons, but it's still 3500 bucks. The billing department is not sure about his insurance. And he doesn't have money."

"How do you know?"

"Writers never have money."

"Can't you sign for it?" I ask her.

"Only when Quinton is off to the restroom."

"Quinton must be going to the restroom a lot," I suggest.

"Perhaps you should make an appointment, there's a glory hole between the second and the third stall..." (there are continuations to this dialogue from which both of us refrain).

Maurice is still pale and seductive, and the IC ambience lends him an air of *right-ship-wrong-ocean* so typical for aspiring playwrights, but he's not in good spirits. He has checked on the blog this morning and discovered that his posts were gone. And the entire blog makeover, he's unconvinced.

"Your deployment of the vampire theme," he says, "you're out of touch, vampires have become objects of love and affection, your comparison of Benson with a vampire, nobody will understand."

"It was Alex's idea," I lie.

"Really?"

"He triggered it."

"Alex triggers a lot, doesn't he?"

I retract, explain. Get things out into the open, feedback, open society.

"That rings more like Alex. But the vampire idea?"

"It was very late when I worked on it. Or very early. The vamps were intended to attract visitors and replace the naked girls."

"And now they *have* replaced the naked girls. Before you know it, Benson has been elected Miss Vampire."

"Not funny."

"Not funny, indeed."

"Benson won't dare if everybody knows."

"The undead get away with anything."

"OK," I say tepidly, "but you're safe here." How safe can one feel as an alien in red meat country with a big, still-active scar across the abdomen. Maurice couldn't even run away if Benson shows up again. Not exactly the moment to tell him about Ray's night at the police department.

He wants to know why I didn't start a *new* blog for the Benson thing. The crawlers wouldn't know it, I explain. "Can't we start a blog together?" he says, "just about writing, I pursue my things, and you write a *true-story* story, every blogger is a budding author, just write up what's happening now. Nobody will believe it, which is always a good start."

He's such a sweet guy, this doing-things-together-thing, it's strange he doesn't have a steady companion who lays tea without being asked and holds his dick in the meantime. Then he adds: "*If* you survive, darling."

"The blog is anonymous."

"Benson found me, he'll find you."

"I'm still more concerned about you," I lie.

"Let's have another look at your vampires," Maurice resets. "How many viewers did you have today?" He grabs the hospital iPad and gets onto the blog's statistics page.

"Queen and country," he says.

"Nobody?"

"Yesterday, we had 80 views, didn't we? You know how many we have now?" He keeps the iPad close to his chest.

"Yes?"

"You've received two thousand, two hundred and fifty five page views since midnight."

I grab the pad. It's not only the numbers. We've got twenty-seven comments—normally I don't get any comments at all—comments from

Russia, California, Mexico, Florida, Georgia of course, both Georgias, there's a comment from this place on the *Black Sea*, and from somebody in the UK. "V for victory," he writes. I read it to Maurice.

"'V' mean vampire," he says, "Brits adore paper chases."

I have a second look. I'm not certain anybody actually read the posts. One comment from Delaware reads "From V2V, beach peach, I'm coming," and there are others who must have misread my dire Benson prophesies as invite to an undead-vaganza, or who think this is part of the Festival Week. I'm reading another comment to Maurice ("I am inspired, nourished, and challenged by your amazing work. Thank you so much for sharing. God bless") when Alex appears in the door.

Judged by his eyes and overall flourish, this is not his day at all, it's worse than yesterday even. But he makes an effort, plants a kiss on Maurice's cheek, circumnavigates the bed, plants a kiss on mine. He has a message, or, more precisely, a few pills. "These pills," he says to Maurice, "should induce problems with your heart beat."

"How about my other problems?" Maurice replies.

"They solve at least one of them, they'll keep you in IC. You take one pill now, and two more before four PM when they must decide whether to keep you for the night. Your monitors will get a bit upset, Quinton needs an excuse."

"Splendid," Maurice says, "but how about tomorrow."

"Tomorrow is another day," Alex says with an air of something between desperation and wisdom. There's not much left of the alpha god today— he's unshaven and looks scrappy and worse. He's so beautiful. I want to touch him, do something to him, don't know how.

Alex returns my glance. "I look scrappy, I know," he says while the door opens. It's Alice, or *Dr. Dyke* more precisely, the head of the ER, who's visiting Maurice. You can be as sophisticated as you want, study internal medicine, wear horn-rimmed glasses, become an in-law of an in-law of the Wagner family, inherit a lot of great artwork with white dots on white backgrounds, when push comes to shove the tricks are always the same. She talks to us as if we are human beings, she's available for eye contact, but she hasn't forgotten yet.

She wants to know about Maurice's scar. We get a good look at his abdomen, Alice is quite satisfied, "Two days," she says.

214

"Anything new," she continues. She has a second look at us, and in particular at Alex. Alex doesn't want to reciprocate at all. "Ask John," he finally says.

I've really lost track, forgot what I told Alice already, or didn't, or shouldn't, so I tell everything again, starting backwards—just (*just*) managing to omit Hunnsbruck and the video installation—so I begin with Alex's idea to revamp my blog as a whistle blower.

"And?"

"It was very late when John made the changes," Maurice interposes, "or very early."

"Which means?"

"I had the brilliant idea of a themed presentation. Something to replace the naked girls. Vampires."

She knows nothing of the naked girls, I have to explain.

"So you dropped the naked girls that made your blog popular? Naked girls will outlast vampires forever, trust me."

She is almost about to elaborate (and Alex is almost showing signs of amusement), but a large flower bouquet gets in the way. "Godehart, you know how to make an entrance," Alice says to the flower bouquet. They've forgiven each other, you can see, the double dildo episode is really a study in side effects, somebody should write this up for the *Harvard Business Review.*

Wagner liberally kisses everybody in reach. He then clutches Maurice's hand and says, "My dear boy," as if he's going to propose.

Maurice looks the part. "How ace of you to think of me, darling," he says.

"You look like you are going to propose," Alice says to Godehart.

"Come to think of it," he replies.

"It'll be the opening of my new script, *Love at First Sight*, very original," Maurice says. "We'll marry in the beginning and it gets better from there on."

"Do not make jokes," Godehart says, "I will make you an irresistible offer, and then you are stuck, or?"

"Like, like…" Alice adds.

"Like…" I add. We can't be serious.

"Stuck like a dildo," Godehart completes with a queenish look at us.

"But in the meantime," Maurice (who may or may not have gotten it) interrupts, "I could write the script for another Wagner opera."

"It's called *libretto*, Maurice," Alex says.

"I cannot compose," Godehart adds.

"The Wagner brand requires a makeover, an update, I'm your man, darling," Maurice insists. It's unclear whether he wants to get married or famous or both. "You need a modern myth. Like, like…."

"I will see what I can do," Godehart says, "but Winnifried, Friedelind, Siegfried, Wieland, Gottfried, Woglinde, Wellgunde, I should not inconvenience you with their names, the more so since they seldom speak with me, we would need their help if we want to give the marque a facelift, or?"

"Most of them are probably dead"—Alex.

"Perhaps that is the reason why they seldom speak with me. Is he getting better well?"—Godehart means Maurice.

"Yes, he is, he's recovering faster than anticipated"—Alice.

"Your work"—Godehart to Alice.

"I thought it had been your work," Alice says, "originally."

"It is frightful," Godehart says, "scareful."

"It isn't over yet," I say. "We've tried to get the DA involved and failed miserably. And Benson is still at it. His partner, Blake Jackson, the other witness, was killed last night"—I throw this into the room, nobody knew, only white trash watches morning TV. Well, Alex knows, I had told him.

"So Blake was Benson's partner?" Alice asks.

"How to explain this?" Godehart asks.

"He lost it," Alex says. "I've known him for years, saw him in action, I've always wondered when he would lose it."

Maurice fiddles with his iPad, holds it up. "We're at the top of the hour, as they say here," he says, "let's see, let's pop in." The newsroom of Channel Two materializes on his screen.

An anchorman and an anchorwoman appear in the beaming studio and greet each other expansively against the backdrop of the police department's parking lot. Assorted vehicles are still parked there, and

Charleze (the local reporter), is still on location. "The top story today is so breathtaking, it is positively, absolutely, and definitively shocking," the anchorwoman ("Olivia") enthuses, "Charleze has more."

Charleze expansively greets anchorwoman ("Olivia"), who expansively greets back. Next to Charleze a man is standing whom we know already thanks to our interest in family blogs. Hunnsbruck is dressed this time, dressed to kill, you'd say, or at least dressed to advocate innovative punishments for police department homicides, so he's emphasizing local roots with a light seersucker suit of modest stripes and cut. The reporter turns to the seersucker suit and introduces him as the youngest DA in the history of the galaxy: "When we arrived on the scene this morning," Charleze says to Hunnsbruck, "having been alerted by vigilant members of the Georgia Beach community to the unsettling traffic on the lot outside the local police department, right here where we are standing, rumors were swirling that an officer has been shockingly shot dead inside and that an assistant district attorney from your office is implicated. Does the size of the CSI vehicle" (pan on the white-cubicled truck) "points to the size of the crime committed inside?"

"Splendid"—Maurice.

"Thank you for having me on"—Hunnsbruck.

"You are always welcome"—Charleze.

And now, in unison: "Thank you"—both.

A moment of recovery, Charleze catching her breath. "The word is, Sir, that Lieutenant Blake Jackson of the Georgia Beach police force was shot dead last night."

"Although I've never had a chance to meet him in person, I am convinced that he is, or was, a truly wonderful person. My thoughts and prayers are with his family and friends at this difficult juncture."

"We have to interrupt briefly for this message," Charleze informs Hunnsbruck, who gracefully cedes the floor to a risqué soda commercial with a curly-blond girl, the wind-surfer back of a hot male (only the back), and a soda bottle. When finally allowed back, Charleze and Hunnsbruck have obviously had a chance to follow the ad on their return video—so Charleze suppresses a giggle when asking Hunnsbruck: "Sir, this is a shocking crime, is it not," (her left hand gesturing, digits splayed, dramatic nail-paint-jobs exposed, the right hand doggedly clinging to the phallic mike) "is it not a shocking crime when a trusted member of the local police force is shot dead while in full discharge of his duties? How do you feel about this?"

"Charleze, let me tell the viewers, the people of Georgia feel terrible about this, and in particular the people of my District, and I, as the DA in charge, feel exactly as terrible about it as they do. This is a shocking crime of which the people of Georgia disapprove strongly. It is, uuhh, illegal. Life is sacrosanct from inception, especially when it comes to the police."

"Can you assure our viewers that your office won't let this particularly shocking crime go unpunished?"

"The people of Georgia know me and my office, and I can assure the people of Georgia that I will work tirelessly to aggressively pursue the perpetrators of this shocking crime and bring them to justice."

"What will be the charges?"

"It's early days, but the perpetrators will look at malice murder, felony murder, aggravated assault, aggravated battery, possession of a firearm during the commission of a crime, maybe on several counts, or more."

"Will you seek the death penalty?"

"We seek the death penalty whenever it is appropriate."

"The people of Georgia will be grateful."

"This is another step ahead in the never-ending battle against crime."

We're interrupted by the studio and another commercial.

"Did you listen to what he just said," Alex says, "about the never-ending battle against crime. It's like saying we're battling infinity, and we will count to three, and four, and five, and go on and on until we run out of numbers."

Not everybody gets it, Alex has to explain.

"You're better off if you don't have to explain your own jokes," Maurice says.

"It wasn't a joke, it was the very opposite," Alex replies.

"May I cut in on that?" the newsroom comes back, "Mister Hunnsbruck, a member of your office has been connected to the shocking events unfolding at the police office. Could you comment on that?"

"The case is being investigated extensively, and I would like to thank Deputy Sheriffs Hartley Hansford, Harrison Thomas, and Jeremy Hicks from Glynn county, Lieutenant Thomas Raybon, Lieutenant Peter Hoyle, and Lieutenant Mario LaStrada from the GBI, and many unnamed others for their tireless efforts. I can assure the people of Georgia that no stone will be left unturned in this ongoing endeavor."

"The people of Georgia will thank you for that, Sir."

"Thank you."

It looks as if we're in for a thank-you *encore* when Olivia says "May I cut in on that"—cut—and we have Olivia in the studio next to a side-screen with a screenshot of Google's search results, the usual listing in blue Google font, and my blog at the top of the page, with words like 'Richard Benson,' 'murder,' 'hit-and-run,' all quite visible and readable. "There have been rumors on the internet that another police officer might have been involved in this. It's only a rumor, for sure, but it's a shocking rumor, isn't it. How do you feel about this?"

Had he been cued on this? Hard to tell: "One of the great things about our country is that we have democracy, and the First Amendment of the constitution protects free speech, including the internet. I'd like to leave it at that."

"I fear we'll have to leave it at that. Thank you for being with us this morning."

"Thank you for having me."

"Thank you."

"Thank you."

"This was Doyle-Ray Hunnsbruck, District Attorney for the Judicial District of South East Georgia." Another commercial takes over.

"What do we make of this," Alice asks.

"He keeps his powder dry," Alex says.

"We had our minute of fame," Maurice says.

"Don't be scared," I say to Maurice because I'm scared.

"We *should* be scared," Alex says.

"Stop scaring Maurice to death," Alice says, "you said yourself this won't hold. This won't hold."

"No, it won't. But it can't wait. Somebody must take care of Benson. NOW."

"Which options are left?"—Alice.

"Alerting the FBI, somebody from the outside"—Godehart.

"The Feds can't intervene unless state borders are crossed"—Alex.

"We can't take the law into our own hands"—Alice.

"Why not," Alex says, "we have stand-your-ground laws now. We stand our ground. We defend Maurice."

"Stand your ground applies when you are at home"—Alice.

"We are at home, aren't we?"—Alex.

"At *your* home."

"Georgia *is* my home."

"You cannot do this, take the law into your own hands," Alice says.

"You talk like the New York Times," Alex replies.

Amy Lou appears and wants to know more about Maurice's cardiovascular system, Alice sends her away. There is a silence. Alice stares at Alex with an mix of anger, affectation, and anguish.

"What's wrong with you," she says.

"Sorry, I didn't mean it," Alex replies.

"What?"

"The New York Times thing. You are right."

"What's wrong with you?" Alice says again. Awkward silence.

"You really want to know?" Alex says.

"Yes."

"I got fired."

"No."

"I got an email this morning. From Harrison. Or his assistant." He produces a page, folded, fumbled, from his pocket, hands it to Alice.

"After careful review of your employment history," Alice reads, "detailed notes and entries recorded by the head of ambulance services, we had to determine that your termination is necessary due to cause of gross misconduct. Duhduh, duhduh. Severe attendance problems for which you have received notifications for several times. Duhduh. Due to above mention and several other reasons it is not possible for us to keep you within this organization. Duhduh. Thanks and regards. Ford Harrison, Director."

"It's a template," Alex says, "they copied this from the internet."

Alice hands the sheet back to Alex, covers her face with both hands briefly. "I will talk to them. You're the best paramedic they've got. I don't know how many lives you saved."

"I would have myself fired a long time ago," Alex says.

"Don't say that."

"Well, it's true."

"What are you going to do?"

"Don't worry," he replies, "I'll figure out something. Go to medical school."

Alice sits down on a chair, points to the fumbled sheet in Alex's hand. "With that as reference?"

"No sweat," Alex says, pockets the sheet (still wearing the themed hospital sweatpants that make him look just great), points at said pants, and continues: "I'll have to, *quote*, return the materials in my possession related to the hospital such as employee card, uniform, badges, equipment, real property, and other unnamed things, *unquote*," and with this, he is gone.

43   CLUTTER, CLUTTER & CLUTTER

E very soap opera has its *homme à tout faire*, be it James Bond ("Q"),
or us ("Jack Horn"). Speaking of James Bond, if you've watched
the earlier movies (there is a new-new Q now, bear with me), you must
have realized that Q's old lab was too small. There was no way anybody
could combine a shooting range for warheads with a workshop for
poisonous pens with an assembly line for Aston Martins anywhere outside
Pinewood Studios. (The newest Q holds court in the British Museum where
they have more space).

Same for Jack Horn. If you ever had a look at Jack's place—he lives in
a rambling farm house outside Georgia Beach with a large orchard and a
big barn where he works—you don't have to enter the barn, you only have
to look at it from miles away—it's like Q's (old) universe, only more so.
There are toy helicopters, coloring books of his three lovely daughters, the
original camera of Toulouse-Lautrec, the screen wall from Startrek, entire
hardware shops, books even, some of his friends write books. It's like the
law firm of Clutter, Clutter & Clutter: there it is, climbing the stairs,
climbing the walls and climbing into the basement where antique premium
cars await repair: clutter. There's no way you could spend a minute in this
chaos and not come away with the idea that Jack is your man when it
comes to harebrained schemes.

There's only one small problem, Jack is homophobic. He accepts me as
an acquaintance—just—but that's where it ends. Jack is a photographer
by training—I once asked him to take some nice pictures of me together
with a long-lost lover, and he immediately assumed I wanted something
lewd.

I'm already driving down to his place—it's still early by his advanced
standards, but we have no time and the Hunnsbruck blackmail is not
something you want to discuss on the phone—when I realize that the only
person I can fully trust with this is Godehart. Only Wagner is crazy
enough. So let's talk to Godehart first. I turn around and cruise back to

Georgia Beach and Atlanta Street. Surprise, surprise. Godehart and Alex are poised in conversation outside, next to the cerulean SUV. They stop talking when I get out of the car. No kissing this time. Conspiracy is in the air, both ways, in fact, I can't discuss my Hunnsbruck schemes in the presence of Alex—although, come to think of it, isn't he telepathic, isn't he going to read me anyhow? Well, he doesn't bite or show other signs of alpha dog disapproval. Instead, he casts a sad glance in my direction before he clutches the cruiser's remote control, taps a hand on my shoulder, and departs.

Godehart pensively tracks the SUV with his eyes. It takes a few seconds until the queenish grin re-emerges. "How are you, my boy," he resets. I tell him of my plan. He is delighted.
"Isn't this all a bit unrealistic," I ask.
"No, not at all, my boy. Better even, yes, it is. Let's go inside and have congress while I explain."

He has already climbed the steps of his porch when he turns his head and adds: "It's so much cooler inside."

I'm still standing there, it takes a little while for the news to sink in. Wasn't it Lincoln who said that your wit decides your life? Or Beyoncé? Or the absence thereof? "Not the dildo again," I say.
"Just, how do you say, a quickie, or? You will need all the training you can get," Godehart says.

Inside, a fresh breeze from the a/c vent lifts us upstairs into the master's chamber. The bed is emperor-sized and the headboard looks like the snout of an oversized truck, gleaming metal that doesn't seem to make sense until you figure the master (or slave) clinging to the chrome grill when congress is in session. Gohard undresses casually, hands me lube and condom. He's a bitch on the bed now, hands clinging to the chrome grill (didn't I just say?), peach butt rutting suggestively upward. "The immediate prospect of sudden, unexpected sex makes you hard, not true?" He shakes his butts as if this were a gif picture on *Fagsmut*. "Fuck me," he adds redundantly.

He is right, the flash of gay yen is flashing. There's no need for foreplay. He's an experienced bottom, I'm already inside, humping his rear. "Ooh yeah, ooh yeah," he answers, "Ooh yeah," and so on. "Fuck realistic reality," he adds to the iambic rhythm of my thrusts. "Perhaps there are a few pockets where reality is still helpful. When you build harp bridges, for example."

"Harp bridges," I say—just imagine us, we're in high gear now, he goes 'Fuck, uuhh, re-a, listic, uuhh, reality, uuhh,' and I go 'Harp, uuhh, bridges, uuhh,' and so on—I don't think it's funny, by the way, harp bridges, did Ben and Gohard ever meet? Anyhow, he fails to elaborate and continues (non-referential speech omitted): "In most sorts of human enterprise reality is just a hindrance. Trust a fifth-generation member of the Bayreuth clan, the hare-brained-er the *libretto*, the accomplished-er the opera."

I am trying to convey a certain sense of skepticism despite the challenging circumstances. He's not listening, though. "Go hard," he shouts, "Fuck Hunnsbruck. Get laid. Go-hard. Fuck, fuck, fuck, uuhh, I'm coming." He withdraws, turns around, and clutches his chimpanzee hammer. There's a parabolic quality to his spasms, the goo lands on his nose, forehead, hair. I'm a quick cummer too (as you know), a few pointed jerks, and my nectar is all over his map. He wipes his nose, smacks his lips. We're both gasping. "Perhaps Hunnsbruck is into threesomes," he laughs.

We've reached full after play now, which means we are resting against the chrome grill, not the most comfortable of head rests, and I don't know what to say. Gohard is stroking his dick again. "How about a re-run," he says, pulling his foreskin in all directions.
"It was great, but I need to save some cum for Hunnsbruck."
"Hunnsbruck," he says, "I forgot. Yes, let us save some cum for Hunnsbruck. Let's get pen and paper." He jumps off the bed and returns with a *Montblanc* pen and a leather-bound, Wagner-iconed notebook (this one even prettier than Howard's lawyer's diary).

"Let us swap meanings about the right use of internet dating sites" he says, "I am a platinum member of Manhunt, so I can help. What age have you?"
"Twenty-nine."

He has opened the notebook, readied the pen, and scribbles my age pensively onto a virgin page.

224

"That's clever," he says, "that's really clever. Twenty-nine. I didn't think you would have it in you."

(I agree defensively.)

"Twenty-seven would be the self-evident choice here, but not the best, because it is also evident to others. So that we are practically forced to choose twenty-six. But everybody knows that. So it becomes twenty-five. But everybody knows that. So it becomes twenty for and so on until one reaches the age of nineteen, where uppity twinks lie about their illegal age. But everybody knows that. So one is stuck. I've seen many a good man stuck at twenty-one, men practically double my age. Whence the wise choice of twenty-eight imposes itself."
"I thought you were talking about twenty-nine."
"Twenty-nine is for advanced players. It shows you know the game."

The number "29" is carefully penciled onto a virgin page of his diary.

"How old are you really?"
"Twenty-nine."
"What?"
"Twenty-nine."
"You lie."
"I swear, twenty-nine."
"Well, if you insist. So long as you are sufficiently younger than he. What age has he?"
"He's the youngest DA in the universe."
"Ach. Legal age, can we hope? Else he could get you arrested."
"He's twenty-eight on his Manhunt page."
"Twenty-eight, Q-E-D, twenty-eight." Godehart is overjoyed.

"Godehart," I say, "we don't have much time."
"OK, let's shortcut the corners. Your position." He writes down 'Versatile.' "I don't have to explain this, I think," he says. "Height: 'Six feet one.' Penis size is related to body height. Built: 'Defined.' Yes, I know, you are near so athletic, but we don't want to overawe the district attorney. Ethnicity: 'White,' better not lie about your skin color. Hair: Tousled."
"I think they mean the color."

"Exactly, a sense of humor is always in the right place. Eyes. You have beautiful eyes, their oscillation between gray and amber, but this is too complicated for Manhunt. You say 'oscillating between gray and amber,' they think you are schizophreen. 'Ask,' then, let them ask. Cock: 'Seven inches.' Seven inches is obligatory unless yours is truly seven inches, whence you say nine. *Eight* inches are very rare and stir suspicion. Availability: 'Sometimes,' we say, else he thinks you're a fast woman. Place: 'Mine.'"

He puts the diary down. "How about your pictures?"

"I'm on my way to Jack, who's a photographer."
"Make sure they don't look too realistic, your pictures, realism stirs suspicion."

I'm already re-dressing. He tears the page from the diary, folds it neatly, and hands it to me as if it would contain a secret formula: "No reason for excitement, you can always make changes when we have dealt with Hunnsbruck. And do not worry, Alex has a reserve plan. I like your plan more, however. Carry him out."
"What's his back-up plan?"
He puts a finger to his lips. "Scout's secret," he says.
"Something to do with Isolde?" I ask.
"She's a scouts secret, don't you know."

44 A SURGICAL STRIKE INTO SEMANTIC SPACE

S o I'm off to Jack again, who should be awake by now.

It's past noon on the fourth or fifth day of this soap, I feel exhausted, dead tired. In parallel worlds I would be lying in Alex's arms, or Ben's arms, or the well-paying arms of an A-level escort client, but I'm not, and without any immediate checks and balances around me I'm practically dying of self-pity when driving up Jack's yard. He receives me with his trademark debonair gesture and offers a glass of whiskey. This won't be my last drink today, I think, erroneously.

Let's recall that Jack once took my tentative request for a partnership picture as an insult to his straight sexuality, so I will have to dance around the issues and explain my case as if this were a surgical strike into semantic space. A space devoid of any motives, reasons, or explanations, solely consisting of noncommittal visual gear pointing at my bed from various angles, everything invisible to the unsuspecting eye, and wired, wireless, of course.

"Uhh huuh," he says, sipping his whiskey. "So you want a video installation?"
"In a sense."
"On your own premises."
"Yes."
"You won't have much traffic in your apartment."
"Should I?"
"Perhaps you should contact the MoMa for your work."
"You mean the *Museum of Modern Art?*"
"They have more traffic. In New York City."
"I'm not famous enough," I say.

"I worked in Manhattan, once had sex with the secretary. Of the director. Twice. My-ooh-my. These people know what they are doing."

"Hiring secretaries?"

"Hiring secretaries. Three times." He smacks his lips, swipes his unruly black hair with his fingers. "A video installation. That could be challenging."

"You are the man."

"Thank you," he says and turns to the Startrek wall we've mentioned earlier. He ignites one of the screens with a remote control and is already surfing on the internet: "Video installations, invented by *Nam June Paik* from Korea, who also invented the *Information Highway*. Today ubiquitous and visible in a range of environments...the only requirements are electricity and darkness..." he pensively quotes a Wikipedia page. "You have electricity in your apartment, don't you?"

"Yes," I say.

"And darkness, how much darkness do you have?"

"Enough."

"Enough enough, or just enough?"

He's expecting an answer.

"Just enough," I say. He swirls the ice cubes in his tumbler, resumes control of the whiskey bottle, makes arrangements for topping up my glass. "Light isn't like booze, you know," he goes, and halts, as if he's waiting for something to click.

"Analogies break down all the time," I reply.

"Somebody should do something about analogies. You know, the bottle is half empty, it doesn't mean it's half-full." I will lose this, I know.

"My God, and you are a college professor. If you have enough darkness, baby, will you have enough light?"

I hand him the half-empty glass.

"Or do we need to install additional light-e-ning?"

"You say."

"Should they be visible, the ligh-heights, or invisible?" His face alights. He hands the glass back to me, un-refilled. "You are aware of the pecuniary implications?" he adds.

I didn't think about money at all, I assumed he would reach into his clutter and produce the required amount of high tech for free.

"It's urgent, right?" He asks.

"How do you know?"

"If it wouldn't, you'd possibly have some time to think."

I take another sip.

"And come up with a better idea than this harebrained scheme of trapping someone *in flagrante* in your bedroom," (he continues).

"It was suggested to me by a lawyer."

"A lawyer? Like in LAWYER?" He's having a fit. "This isn't a joke, right?" He chokes on his drink, I have to save his life and slap him on the back.

"Blackmail, you know, is a crime," he adds when he has recovered.

I blush. Jack seizes the moment. "Think at least one kay," he says.

"One kay," I say, "you mean kay as in kilo?"

"I mean as in dough, cash, or other stores of value."

"I'd thought you just reach into your..." I point at the reality around us, "...into your reserves and produce the required amount of visual technology for free."

"Yeah," he says, "with your familiarity of my *reserves*, why don't you try yourself." He gestures at a heap of electronic equipment two feet high, a catcam or two could easily idle inside. Then he reaches for his remote control, flips another screen to life, and a close-up of the barn's interior appears. He starts a third screen, and a different perspective of the same clutter drifts across the screen. He points in the air. "All catcams are all in use. Think of lavatories on an airplane."

"You really need this?"

"On orders from *Homeland Security*. It works like an electronic bracelet. I'm on parole since I built a nuclear time machine."

"They believe in time machines?"

"They believe in everything, just to cover their ass. You say *boo*, they believe you, just to cover their ass."

"One kay?" I ask, "As in thousand bucks?"

"Kilo," he says, "is the measure of weight in the metric system. One kilo was the weight of a cube of pure water, ten centimeters wide, deep, and high, at the temperature of four degrees Centigrade. You want to know where centimeters come from?"

"A thousand bucks?"

"I'm also part of the equation."

We shouldn't be surprised, throwing good money after bad money is what soap operas do for a living. OK, hold on, my credit cards are maxed out (a third of my pay goes to credit card arrears, it's a vicious circle, the escort service is not a joke).

A thousand bucks. Whom could I ask? Godehart is rich. If I'm getting serious about escorting, steady johns like him provide the bottom line. But Godehart didn't pay me this time, perhaps I have been elevated to his exalted station where money plays no role.

Alice? She's rich, too, with Eleanor's dotted spots in Godehart's basement. I cannot ask her, though, I would have to explain, impossible. Somebody else? I have no friends. How about Alex? We had a walk on the beach, he told me about his depression, critiqued my metaphors, held my hand, we've known each other for four days…

So I call Alex. I'm in panic, there's no time to think up lies about ailing uncles. We are lucky, Alex is *not* on voicemail. Sure, thousand bucks, no problem. He sounds like he's happy to get rid of his stores of value. Cash? He's not at home now but he'd have to hit Walmart anyhow, he'd see me there in ninety minutes, at the other exit, not the food, the exit for camping gear and lawn mowers.

I explain to Jack, who can't suppress a happy grin. "You're really in a hurry, ain't you?" It's my lucky day, he explains. He'll get the equipment from *SpiesAreUs* and will install it as we speak. "When is your *flagrante* taking place," he asks.

"It all depends on you," I say, "since," I say, "I need some nice pictures."

"Pictures?"

"Yes."

"Of *Snow White* and the seven dwarfs?"

"Yes."

"I don't do dicks," he says.

"No, just nice pictures."

"Why don't you take them yourself with your i-ding, do some *selfies*."

"My cell phone is nokia."

"*Is-no-ki-a*," he echoes. "'Nokia' as an adverb. Not bad. Could make the Urban Dictionary."

"You think they pay, the Urban Dictionary?"

"Give it a try."

"I really need a few pictures."

"OK," he says, "I'll throw a few pictures into the deal."

He must have been overcharging me big time with his thousand bucks, I'm a bad negotiator.

He directs me to a large paper backdrop rolling off the wall, flips two Klieg lights, and points his *Nikon D3x* in my direction. He isn't even snapping, the thing is on speed repeat.

"In the past," he says, "you would think first and then shoot. Now it's the other way round." Then he adds, as if bowing to conventions: "Give it to me, baby, give it to me." He's already done. "You no longer have to think at all, in fact, you dump the whole set on *Tumblr* and see which ones bounce back through *re-blogging*, those are the good pics. But the feedback takes weeks, we don't have the time."

We're sitting at a long desk that had to be cleared of the worst debris (think of *Jurassic Park*, one of the best scenes, when *Attenborough* wipes the messy desk of the greedy programmer), and downloads the pictures from his Nikon. He flips through the pictures at high speed—he has me spinning like a dancer in a silent movie. "Hold on," he interrupts himself, "I forgot."

The screen changes to Google's search window. "As outlined earlier, one should let somebody else do the thinking," he says. "Who's going to make our life easier? The Windsors. That's *it*, the British dynasty." He googles for "Windsor porn pictures," and arrives on a page with royal obscenity involving all members of the dynasty, in particular an elderly woman with petrified white hair. "How many have jerked off on Elizabeth, you think," he asks as if expecting an answer. "I wonder whether the Queen realizes."

"The porn torsos have already been taken care of, that's why we do this," he says, "there are professional secrets to this." A picture of *Prince*

Harry is saved to the work space, a royal member of seven true inches at 35 degrees. "This is the magic angle, especially girls love this angle. It's about anticipation. You play chess, right? The threat is stronger than the execution. A dong like this, they can't take their eyes away from it. I'd always made sure I undress *before* I was fully erect. Which meant I had to strip all the time, practically speaking. In my days."

He drags the picture onto the gray Photoshop canvas. "It's for a dating site, right?" I don't answer. "Don't worry," he says, "our sex has dating sites, too. They are easy, the pictures are never large." My head is cut off and placed on top of Harry's torso. Then it disappears. "A mask," Jack says, "you're masked now. I'll invert the mask, then rub it away where I need to." He describes tiny circular jerks with his mouse (just imagine you'd read this 30 years ago: 'he describes tiny circular jerks with his mouse'), and my face reappears, jerk by jerk.

This is going to be iffy. I look like shit, like I haven't slept in days. "Don't worry," he says. My face is split into color bands, the red band glows a bit more under his touch. The pointer morphs into a tiny makeup brush that does wonders to my face. I'm filtered, rendered, sized, brightened, saturated, contrasted, intermittently he uses the mouse, even, although it's usually an interplay of *control* and *alt* keys that does the trick— that's the way to tell the men from the boys, boys use the mouse. A few more adjustments, and I'm looking like—I'm looking surreal now.

"I'll save you with a loss of quality, that'll save your day." And, indeed, a reborn semi-erect hunk appears in a new window against a creamish-colored bookshelf that I don't own.

"That's not my bookshelf," I say.

"He'll be too aroused by then to think about books," Jack says.

He's enjoying this. "How many pictures do you need for the locked section," he asks.

"We need three or four," he answers himself.

"You do a lot of internet dating?" I ask.

"In the past I didn't have to," he replies, "and in the future she won't let me."

"She?"

232

"My wife. And in between it's just one moment in time." He raises his hand. "Watch out." He presses his thumb against his ring finger. "Now," he says, and snaps. "That was the moment. Life's over."

"You love your wife?"

"Love's like an electronic bracelet."

"Analogies break down somewhere," I say.

"My only consolation," he says.

Jack pulls down more royal members. Half an hour later we're done. He rises. "Let's get rolling," he says. "I'll sweep *SpysAreUs* for the gear. I have an account there, but need to pay them asap. Make sure you collect the money on your way home. We'll reconvene at your place, you pay, I play, then you play, and then you possibly pay for it, but that's life. See you later."

I'm late.

I forgot about the time. I have to call Alex, but I forgot to recharge the cell. Let's hope he's patient and waits for me. Not exactly his forte, patience. I hate my cell-phone.

I slide onto the Walmart parking lot and drive up to the entrance, no, the other entrance where we are supposed to meet. Nada. No Alex. I find a parking space for the truck and return on foot. Still no Alex. A brief glance at my wristwatch. It's minus hundred feet. It's minus hundred feet since I pushed the wrong button on the *Suunto Altimax*, a present from a long-lost lover, the same slut that inspired my asking Jack for an innocent partnership picture.

I feel a hand on my shoulder. It's not Alex, it's Neill, the rice queen from Godehart's party, the guy who called the ambulance with Alex on board. "We haven't had a chance to talk," he says, "what happened to Maurice?"

"He survived," I say. "So far."

"Really bad fuck. Terrible," he says.

"You haven't seen a guy..." I describe Alex, "the green-eyed paramedic who came to pick up Maurice at the party, you haven't seen him?"

"No, I haven't." A jaded sense of *déjà-vu* appears on his face.

"I have an appointment with him."

"Yes," he says, "apparently." Both of us look around.

"He drives a Toyota Prius," I say.

Last time, at the party, the ambient light was sort of forgiving. Today, in the aggressive sun of an early afternoon, Neill's long neck shows creases of weight loss. There are lines of exhaustion on his face. "What do you do at Walmart," I say, just to say something, "why don't you shop at Nordstrom?"

"The nearest Nordstrom is in Atlanta," he says and scratches his neck, drawing my attention (or what's left thereof) to a spattering of reddish, ill-defined lesions on his shoulder blade. I've seen this before, once, in a sauna. And on the internet when I checked later. *Kaposi*. AIDS.

"Itching?" I ask.

"Not really," he says.

"You should go see a doctor," I say.

"I have."

For a moment I think he folds.

"I take medication," he says, "Complera, Norvir, and Dermavir."

"It's curable now, right," I say—I know it isn't really.

"Well," he drawls.

"What's your life expectancy?" I ask (terrible, John, how can you possibly say this).

"I'm proactive," he says.

"The earlier you start taking antiviral drugs, the better."

"I'm past the point of return," he says, "but I'm just back from a meeting with the mayor. I want to give back to the community."

"What did you get from the community, then?"

"We got wealthy on real estate. The stretch of land behind the beach, right down to Simons River, for example, it's worth a solid eight digits since Connecticut discovered we're only a few miles from Florida."

"You own the cruising area?"

"For example."

"So that's why there's no buildup."

"I just made the deed over to the town. They're going to create an award in my name. The Neill Palmer Memorial Award. No strings attached."

"You're not dead yet."

"Well, forget the 'memorial.'"

"How much is it, the award?"

"Hundred kay."

"Gee-whiz. What do I have to do to get it?"

"Get yourself elected King Dracula. Or Queen Dracula. It'll go to the festival this year. For the winner of the vampire contest."

I'm getting aware of a cerulean SUV right at the center of my field of vision. Isolde is parked quietly on the best space of the entire lot. Of course, Alex is driving Godehart's SUV. "Sorry," I say and abandon Neill.

I find Alex inside, sleeping on a bench. He still looks unshaven and scrappy and beautiful, but his countenance appear more at ease, the tension between the eyebrows is gone. I touch his elbow and plant a kiss on his forehead. Yeah, he slept, stupid. He's falling asleep at impossible hours. Funny Walmart security didn't do anything. "You don't look like a bum, they don't treat you like a bum," I say.

"I *do* look like a bum," he says. I apologize for being late.

"Let's get the money," he says and directs me to the ATM across the aisle. We have to wait in line. First time we do something really mundane together. I feel his proximity. "Why do people need cash?" I say stupidly, but Alex isn't listening.

"You've heard of Torre's observation?" he asks.

"No."

"The other line is moving faster."

There is only one ATM. "There is no other line," I say.

"So, I'm right."

"Huh."

"There is no other line. Nothing to refute me. It's vacuously true, my statement."

I don't know what to say, or I don't dare. It's our turn. "Thousand bucks, right," he says. He feeds his credit card to the machine and enters a pin code. A number appears on the display, something around $1,200.

"That's your balance?" I ask.

"Guess so."

"You've got no money left," I say.

"Don't worry," he says and digits the dollar amount into the keypad. Greenbacks appear in the dispenser tray and are handed to me.

"Let's go," he says, "I've got lots of things to do."

"What are you doing with Godehart's truck?" I ask as he climbs back into the SUV.

"I need it."

"Godehart said you had a plan for RapeDick."

"Did he?"

"Yes."

"He's not supposed to talk."

"He didn't explain."

"He doesn't really know."

"What you're up to?"

"Do you really want to know?"

"Yes."

"I'll take care of Benson, and then I'll take care of myself."

He shuts the door and drives off.

A shopping cart appears in my field of vision, or what's left thereof. The cart is pushed by a Walmart-sized woman with a toddler of uncertain gender at her hand. The cart has a crazy wheel and swerves sideways despite her efforts. A second toddler occupies the cart's baby trap and jiggles his naked feet against his mother's midriff. The woman seems to know me, no idea where we met. Look what I got, her face says while my field of vision continues to shrink. There are six-packs of choco milk, bags of frozen fries, six-packs of beer, crust-less Winkies, generic pintsized Colas, Luncheables, moonpie cookies, frozen donuts, frozen tacos, crust-less white bread, Walmart Twinglets, frozen American pizzas, muffins, plastic peanut butter bottles … I'm losing concentration. Something's wrong with the first toddler. He hangs back. "Come on," his mother says, "mommy is in a hurry."

"Wheel, wheel," the toddler whines and pulls at mom's hand. They're holding up traffic. The traffic consists of a shiny SUV of unusual color. The driver's door swings open, Alex gets out, walks up to me, and says: "John, I'm sorry about what I said. I didn't mean it."

There's more traffic, a Walmart motorcade is building up behind the Google SUV, someone blows a horn. "Later," Alex says, and is off again.

I have the rest of my life to call him immediately, but the cell is dead, as you know.

237

46   LOOK, MUFFY, HE BROUGHT HIS INSTRUMENTS

A lex will take care of Dick Benson and then take care of himself. Benson's just an excuse. But he may need an excuse. Somebody has to take care of Benson first.

I won't have much time.

We have to pay Jack (check), have him install the candid cameras (check), look great on the pictures (you say), place the Manhunt add (check), wink on Hunnsbruck (it's called "winking," this knocking on a Manhunt door), wait. The phone rings (recharged, partially), Hunnsbruck hasn't my number, it's Ray. He's still at the police department. The cops are going to release him, but only if he provides a credible address. How do you mean? I must come pick him up and convince the cops he's staying with me. I can't, Ray, I'm waiting for Hunnsbruck. Who's Hunnsbruck? He doesn't know, fortunately. Does it matter? We're in absurd territory anyhow. How many people did you need to wait for *Godot*? Did Godot ever show up? Okay, Ray, I'm coming.

There's some official who's happy to see me. Ray didn't have a shower or anything in a while, he's more smelly than usual, he stinks. They need to get rid of him and accept my word that Ray will stay out of trouble if I'm next of kin and sign the form here, here, and here. We are released.

"Where do I take you, Ray?" I ask him.
"Dunno," he says. We're driving down Canal Street. I would have to turn left on Georgia Avenue to take him to my place, or turn right to take him back to Lake Gerard Park, which is not a bad address if you think about it, only a few steps from the Blue Moon.

Unlike Ben (when I picked him up on Monday), Ray knows where I live. He had spent a night at my place and gotten hold of the spare key. It took me a while to get rid of him, make up a story, my aunt would be staying with me, or something, but he understood, he's low-information but sensitive. That was four years ago (why did my life end at twenty-five?).

We've reached the junction of Georgia Avenue. I concentrate on the traffic, a bit more than necessary, and turn right. We go past the traffic circle, past the afternoon traffic jam, turn left on Lake, left on First Street, and arrive at the park. I have to steal a sideway glace at Ray now, his little head, the flat, roundish face, the salt-n-pepper hair, the tiny hands resting on short thighs. He's staring through the windshield, he knows I'm looking at him. He must be forty years old at least; he may not even know his birthday although he's certainly lying about it. He's not going to last long. I can't step out, saunter around the truck, open the door for him, can I? Ray has found the handle, pushed the aging passenger door for what it's worth, said "see you later," and disappears among the conifers of the park.

Better get going. I make a U-turn on Lake, and turn left on Atlanta to avoid the traffic on Georgia Avenue. That's a mistake. It takes me past the Blue Moon where I met Ray for the first time, ten years ago, coming home during the Easter break, when he was still ageless, his hair still black-black, and I bought him a drink on my Dartmouth scholarship. How come we both lost out, he at Lake Park, me at SGC? How come he never got in trouble with the law before? Every other day he would possibly find someone who'd take him home for a fuck—it's not his thing—take him home and let him have a shower and fresh underwear perhaps. He was a regular in the park then but is stuck there now, nobody's taking graying oriental boys home, it's a law. And the cops, it's a law, too, they are supposed to do something about smelly aliens. They book him in again, or, hard-working as they are, shirk the official paperwork. 'We warned you.' He won't forget. They won't rape him, though, let's hope.

You are a piece of shit, John, you are a piece of shit.

There's no space for a U-turn. Not a good excuse. I turn on the first private driveway for a K-turn, the tires shriek. The driveway looked empty from the street but has been hiding a gleaming Audi A8 parked in the back. I over-hit the brakes and find myself next to the side porch of a

Victorian lady, gingerbread behind a budding hedge of roses. A female face appears above the hedge. Blond hair, gray eyes. She looks shocked, shocked. Her eyes travel to the Audi. The Audi looks shocked, too. The female face wants to talk, the side window is in the way. A second face appears, dark hair, blue eyes, same posture. These women can't be standing upright, their heads barely clear the hedge, they are on their knees somehow. The first face turns her hand in a circular gesture. I lower the side-window. I look at an expensive five-digit hand, the engagement ring alone. "Look at him," the second woman says.

"Ladies," I say, "I'll be out here in a sec, apologies."

"No, no," The second woman replies.

"What happened?" the first woman says.

"I'm trying to make a K-turn, apologies."

"What happened?" the first woman insists.

"Nothing, Ma'am. I didn't touch your car."

"I heard a noise."

I have trespassed and interrupted some interesting goings-on porch-wise, I can't just drive away. I get out, walk up to the Audi, fondle its rear, especially the *soi-disant* bumper, and say: "Look, the rear is completely unblemished."

I should have been more careful in my choice of words. "My rear," the second woman echoes, "unblemished. He's cute, Muffy."

"Look yourself," I say. Ambivalence is growing upon me until the second woman—her name is Jane, as I will learn presently—until Jane rises to expose a pair of full, fresh, naked boobs. She's even wiggling them briefly, you'd almost expect to hear the sound of jingle bells. Muffy, still hesitating, casts a lateral glance at her girly friend and rises as well, exposing a second pair of principle female attributes. "You owe us," Muffy says.

That's the problem with *soi-disant* lesbians (if you can believe the porn sites), you never really know whether they mean it. "Come hither, young man," Jane says (*hither*).

"I'm really in a hurry," I say.

"You owe us," Muffy insists.

"Perhaps we can discuss property rights later," I say, "I'd love to come back, trust me."

"You think we trust you?"

Jane's hand appears on Muffy's naked shoulder as her eyes vise my crotch. "Look, he brought his instruments, Muffy," she says. A poignant moment. "Don't be shy," she adds in my direction.

"What do you expect me to do?" I ask.

"Care for a cup of tea?" Muffy asks. She's apparently the host. "This is my friend Jane." I feel obliged to climb the three steps up to the porch deck where a wide, linen-covered lounge-bed awaits me. "Sit down," Muffy says. "I'll have to get a cup for you," she continues and disappears.

In all this excitement I forgot to remark that both women are, indeed, completely naked, sporting youngish, scented bodies and attitudes to match. I sit down next to Jane. Jane, tactfully, refrains from any further action until the hostess returns with a tea cup in one hand and … a Siamese dildo in the other. "You got this from Luke's convenience store?" I ask foolishly. The ice is broken. Consenting adults, unite.

Now, let me be clear, this wouldn't be my first shot at straight sex, plus, as a budding escort, you'd better be versatile anyway. But I need some spare cum for Hunnsbruck. Let me count, how often did I come today? I'm trying to concentrate but fail, Jane has already unbuckled my belt and unzipped my fly and is fondling my erective organ. Muffy takes care of my T-shirt. "Lie down, young man," Jane says, "relax." That's not what she means, of course, but I give in anyhow and raise my butt. Jane pulls my shorts. A throbbing hard-on points at my navel, it must be my own. Another vain thought of Hunnsbruck, the last one for the next twenty minutes. Both women are kneeling next to my haunches as I expect a Siamese blow job, but that's not going to happen (wait). Instead, they inch up to my cheeks, Jane from the left, Muffy from the right, until their pussies lock onto my ears, whence the girls fold their knees in sisterly lotus behind each other's backs. A gentle, rolling movement of their underbodies engulfs my head, a belly-dance done by their bottoms.

"Can you hear the waves," Jane asks.

"Who told you this?" I manage to say.

"Nick," Muffy replies. By then, they've stirred up quite some excitement, both in themselves—I can hear the blood romping in their veins—and in yours truly, who can barely handle himself. They finally unfold, inch lower into fellatio position, and plant kisses on my cockhead.

241

Anticipation is key, passion grows—until Jane finds a chance to say "he's beautiful," and Muffy finds a chance to answer: "And large."

"Who is Nick?" I ask. They must have joined forces before. "Our master," Muffy replies. Nick! Nick who sent me the naked girls on the blog? Is he leading a secret life?

It's time for the higher level. Jane assumes horseback position, fitting her squishy pussy around my restless dick. Muffy does likewise at my upper end, planting her pussy on my lips. Jane rides, Muffy slides. I fuck, I suck. "Uuhh, uuhh," Jane goes. Juices are flowing, pricey housewife perfumes (Opium, Fahrenheit) mix with the natural scenting of happy vaginas. The neighbors could hear us. "Uuhh, uuhh," Jane goes again, louder this time, Muffin joins: "Uuhh, uuhh." I do what I can, a multiple orgasm is in the making. Jane comes deep down in her vagina, Muffy comes right up there with her neat little clitoris in my mouth. Jane groans, Muffin moans. I'm trying to hold—they sure want me to come over their shapely breasts, Jane has released me, but before anybody can get hold of my dick it has happened already, I'm spouting into the suburban air of Georgia Beach like the fountain of *Djerba*. It takes a little while, fortunately, the ejaculation of ten, fifteen spasms of pristine man milk, so both girls find time to get in position and meet my final squirts with their up-market bosoms.

Jane creams her index finger through the jizz on her boobs, then sucks her digits as if this were a cooking show. Muffy mimics Jane's movements and appreciation. And now they move into frontal position, cross-legged again, facing each other, torsos erect, boobs in attendance, four nipples touch, four breasts meet, and rub, and do squishy rounds in squishy cleavages, and now the girls finally kiss an interminable French kiss, two lusty tongues traveling deep into lesbian terrain, exchanging and blending the fluids of tripartite lovemaking. They can't be serious, these girls, or they are, it's possibly both. We're done.

A sensual moment of contemplation follows, regrettably interrupted by Jane's stolen glance at the idling dildo on the coffee table.

How to get out of this? You know, I'm not good at transitions. "I charge ten dollars but am willing to negotiate," I say. And yes, they get it.

"He's funny," Jane says.

"He's sweet," Muffin says.

"I really have to go," I say, "This has been an inspirational moment of my life, ladies, my new web site will be up in an hour, A-level-escorts-georgia-beach-dot-blogspot-dot-com. One word." I point at the dildo.

"Cool," Jane says.

"He's hot," Muffin agrees.

"Ladies," I say, still dressing—dressing, the new way of saying goodbye. We're friends now, they help me with the T-shirt. "A-level-escorts-georgia-beach-dot-blogspot-dot-com. One word," I repeat.

"We have lots of friends," Jane says and gives me the high-fives. Talking about desperate housewives or desperate assistant professors. It's hard to believe how I've changed in five days.

I'm back in the truck, back up, gently, gently, out of the driveway, turn, reverse, and return to Lake Gerard Park. I can't find Ray until I find him dozing on a bench, tucked away on the northern side of the lake. As if the cops couldn't trace him here.

"This is your bench?" I ask.

"Yes," he says.

"You can't stay here."

"I know."

"Okay," I say, "you come with me. It's for a few days, we'll have to find a permanent solution."

"Sure," he says. I take him home.

47 MY DICK HAS NEVER BEEN THIS FLACCID

The desperate housewives have revived my spirits—somehow we're going to save Alex, even though he's still on voicemail. Should I leave another message? Depressive people hate phone calls. He knows that I want him to live. I drink another cup of coffee while Ray snores in the spare room. I have to keep promises. It's official. Yes, I knew it, the address

Alevelescortsgeorgiabeach.blogspot.com

is still available. A fitting email address is duly created.[1] The photo that Manhunt didn't like (*Leadro*, a Brazilian super model) serves as the header, there are so many escorts working for us, you know, especially Brazilian ones. A side post with a *Contact-Us* link is in place (perhaps I should get a second cell phone). The rates, yes, the rates, I have no idea. Let's consult the interwebs. $200 for an "incall," $250 for an "outcall" appears to be average. Per hour. I have to make up at least three posts, any self-respecting escort has a website with his latest adventures and feelings. '*Let's call her Barbara,*' is the heading of the first post that serves as template forthwith, followed by '*Let's call him James,*' and '*Let's call it quits,*' the last one telling the educational story of a fuck abandoned for financial reasons. And, yes, girls, a first click materializes from nowhere, or more precisely from Georgia Beach. The *URL analyzer* confirms my wistful thought, the click comes from *32 Atlanta Avenue*, Muffy's home.

I'm almost done (still need to register the 'Alevel' email address on the *Opera* browser) when the Manhunt alert signal sounds ("winks"). Hunnsbruck? Yes, it's mec-six-lying-dashes. Let's chat. He likes the color of my eyes. He wants to know more. Seven inches, truly? Well, internettishly. He understands. He likes my pictures. He's around. Pictures

---

[1] Alevelescort@gmail.com

can't lie. Tonight? Tonight. When. Where. You know Georgia Beach? He has GPS. Sure. He's in a hurry. Important meeting. My address: *42E, Boat Lane Road*. Downtown? Almost. Fifteen minutes.

Let's try to calm down. Let's see what Jack has done. We have four catcams pointing at the bed from various angles. Anything that gives us away? The cat-cams are tiny insects tucked away in the upper corners of the bedroom, bitsy black spots but duly in touch with a router sitting on top of the PC box. The PC is on. The computer screen looks like a closed-circuit display above the counter of a 7-Eleven—four rectangles filling the screen with four versions of an empty bed. Let's test this. Yes, I can recognize myself. I unzip briefly. Yeah, that's my dick. Everything goes to the hard disk. Let's hope we won't have a power outage.

How are we are going to do this? We are going to have sex with Hunnsbruck, right? On my bed, but not on the kitchen table. We have a fair amount of practice, *n'est-ce pas*? Then what? My chest still oozes with his cum, say, and I half-rise, lean on my elbows, rest my head on the back of my hands, and say 'Doyle-Ray, have you thought about the ramifications?' Not a bad opening. He's puzzled. How do I know his real name? I get up and follow my softening dick to the computer, open the SpiesAreUs window, and say 'Have a look.' He's irritated a bit until he realizes what's going on, it may take a while before he recognizes himself. What if he doesn't recognize himself? He's in a hurry. He's already dressing. He's feigning ignorance, or not feigning ignorance. He isn't going to say 'I don't know what you mean,' no, he's tying his brogues and buckling his belt and adjusting his tie and departs. He might even say '*Ciao*,' just to vex me. What's next? I should ask Howard's lawyer. I don't even know the guy's name (the lawyer's). Okay, so while Hunnsbruck is about to leave, I tell him this was all Trevor Howard's idea. That will scare him, right? Remember yourself, John, your timidity? You won't even have the nerve to confront him with the evidence, let alone with pertinent questions.

A short crescendo in Ray's snoring interrupts my brittle thoughts. This is not going to work. Let's call the whole thing off, Alex isn't dead yet. I'll plant myself next to Alex, I'll chain myself to Alex, and say: 'Alex, you know, I know …'

The doorbell rings.

I crash Ray's door, shake him, and yell: "Don't you snore, don't you snore, it's a matter of life and death. Stay in your room." I dart to the intercom. "It's me," the voice from Channel Two says. I dart back to the bedroom and kill the spy window on the computer screen.

Steps on the landing. A larger pair of sunglasses, accompanied by the seersucker suit we know. "John," he says and shakes my hand. Mec-six-lying-dashes has done this before.

"John," I say. He laughs.
"Your real name," he asks.
"Unfortunately."
"It's okay."
"A drink?"
"Yes, a drink."

One beer is left in the fridge. Hunnsbruck takes note (eyebrows). What can I say? I'm doing my best, pouring the beer gingerly in pursuit of the optimal foam while thinking of Alex, the last recipient of this treatment. Just for symmetry, I pour myself a glass of water. He's self-assured, we wouldn't know he's in the closet. He isn't blackmailable as long as he doesn't tell anybody he's in the closet.

Hunnsbruck sits down in Alex's chair and says: "There's a problem with your door. Your main entrance below, it won't close."
The foam is his glass is still rising and may spill over one day. What to say next?
"The foam in your glass is rising and may spill over one day," I say.

He feigns concern, but the foam stops at the rim of the tumbler. It's possibly easier to move forward and have Manhunt-sex than to call the whole thing off. Wait, I could use Ray as an excuse, knock on his door, drag him into the kitchen, explain his case, mention Trevor Howard, move on from there. Too late, Hunnsbruck has already said: "Let's move on" and asked for directions to the bedroom. I point to the open door, you can see the bed from here. My dick has never been this flaccid.

246

What would *you* do, reader? I mean, what would you *do*? You have studied escort blogs before, flaccidity is never an issue. 'Must post an honest post on the A-level blog,'—I think the penultimate John-thought of this episode—'titled: Let's call it pendulous.'

I just can't. I need a drink. The conversation has died, Hunnsbruck is waiting for the go-ahead. "I need a drink, John," I say, "I'll be right back." Whatever he thinks, let him think. He's still wearing his shades.

Three minutes to Luke's store if I run, two minutes to buy a bottle of wine (the strongest stuff Luke sells, as you know), five minutes back (exhausted). I'm sweating, the elevator's unrepaired.

Something is not right. There are bunky, woody sounds coming through the door. I open the door. Three people stand around the kitchen table, shoulders bent forward, all breathing heavily as if I've interrupted a *Laurel & Hardy* flick. In this order, Doyle-Ray Hunnsbruck, still wearing his shades, Ray Mayang, naked, and Dick Benson, in full gear. Benson holds a tactical knife. Bensons turns slowly around. "He's coming for you," Hunnsbruck says. Ray shivers. Hunnsbruck is calm. Benson trembles slightly. Benson turns his head, faces Hunnsbruck again. Hunnsbruck raises his arm and removes his shades. A split second of absolute silence follows, the world has come to an end. "You can't kill us all," Hunnsbruck says. Benson's tense body jerks, turns, and the contorted baby face pushes past me down the stairs. I stand there, frozen, feeling my heartbeat.

"I think we'll have to leave it at that," Hunnsbruck says, puts his shades back on, and departs.

R ay plops down onto a chair. I can't help it but cast a glance at his miniature organ. He crosses his legs.

The sun has set some time ago but the water tower hasn't and is softly recasting the lights of downtown Georgia Beach. I explain a bit about Hunnsbruck. Ray shivers. "I thought he was coming for me," he says. He gets up, walks to the sink, bends over. He tries to be sick. There is no vomit. He returns to his chair. Both of us listen to his tummy. It takes a while.

"I hungry," he says.

"You know the way to the fridge," I reply.

The appliance contains a bottle of ketchup, a glass of mustard, two slices of cellophane-foiled burger cheese, and dark-greenish, un-cerulean spots in several locations. Ray studies this carefully. "Have a shower and get dressed," I say, "We'll go to Mamma Mia." I sit there, waiting for him, shivering as well.

We're already on our way to Mamma Mia's diner when my head finally clears. Perhaps Alex is at home, I could ask him to join us, he must be hungry too. I take the shortcut along Miller Road, his place is barely two minutes away. The white Prius is parked in the driveway. Isolde is nowhere to be seen though, and the bell goes unanswered. The door has been repaired and is locked. I call his cell. I can hear it ringing faintly through the dark windows of the second floor, an archaic analog ring tone, the sort of sound that always eludes me when I'm trying to change ring tones myself.

I get back into the truck. "You love him, right?" Ray asks.

"Yes," I say.

Bubble lights stroke the longleaf pines when we arrive at Mamma Mia's parking lot. An ambulance and three police cars are parked at odd angles near the entrance of the diner. "The odder the angles, the odder the event," I say to Ray in one of these remarks I usually come to regret. This is the parking lot that saw Benson's ex mortally injured in a hit-and-run.

Patrons of the diner have poured outside and are milling around. I lower the window and ask a woman. She's holding a slice of pizza. The cheese drips. She takes a bite before she answers. She takes another bite. A drip of cheese ends up on her left Nike sneaker, she's distracted.

"Stay in the car," I say to Ray and get out. "Somebody got hurt?" I ask a cop. He's staring into the distance. Then he adds: "They won't get away with it."
"A police officer?" I ask.
He nods in the direction of the ambulance.
A gurney is about to be hoisted into the emergency vehicle. This is serious. The casualty is wrapped up in sheets and fed oxygen through a mask. Gray noise fills the air, another cop talks on a walky-talky. The victim's face is partially visible. "Dick Benson?" I ask.
"They won't get away with this," the cop replies.

I knew, I just knew. I find the cell in a pocket and dial Alice's number. She answers. "Alex is committing suicide," I say.
"In your presence?"
"Benson got hurt in a hit and run."
"Benson?"
"I know, Alice, I just know."
"Where is Alex?"
"At home."
"How do you know?"
"I know, I just know."
"Okay," she says.
"You agree?"
"Yes, no, yes. He's a medic. OD. I send an ambulance."

Three minutes to Alex's place. The neighborhood is dark and quiet. A dog barks in the distance, a second dog responds. I get out, don't even try the doorbell, ram through the rickety door with my shoulder. I'm upstairs already. I forgot where the light switch was. I stumble, fall onto something, hurt my face badly, get up, stumble again, hurt my knee, have trouble getting up. Somehow I've fought my way to the bedroom door. I feel up the frame, find the light switch. Alex's bed is empty.

He must be here. Or at least he was if he's dead now. He is nowhere, not in the den, and not in the kitchen corner. I enter the bathroom; he's lying on his back on the wooden planks, legs sideways as if he's sleeping. I can't feel a pulse. Laymen can never feel a pulse. I slap his face, hard. "Wake up," I holler, "wake up." There's a flutter in his eyelids. I slap harder. The green eyes are open. For a sec. "Stay with me," I shout, and slap. "I love you, Alex" I shout. He's slipped away. Where's the ambulance? I call Alice again but get nobody at first and then a different voice. It's Roxanne, the emergency receptionist.

"Where's Alice?" I ask.

"Dr. Sandeman, you mean."

"Dr. Dyke, whatever."

"She's in the trauma room. Some cop got hurt badly."

"The ambulance," I say, "the ambulance."

"They just called in, they can't find the place, there's no street number they could identify," she replies.

"They don't know where Alex lives?"

"It's Alex?"

"Yes, Alex. Call them. Alex. Alex has OD'd himself."

"Is he dead?"

"No, he's unconscious."

"Unconscious?"

"Call them."

There's no answer, we got disconnected.

I pocket the phone, run down the stairs. We can't wait, we have to get him to the hospital. Alex, the hunk, is too hefty for one person, I need Ray. I've just opened the front passenger door as the ambulance approaches. I sway with both arms. They are already past, haven't seen me. I grab Ray's arm, drag him upstairs. My phone is trying to say something, I dig in my pockets, but it's dead when it reaches my ear. "You take the feet," I say to Ray. I pull at the arms, Ray's sort of pushing, this is low budget, but we get him across the den and onto the landing. His body slides down the stairs, it's ugly, his head bobs on some steps. We have him lying next to the truck now, the passenger door is open. The seat is up there, two feet in the sky. Another ambulance is coming from the opposite direction, the same ambulance. A ~~deer~~ scum squirrel with suicidal tendencies jumps right into the headlights. They will see me this time. Tires yell. The side door pops open, it's Amy-Lou.

"You?" I say.

"They are short a paramedic," she says. "Where's the patient?"

"Next to the car."

"How?"

"He's unconscious."

"How?"

"OD, I guess."

"Blood, injuries?"

"No."

"OD. How do you know it's self-inflicted?"

"I know."

"*Copper*, stretcher," she yells to the driver, the same guy who partnered with Alex at Godehart's party. She feels the pulse. "Not great." Alex is rolled onto the stretcher and hauled into the meat wagon. She feels the pulse again, purses her lips. "His shirt." Copper cannot find the box cutter. Seconds crawl. Amy Lou retrieves a Swiss army knife from her pocket, hands it to Copper who gets the blade under the neck line of Alex's tank top and cuts it open from top to bottom. The cloth gives way along the midline and falls to the side. A sheet of paper appears, tucked under the waistband of his shorts.

"*Felo de se*," Amy-Lou says, and hands the sheet to me. "Read it," she says, "it may tell us things. About the method. Read it."

"Where's the oximeter?" Copper hands her a large, fancy pencil sharpener that fits onto Alex's left index finger. An electronic display springs to life, digits and a wave curve. Amy-Lou is handed two oval plastic sheets, electric blue, dangling from thin black cables. The sheets are fixed to the corners of Alex's still-seductive pecs. "Heart monitor," she says, "can also do defibrillation."

"Rhythm normal, pressure low," she says to Copper. "Anything in the letter about the method, the substance?"

I'm a failed academic who knows how *not* to read things, I fly through the text. Nothing specific. "Nothing about the method," I say.

"Never been a method actor, Alex," she says.

251

"Gastric lavage," she adds in Copper's direction. Copper hands her a plastic tube that goes into Alex's mouth and deeper. She connects the tube to a device on the rack along the side and hits three buttons. "Get the stuff out." The tube gurgles. "We don't pump, we rinse."

"Actidose aqua." Copper finds a polyethylene bottle in one of the drawers. Amy-Lou pushes a button, the gurgling stops. She unscrews a plug, pours the bottle's contents into the aperture, pushes another button. "Activated charcoal, one teaspoon has a surface area of ten thousand feet. Neutralizes everything. Sucks it up."

There's a mild screech in the air all of a sudden, as if Alex's finger is trying to tell us something. Alice turns her head, stares at the oximeter. "Not much left of him." She pushes another button, pulls the tube. She cups her hand on Alex's forehead, moves her index finger along his hair line. "Alex," her eyes reflect the overhead light. "Why, Alex." The device at the end of the defib cables changes its tune into an aggressive beep. "Pulse," Amy Lou says, "Where's the pulse? CPR!" she yells at Copper, bends over Alex's chest and plants vigorous kisses on Alex's mouth, hyper-French kisses I've never seen before.

She's standing next to Alex now, both hands on his sternum, one hand folded around the fist of the other, and she pushes, pushes *into* his sternum, attacking Alex's chest for all she's worth, pumping. And now she's mumbling. "Another-one-bites-the-dust, another-one-bites-the-dust."

The pencil curve is dead but the digits are still alive. "1:13" says the display when Amy-Lou breaks. "Fuck," she says, "fuck." Our eyes lock briefly. "All clear." Copper is pushing a button. Alex's body jumps, and jumps uncontrollably. He is alive again. For a sec.

Amy-Lou resumes resuscitation. "Another-one-bites-the-dust, another-one-bites-the-dust." 2:25 now. "All clear," again. Alex jumping. Silence. Three minutes. The world has come to an end.

It's stupid, but I press myself along the side-rack past Copper, bend over with some degree of circumspection, and plant a kiss on Alex's forehead. Good Bye. Stupid.

"I feel something," Amy-Lou says. The flat sound has ceased. "Kiss him again." I kiss. "Atropine," she yells, "Norepinephrine." Syringes, motions, split seconds. "All clear." Alex-jumps. "I feel a pulse," Amy-Lou says. "Endotracheal intubation." A tube goes into Alex's throat. I try to read the letter. I can't. I can't. I think I discern the words "normal," and "effort," "Benson," and "Sorry," ("SORRY," capitalized); there's no signature.

Amy-Lou resumes her pumping.

I peek across the body at the pencil display. There's life in the curve. "Adrenaline." Amy-Lou is still pumping, "Amiodarone. We have rhythm." A few preparatory gestures and a syringe go into Alex's arm. "More oxygen, 40, 45." "They rarely come back," she says.

We stare at the display some more. "Stabilizing," Alice says, "almost four minutes, let's hope for the best."

I still hold the letter in my hand.

Another look at Alex. He appears alive. We're rushing back to the Hospital. "Almost four minutes," Amy-Lou says again.

I don't know how but Maurice gets it immediately when Alex is wheeled into the room, he almost throws up. I grab his hand.

Amy-Lou pushes the bed past the British patient to the station at his right, next to the window, and connects the catatonic Alex to the IC equipment. She exits, then returns with a chair on wheels, the "Serenity Chair,"—a recliner chair, "for you"—and disappears again. I still stand there, next to Maurice, and listen to the contemporary music of life (synthetic beeps and pings from the monitors).

The door opens again and another, unknown nurse pushes another bed into the room. Another patient with a round, flat face covered by a breathing mask linked to a pressure bottle sitting on his abdomen. Various limbs are wrapped up in plaster, two limbs hung into medical space at odd angles like in a cartoon of *Grey's Anatomy*. Maurice is the first to recognize the new patient. "Benson had a serious accident," I say to Maurice, who is in no position to process this piece of information in any meaningful way. "Your patient has tried to kill, tried to murder Maurice here," I say to the nurse. The nurse links Benson to the vacant bed station opposite to Maurice. Maurice sobs.
"Where's Amy-Lou?" the nurse asks.
"Your patient has tried to kill, murder this patient here," I repeat.
"Stuff happens," the nurse says. He checks Benson's eyelids, tests the airborne limbs with his curative touch, and adds: "He can't do much harm now."

He's done, the nurse, and leaves ("Good night").

Where's Amy-Lou? I don't dare to leave Maurice alone with Benson.

Alex is still alive. Everybody is still alive. Benson is quietly breathing under his mask, lightly snoring. Maurice is sobbing. Benson's snores are coming alive, interrupting themselves, resuming rhythm. A deeper, longer snore punctuates his performance now and then; he's apparently dreaming.

This is really happening, Benson's not a wraith. Twenty minutes go by, or more. A red-eyed Amy-Lou appears in the door.

"What happened," I ask.

"I was kept on the phone," she replies, wipes a tear, "Gretchen."

"Gretchen?"

"My girlfriend."

Amy-Lou has never seen Benson. She holds some paperwork absentmindedly in her hands. Yes, patient X. She looks very tired. Maurice is still sobbing.

"Maurice needs a tranquilizer, a serious one," I say.

"Yes," she replies, waves Benson's sick-sheet, disappears, and returns with a serious-looking syringe that goes into Maurice's arm. Maurice stops sobbing.

"Later," she says, and withers away.

The room's layout is almost quadratic, four bed stations, Maurice and Alex next to each other on one side, Benson on the other side. I push the serenity chair past Alex's bed and arrange myself between him and the window, facing Benson's bed across the room, avoiding having the monster in my back.

We are all sick. Worried sick, sick at heart, sick in the head, sick of the fluorescent overhead light. It doesn't matter whether this is a dream or not, ghosts walk across the room. This goes on for quite a while, perhaps a few hours. Then the door swings open again and a new nurse appears with a small, khaki-clad man in tow. He's wearing a uniform, and the shape of his Stetson points to an affiliation with the regional sheriff office. The nurse checks the sick-sheets clipped to the bed-ends. The choice falls on Richard Benson, who is methodically disconnected from his IC gear under the watchful eye of the smallish deputy. Two other men appear, another nurse and another deputy, the nurse pushing an IV stand and holding some IV pouches that are fixed to the stand and connected to Benson. There's a ceremonial quality to this, it's like Benson's being prepared for some Mayan sacrifice. The team is ready to roll. Benson's bed wheels are un-clicked, one nurse pushes the bed, one pushes the IV stand, the two deputies secure the perimeter. Nobody says goodbye, somebody closes the door.

50 SOMEBODY TRIED TO KILL ME, POSSIBLY MYSELF

There are many moments in life when you know you're awake, and this is one of them. A narrow sound drips from the monitor above Alex's head. I'm not dreaming.

Alex is stretched out on the bed, tangled-up in IC hardware, supine (not much choice there). His face is pale and unshaven. You've possibly seen enough art house flicks to know how demi gods look in the wake of a suicide attempt. Alex doesn't quite look the part though, at least as far as I can tell from my point of view, still slouched below the horizon in the recliner. He seems awake.

"Alex," I say. He's trying to turn his head, the oxygen mask is in the way. I get up, bend over the bed, unsure whether I should remove the mask. He's realizing his encumbrance, grabs the mask with one hand, pulls on the rubber band with the other, and frees himself. He pushes some button on the side of the bed, his head rest rises until he's half-sitting. His eyes are fairly empty but far from desperate. He looks like the victim of a significant night about town, roughly.

"Alex," I say again. He stares at me as if he's somebody else.
"Who is Alex," he says.
"You, Alex."

He looks puzzled. Yes, expression is returning to the most colorful eyes in the world. I touch his forehead, he follows my movements. The last time I shed tears was when I didn't read his suicide letter—that was when he was dead. Now he is alive. As if I haven't cried enough in this soap, tears dripping down my cheek, onto my T-shirt, even onto his nose.

"Sorry," I say to him, "I didn't get enough sleep." He appears mildly puzzled.

"I'm thirsty," he says. I pour a glass of water from the sink next to the door and hand it to him.

The door swings open. This isn't Quinton or Amy-Lou, whose entry styles we know so well by now, it's Alice. Her horn-rimmed glasses are still in place, but Dr. Dyke went home earlier. Alice should consider wearing contact lenses, she's still a beautiful woman in a fundamental sense, a person who radiates mental and emotional substance—okay, the hips are somewhat in the way, but I could introduce her to my gym (where I haven't been in a week, despite my promises to Howard). She can't see Alex at first, I'm obliterating her view of the water-drinking patient. She looks at me and then at my T-shirt. There's a second until she realizes the innocent nature of the wet spots, and another second until she realizes Alex is awake. "Alex," she yells. She looks at me and grins. She cries and grins. What must the world be thinking of us? This is the best moment of my life. And Alex? What is the world thinking? Alex looks at us like sitting on a bench in the park watching kids at play. "You should eat something," Alice says to him. "Something light, like biscuits."

"I'm not hungry," he says.

"I'll get you something anyhow," she says and rings the nurse button. We stand there, breathing, recovering. The door swings open, compliments of Quinton Hayes.

"Alex," Quinton says, or blurts.

"Who is Alex?" Alex asks.

"You are Alex," Alice replies. "I am Alice."

"You are Alice," Alex says.

"You've no idea who I am?"

"Nope," Alex says.

"This guy?" She points at me.

"Nope."

"This guy?" She points at Quinton. "*Idem*," he says.

"Right," Alice says to Alex, and then to Quinton: "Let's get him a few biscuits and a cup of tea." Quinton futzes with the IC paraphernalia, replaces an IV pouch, exits.

"Listen," she says to Alex, "I think we got some work to do. How do you feel?"

"I feel drowsy," he replies. Alice casts a brief look at the monitors.

"You look better than I thought," she says, "much better. Tell me again, what's your name."

"I told you already."

"No, you didn't."

"I told you I don't know."

"I think you have amnesia," she says. "Do you know what amnesia is?"

"Yes," Alex says.

"What is amnesia, tell me."

"The loss of, or the inability to recall, memory content."

"You are unable to recall your name," Alice says.

"Is it relevant, my name?"

Alice turns to me as if she needs reassurance. "John, he can still think," she says.

"You're joking?" she says to him.

"I'm not joking."

"You know where you are?"

"In a hospital."

"Where?"

"In an IC unit."

"I mean the location, the town."

He thinks for a while. "No. Yes, hold on, we're in America."

"How do you know?"

"We speak American."

"Where in America?"

"In the South. John has a light Southern drawl, the nurse had. The flat vowels of the coastal region. We're in Georgia, on or near the coast."

Quinton reappears with a tray of cups, biscuits, and a tea pot.

"Quinton," Alice says to him, "you know Alex well."

Quinton, who's picking up on the half-merriment in the room, deposits the tray on the over-bed table, looks around, hones in on me, and, speaking mostly to my T-shirt, says "Yes." There's a touch of camp in his voice. Perhaps I should donate this shirt to the hospital and have it framed and hung on a wall, in the corner for off-color jokes.

Says Alice: "We need somebody to assure Alex of his first name."

258

"Amnesia in cases like this happens all the time. Should blow over soon. Nothing to worry about," Quinton replies. "Do you need anything else?" Alex shakes his head.

"Well, till later then," Quinton says, and disappears.

Alice pours tea and drops a piece of sugar into Alex's cup.

"You know me," Alex says.

"Yes, I do."

"You know me better than an attending physician would."

"Yes, I do."

"Even though you *are* the attending physician."

"No. Yes. The intensivist is the attending physician. I run the ER. I'm doing the night shift on a regular basis. We know each other well since you were a paramedic on the ambulance service."

"Paramedics and doctors rarely socialize."

"You do not know your name but you seem to know a lot about hospitals."

"As I should." He sips his tea. "As a paramedic." We're back to square one, does he *know* he's a paramedic, has he just learned it?

"Listen, Alex," she says, "We'd like to find out a bit more about your amnesia."

Alex casually sips his tea. "You're aware you're suffering from amnesia."

"Sure, the name, my name. Provided I have one." He grins.

"Anything else that comes to mind?"

"Yes Dr. Alice, I'm in IC and don't know why."

"But you remember my name."

"You told me."

"How about him?"—she points at me.

"John."

"You remember his name?"

"Yes"—he remembers my name—"You addressed him as John."

"So you don't remember his name."

"Well, I do."

"From a few minutes ago."

"Yes."

"Not more?"

"No." Alex looks at me as if we met fifteen minutes ago.

"Okay, so, for all we know it's not anterograde amnesia," Alice says.

"Well," he says, "it's not anterograde in the sense that I am able to recall events dating back 15 minutes. How about events dating back an hour, or five hours."

"In cases of anterograde amnesia, the window is typically one of a few minutes."

"With neural disorders one never really knows, there are always exceptions."

"We will have to do some thorough testing on you, anyhow."

"People waking up in IC with serious amnesia have typically suffered oxygen deficiency or traumas. I'm not a *smashola*, right?"

"You don't remember anything of an accident?"

"No. You have a mirror?" There's a hand mirror lying on Lady Dy's bed table (Maurice is still sleeping off the sedative of last night). Alex studies his reflection superficially and hands the mirror back to me as if this is the answer.

"You appear to have retained some of your medical knowledge," Alice says.

"Some of this knowledge tells me something is wrong," he answers.

"How about other parts of your knowledge?"

"What is my etiology?"

"We'll get to that soon."

"I am a paramedic, right?"

"Yes, Alex."

"I worked here?"

"Yes."

"Work or work*ed*."

"It's a long story."

"When did I stop working here?"

"We'll get to that soon."

"Why not now?"

"Stop it," Alice says, "what's wrong with you?"

"You're disingenuous," Alex replies.

Alice stares at him with a mix of disapprobation and relief.

Alex puts the cup away and embarks on an inspection of the IV stand next to his bed. He stretches his limbs, very consciously, deliberately. It's not the casual, feline stretching of his perfect body which triggered my hopeless crush five days ago. He rolls his head in all directions. He turns around, peeks at the real-time encephalogram on the left monitor. He turns the other way, studies the display of another, smaller device with the name *Phillips* on it.

"You ask me what's wrong with me," he says to Alice. "I tell you what's wrong with me. Somebody tried to kill me. Possibly myself."

"You need a rest," Alice says.

"It's not so difficult," Alex replies. "The naloxone drip points to an opioid overdose, possibly by a synthetic agent, oxycodone perhaps. I have been poisoned, either by myself or somebody else. In younger people, death by suicide is twice as likely as death by homicide. Two to one. But that's not all, few homicides are done by poison, less than ten percent. Which brings the odds of suicide in my case to…duh, duh, duh…twenty nine to one, roughly. Suicide. *Felo de se.*" He sips his tea. I'm surprised anything is left in the cup.

"OK, Alex, let's face it," Alice replies. "But you survived."

"Unless this is heaven. Who knows?" He laughs.

"Don't be silly," Alice says.

"Perhaps you and this guy are part of the reception committee that eases suicide victims into celestial life." He points at me.

"Suicide is a mortal sin," I say.

"Or hell, what's the difference."

"We are real," I say, "trust us."

"Heaven is also real, look around."

"It's not a joke, Alex," Alice says.

"Joke," Alex replies, "remember this joke, this biologist somehow talking to a lemming, and the lemming somehow talking back?"

"You must be tired, Alex," Alice says.

"Sort of."

"You know, Alex, *I* am tired. Really. And John here, he's tired, too."

"You've somehow been involved in this, right?" Alex asks.

"Yes, to put it mildly."

"You want me to go back to sleep?"

"Yes."

"Okay, I'll be sweet, but I haven't conceded my point."

"Which point?"

"That we are in heaven."

"We have him back," Alice says.

"I was like this before?

"On a good day."

"And on a bad day?"

"On a bad day, you would sometimes relent. Give in."

"This is a good day, then."

"A very good day, by recent standards."

"I rest my case, then, for the time being."

And with this Alex stretches like a cat, operates the side button for the headrest, goes back into horizontal, and closes his eyes.

51   FIND YOURSELF AN ALLY

L et's cut corners and tie up a few loose ends like (a) what happened to Dick Benson, or (b) what is going to happen to Maurice, or (c) what happened to Ray, or (d) what happened to everybody else, or (e) what's going to happen next?

(Ad a & b) Maurice has been kindly informed of his impending discharge from the Memorial. He's fine. Everything will be fine, Benson is in the able hands of the sheriff who will have him transferred to the Augusta Prison Hospital. Maurice is in the able hands of his next of kin, John Lee. He can't stay in his one-room apartment off Philadelphia Street all by himself for the moment, and there are still problems with his insurance. John will take him in. An outpatient nurse will drop in on us twice per day for post-surgery treatment. The ambulance is ready.

(Ad c) Which brings us to Ray. Ray will be kindly asked to spend the night on the couch in the kitchen den since Maurice needs the spare bed. I'm not going to kick Ray out, at least not during the next few minutes, the more so since he won't be there anyhow because he doesn't have the key. Yes, he does have the key, it was on the key ring that I left in the ignition of the truck. And Ray is at home since he had the guts to climb onto the driver's seat after our departure, shift the transmission handle into "D," and turn the steering wheel into the direction he wanted to go. He didn't even spend the night at the Blue Moon.

(Ad d) What happened to everybody else? That would be me, John Lee, of Georgia Beach, GA, 29 years old, assistant professor of French, who met Alex Iglesias 24 hours ago in the hospital, when he (Alex) took kindly notice of yours truly.

(Ad e) What's going to happen next? Let's find out. Alex is no longer in IC but has been transferred to the trauma ward, where blood tests and the surgeon can't find much wrong with him, except for the usual amnesia. A *Mental State Examination* (MSE) will be administered by Dr. Karen, but Karen called in sick and will be replaced by a social worker. Her name is *Mary-Ann,* and she has the right diplomas and has already arrived. I'm next of kin, correct? Sure, I'm the next of kin from central casting, Maurice

Dymond, Ray Mayang, Alex Iglesias, you name it, we could be brothers. We're actually congregating in Maurice's former room 3-16, the room of Benson's murder attempt. I tell Alex who kindly takes note, there's even a question mark in his eyes. Alice has called, she'll drop by later.

Mary-Ann has the right diplomas, but not quite. Her reach under the Georgia statutes extends no further than the Mini-MSE questionnaire, and she would like to know whether Alex is overweight or emaciated, whether he is unshaven (yes, under the circumstances), there are no wounds, he's dressed for the occasion, and so on. His mood, yes. "Your mood?"

"Fine."

"Apathetic?"

"Fine." The new Alex again, although the old one could also have done it—generating just the right amount of ambiguity by means of verbal parsimony. Fine.

"Agitated."

"No."

"Tense?"

"No."

And so on. Something must be wrong with him.

"Other signs."

"No."

"Ambivalence."

"No."

(I would say 'yes' but am not asked). And so on.

What do you do with patient patients? You proceed. You dig into your administrative tote bag and issue a little blue booklet that you hold up as if you're from *Jehovah's Witnesses*. Then you lower the booklet into your field of vision and read from its pages: "Today may feel like the hardest day of your life."

"It feels more like the *second* day of my life," Alex answers, but Mary-Ann ignores the clue, concentrates instead on the next quote: "You have seriously thought about or perhaps attempted to end your life. You may be exhausted. A common experience after surviving a suicide attempt is extreme fatigue. You may be angry. You may be embarrassed or ashamed. The attempt itself, the reactions of other people, transportation to and treatment in an emergency department or other healthcare facility—all these can be overwhelming to you right now. But, recovery is possible and all the feelings you are probably experiencing right now can get better."

"Say that again," Alex says. A moment confusion reigns until Mary-Ann's body language threatens a repeat performance; Alex catches her just in time: "Only the last sentence."

"But, recovery is possible and all the feelings you are probably experiencing right now can get better."

"You sure about the punctuation?"

Punctuation, she is not so sure. "There's no comma after the 'possible,' right." No, there isn't. "Don't you think there should be one?" It takes a little while until she declares defeat. Alex, we have you back.

Yes, we have him back: "And the extension of the second noun phrase, provided we did insert the comma after 'possible,' you sure there's no shifting sands happening in the second noun phrase?"

"Shifting sands?"

"In that the extension of the 'feelings' you've so courageously quantified shifts underhandedly when we move from experience to improvement, I mean your 'getting better'?"

She looks at me.

"He's not schizophrenic," I whisper to her, "don't worry, he does it all the time." She is not so sure.

"You don't feel depressed at all, Alex, right?" I ask. "Not at all, right?"

"Not at all."

"How do you feel?"

"Great. As if I'm floating." He turns to the social worker. "Carry on."

We learn that there is a shortage of hospital beds in many parts of the country, but the mental health-care providers will "work with" you, "if appropriate," and "create a safety plan as part of your discharge instructions," and make sure they have your phone number and, yes, one more thing: "it is very important that you have at least one person in your life who can be your ALLY. This must be a person you trust and can be very honest with—especially if you start to have thoughts of ending your life again. Family members or a close friend can serve this important purpose."

"Work with me," Alex repeats.

She looks at me. "Your brother?"
"No," I say, "just a friend."

She looks at me again. She's evaluating me, carefully, to the best of her abilities. You can see her wrestling with the rules of inference. Alex can see it as well.

"How about your family?" Mary-Ann asks.
"How about my family?"
"His family is okay," I say.
"They work with me," Alex adds, "ask John."

The door opens, and Alice, not in her white coat today, projects a matt-green paper box into the room, follows the box, and says: "Alex, Alex." She looks younger today, she possibly slept well. I'm reneging on my contact-lens observation, she should keep the horn-rimmed glasses.
"I'm Alice," she says to the social bureaucrat.
"You're his mother?" Mary-Ann asks.
"More his sister," Alice says, "we're brothers and sisters, in a sense."

Mary-Ann is very pleased to meet a better next-of-kin, the more so since her time is up, there are more suiciders out there that need her assistance. "I just said to"—a brief look at her sheets—"Alex, Alex, how important it is to have an ally, a member of your inner family, whom he can trust if thoughts of ending his life again cross his mind." She raises the suicidal brochure one more time (the brochure is printed in steely, assertive blue, hex value #2900a7), hands it to Alice, and gracefully exits. Almost. "I think Alex is ready for discharge," she says. Goodbye.

"Macaroons, Alex," Alice says and hands the box to him, "your favorites." Alex is mildly perplexed.
"I see. My favorites? Interesting." He opens the box—yummy stuff in understated colors—and offers one to Alice who does not hesitate.
"They are certainly *your* favorites," he says.
"How do you know?" Alice replies.

266

"Have another one." Alice obliges. I feel ignored. "John," he says to me, "you were my friend, right. Do I like macaroons?" He extends the box in my direction.

I have no idea. "Yes," I say. I briefly consider whether to decline the double-decker sweet, then accept it.

He finally puts a macaroon in his mouth, munches tentatively.

"My favorites," he says. "Sure. Great. Thank you."

"John, you said you were my friend, right?" Alex asks.
"Yes."
"You *are* my friend?"
"Yes."
"How about my family?"
"Good question," I say.
"How old am I?"
At least, I know his age. "Twenty nine."
"I'm twenty-nine. Just attempted suicide. There's no family to speak of? To work with?"

I'm chewing on the sweet. What do I know?
"They live somewhere else," Alice says.
"I could be married, right? Have children?"
"You have no children."
"How about a partner, a wife?"
"No wife." she says.
"Figures," Alex says, "she would be here now. I could be divorced, though. Not divorced?"
"Not divorced," Alice says.
"You've heard this social worker," he says to me, "I need an ally. How about girlfriends."
"Girlfriends don't make good allies," Alice says, "I speak from experience." She looks at me. "Alex, you'll have to do with us," (she rests her hand on my shoulder) "John here, and myself. We're your allies."
"Thanks," Alex says. He seems unconvinced. He seems so unconvinced, Alice has to add: "All the girls I know are in love with you."
"You are a girl, too," Alex says, more matter-of-fact than joking.
"Yes."
"You are not my partner, right. Never been?"
"I'm lesbian," Alice says, "I'm a dyke."

267

"Right," Alex says.

"How to explain this," Alice says, "Here, John, here, he's your partner."

Don't ask me how Alex ~~looked~~ glared at me. "Right," he says. We're cool.

**

We're in the truck now, I'm taking him home. He has been discharged with an appointment for the suicide officer to work with and the stern warning not to go back home immediately where bad memories could overwhelm him. Alice had cast a last, critical glance at my T-shirt (still the old one, no time for the launderette), asked for my address and indicated she will swing by tomorrow. She has talked to Harrison, the hospital director, who had already revoked Alex's dismissal, his assistant had trespassed under his name. Alex could have had followed the conversation but isn't really interested. It's hard to tell what he's interested in, certainly not in me. He's floating. He's interested in the sky.

"You remember about Georgia Beach?" I ask while turning onto Route One. No, he doesn't, at least not clearly. So I explain a bit.

"We're going to your place, right?" he asks.

"Yes."

"But we don't live together?"

"No."

"But we are partners."

"You've heard Alice."

"Since when?"

"Some time," I say, "let me think."

I'm not only lying, I lost count. Was it five days? Six days since we met in the dunes?

"Sexually. We are sexual partners?"

"We were."

"Interesting." He stares through the wind shield, not unlike the way Ray stared through the same shield two days ago.

268

"Listen, Alex, I have to tell you, my place is a mess." I explain about Ray (on the couch), and Maurice (in the spare bed). Next of kin.

"We'll sleep in the same bed, then?" he asks.

"Yes."

"Don't get me wrong."

"We have not much choice at the moment."

"I don't want to sound old-fashioned," he says, "but the prior probability of me being gay is what, five to ten percent."

"*Prior* probability," I say.

"In the absence of additional information."

"…" (I almost say something).

"But I don't have it," he says, "the additional information. How do I know I'm gay?"

"Didn't Alice tell you?"

"Alice told, me, right."

"What can I say, it's really not my fault."

"Not your fault," he says.

"I love you," I say.

"You love me, right. I love you too, I guess, right?"

The cell rings. It's somebody for the escort service. The A-level escort service, serving Georgia Beach and environs, internet-based, family-owned. The first paying customer.

Alex is not interested in my phone conversation. He is still convalescing, he'll have a nap.

Nick's Restaurant occupies the most important location in Georgia Beach on the corner of Georgia Avenue and the boardwalk, a fact that won't surprise you if you met the charismatic, handsome, and extremely straight owner who sent us the naked girls (for the blog), and who has resurfaced recently as an intimate acquaintance of Muffy & Jane. Nick's joint is also the largest eatery on the planet— expansive multileveled decks, multiple bar rooms, multiple beer gardens, a stage (rock stars, bikini contests), views (beach, sea, Noonan statue), and *Georgia Crabs* as the principal special on the menu (I explain later).

We are not there yet. Alex is sleeping in my bed, whereas I, who could be lying with Alex, not euphemistically lying with him, mind you, just literally—not doing anything special, just being there, next to him—while I could be lying with Alex, I'm lying with Chris, my first market-rate-paying A-level client. More specifically, I am posing, stark naked, as far as I can tell. I was still half-dressed when Chris got hold of the *Sinvention Deprivation Hood* which is now strapped over my head and which, as she explained beforehand (I cannot hear her now) offers a sensation of "complete nothingness" and "confinement." So I had to infer, mostly from *proprioception* (the sixth sense of the position of the limbs), that I was being disrobed, and strapped to something (I caught a glimpse of a mega-sized mahogany cross fastened to the bedroom wall with restraining cuffs on each arm).

So now I'm inferring from my sense of hurt that I'm being flogged, or flagellated, since how else would you interpret the repeated sensation of searing pain on your skin, on the chest, mostly, but also on the upper arms and the thighs? I don't know whether I'm aroused—that's the idea, right, this isn't going to stop until some sex act is being performed, so I'm trying hard to let it flow and absorb the pain, like Wall-Street types would absorb human contact to get at their bonus. The searing stops, alright, and I feel something near my groin, a hold around my dick, moving up from the shaft to the cock-head, and a mild contraction of the cock-head under the influence of outside forces (a kiss?), and a repetition of gesticulations that would remind a saner person of oral sex, whereas I have lost my mind to nothingness and confinement and also my erection since I'm in the throes of a searing claustrophobia. This goes on for a while until it stops. Searing and burning of skin resume, and if there ever was any playfulness during the first round of this *BDSM* it's definitely gone now, the novice slave experiencing a dominatrix of mounting anger living out her darkest instincts on the hapless A-level escort.

And when we're finally done she wouldn't even pay. "No erection, no compensation," she said. Rhymes a bit. "Basic," she added.

So I'm crawling home in my truck, where a new and improved Alex awaits me. He had a good nap and is completely suicide-free. "Let's go for a walk," he says. Ray is shopping (Maurice gave him some money). Maurice himself is enthralled in his Freedom Fries script, informing us that he has Doubya now reading Krugman's "Depression Economics" while Laura is about to call *Dick Cheney* and everything "is going pear-shaped." I have no idea what he's talking about and no time to change clothes.

I can barely walk (there's even blood), but I can't explain, obviously. Georgia Beach has a beach, he knows. How to get there? John will know. So I'm hurtling next to Alex along the Davis canal in the downtown direction. He puts his arm around my shoulder as if he's testing his sexual preferences—or perhaps not, since there's this distinctive camaraderie to his touch that football coaches and oncologists are so good at.
"John," he says.

We shortcut in lockstep through the ghetto of Georgia Beach, black kids play soccer. He's leading, in fact, although he's unsure about the direction. "John," he says again. "How do you do."
"Fine."
"You don't look the part."
"I'm exhausted," I say, "It'll blow over."
"I understand. You were with me, right? Then. When it happened."
"Yes."
"You discovered me?"
"Yes."
"It's you who needs to recover, really." (I know, I know).

"How do *you* feel?" I ask.

"I'm floating. Still. Like this morning. Like I said. I haven't conceded my point, you know, I could be in heaven. A depression did me in, right? I don't feel depressed at all."

"It looks as if the amnesia has taken care of your depression."

"Yes. Looks like."

His touch lightens. "So, we are partners?" he asks with this new, unbalanced expression in his eyes.

"Yes, in a sense."

"In a sense...In which sense aren't we?"

"We're not in a civil union, say."

"We couldn't, Georgia doesn't recognize civil unions."

"We're not living together."

"Today we did."

"Ask Alice."

"About what?"

"Our partnership."

"We could be wearing wedding bands, or partner bands."

"I don't like rings."

"Or go on a honeymoon. We could have gone on partner moon, honey." He grins.

"Yes."

"Did we?"

"We had no time."

"Or a mini moon."

"I don't know," I say, "mini moon."

"Like *mini me*. For people who are too busy for a full moon."

"Honey-wise?"

"Honey-wise. *Mike Myers*, mini-me. Did we go for a mini-moon?"

"In a sense."

"In a sense?"

"We went for a walk on the beach. That was our mini-moon. You talked about destiny. You said it was destiny that we met."

"Where did we meet?"

"In the dunes."

"Which dunes?"

"The cruising area."

"We met in the cruising area. Let me think. Meeting in the cruising area, not a bad idea, in fact, it would at least confirm my sexual orientation."

"Yes."

"But it wouldn't be destiny. It's what gays do, meeting in cruising areas for casual sex."

"You meant the second time we met. That was destiny."

"How did we meet the second time?"

"You were on the ambulance, the ambulance that picked up Maurice."

"Maurice?"

"Maurice."

"Maurice is still bedridden."

"Yes."

"He collapsed, what, a week ago, I guess."

"I lost count," I say.

"A week is seven days."

"Seven long days."

"We must have been busy."

"You could say that."

"Like calling each other."

"Yes."

"But too busy to register phone numbers."

"You know how it is."

"There is no John contact on my cell phone."

"I wouldn't know. We called."

"Or exchange emails. There is no message from you in my inbox."

"Perhaps you deleted them."

"There's no message to you in my outbox."

"I don't know."

"If Sherlock Holmes, say, would enter your apartment in hot pursuit, or cold pursuit, more like him, if he would enter your apartment in search of any evidence of your relationship with a certain Alexander Iglesias, if that's my name, what would he find?"

I am saved by Nick. We have arrived at the head of Georgia Avenue where Nick is standing next to the restaurant's main inlet, admiring a backed-up stream of patrons as if he is starring in a movie about himself. I'm able to write this up now; I wasn't able to think it then because I had been doing what people in my situation tended to do before they had a chance to hear my story, people who had been beaten up by an ill-

273

tempered dominatrix and were subsequently questioned by the amnesia-challenged love of their life about sexual preferences. Those people would not hold their chin up high and alter the angle of the head backwards, exposing the neck, which is a signal of strength, resilience, resistance and so on. No, they would look at their dirty sneakers, and then let their eyes travel along their legs and past their pelvises and other parts of their bodies where a sense of still-searing pain would be confirmed by strings of rust-colored goo seeping through the fabric of their clothes. Alex hadn't noticed those strings yet, but would surely do so soon. And I guess I was smelly. The sour smell of sweat enhanced by the metallic odor of drying blood, and perhaps even a whiff of the up-scale leather of the Sinvention Deprivation Hood still lingering in my hair.

Nick, right. I had met Nick first on the internet several years ago and then in person after having posted a review of his restaurant with redundant questions about the authenticity of his Georgia Crabs, a post that prompted a disarming message regarding his upbringing in Maryland and the freedom of speech. His Georgia Crabs were, it transpired, legal immigrants from the *Chesapeake Bay* prepared according to a recipe from his mother.

Alex isn't gay anymore, but he urgently needs to take his eyes off my clothes, so I introduce him to Nick. Nick has the brilliant idea that we're hungry and ushers us past the queue and the Maître d' and cannot find a table for us because Nick's restaurant is packed, packed even more than usual on a Saturday night. I discover a familiar face in the crowd, Amy-Lou. It isn't her day, exactly. She's looking very sad, as if Alex's depression has jumped bodies during the CPR, but she manages a smile when she sees me and switches to a wide, proud grin when she recognizes Alex. Nick finds a waiter to squeeze in two chairs somehow next to and opposite to Amy at one of the long picnic tables shared by tipsy tourists and orders crabs and white wine for us.

Alex is seated next to Amy-Lou, I'm seated cross-table on the other side. Bottles, tumblers, cans, dishes, newspapers everywhere, even on the tables (the crabs are served with a newspaper that provides a repository for the carcasses; you eat with your hands). People happily share around the table, so many people wanting to share reminiscences and food and dirty jokes, there's a certain dynamics that feeds on the decibels and the booze and itself. The stage is not far away, and Nick, having donned the wig of an elderly rock star, is already singing *Don Henley's* "Boys of the Summer," and winks at us with his left eye.

So, there we are. Destiny again. Amy-Lou's a bit puzzled at first that she has to be introduced to an Alex whom she knows so well, but that's the way it is for deputy head nurses of IC units who bring the dead back to life. Anyhow, she's alone—didn't she have a lesbian lover somehow, Gretchen? We will learn later that they just had a fight—and she's taking things increasingly lightly, the more so since she's not so alone any more with Alex nearby. Alex has taken an immediate liking to her. "I've been the victim of a serious suicide attempt," he says.

Let me interrupt myself briefly and tell an anecdote to calm us all down. I once met a guy, a fairly distinguished British economist, whose three big problems were that (a) he had written one famous book, but only *one*, (b) drink, and (c) the fact that all his friends had won Nobel prizes (some even uneconomical ones, like *Francis Crick*). He's visiting the University of Maryland (yes, Maryland again) and the department of economics needs a new chairman. Robin, that was his first name, Robin, as an outsider, would be the ideal candidate for the job. So he's invited for an interview with the provost. It's already ten o'clock in the morning and Robin is completely drunk. He's so smashed, he cannot speak. The provost makes him an offer he cannot resist. Robin cannot answer. Robin must be raising the ante, the provost thinks, and so improves on the terms of his offer. Robin still mum. This goes back and forth for a while until Robin finally manages to say "yes" to a compensation package of seismic proportions. I kid you not, he told me the story himself.

Analogies always break down somewhere, and this one breaks down immediately, except that Amy-Lou doesn't know what to say. She laughs, finally, and leaves it to me to explain who saved lives here. Life. Us escorts is always glad to assist, although lending a helping hand going forward will be complicated by the rising decibels around the table. Never mind, Alex is very grateful to Amy-Lou. He enjoys life now, a lot. He's completely depression-free. A lot.

Anyhow, I am sitting infinitely far away on the other side of the wide table and try to eat my crab. The trick is, the crab is battered in a mix of herbs and spices that stick to your fingertips as you are undoing the carcass and then rub off on the crabmeat as you progress. The secret is thus in the spicy mix, which is mixed according to a secret formula, a formula for which people will kill in the next part of this soap opera (perhaps). I'm saying this because I really need you to stay tuned although you must be tired by now, the *x*-th time in six days that your narrator is doing the same trick on you, having himself casually ditched by the love of his life for extraneous reasons.

I know, the messiness of my eating won't make me more attractive in Alex's eyes—and, of course, he's considerably less messy with his own crab. Amy-Lou, who had hers before we arrived, has all the time in the world to behold Alex's dexterity with starry eyes, not to mention his other qualities and attributes. It's unbelievable how Alex fingers the seafood while his green eyes are sunk deeply into Amy-Lou's peepers. This goes on forever, until the lovebirds remember me, and, by implication, my T-shirt, which, in the meantime, must have acquired the flavor of a *Jackson Pollock* painting done in real blood (Pollock had these fantasies about using blood and sperm for his paintings and actually lived them out, according to some sources).

Amy-Lou points at it (my shirt), and Alex points at it, and they giggle—almost giggle, you can see them trying to stay polite—only one of them asking pointed questions (I forgot which one). And I, although I should not be able to understand them, the questions—drowned as I am in the drunken decibels around me—I'm answering too impulsively to make any difference. For a brief moment I understand the meaning of 'queer.'

Amy-Lou must have some second thoughts now, puzzled as she should be by the difference between my stains today and the cum-spots three days ago. But she is taking another gulp of chardonnay while I am distracted by the thought that the original cum-shirt could have swayed Alex if only I would have shown it to him ("Here, Alex, this is your jizz"). And then Amy-Lou points at me again, with her right index finger (her left hand is busy somewhere else), and I know, I just know what she is saying to him although I cannot hear her.

"He proposed to me, you know, John proposed to me a couple of days ago," she says to Alex and giggles again. Both laugh and giggle and swill the wine, and all inhibitions are gone, and he's holding her hand, and the lonely cum-squirrel gets up and runs away.

The sun has set in the meantime and on my life. So I stagger through the street lighting of Georgia Avenue, turn on Second Street and then on Philadelphia. This is the shortcut to the other side of the canal and will get me up to the overpass next to the condo. Jumping off that cliff would be the first fail-safe suicide opportunity coming my way. You remember that joke, Wile E. Coyote talking to a lemming.

Some bum staggers down the sidewalk ahead of me, whistling an old tune, off-key. I realize it's Neill, the rice-queen-to-riches person from Godehart's party, tootling a *Springsteen*-song from this *Tom Hanks* movie. I'm trying to sneak past, but Neill recognizes me and grabs my shoulder.

"John," he ~~says~~ slurs.

"Neill," I say.

"How are you," he says, over-accentuating his speech.

"Good," I say.

"Good," he replies, using my shoulder as support, "what's up man?"

"Not my day," I say.

"Did you find Alex?"

"Huh?"

"Alex, remember, the other day." Right, at Walmart, I had asked whether he had seen Alex.

"No," I say. I need to get out of this and die quickly. He starts whistling again.

"Philadelphia," he slurs, "brotherly love."

"I know," (I've never been good or effective with drunks despite my own alcohol intake).

"Philadelphia," he slurs, "I saw the doctor yesterday."

"Sure," I say.

"My count is below hundred now," he slurs.

"Your count?" (stupid, John, why do you ask).

"My count. CeeDee. CeeDee four."

As a raving homosexual I should know about these things but don't, exactly.

"CeeDee," I say.

"Helper cells. Tiny little cells. For your resistance. The virus kills them."

"Sure," I say.

"Don't be offended."

"It's not your fault," I say.

"I'm going to die."

"Nobody dies of AIDS anymore, you'll be all-right."

"Multiple strains, I've got multiple strains. HIV strains. Too many. Medication … control … overwhelmed."

"I'm sorry to hear that."

"I'm one cold away from dying. Or one cancer. Opportunistic cancer"—he over-accentuates again, 'Cancer'. "I'm going to change my will, leave everything to AIDS."

"You can't leave anything to AIDS, it's a disease, it's not a person, or a charity."

Speak first, think later. I don't know how to explain this, but saying this I suddenly realize that the old John is still around, the John that lived 29 years without Alex, the John who's *not* going to die tonight because he's a coward and also because some of his secondary cockiness is still left in him. So I won't jump off the cliff tonight, instead I will use the direct route home through the ghetto and go to bed. Goodbye, Neill, change of plan.

"I'm going to change my will, leave everything to AIDS," Neill repeats.

"You should leave something to Ray," I say, "he needs money, Ray," (perhaps I could claim a commission).

"Ray?"

"Sure you know Ray, the oriental boy, the Malay, sure you know him, he's been around forever."

"There are so many Rays," he slurs, "they're all called Ray. Or Jason."

"I'll introduce you," I say, "Ray needs help." Impossible they haven't met biblically.

"We all need help. I'll leave the money to myself," he slurs.

"You can't do that either."

"I'm scared of death."

"Yes. We all are."

"You have a knife?"

"A knife?"

279

"A knife."

(I don't, of course. I don't even own an AK47.)
And now I'm thinking the worst thought of this soap. An unspeakable thought.

I have a knife. I had a knife. The Swiss army knife from the ambulance. Amy-Lou's knife. I kept it. I picked it up when we left the ambulance, absurd, but that's what you do when people die. I feel in my pockets. I didn't change my shorts, right. Yes, there it is, the knife that Copper used to cut Alex's shirt. I hand it to Neill. Neill pockets the knife, haphazardly.

"Ray needs money," I say, "You can find him in the Blue Moon," (other direction, we would have to part ways, regrettably).

"Blue Moon."

"Darkroom, Blue Moon."

"Darkroom."

"You can find Ray in the darkroom, always."

"Yes, I remember Ray."

"Ray Mayang. Leave your money to Ray."

"You have something to write? For the will."

(I don't, of course, I didn't even bring the cell-phone.)

I paw my shorts. This cannot be. The oblong touch of a pen. I feel it in the pocket, father's ballpoint from his Chevy. I hand it to Neill. "And paper, I need paper," he slurs. It doesn't matter now. We've reached the end of an absurd play, Godot has finally shown up. I paw my shorts again. The back pocket rustles. A sheet of paper. Used. Alex's suicide letter. It's no longer needed. I hand it to him. "You can use the other side," I say.

"I'm lost," he slurs, pocketing the fumbled sheet, "which direction?"

"The Blue Moon?"

"The Blue Moon."

"That way," I point. "Take care," I say, "stay in touch." He staggers away.

D id the doorbell ring or not?

Wasn't it *Sarah Palin* who once said that history repeats itself as a farce? Or as romantic comedy? There's always a moment when you know you are awake, but there is no such thing when it comes to sleep, or doorbells. Did the doorbell ring or not?

There's a reverberation of the mattress, like somebody's sitting down (Ray must have answered the bell). Or lying down, or getting under the blanket, or somehow sidling up to me.

That's all I remember until I wake up with serious morning wood. I am still alive. And I had a wet dream. Apparently.

What is it when you wake up to the sound of a campy voice from the kitchen that informs another voice, a politely listening voice, ("uhuh, uhuh"), about the mental voyage of a certain Doubya Bush, and how he got kidnapped, and escaped, and got divorced, and fell in love with the voluptuous dean of Berkeley Law School (female?), who's going to be appointed to the Supreme Court by Barack Hussein?

Anyhow, the smell of the fresh coffee is wafting into my room. The people in the kitchen should be cool about morning wood, but I'm shy, so I make noises, suggestively, hoping somebody will take note, the door's agape, they might hear me. And yes, it worked; a shadow darkens the bedroom door and a cup appears on the bed-side table. This is the first time in my life (I'm exaggerating). This is the first time in quite some time I'm on the receiving end of breakfast in bed.

I drink the coffee and wait for the boner to subside. I have never been fully at ease with my dick (save during sex), but the thing behaves, subsides, and I can take a leak. I enter the kitchen and Alex stretches like a cat. "More coffee?" he asks, gets up, and pours another cup for me.

Maurice doesn't want another cup. He's still feeling weak, he says. "Shall we resume our conversation later," he asks a bit too considerately and drags himself back into the spare bedroom. Ray's lying on the couch, half-asleep, until he realizes that my bed is no longer occupied. He disappears in the direction of my chamber. I take the chair next to Alex. We're both watching the water tower. We could be brothers.

"The water tower," I say to Alex.

"Yes, I know," he replies.

"You remember?"

"What?"

"Us, talking about the water tower?"

"No."

"How do you know, then?"

"I know about the water tower, and Georgia Beach in general, just get confused about directions. Directions appear to be borderline. Amnesia-wise. Forgot everything about my personal life, remember a lot about everything else."

"You like the water tower?"

"You like it?"

"I'm like the only person in the world who doesn't like the Sydney opera house."

"The Sydney opera house, right. Don't remember whether I liked it or not. Let me think. Let me get it on my mind's eye. Looks like a clam, right, several clams, clams playing domino, right?"

"Sort of."

"You have a picture somewhere?"

He looks around. His eyes fall on the iPad on the kitchen table, the i-thing he gave to me the night before his suicide. "Let's have a look," he says, grabs it, hits the touch screen a few times. The internet isn't willing though, *Safari* returns an error message.

"You've got no Wi-Fi?" he asks.

"Yes," I say, "but never had a chance to use your pad, it doesn't know the WEP code for the Wi-Fi connection."

"This is my pad?"

"Yes, you gave it to me, the day before your, uuhh, accident."

"Right," he says and hands it to me.

I be-fumble the thing under his critical eyes. He's patient. Well, he shows a certain degree of patience. "Listen," he says, "whatever happens, I really love you."

He looks at me, taken aback. "What?" he says.

It's the i-thing. The pad that talked.

"It has your voice," I say and hand it back to him. He taps on the screen a few times.

"It's a recording," he says, "This is my voice? I don't recognize my voice." He pushes two buttons, says "This is my voice," pushes two more buttons, and replays his words. "This is my voice. I must have recorded it. Yes, here, on Wednesday, 5:33 PM. Last Wednesday. Interesting. I'm in love. Or was. I wonder whom I was talking to."

"You were talking to me."

"Why don't you give me your WEP code so we can have a look at the Sidney opera house?" he says.

"Why did you come back?" I say.

"Amy-Lou gave me a ride."

"In the early morning?"

"Yes."

"Why?"

"Well, she did."

"Why?"

"She had to go somewhere. Something about her friend. Gretchen. She got a phone call. She didn't explain."

"So she dropped you?"

"She gave me a ride. She lives in Lewes. Would be too far to walk."

"Sex was great?"

"Sure it was. Always is."

"How do you know, with your amnesia?"

"You're troubled by the quantifier?"

"The '*always*,' yes."

"No so difficult, in my case. I had sex three times in my life. As far as I remember. Twice with her, once with you."

"With me, you had sex with me?"

"Well, perhaps not under the most stringent of interpretations. You were asleep. But I got between the sheets, got an erection, penetrated, had an ejaculation. I didn't want to wake you up, you must have had a rough day yesterday. You slept through the whole thing. We got laid, yes."

"So it wasn't a wet dream then."

"You came as well?"

"There were some traces."

"Interesting. Sheer serendipity. Didn't want to wake you up. Screwing without fucking, cool. Didn't know I had it in me."

"It's a well-known technique, invented by the Knights of Malta."

"Really. I didn't know. Who knows. Apes could have invented it. Possibly did. Great sex."

"You'll do it again?"

"Now?"

"The bed is occupied."

"We should let him sleep, Ray."

"We could go to the beach, Alex. Have sex in the dunes."

"Sure, John," he says.

"You surprise me," I say. "Yesterday you sounded not so sure."

"I haven't conceded my point."

"Of not being gay?"

"Of not being in heaven."

"How do you mean?"

"I never conceded the point. Remember, our discussion two days ago, in the hospital, whether I'm dead or alive? Post *felo de se*? For all practical purposes, I could be dead. I could be in heaven. This is heaven. Alice is heaven. Maurice is. Ray is. Amy-Lou is heaven. You are heaven."

"It wasn't heaven for me, yesterday, believe me."

"Let me think. You have a minute?"

"Yes."

"Can I string sixteen sentences in a row?"

"Yes."

"Some people thought seriously about this. *Leibniz* say, the guy who also-invented the calculus. Leibniz held that ours is the best of all possible worlds. Was much-maligned by *Voltaire*, of course, whose arguments were pure rhetoric, Voltaire's. In the same mold as the arguments for Intelligent Design. Anyhow, the trick is, the trick of the possible world argument, even God is constrained. But he's around. He created this world. So it's the best of all possible worlds. Assume. So it doesn't matter whether it's heaven or hell, for as long as it's the best of all possible worlds. No big deal, I mean, I'm sorry for you, of course, I know we misbehaved, Amy-Lou and I. I know. She knows as well. She's sorry, I think. I'm sorry."

"You had this French guy, Sartre, who said '*l'enfer, c'est les autres'*."

"Meaning?"

"Hell is other people."

"See, that's my point. We are sorry. We'll ask you to be our best man at the wedding."

I believe it, I believe it—for a second, seven seconds, fourteen seconds—he is aware of this.

"You love me," he says twenty seconds into this.

"Yes, I do."

"See? This is heaven."

"You heard what you said? On the pad? You know you said it to me?" I ask.

"You're not a good liar."

"I'm not lying."

"That's what I mean."

"Huh?"

"There would be too much of a story to make up. It must have been you. The night before the suicide. It was you, of course. Perhaps I recorded it on purpose. Just in case. Only 10 percent of suicides by OD are successful. Let's go to the dunes, have fun."

I'm skipping a few details now, we're off to the beach, find a parking space, and are already walking southbound along the waterline, our dirty sneakers being played with (and partially cleaned by) (the) immeasurable Atlantic ocean.

"Look," I say, "you don't have to love me."

"Obviously."

"You could have changed your mind. Your amnesia could have changed your sexual orientation."

"Would it matter, the sexual orientation? For as long as I love you?"

"Sure it would."

"Think this through," he says. "Consider the chance of me being gay, provided I love you. Compare it to the chance of me loving you, provided I'm gay."

"Yes."

"Look at the odds."

285

I have to think. I'm still thinking when he interrupts me: "And you don't want me to love you because Alice called and dropped more hints while you were out."

"Alice called you?"

"She called *upon* me. Us, in fact. Brought me some clothes. And the cell phone. She had been to my apartment. She regretted your absence. I had to explain."

"You explained my absence? How could you have known?"

"I didn't. There were some cues of course, with hindsight, which I didn't have at the time, the hindsight, by definition."

"Of my engagement yesterday afternoon?"

"If that's the word, engagement, I mean the time you must have spent in the company of one or more persons involved in activities that any disinterested observer would qualify as BDSM."

"How do you know?"

"I got a glimpse at your naked body this morning. Not to mention your T-shirt yesterday."

"Well, it wasn't exactly an engagement."

"It wasn't an engagement?"

"It was an out-call."

"An out-call?"

"Yes."

"And what is that, an out-call, if I may ask?"

"It pays. An out-call pays."

"How much?"

"Well, she didn't pay."

"She?"

"Chris, she, yes."

"And you get all worked-up about sexual preferences."

"Money has no gender."

"Why do you do out-calls?"

"Because we need the money."

"We need the money?"

"Yes, I'm about to lose my job, and you lost yours."

"So we are driven into prostitution by destitution?"

"Yes."

"Best of all worlds, come to think of it. Perhaps Voltaire had a point, after all."

"Yes."

"But it wasn't prostitution, after all?"

"How do you mean?"

"She didn't pay."

"No."

"Why?"

"I failed to maintain an erection."

"During BDSM. You failed to maintain an erection during bondage, dominance, sadism, and masochism."

"Yes, during BDSM. If you will."

"Well, at least you were not cheating on me." He rolls his head.

We're still walking down the beach. The alpha dog picks up a pebble, sends it off with a flip of his hand across the water, where it obliges, naturally, re-bouncing, traveling along the ocean surface till it reaches the end of the world.

"So, John, let's reset. You wouldn't want me to love you because Alice told me to do so?"

"No."

"And you wouldn't want me to love you because it would hurt you too much if I don't?"

"Huh?"

"Let's simplify. Would you love somebody because he loves you?"

"Possibly not."

"Would you love somebody because he brought you back from the dead?"

"Amy-Lou brought you back from the dead."

"She said *you* did."

"*She* did. *She* performed the CPR."

"She said it was *your* kiss. You kissed me back to life."

"I didn't kiss you back to life. I planted a kiss on your forehead to say goodbye. You were dead then."

"So, I'm right then."

"How?"

"You didn't kiss me back to life, Amy-Lou didn't bring me back from the dead. Q-E-D. I'm in heaven. Everything is heaven. Even you are heaven, not cheating on me despite the challenging circumstances of an out-call."

"And so are Amy-Lou, and Alice. According to your logic."

287

"Who didn't cheat on me either."

"You know what I mean. Why should you love me?"

"Because, John, you are unique among us angels. You are the only angel who *needs* my love. Who *wants* it. Why shouldn't I love you back? We're in heaven together. Wishes are fulfilled in here."

"I didn't know."

"Now you do," he says and rolls his head again.

He halts his steps. No, he stops. It's in between. We've arrived at the gay beach. He turns sideways, we're facing each other. He touches my cheeks, plays with my tousled hair. He squeezes my nose. He touches my absent love handles, just to make sure (I guess). He slips a finger down my tummy, almost reaching an erogenous zone. He looks at me, from top to bottom. His eyes drift out to the sea, return. He stares at me with his new, unbalanced eyes. He embraces my cheeks again, squeezes his lips onto my lips for a kiss. "I love you," he says. He embraces me fully now, his arms around my body, his tongue traveling deep into gay territory, he kisses, touches, embraces my mouth, my selfishness, my cynicism, my innocence, my stupidity, my soul.

All this takes quite some time since it is done in slow motion. As mentioned earlier, we're on the water's edge, the surf plays with our sneakers. Next to us, a Georgia Flamingo picks on a worm (C. Elegans).

There is some funny, clappy noise. I turn around. Alex is kissing what he can with my face turned to the beach crowd, so he kisses my right cheek, and the flank of my nose, my ear, it's quite funny. There's this guy standing there, a young black queen, and he claps, and points at us, and asks his pals to rise. "Give them a hand," he yells at his beach friends, and they get up and start clapping. It's an ovation. Somebody sings "Love, love, love." Others join. The entire beach sings "Love, love, love." Alex pivots, we're both facing the crowd. Shall we bow? The queen yells "Author, author," but nobody comes forward. I'm not sure what to do. A man approaches, a bear, hairy and tummyish, he holds something in his hands, in both hands. Flutes, it turns out as he comes closer, champagne glasses, filled with bubbly, and it is, yes, it's the bear from the beach towel, the beach towel that was wrapped around his private parts before I grabbed it and ran away with it to save Maurice's arse. The bear hands one glass to Alex, the other one to me.

"Cheers," Alex says. We sip. "Cheers," the bear says as a third glass appears mysteriously in his hands, then adds, "Where is my beach towel? Please enlighten me."

"It's possibly still where I left it," I answer, "I took your towel to save somebody's ass, but the arse was gone when I came back. Although it's not an ass. It's a Brit."

"Where is it, my beach towel?" the bear insists.

I take the bear to the dunes, holding on to my glass, Alex follows, holding on to his. This is where we met, him and me, Alex and I, right here, at this spot, which changed our life forever, seven days ago, we had no idea. We traipse across the accumbent ivy. The towel, didn't I just hang it over some unassuming branch of this pine tree? Remember this pine tree? Yes, I did, and there it sways in the breeze in all its Nordstrom glory, blending perfectly well with the nature around it. I lift it off the branch and hand it to the bear. "My name is Albert," the bear says.

"My name is John," I say.

"My name is Alex, I guess," Alex says.

The bear raises his glass.

"I'm ticklish," he says.

The end (of Part I)

Readers, are you still there? If you are, and if you liked the book (and if you have a moment to spare), I would really appreciate a short review. Your help in spreading the word would be gratefully received.

You can also stay up to date with the latest developments around the *Green Eyes* by subscribing to our mailing list:

http://morefreedomfries.blogspot.ch/p/mailing-list.html

Acknowledgements

Thank You, first and foremost, to *Joe Phillips*, whose picture *Latino Boy* inspired the book. I had started a new blog and converted it to Blogger's *Dynamic View*, whence it froze (Chapter 19). Three month later I tried again, and voilà, the blog unfroze, and first thing I posted Joe's beautiful picture. Then I thought: 'Why not tell the story behind the picture?' So I wrote that story—the unprintable Chapter 1 of this book. The chapter ended on a cliff hanger, so I had to continue, and when I had reached Chapter 7, I knew I had the plot for a novel.

Thank You to Christine Bally, Glenn Charlow, Tony Foster, Scipio Garling, Kate Hardy, Elizabeth Morrisey, Peter McKinley, Cathy Ulrich, and Michael Williams for helpful comments on the manuscript. *Thank You* to Michael Biron and Perry LaPotin for additional support. *Thank You* to Dr. Andreas Hirschfeld-Warneken of Heidelberg and Dr. Michael Merport of Cambridge, MA for advice on medical issues—all remaining errors are mine.

Thank You to Rehoboth Beach, DE, for serving as the model for Georgia Beach, and *Thank You* to Hilton Head, SC, for serving as the model for the beach of Georgia Beach.

About the Author

In his former life, Michael Ampersant ran the *Applied Logic Laboratory* at the University of Amsterdam, NL. He's living on the *Cote d'Azur* now where he writes erotic prose. The *Green Eyes* are his first novel. There's a follow-up to the story, almost completed ("*This Is Heaven*"), which will show, among other things, the unsettling relativity of *happy-ever-after* (endings). And should you wonder about all the brackets: yes, Michael taught LISP for a while.

www.ingramcontent.com/pod-product-compliance
Lightning Source LLC
Chambersburg PA
CBHW030652260626
47157CB00007B/2606